This is a work of fiction. While some of the places and people are real, names, characters and incidents are creations of the author. Any resemblance to actual events or persons, living or dead, is coincidental.

ISBN: 978-1-7335379-0-2

Pink Revolution

I

II

For the wonderful and patient Susan, who puts up with this process.

Contents

PINK
REVOLUTION

CHAPTER 1

Lost Parents

Pierce Morrison Buckman wasn't a 9-year-old hopelessly lost in Washington, D.C. He knew exactly where he was. His parents, Jane and Robert, were the ones who were lost. He informed them of the reality when his mother had wiped away her tears, the paralyzing panic had subsided , and the security force of the Smithsonian had returned to the responsibilities of supervising the vast collections.

Kids didn't run freely in the Smithsonian, and 1976 was different than any other year in the Smithsonian's history. The republic was in the midst of celebrating the Bicentennial anniversary of independence from the British.

Jane and Robert did not yet fully understand the child they had always believed had been conceived during a night of passion in the arboretum of Crossroads State University in University City, Iowa when both were young college instructors working on post-grad degrees. Pierce was fearless, independent and insatiably curious. This wasn't the first time he had wandered away with his own agenda and certainly wouldn't be the last. He had walked off to check out something of interest. Everything seemed to interest the precocious kid.

Pierce knew exactly where he was and what he was doing. He had things to see, learn about and experience. He was paying scant attention to where his parents were or what they wanted to see. He was oblivious to their world and every other world except the one revolving around himself.

The National Air and Space Museum was new in 1976. Pierce

could have lingered several days just in that one museum. He had also wandered the special exhibits that were part of the Smithsonian's Bicentennial celebration.

His parents knew he would be mesmerized. It was the reason Jane and Robert planned their trip to Washington, D.C., as had millions of others, to experience the celebration going on throughout the country. The Buckmans predicted Washington, D.C. would be the epicenter. They drove from Iowa in their yellow Datsun station wagon with Pierce and all the camping equipment they could fit into the car around the boy. They had reserved a camp site in College Park, Maryland a year in advance. They ate breakfast there, packed lunches in the morning to carry along and ate in the city at night before returning to the campground exhausted. Pierce would awake refreshed and ready to explore again.

Pierce's frantic parents, with the assistance of Smithsonian security and Washington, D.C. police officers, found him several hours after he walked away. At the moment he was finally tracked down, he was intently looking over a Bicentennial exhibit called Signs of Life: Symbols in the American City. The exhibit explored both historic and contemporary signs in American life. There were signs and symbols from the American home, signs from the developing commercial strips of American cities and from a streetscape of an urban city. He was overwhelmed by the expanse of the collections. Pierce had been to the Iowa Agricultural Exposition, usually referred to as The Fair. The Fair was nothing like this. The Buckmans couldn't really punish their son for being inquisitive. They encouraged his curiosity. They set ground rules for the rest of the stay in Washington.

The Buckmans didn't let Pierce out of their sight again in Washington, D.C., New York City or Boston on their way back to Iowa.

"Pierce, you at least have to stay in the same building we are in. When you want to go somewhere else, find us and tell us," Robert said, crouching down to his son's eye level, his arm gently around the back of the boy's head. "You can't just take off. It's not like being at home in University City. You scared us.

A lot of people were looking for you."

"You were scared? I was never scared. I just kept looking at stuff and figured you would find me," Pierce said.

He wasn't done with surprises for the day.

"Did you see the queen lady? I did. She patted me on the head," Pierce reported with a nonchalance that made it sound as if he saw royalty every day.

"What? What are you talking about?" Jane asked.

"I was looking at something and all these people walked up and there she was wearing this round hat ... not like a cap ... a hat. She had a pearl necklace. Some of the pearls were as big as marbles. Everyone was making a big deal about her being there. There was a guy in a robe with her and he seemed to be leading the tour. Why would this guy be wearing a robe in the middle of summer?" Pierce wanted to know. "The queen lady smiled at me, then she patted my head."

On July 8, 1976, Her Majesty the Queen of England did visit the Smithsonian as part of a six-day visit for the Bicentennial of the revolution. Other than Pierce, the Buckmans didn't see the queen. The "guy" in the robe was Warren Burger, Chief Justice of the U.S. Supreme Court. Burger and his wife, Vera, were the official greeters when the queen's contingent arrived at the Smithsonian.

Thirty-one years later on the day he officially took the oath of office as the junior U.S. Senator from Minnesota, also Burger's home state, Pierce Buckman talked with the media about walking away and causing a panic for his parents the first time he visited the nation's capital. He recalled seeing the queen and being overwhelmed about being in Washington at such an exciting time.

It was a good story.

"I think I can find my way around," he told reporters. "I could when I was 9 years old. Everyone else was lost, not me.

"We saw everything, the museums, the monuments, the Capitol, White House. My parents just followed me around. They turned me loose with those restrictions after the day that didn't go well. In some ways, I felt like I found my place on that trip and my parents found me, quite literally.

"I was fascinated by everything I saw. It was like this geeky kid with the glasses, who sometimes got picked on as the nerdy kid in class, had found his place in the galaxy. You figure out when you visit museums that quite often it's the geeky kids with the glasses who do something special."

Pierce Morrison Buckman was now carrying the flag of the progressive wing of the Democrats in his second term as a United States Senator. He had a well-earned reputation of being sharp politically and sharp-witted and sharp- tongued when sharpness served his purpose. He had fought impatiently for universal health care, unsuccessfully so far, won on a minimum wage increase nationally, lost on any expansion of gun control but hadn't given up on the issue, and won on renewal of children's health insurance.

He had been turned loose by progressives, just as he had been during his first visit to Washington, D.C. by his parents.

Buckman was now 50 years old and he was being encouraged to expand his progressive horizon. One March night he told the Smithsonian story again to his friends, Carol and Jack Holton, when they met in the Holton's mansion on Lake Minnetonka in the Twin Cities. He asked his friends if he could stop by for a conversation. They invited him to dinner. They knew where the conversation was headed. It really wasn't a revelation Senator Buckman was about to share.

They knew him well. They had first met him when he announced he was running for the Senate, his first attempt at elective office. If you were running for anything in Minnesota as a Democrat, you wanted the Holtons on your side. They had become friends, but in politics you also need financial support and the Holtons had the financial position to be generous financial supporters.

"You are going to do it aren't you?" Carol Holton asked. "Are you crazy? I can think of at least 50 reasons off the top of my head why you shouldn't."

"Only 50? I've thought of more than 100," the bespectacled Buckman said with a wide grin and a chuckle. He wasn't the best-dressed U.S. Senator. When he met with the Holtons, he wore the usual ensemble of a T-shirt, baseball cap over his bald, shaved head, jeans, no socks and gym shoes.

"One, we both know you are going to suck at selling yourself. That means you will also be terrible at asking for money and you are going to need piles of it. You barely had enough to get elected to the U.S. Senate. No one could remember a more bare-bones campaign for a winning U.S. Senate candidate. You were driving around in a beat-up RV that was junked, for what, $1,000 in parts at the end of the campaign? About half the time you were late for campaign stops because the RV had broken down on the road again somewhere a mile from nowhere. Pierce, you don't have the gigantic ego … arrogance … for this kind of thing. I think you have the toughness, but come on, what is so bad about being a U.S. Senator? You've introduced legislation and walked across the aisle to get it passed. You have made a difference in peoples' lives. You were willing to cross the aisle and at least talk with the opposition. You got the minimum wage to $10.35. Not $15, but $10.35 has made millions of people more comfortable. Not bad. You did that. You have done a lot already. You can do a lot more where you are now.

"You know that if this fails, you may never be a U.S. Senator again. You may lose the seat forever. To win, you will need to be in Iowa. That means you will be criticized for not being in Washington for votes. It has happened to others who thought they wanted to be President of the United States.

"You'll be called every name in the book."

Carol Holton was on a roll. She wanted to know if Pierce Buckman really had the desire deep within him to get through the process that could be brief and painful. Was he capable of maintaining the drive required to campaign for more than a year, almost two, if he was the eventual nominee? Even if he did win the Iowa Caucus, the victory might not make much of an impression anywhere else. Senator Tom Harkin, after all, won the Iowa Caucuses at home and couldn't turn his campaign into much more than a footnote in 1992 when a virtually unknown governor named Bill Clinton surged to the nomination and into the White House.

"I think you lack the ego to want to be president. Do you

truly believe you have the desire to go through the … let's call it stupidity … to be elected president?" Carol Holton asked. "Honestly, I question your will to go through the lies, deception, name-calling, scrutiny and the incredibly nasty stuff that will be done to you and said about you. You, in particular, will be a target. You would be the most progressive president since FDR and maybe ever. You'll be slammed with every liberal slur imaginable, and a few more that will be created especially for you. If you somehow win the nomination, you are going to be running against the position, resources and incredible power of a sitting president. Even if Jack Rushton is a buffoon, which he is, he will be the incumbent. He'll be *their* buffoon and they will still support him. That comes with a lot of power and advantages in a campaign. Even in your own party you will be considered to be the extreme left candidate. A socialist like Karl Marx. Not Groucho Marx … he was funny. Being compared to Karl Marx is not as funny. And there will be plenty of others running against you for the nomination. Do you really want to go through all of that? Is this really your time? You could be embarrassed, disgraced.

"How are you going to explain that your wife was once a graduate student and you were her advisor? You weren't exactly professional with that professor-student relationship."

Done with the grilling, Carol got to the point she really wanted to make.

"One more thing, and we'll open the wine. If you do this, I believe we're going to be close friends with the President and First Lady of the United States. I think you can win. You know that I will do everything I can to make that happen. We love you. I can't think of a single person in this country more capable of doing great things than you … both of you."

"Pierce, what do you need from us?" Jack asked.

"Your support is the perfect place to start," he said, looking over the top of his glasses. He unconsciously pushed them up on his nose.

"Pierce, raising piles of money isn't in your makeup. You sure aren't going to buy a national election but you will face people who will try," Carol said. "As much as we support you, what we can do legally will be a drop in the bucket. You would need to come up with hundreds of millions of dollars to reach Inauguration Day."

The senator listened intently as Carol shared what he knew was an accurate assessment of his candidacy. He was not being told anything he hadn't already contemplated himself. He would need to be an entirely new face, a new type of candidate with a fresh coalition to have any chance to even make it to the night of the Iowa Caucuses in 11 months. His message would have to be different. Less polarizing, more inclusive. To be elected, he understood he would need a unique patchwork quilt of support from liberals, one-issue advocates of the environment, gender rights, women's rights, progressives who believe government programs can make lives better, and he would need every Republican who could be convinced that the president, as Carol Holton so capably expressed it, was indeed a buffoon.

"Carol, you make this all sound like so much fun," Pierce said, chuckling again with a toothy grin that observers would soon recognize was occasionally used as unspoken sarcasm.

Now more serious, he said, "I want to be different. I don't want to run because of ego. I don't want to run because I can. I want to do something important for people. That would be my entire focus. I want to make a positive difference in this country. I want to make a difference in peoples' lives. For once we're going to talk with some foresight and vision. At least I am. We're going to talk about doing big things and doing the good things we do now differently.

"For decades our leaders have pretty much taken the path of least resistance. We never look ahead. We only respond to a crisis as it develops. We manage from crisis to crisis. Our politicians are often more interested in being re-elected than doing something important. We don't think big. Not like Lincoln, FDR, Eisenhower, LBJ did. Take just one issue … universal health care. We are so absolutely terrified of health insurers and big pharma we don't go far enough to ensure everyone has access to affordable, high-quality health care. No other industrialized country in the world has an inefficient, expensive system like ours when it comes to our citizens' health."

He paused briefly, capturing more of the messages he had already been forming as he considered a campaign for president.

"I can pretty much promise you that everything you said would be true. I could be embarrassed. This could end my political career. But you know what? I loved teaching. I could go back to it until I retired and be perfectly happy. I need you with me. I need your friends and the organizations you donate to with me. I need your media expertise and your influence. I need every lefty, gun control advocate, communist, progressive, socialist, tree hugger, American Indian, immigrant who can legally participate in the process, gay and transgender rights advocates, health rights advocates, green advocates we can round up across the entire country. I need the underserved, I need the young, the silent dreamers, the passionate activists on every college campus who will knock on hundreds of doors, have them slammed in their face and keep knocking. I need the kids who graduate with $50,000 in college debt and prospects for only a $25,000-a-year job. That is the only way I could ever be elected president. Those are my people. Shouldn't be that hard, should it? And, right now you could end my candidacy before it starts by repeating any of what I just said."

"How much to get to Iowa?" Carol asked, no longer dancing around the most important conversation of the night.

"You are right, you know. I suck at this part, but I'll get better. At minimum, several million," he said. "But if we can gain some momentum before caucus night, I'll develop credibility as a candidate and support will grow. These days, with social media, you can put together a strong campaign with smaller donors. Others have done it that way. That is my game plan."

"I think you can get that much but we might have to form a political action committee and that means you'll be taking 'PAC money,' which comes with negative connotations," Carol said. "Why don't you explore Iowa, set up a campaign website and solicit contributions from small donors at least to get started. I'll contact a few of my friends and we can at least get you start-up funding. It will probably take a lot more to do it right but we'll do our best. What else?"

The senator answered quickly.

"Do you have any space for a campaign headquarters? We need room and it needs to be wired. We're going to have to do this from the ground up. That means volunteers with computers and cellphones with unlimited minutes. Heat would be nice. Other than that, we won't be too picky."

"We have a former warehouse that will be developed into high-end condos. How about 40,000 really bare square feet in St. Paul?" Jack offered. "Two stories, no elevator. At least not one that works. Can we give you the space for free or do we have to charge you something? We'll get it wired."

"I honestly don't know if we are required to pay for the space," the senator said. "We'll have to check it out."

"You'll make a great president. Now, who wants pie?" Carol asked.

CHAPTER 2

Calling All Liberals

Pierce Buckman and Carol Holton spent the next day working the phones. Carol was persuasively asking for money from her friends. The senator was making and taking calls from a lengthy, hand-scribbled list. In his position, as one of the least affluent senators, he agreed to one political action committee.

His first calls were to recognized liberal activists, including union executives, big city progressive mayors and council members, teachers' union executives and activist college professors and administrators he knew personally.

He designated two young idealists on his Senate staff as the first campaign workers, officially moving them from his senate staff payroll to his campaign organization. They were told to get to Minnesota as quickly as possible. Their first task was to build a "Buckman for President" web presence with a secure social media platform able to take and process donations. He kept reminding everyone that this was purely exploratory. No one believed him.

And, the senator made a call to Carl Lyon, editor of the Big River Beacon in Big River, Minnesota.

"Carl, this is Pierce. How is everything going in Black Bears country? Any scandals at Big River State brewing? Any buildings burning or U.S. Senators having heart attacks in Big River these days? Anything worthy of a First Freedoms nomination?"

"Senator, how are you doing? No, it's just routine right now. Routine is OK after last year. Why don't you come up here and announce you are running for president? We need a big news story. Mona will cover it for us. Heck, I might write again. You are doing it, aren't you?" asked Carl.

Carl and Susan Lyon had been around the senator several times since he survived what could have been a fatal heart blockage in Big River. Susan, an emergency department nurse at Northwoods Regional Medical Center, had helped save the senator's life. The senator's heart attack was already a legendary event at Northwoods Regional. Buckman had not taken for granted the care he had received there. He called her often. They had a bond.

In decades of being around politicians, Carl had never had admired a politician more than he admired Senator Pierce Buckman. On the day the senator and Minnesota Governor Glen McGrath walked Big River street after a deadly summer storm that killed eight people, Carl watched Buckman listen to stories of loss and survival. The senator listened much more than he spoke. He hugged people who were heartbroken after losing everything they owned, shedding tears with them. He said he would help and he delivered.

The storm ravaged the gorgeous town, transforming it for decades to come by taking out thousands of acres of mature forest. Big River's citizens needed both moral support and the tangible support of their U.S. Senator. Buckman provided both. His compassion and his ability to get things done made an impression on Carl and the people of Big River, regardless of party affiliation. Buckman worked to provide tens of millions of dollars of relief for the region at a time when the parties could barely agree on what day it was.

"Officially, I would say, quote, 'there will be plenty of Democratic candidates I admire and I will support a campaign to end the damage Jack Rushton is doing to the country.' At this time, I haven't decided about my political future. I'd call it an exploratory period. But I'd like you and Susan to come to St. Paul to talk with me. I need you both.

"If I'm going to do this, I want a biographer who can get a book out by the time of the Iowa Caucuses. I want you to write it. My parents will give you access to photos, school grades, that kind of information and I will give you plenty of time for interviews. I want you with me every step for the next few months before the Iowa Caucus date. I know you wouldn't do this without Susan being involved and with you. I wouldn't want it any other way. Lord knows I probably need medical monitoring, and Susan can advise me on issues we have as a country with access to affordable, quality health care. She knows that issue. Jack Rushton believes big insurance and big pharma should run health care and doesn't care if millions are left behind. We're going to fight every day for universal health care.

"I also want you to advise me on media issues. Keep me in the media, but out of trouble."

"Senator, I can't be the media face of the campaign. We both know that," Carl said. "I can help you find the right person but it can't be me. You need a younger person ... attractive, articulate, tireless, capable of staying on message and capable of manipulating and obscuring the message when the need arises. I've only got one suit, one sports coat and a couple of dress shirts. One of the shirts *might* be clean. I'm not your guy to be out front for you publicly. You need someone with much more energy and thicker skin. At my age, I no longer have enough of either. I bruise easily now and for no apparent reason. You need someone driven and totally invested in Senator Pierce Buckman. They may not have guzzled the Senator Buckman fruit juice yet but they know the color and the flavor. Absolutely, I would like to write a book or two if this effort goes the way I believe it will, it will be an incredible first book for both of us. I am with you; I can't think of anything I would rather do than get Rushton out of office. On second thought, I can think of one thing I would rather do. That is to get a guy in the White House who will make a very good president."

"Talk with Susan and give me a call," Buckman said. "If I do this, I think we're going on a long road trip. Have you got about nine more years in you?"

"Not even close. I think I can make it about 18 months to January 20 when you deliver your first inaugural address. Can I possibly contribute a word or two to it?" Carl asked.

"As long as you don't plagiarize anyone," Buckman said, laughing.

"Then I'm not doing it," Carl said. "Why re-create something that has been said perfectly?"

There was no doubt in Carl's mind that Buckman was running for president. He was excited by the thought of being any part of a national campaign. He called his wife of nearly 40 years with the news.

"He wants what?" Susan said. "No shit. When we came here I thought maybe it would be our last adventure. Maybe not. Can we afford to do this? I would love living in the Twin Cities, I know that."

"We didn't talk money. We should be comfortable, and maybe there will be some money if the campaign draws attention. We are both eligible for Social Security if we have to start collecting," Carl responded. "He wants us to come to St. Paul and talk with him soon. Are you good with this? If you are, I will call him tomorrow."

"Let's go," she said. "Even if it isn't much money, we'll find a way. I'd probably pay to be part of this. This is what you call your life-defining moment. Tell him we're in."

Pierce Buckman had more calls to make. He needed to find a social media team. If one of the team members had a cybersecurity background, even better. He eventually would need to find someone with experience in staging political events, although he had already decided his campaign would look much different than the norm. He wasn't going to be waving flags at every event and flying in a private jet. He was going to do what he did to get elected twice from Minnesota to the U.S. Senate. He would talk with people face-to-face, and from the start it would be clear to voters where he stood on key issues. He would have to do it on a modest budget.

He needed millennials, lots of them, and he needed them quickly. He needed energetic, driven young people who would buy into the campaign and drink the fruit juice as Carl had suggested. He needed young people who would work 18 hours a day and drink two or three more hours before crashing and doing it all again the next day.

You don't become a U.S. Senator without developing contacts immersed in the national political scene who know how to run a winning campaign.

Buckman wanted Gerald O'Malley, a rumpled, pudgy, hunched over veteran of national campaigns. O'Malley was usually angry at someone, always looked like he was in need of sleep, which he always was, and was brutally honest and demanding. He drove staff to the point where they had a deep desire to jam shards of a broken beer bottle through his heart, another through his brain and finish with a glowing fireplace implement jammed up his ass. Oh, and he was known to have a drink or 17 of them when he had someone to drink with who could tolerate him in the slightest and buy most of the drinks. Grandpa Sherm's Barrel Bourbon and Diet Coke was his drink of choice. It had been suggested by young staffers on campaigns he headed that one day at a campaign event he was likely to drop dead of a heart attack or stroke. More than once he was the odds-on favorite in a campaign staff's office death pool, although the senator himself might be considered a worthy contender in his campaign because of his heart history. O'Malley also was legendary in political circles for his ability to win.

A brilliant strategist, O'Malley was a walking digest of political facts, figures and contacts who could get things done. He had a notebook jammed with everything from contacts from Iowa precinct leaders to cellphone numbers for Democratic governors, congressmen and key state officials. He wasn't hostile toward the latest technology. At night in bars about to close he would transcribe his scribbled notes and the day's new phone numbers into a campaign update email and into his digital contacts. When he dug a few dollars out of his right pants pocket indicating he was about to spend money, which he rarely did except for his first drink, 10 scraps of paper with phone numbers might float out to the ground. Anyone who found those scraps would likely have immediate access to one or more of the most influential Democrats in the country.

O'Malley didn't do what he did for financial gain any longer. He had become comfortable financially by managing winning candidates. He had written a funny, irreverent book he protested was fiction about being on the road with campaigns. No one else thought it was fiction, especially not the people he was writing about. The book made the top 10 nationally. He wasn't exactly telegenic but was a frequent and popular guest on cable news networks because of his expertise and his lack of restraint when it came to the opposing party. His agitation toward the right made good television. After the book, he became a popular speaker for a standard fee of $15,000 a night on college campuses and at state Democrat gatherings. He could get the party faithful wound up. He was worth the speaking fees, which became his ticket to financial security.

The candidates themselves didn't win. In Gerald O'Malley's brain, he won for them. Often, he was right. He had somehow guided some really bad candidates laden with baggage into office against overwhelming odds. The Bostonian, who worked only for Democrats, now ran campaigns because he enjoyed the sport, the fight, the grime of politics. Winning was his high of choice. He claimed he could give up drinking but never politics. He liked the long days, late nights, the banter. Truth be told, he enjoyed being around the idealistic kids who gravitated to campaigns. He thought their youthful enthusiasm drove him. He passionately enjoyed beating Republicans, particularly incumbents who people believed were untouchable.

Buckman was considering trying to pull off the ultimate beatdown by beating an incumbent president. He thought he could land O'Malley because the organizer would be attracted to a campaign most observers would say had no chance. Buckman knew he needed to get to O'Malley before another Democrat, probably New York Governor Mike Clarke, or former Virginia Governor Karla Foster, did. Clarke was already considered the party's front runner to take down Rushton and win the White House.

Buckman made the call.

"O'Malley, I need you. I'm running. You are the first one I've said that to out loud. Let's hit the road. We have to get Rushton out before he does even more damage to the country," Buckman said the first time they talked on the phone about forming a campaign staff.

"Senator, I'm not sure you can win the nomination, let alone win the White House. I want to end Rushton's political career as much as anyone but I'm not sure you are the one who can do this. You are on no one's radar. You are no centrist. You will be ignored by Rushton, at least initially. That isn't necessarily a good thing either when you are trying to engage him in a fight. You will have to work your ass off in Iowa and concentrate on the silly caucuses there. If you don't win there, you will probably be done. If you do win there and become a real threat to Rushton, then the fun begins. His people will absolutely abuse you if they believe you are a threat. Kind of sounds like fun to me. Rushton is not only an ass, he is a dangerous ass."

"Come to the Twin Cities and talk with me or I'll come to Boston," Buckman said. "We have a headquarters, or will have, and I have just enough money to go across the border and start finding supporters who will show up on caucus night."

They talked a while longer about the senator's positions on the issues. There were no real surprises. Senator Pierce Buckman was widely known as an unapologetic progressive who would push for universal health care, look for ways to put the regulatory hammer down on Wall Street, push for big public works projects reminiscent of his favorite presidents, FDR and Eisenhower, and advocate free college educations for every American kid who wanted one, in exchange for public service.

He would demand that big business and the wealthiest Americans pay their fair share of taxes.

He would advocate for reduced military spending by eliminating waste, reducing civilian personnel, and staying out of other countries' issues except for using diplomacy to help alleviate tensions. He had gone on the record favoring an immediate 10 percent decrease in nearly all departments. He believed there was at least that much waste and over-employment, probably much more. He also knew the 10 percent decrease in costs across the board would allow him the resources for the other things he advocated. He was a pragmatist about big projects. They would have to be paid for without a huge increase in taxes.

Buckman believed the federal government was bloated with programs and bureaucrats who would be hard-pressed for an answer if you asked them, "what do you do for Americans?"

"What don't I know about you? Any skeletons?" O'Malley asked, giving his first indication he was interested.

"I had the heart scare. Everyone knows that. I'm told I have at least one other potential issue. Maybe two," he said.

"OK, give it to me."

When Pierce Buckman, Ed.D. was a professor of political science at Big River State University, he was advisor to graduate student Kim Wakefield, a smart, attractive 23-year-old. What began as a platonic student-professor relationship developed first into more of a social relationship. They were careful. Mostly they hung out with each other. Their relationship became intimate. The relationship was eventually apparent throughout Big River – there are not many secrets on a college campus in a small town -- but not much was thought about a 38-year-old professor with a 23-year-old student. Both sets of parents approved when they realized how happy their children were.

"We fell in love. We've been together since. We're married. I don't regret a second of our relationship and if people are so narrow-minded that they don't understand, I'm OK with that. Support someone else."

"And the other thing? Drug rehab? A felony?" O'Malley asked.

"Kim is pregnant."

CHAPTER 3
Leaving Big River

The excitement of Carl and Susan Lyon was obvious when they arrived early to walk through the ramshackle warehouse soon to become the national headquarters of Buckman for President. It was an empty space except for neatly stacked tables and chairs in one corner. A thick layer of dust, more black than gray covered everything except the tables, which appeared to have been delivered overnight.

It looked like the building was abandoned years ago. Carl counted seven broken windows on the first floor alone. It was still winter and the space was cold, without a working furnace judging by the temperature, and no one looked at the restrooms.

"At least there are restrooms. I think I have found my first role of this campaign. I'm going to start cleaning up and organizing this place," Susan Lyon declared.

Carl knew his wife of four decades was just the person to take on what appeared to be a huge task.

"Can we please put heat near the top of the priority list?" Carl said, clapping his gloved hands.

Senator Pierce Buckman was often late. Those who knew him referred to it as "Pierce Time." It was a habit developed in two campaigns for the U.S. Senate. He rarely made it to campaign events on time and usually was reluctant to leave before everyone got a chance to talk with him and share their story. He was consistently late for the next event. He didn't just talk to voters, he listened to them, carrying a notebook and pen in his left pants pocket. The pens frequently leaked and ruined the slacks. Sometimes he took notes on his mobile device. His notebook typically had names, phone numbers, email addresses and notes to himself about the issues people shared with him.

Today he was running behind schedule by 20 minutes. The senator ambled into the warehouse holding hands with Kim. He wore jeans, a long-sleeved shirt, wool coat, sneakers, no socks and a Minnesota Twins baseball cap.

The senator usually looked like a college student, not a college professor, nor a United States Senator. His face and physique were younger than his age.

"Kim, are you …?" Susan Lyon asked.

She was beaming. "Three months," she answered.

They hugged. Carl shook hands with the senator and congratulated him.

"Well, that will be something different for a presidential candidate," Carl said. "When was the last time that happened?"

"Jackie Kennedy, 1960. In the general election," Buckman said. "John Jr. was born the same month as the election. I had to look it up. It isn't some political stunt on our part, although maybe it will win us the pregnant women vote in Iowa if I run. We'd been practicing for a while."

Kim Wakefield, who preferred using her family name, and Susan Lyon set up tables and chairs. The senator and Carl sat down at one of them.

"You know I need a biographer. I want to write a book about the campaign from our personal experiences and my positions on the major issues … fair taxation, universal healthcare, universal living wage, public service in exchange for college or trade school tuition, improving public schools, a public works initiative, reducing our role as the world's enforcer and reduced military and defense spending. We'll share the author credit. I want you and Susan to go on the road with us to Iowa and we'll go from there. I want you to help counsel me on media strategy and help get the right message to the right people. Your media contacts will help. Susan can monitor my health and Kim's and advise me on health issues. The campaign will pay expenses. There isn't much more at this point financially. Maybe later we will be able to pay you if we are able to raise money. Let's hope."

"Senator, we're all in," Carl said. "We already decided. We need an adventure. We believe you will make a great president. We've already told people at work we'll be back only briefly. They don't know what we're doing."

"You need to call me Pierce," the senator said.

"No, senator. You have earned the title and it should be respected. It always will be by me. You are Senator Buckman and in 18 months you will be Mister President. We're going to do whatever small things we can do to make that happen," Carl Lyon said. "I knew it when you visited Big River for the memorial service for the hockey player, and I knew it when you walked and talked and cried with the people of Big River after the storm. You are going to be President."

"Your wife has seen me naked," the Senator said with his toothy grin. "Will that be a problem with our relationship?"

"No, she told me. She said it wasn't a big deal," Carl said.

"Ouch," Pierce said.

"Ever been to Iowa?" he asked Carl.

"As a sports reporter, I'm sure I have been through it. Green in summer, white in winter. Is that the place?"

"Same one. Have you ever been to the Iowa Agricultural Exposition? It kind of kicks off the Iowa Caucuses," the senator said.

"I've seen at least two versions of the movie. Does that count?" Carl said.

"Pat Boone, Bobby Darin, Ann-Margret…I love that movie. But that fair was in Texas. Hey, maybe Pat Boone and Ann-Margret will appear with us at the fair. Celebrity endorsers," Buckman said.

"Well, I know it won't be Bobby Darin. That could only happen on election day in Illinois," Carl said in a droll voice, knowing Darin had died young in the 1970s.

"We're going down to Iowa to get a start. I'm not announcing formally for a while. A few weeks anyway," the senator said. "Go home and pack and be back in a few days."

The Lyons decided to keep paying rent on the lake house. They loved the cozy house and didn't know how long the

Buckman campaign would last. Maybe they would be home long before Iowa Caucus night if Buckman couldn't gain any traction or funding. They each packed a couple of bags. The temperature was in the 40s but they sat on the dock in their regular chairs, wearing their winter coats, and shared a bottle of wine.

"We'll be back, Carl. It might be a while, but we'll be back. We will, won't we?" Susan asked wistfully.

In the morning they both went to work and broke the news. It wasn't the best way to leave jobs they enjoyed. They had told their employers that they were considering exciting opportunities that they couldn't pass up. There would be no two-week or even two-day notice.

"Carl, I totally understand. I'd do the same thing myself. I'm envious. This is something you can't pass up," said Beacon publisher John Casey, who had revived Carl's career after his previous paper, the Colorado Sentinel, had failed. "We appreciate everything you have done here. It has been an incredible run and too brief for me. To come here and do what we've done together is amazing. We won a First Freedoms Award from out in the middle of nowhere. I thought you'd have been gone soon after that.

"Get out of here and go get the senator elected president. We know him personally. He'll make a great president."

Carl was emotional as he walked out of John Casey's office and into the newsroom to tell Mona Vanhoutenbeck, one of the people who had helped the Big River Beacon receive national journalism recognition for its coverage of a convergence of events. They had covered the senator's life-threatening heart procedure and the tragic death of Brandon Trent, a Big River State University hockey player who died of sports-related concussions and hypothermia, found lost in a forest after another brain injury. The Beacon's coverage of the deadly summer storm also earned national attention.

Mona had tears flooding down her cheeks. She was sobbing as she tried to talk. Carl tried unsuccessfully to stop his own tears.

"Mona, you are a fine reporter. Our experiences here will be memorable because you were here. I'm sorry this is happening

21

so quickly but it's an experience we can't pass up at this point in our lives," Carl said. "We'll be back. The next time we are here Senator Buckman might be President Buckman."

"Carl, we'll all miss you. I'll tell everyone else," Mona said.

By 2:30 p.m., Carl and Susan Lyon had locked the doors to the lake house. They stopped in front on the long gravel drive. Susan always cried at moments like this.

"We'll get to come back, won't we?" she pleaded again through her tears.

They stopped and looked around. They pulled down the lane. They passed the iconic sculpture of Paul Bunyan and Babe the Blue Ox, who inexplicably lacked ox testicles, as they discovered on the day they arrived in Big River. That hadn't changed. They didn't even know where exactly they were headed except that they needed to find Highway 2 past Cass Lake, the Leech Lake Band of Ojibwe settlement, and south to the Twin Cities. They soon got accustomed to the uneasy feeling of not knowing where they would spend the night.

CHAPTER 4

Joining the Campaign

Carl and Susan Lyon found what they were convinced was a great online rate of $99 on a downtown Minneapolis hotel room. They checked in at 8 p.m. and immediately went for a walk. There was a basketball game Carl was sorry they had missed by a couple of hours. The downtown was bustling. People were on the sidewalks headed to restaurants and clubs.

"A big city again. As much as I love that lake house, it feels good to be back in a city," Susan said.

A text message to Carl's phone at 10 p.m. from Senator Buckman filled him in on details for the next couple of days.

"Meet me at this address at 8 a.m. You can live in boat house of Holtons. The Holtons are great. We'll start talking about book. This weekend we're going to Iowa."

"Hoodie's parents," Carl said, explaining the message about their new temporary home to Susan. "You've heard me talk about them. Apparently, they live in a bit of a shack on Lake Minnetonka."

"Does that mean Hoodie knows the Senator is going to run?" Susan asked.

"I'm guessing it does but really, this won't be a surprise to anyone," Carl said.

Hoodie was Jason Holton, senior reporter for the Minnesota Standard and son of Carol and Jack Holton. Carol Ann Collier Holton was a board member of the now publicly traded but formerly family-owned Collier Communications. The Collier family was once one of the most influential U.S. media families in an era when families often owned large media companies.

Carol Holton was much more interested in causes important to her – the hungry, homeless, mentally ill – than she was in the media business. Those were also people Senator Buckman was interested in serving, not the rich and privileged.

Jason Holton was quickly attached to the Hoodie nickname when he showed up in Big River to cover the unusual death of hockey player Brandon Trent. Hooded sweatshirts were all Jason Holton seemed to have in the wardrobe. He made another impression while in Big River. As quickly as he became known as Hoodie was about how quickly he wooed Lisa Fitzgerald, a former Big River State athlete herself who became one of Carl Lyon's star reporters. Hoodie and Lisa were now engaged and lived together in his moderately sized but expensive downtown condo. When Lisa left the Big River Beacon for the Standard, photographer Daniel Fallsfeather also landed at the Standard.

The Beacon gang was back together only miles apart. Carl Lyon had no plan to renew the relationship until after the first excursion to Iowa. He didn't want to be in a position to say anything or hide anything about why he was in the Twin Cities and why he and Susan were headed to Iowa.

At 6:45 a.m. Carl and Susan pulled on to the stone road leading to the front of the Holtons' estate. They had never met the Holtons.

"Not much in common with our little lake place, huh?" Carl mused as they hesitated for seconds in the car looking over the two-story Tudor style property spread out in front of them. "I've just heard about it. I've also heard they are very nice, down-to-earth people who just happen to have a lot of money."

Both of the Holtons greeted the Lyons at the tall arched doorway.

"Come and have some breakfast with us and then we'll show you the boat house," Carol Holton said. "We're glad you are going to be helping Pierce. He needs people he can trust. He likes you. So does Jason, or as you can him, Hoodie. I like that nickname. Not sure he does. Isn't that boy something? He even dresses that way in the newsroom in meetings with high-level corporate management. Not always in summer, though. He must also own about 100 T-shirts. He switches to those in summer."

"One heck of a reporter. So is Lisa," Carl said.

"We love Lisa," Carol Holton said. "She is doing very well at the newspaper. She is getting a lot of great stories and she can handle them."

After a breakfast of coffee, juice and rolls, the Holtons conducted a tour of the main house. It was pretty much as Carl expected after hearing Lisa Fitzgerald's vivid description. The house had the look of "old money." It was understated opulence, or maybe it seemed understated because the Holtons were so understated themselves considering the family's wealth. The last stop was the boat house apartment on the second level of the wood and concrete block building on the shore of Lake Minnetonka. It was essentially an efficiency apartment with a combination living room and bedroom, mini-kitchen and a bathroom.

"And you are free to use the pool, gym and workout room," Carol Holton said pleasantly. "In fact, the gym is where Pierce will be meeting you this morning. I think his plan is to get some exercise, talk a little about his life and why he is running and then hit the road to Iowa. He says he thinks better when he exercises. He said there is medical evidence. You'll get used to his quirks."

"The senator is right about the physical and mental benefits of exercise. Are you joining us in Iowa?" Susan Lyon asked.

"Not this time. Maybe another trip," Carol Holton said. "One of our nephews, Ryan, will be driving you. Pierce has bought another used motorhome. Well used. At least this one looks like an upgrade. Not like the junk he was driving when he was campaigning twice for the Senate. He'll probably have it this morning when he gets here. Being superstitious is one of those quirks I was talking about. He knows he won when he had a beat-up bus. No surprise he followed form.

"A couple warnings about Pierce. He hits the stationary bike hard … he says it's an old habit from wrestling … and he talks fast when he works out and when he is excited. He does it when he campaigns, too. The faster he talks, the more passionate you know he is about what he is talking about. Got a recorder?

You'll need it.

"He's got some other eccentricities...don't we all...but him more than most. And he has no fashion sense because he doesn't care. He would wear jeans to the Senate chamber I think. He may have. He rarely wears socks."

By the time they walked back into the main house after checking out the boat house and the gym and indoor swimming pool on the property, Senator Buckman and Kim were at the breakfast table having juice and rolls. They had just walked in the front door without knocking.

"Who is ready to go to Iowa? Let's go win the minds of some voters," Buckman said with that electric smile.

CHAPTER 5

Heading South

Carl thought Carol Holton had understated Buckman's workout routine. The senator arrived at the Holton's' at 5:30 a.m. the next morning. He cranked up the music, classic rock 'n' roll, and hopped on the stationary bike. He rode with a vengeance, up on his toes at times, like he was a kid late for a baseball game. He didn't stop for 45 minutes. Sweat rolled off his shaved, now uncovered head. His T-shirt was soaked. He went from the bike to a jump rope for another 10 minutes. He cooled down with a few laps in the pool.

Carl didn't try to keep up He walked his standard 40 minutes on the treadmill at his standard pace of 3.1 miles per hour. He got off and turned on his digital recorder. He took photos of Buckman working out.

Susan Lyon took the senator's pulse and blood pressure; 120 bpm and 128 over 82.

"Good job," she said.

"Do you always take this so seriously?" Carl asked him.

"I guess I do. Goes back to my wrestling days and cutting pounds to make weight. It makes me a little nuts to not exercise every day. I guess I'm a bit obsessive about exercise. If I don't work out, it doesn't feel right, like l have forgotten to eat or sleep. When I ran for senate there was a bike on the RV. I like this bike. We'll load it up. I think when I exercise. It motivates me. I come up with a lot of ideas; some of them good, some of them really out there."

"What do you think about?"

"Mostly I think about how I would like to make things different ... have an impact on peoples' lives. I think I told you, or maybe it was Carol, that it frustrates me as a senator to always be reacting instead of acting. Our Congress often lacks vision. We lack vision often as a country because our leadership does. We don't have enough dreamers. We don't think big. We either react to a crisis or do nothing. There doesn't seem to be anything in between. And that seems to be fine with this president. The guy has no vision. Congress used to do big things working with the president. Congress could find a path to common ground. There was legitimate give-and-take negotiation that accomplished something good. Lyndon Johnson, Reagan and Tip O'Neill, people like that, could get things done despite strong opposition. Sometimes they would negotiate. Other times they would impose their dominating will and people would get in line. Now, no one gets in line. Now it isn't opposition, it is hard-headed, entrenched partisanship. We've got this political mentality that we can't let the other party accomplish anything. They can have no legacy on our watch. Everyone is afraid to cross the aisle to get something done for fear it will cost them an election when they run again."

He continued nonstop for a few more minutes.

"That's something that makes me different. I honestly don't care about the next election. To me, the Senate is public service. Being mayor is public service. Being a state representative is public service. It isn't a career for me. I don't want to just be elected and re-elected for the position and the benefits. I want to accomplish something. That attitude gets me in trouble sometimes with the party people who value the seat and not necessarily the person in the seat. It's about control to them. Not to me."

He was jumping rope at a fast pace and still was explaining why they were about to head to Iowa looking not for voters, but for activists who would show up at a meeting hall, a church, a school, or in some cases, someone's house, on February 1 for the Iowa Caucus.

The Iowa Caucuses are different than other political events. It might be a night with a wind chill of minus 20, or maybe it would be pouring rain. Iowans gather and are coaxed by a neighbor or friend, or maybe a graduate of the local high school back in town for just caucus night, to support a candidate.

At 1,681 caucus sites around the state, the events begin with a recitation of ground rules and instructions.

After the cookies and soda, or maybe slow cookers full of sloppy joes or taco meat, the "vote" takes place. It's more taking a stand than voting. Whomever is running the particular caucus site asks everyone supporting one candidate to stand in one part of the room. Supporters of the other candidates are instructed to stand in other areas.

Candidates who have failed to get their message through the campaign haze after months on the road, after spending millions of dollars, are ignominiously labeled as "not viable" at the caucus sites. Stick a fork in them, they are done. At that point supporters of candidates with enough support to be viable will try to coax the supporters of the rejected candidates to their group. Supporters of each individual candidate raise their hand and are counted or line up and count themselves by voice. The caucuses don't even decide that much or have much of an impact on who is elected president. The purpose is actually to decide the number of supporters who will represent a candidate at the county party convention. What is reported at the end of the night are caucus tallies for each candidate and delegates. From there, representatives of candidates are chosen for the state convention and then national party convention.

Caucuses are an awkward process at first glance. Second and third glance, too, for that matter. They can appear to be organized chaos. There are no polling sites and no voting machines. Go stand with your candidate's group and you are counted. The party faithful watch each other closely for impropriety. Disputes about rules and counts aren't unusual. It is a good thing caucuses usually last only a couple of hours. Any longer and fist fights might break out.

Post-caucus speeches are made even before the remaining viable candidates scramble out of Iowa to New Hampshire, the traditional first state with a primary vote. Everyone claims to have won something, although some candidates quickly announce they are "suspending" their campaigns while speeches are being made by the winner and other top tier finishers.

Buckman understood the Iowa process better than many politicians who thought about making a run through Iowa. He taught the process as part of the college political science courses.

"These gatherings can make or break a candidate's chances," Buckman said. "The first two or three finishers in the Iowa caucuses can realistically advance to primary states. The others might not make it to the end of the week before announcing they are suspending their candidacy, whatever that means. They aren't suspending anything. They are done. They are going home beaten. You spill guts, spend months campaigning in Iowa, only to get your ass handed to you. Those who suspend their campaigns usually have one or two good reasons. They are humiliated. They shake all these hands, make all these stops, expose themselves to the world and spend long days for months and find out they still haven't made an impression. It's a painful, life-changing rejection. Like getting rejected by your preferred prom date, or worse yet, having her leave you on prom night to make out in the corner with some other guy. Second, they have no traction and will soon have absolutely no ability to raise the funds necessary to continue to New Hampshire."

This was becoming a college classroom lecture. Carl was intrigued.

Buckman said the Iowa Caucuses had a sketchy record of picking eventual presidents.

"Sometimes the Iowans – not really a lot of them either – have given candidates credibility and launched them to the presidency. Other times, they somehow decided a relatively unknown candidate was their favorite," Buckman said of Iowa voters. "Candidates can win in Iowa and disappear before the national convention.

"Iowans enjoy their status as the first test of a candidate. It's a special role. It is part of their identity as Iowans. They may see the candidates dozens of times starting 18 months or more ahead of the next caucus night. It's fun and exciting. But there is often national criticism, especially when Iowans give the country a

Jack Rushton. The argument then is that Iowa has exaggerated importance and should be just another stop on the schedule of a campaign; certainly not the first measurement of a candidate. The state doesn't have a large population, is not particularly diverse and the process is odd.

"The national Democrats want to update the Iowa process this time. They are looking at that lack of diversity and lack of access and asking the state Democratic officials to make changes. They are being asked to come up with a method, probably web-based, to open up the process to more people. The caucuses may have an entirely different look and feel this time. That probably is a good thing, depending on how it works. And, whether the changes actually do work.

" The Iowa advantage is that it truly is a swing state that can go either way in a general election. On election night, Iowa often makes a difference. It happened when Iowa went for Rushton and helped put him in the White House. While usually thought of as a rural ag state, the demographics of Iowa are changing. The cities of Iowa now can carry elections and they are often Democratic Party strongholds. Or they used to be before Rushton won Iowa and won a couple of the largest counties. In the rural areas, the Republican Party is dominant.

"Iowa border states Nebraska and Illinois rarely see presidential candidates for basically the same reason. They are both one-party states. Only Republican candidates would be likely to spend any time anyplace west of Lincoln in Nebraska. It's the opposite with Illinois. Illinois is rarely 'in play' for a Republican presidential candidate, although the state will occasionally be fed up with corrupt Democrats and throw them out just before they head to prison.

"Iowans will tell you their state is a good place to start the process because Iowans are smart people who will capably analyze candidates for the rest of the country. Some Iowans vet the candidates. OK, honestly, a very small number of Iowans actually participate. About 10 percent of voters. That's one of the reasons behind the expected changes."

But if it's March, 10 months before the Iowa Caucuses, you go to Iowa if you believe you have something to offer the country as president. Buckman was considering a campaign. Naturally, he was headed to Iowa.

"Besides, it isn't that far away," he explained.

There was little money at the beginning and even less of an organization.

On the day of the first trip south from Minnesota, Senator Pierce Buckman had his driver, Ryan Holton, the Lyons, and himself on the road. Two of his Senate staffers who were now in Minneapolis and a couple of college kids had started making phone calls and researching places the RV could stop to find a few voters. That was his national campaign staff, plus the pregnant Kim Wakefield, who stayed in the office to make phone calls and research where other candidates had stopped in Iowa over the years.

The initial list Kim and the kids came up with included factories, colleges, service clubs, diners and the names of activist Democrats willing to host an event for friends and neighbors in their homes.

"You've got about five colleges and a bunch of factory gates you can stop at between here and Des Moines," Kim reported as the 2007 model motorhome with 85,000 miles on it crossed the border into Iowa. "We've got you five or six small house parties set up in the next week, and the kids have a list of about 20 diners and truck stops. We're working on some service clubs that will allow you to speak at luncheons."

"Carl wants to know if we can stop at any college town bars?" the senator joked.

"Sure, in University City. Take him to the arboretum. Are you really going to share that story your parents told you about how you were conceived?" Kim asked. "Won't it embarrass your mom?"

"She is the one who first suggested I tell the story," the senator responded. "Those old hippies love that story. My middle name is Morrison after Jim Morrison. You know what one of the most popular songs of 1967 was? Light My Fire. That tells you a bit about my parents. I'm going after the old hippie vote.

"I'll use that story early and often. Thanks for setting a

schedule for us. Buy pizza for the kids. Love you and we'll see you in a few days."

Senator Buckman had never publicly shared what his parents had always told him about his conception in the arboretum on the campus of Crossroads State University when they were graduate students teaching classes. He now told the story to his new biographer.

"I wasn't really well-planned," the senator said, starting what would become a very natural conversational style he had with Carl Lyon. The senator was starting his story at the beginning.

"My parents were struggling, married graduate students in education at Crossroads State University. They were grad assistants … my dad in biology, mom in English. I'm a third-generation educator. Anyway, in a few moments of unrestrained passion they say they made me in the arboretum of Crossroads State. They said the moon was out, it was summer and they got swept away.

"I'm making one of my first campaign decisions right now. We're stopping at the arboretum. I've never done that. My parents got jobs teaching in high school, then college teaching positions in Minnesota when I was 12."

The RV didn't have GPS. Ryan Holton, their 22-year-old driver, was fascinated by the story. He stopped the vehicle when he turned on Sunset Road off Highway B10 in University City, Iowa, the home of Crossroads State University of Science, Technology and Agriculture, usually just referred to as Crossroads State University after numerous name changes over the history of the institution. The historic site of Jane and Robert Buckman's hanky-panky was hidden among other campus sites.

"We are definitely stopping," were Ryan's first words other than singing in the past three hours. "Someday they will put up a plaque that says President Pierce Buckman was conceived by this tree in 1967."

Ten minutes later they rumbled south on College Boulevard into a residential area. On the right was a well-groomed area of rolling hills and mature trees. One thing they could do at Crossroads State was grow anything from the ground.

"That's it," Ryan said excitedly. "Which tree?"

The senator laughed, throwing his head back as he broke up.

"Ryan, they never told me. They are in their 70s. I doubt they remember but we can call them," Buckman said.

So, he did.

"Mom, we're in University City by the arboretum. We want to know where I was conceived. Any idea?"

"Oh Pierce, that is funny but it was more than 50 years go. We love you son. We adore you. You are our sun, moon and stars. Our only child because we couldn't handle another like you. Our world revolves around you. We are mere planets in your gravitational pull. You are the coolest thing we have ever created. But you won't find a manger and the Heavenly Hosts hovering above it. Even if I was there I don't think I could find it. We didn't go looking for a place to conceive you. That wasn't the plan. There was a blanket, a full moon and cheap wine involved. In fact, there was no plan. Obviously. But if you look for two empty bottles of cheap wine, that might be the place."

"Love you mom. Can you and dad come down to Iowa with Kim? I'll take you to the arboretum."

"Not this time but we'll come down soon and tell stories about you."

"Senator, are we really telling this story in public?" Carl asked.

"Sure. Local flavor. Even the neo-cons have sex. Rushton has had sex. I've never seen it myself and can't imagine it, but I believe it happens," the senator said.

They got out and walked around on a trail for a few minutes. It was their first campaign stop in Iowa. There wasn't another soul in sight at the moment.

"Your advance people have got to do a better job," joked Susan, who had been looking up Iowa media outlets and starting a list of media contacts when the conversation about the senator's conception attracted her attention.

"So, this is where it all began," the senator said, like he was guiding a biology class of middle school students on a field trip.

As they headed back to the RV, they saw several young people bicycling on the trail.

"Senator Pierce Buckman...how are you today?" the senator

said, extending his hand.

"Minnesota, right?" one of the bikers asked. "What are you doing here?"

"Well, you know that Iowa Caucus thing that comes around every four years? I'm considering running for president. But enough about me. Tell me about yourself. What would you like to see a new president do that would make your life better?"

"How about starting with the cost of college? I'm a graduate student. I'll have about $45,000 in student debt when I graduate. I figure that will take me about 20 years to pay off. That's if I can find a job."

Buckman had switched on his professional identity. He was no longer joking around. He was engaged. He was listening. He was thinking.

"Yeah, you know what a first-year teacher makes?" said another of the bikers. "Iowa has a good reputation for its public schools and Iowa high school kids are usually near the top in standardized test scores. But a first-year teacher might not make $35,000. Pretty tough to pay off those student loans."

"Let me tell you what I would do," the senator began. "I want to start by making the first two years of college or trade school tuition free for every American kid who qualifies. We can do that. We can do that by making sure businesses and the wealthiest individuals who need the skills developed by the kids like yourselves are paying their fair share of taxes. They should look at it as a jobs program to maintain and grow their businesses. We can make loans for the next two years no-interest loans. And we'll make them forgivable if you serve in some way. I'm not only talking military service. I'm talking about community service, the Peace Corps, AmeriCorps, Habitat for Humanity, tutoring kids in reading, working in day cares, working as para-educators and volunteering for global service like paid internships in foreign countries. Serve for two years with authorized, legitimate service agencies and two years of college are paid."

A stump speech was being developed.

"Students your age will be better prepared for college after two years of service. They will have better life experiences when they start or finish college. They will be more successful and more mature. The dropout rate will decline. We can get our economy stimulated by producing a highly skilled, passionate, work force. New employees will come with a strong work ethic and with valuable life experiences like problem solving to benefit their employer."

Ryan Holton had information cards in the RV. He got them out with a clipboard and had all four of the cyclists sign cards with names, addresses, phone numbers and email addresses. Their data base was started with four names.

Carl Lyon took notes about the conversation.

The Senator wasn't done. From the arboretum, they drove to the central campus and found The Center. The Center at Crossroads State is one of the landmark features of a campus that often makes lists of the most scenic in the United States. He walked into the food court and went table to table, introducing himself. He stopped in at the bowling lanes where a bowling class was in session. He rolled two frames with no gutter balls and posed for photos with the students.

They stopped at the Sound Stage, The Center's bar and live music venue. Carl made a note to visit the place on a weekend night.

The senator interrupted students who were studying quietly. He asked about what they were working on. He told them he was a college professor. He introduced himself to the employees of the campus bookstore and the convenience store in the lower level.

Susan and Ryan got as many contact cards signed as they could as the senator moved quickly throughout the grand stone building.

The last stop of the day was for dinner at a legendary local restaurant, one of the highest volume restaurants in Iowa. If you were in University City, you ate at this place. Again, he went table to table introducing himself. No one complained about the intrusion. He made sure he talked with the fresh-faced wait staff. He asked a manager to take him to the back-of-the-house.

"So, this is where the magic happens?" Buckman said as he talked with the staff. "If you were responsible for what we just ate, you guys are doing a great job back here. Are any of you students at Crossroads?"

Several indicated they were.

"You are wondering why this guy is back here bugging you. I am Senator Buckman of Minnesota. It is about 10 months away, but I want you to get the night off and come to the Iowa Caucus. I want your support. I want you to get out your phones when you can and schedule it … February 1, Iowa Caucus. The president we have now doesn't really understand what you are doing to earn a college degree. He doesn't seem to care if you have $30,000 or more in college debt when you graduate. The people he cares about are often not working very hard for millions of dollars every year, certainly not as hard as you work.

"I've worked in places like this. It's hard work for not a lot of money. I helped raise the minimum wage nationally and we'll keep working. I think we can get it higher. You'll hear about something called a universal living wage. I would support that. We're going to work on a plan to reduce student debt. I have some other ideas you will like but I need your help on caucus night."

It was nearly 9 p.m. before he had shaken the last hand and taken the last photo. He wasn't done yet. By 10 p.m. they were at the main entrance of the largest hospital campus in Des Moines as employees left work and others arrived.

"Pierce Buckman, U.S. senator from Minnesota," he said as he stuck out his hand.

Most just brusquely passed him. Only a few stopped.

"Tell me about your job," the senator asked as the employees walked past him.

He seemed genuinely interested in what they had to say if they took the time to stop.

"You know those rude women who brushed past you without shaking hands probably were carrying MRSA out on their skin," was Susan Lyon's snide comment later. "Or c-diff (clostridium difficile). We just saved you from a possibly dangerous infection."

Kim Wakefield had booked four rooms, one a suite, at a moderately priced extended-stay motel in suburban Des Moines. At least there was enough money from the Holtons and their friends to make sure everyone had their own room. The rooms were comfortable with small galley kitchens. And there was free breakfast. This was a campaign that apparently would be fueled by free cereal, fresh fruit, pastries, toast and juice. They made a habit of bagging up extra items for the road.

On the first full day of campaigning in Iowa, Kim had scheduled a house party in Des Moines, a Democratic Party event in Iowa Falls and a talk for educators and political science students at the North Iowa Teachers College in Cedar Falls.

At Ellington Community College in Iowa Falls, the motorhome pulled up and stopped. The stop wasn't on the schedule. Students taking advantage of an unusually warm day for March were surprised that a U.S. senator approached them.

"Senator Pierce Buckman. Tell me what you are all studying," he said, grinning.

One of the students said she was an agricultural business student. Another said he was studying wind power maintenance.

"What a good thing to study in Iowa. We have seen hundreds of wind chargers. Someone has to keep them running," the senator said. "What I would do if I run for president is make sure we support new and renewable energy. How long is your program?

"What we're going to do is pay the first two years of college for everyone who wants to attend a college or trade school or learn a skilled trade," the senator continued. "And the next two years will be paid for if you serve the country in some way. Not just the military, but in an approved service initiative. You might work in a national park for two years, or in a blighted area of a city in a preschool, or as a paraeducator, or in the Peace Corps in a foreign country where you can used what you have learned in college."

More students gathered around.

"Any nursing students here? If you want to be a nurse, we'll help you get there and help you advance your education. We are headed for a nursing shortage but our president apparently isn't concerned."

Buckman was excited and talking quickly.

Carl and Susan were trying to get the senator back on the bus. So far, he was only 20 minutes late for a stop at the Pie Ponderosa, a pizza place in Iowa Falls.

Ryan turned the key and got only grinding noise. The

motorhome was going nowhere in its present condition.

"Starter or battery, I'd say. We're walking," the senator said. "Ryan, call for service."

It was a few blocks from the community college campus to the pizza place. Several of the students strolled with the senator. They asked questions about his health care plan, the environment, more about his two-year service program, and his thoughts about immigration reform.

Carl Lyon counted 21 people at the restaurant. There was pizza, soda and beer available. The senator, now 35 minutes late, made a brief opening statement that was interrupted by a silver-haired woman relying on a walker.

Her tone was noticeably confrontational as she asked, "Excuse me, but who are you and why should I support you and not Mike Clarke? Mike Clarke can beat Jack Rushton. He almost did before. Can you beat Rushton?"

The senator was unfazed. He had an answer and explanation Carl Lyon would later remember as the moment the senator defined his acceptability as a candidate. He might not last long in the process, but he had a message. Ryan Holton had Buckman's reaction on video.

"I am Senator Pierce Buckman from Minnesota. I was born in University City, Iowa. My parents are graduates of Crossroads State University. They taught as grad students while they were students there. They had me and eventually became college professors in Minnesota. We moved to Owatonna. I was also a professor at Big River State University in Minnesota in political science. About 11 years ago I had this crazy idea that I needed to stop being only an activist with strong opinions and actually do something instead of just talking.

"What I did was run for the United States Senate. No money, no plan, no political experience…just a bunch of progressive ideas. Probably a lot like the people in this room at this moment, most people didn't believe I had a chance. They were right at the time. But I did have a message and I still do. I was able to build a coalition of supporters. I went to every corner of the state. Went to all of the American Indian reservations. Went into the neighborhoods in the Twin Cities where people just try to survive from day to day and usually don't vote. They voted for me by an 80 percent margin over opponents. I went to the colleges and was able to attract hundreds of students who went to work as volunteers for me. I have been elected twice, which really isn't important to me. What is important to me, every day, whether I am in Washington, D.C. in the Senate chamber, in Minnesota talking to a Republican voter, or in a pizza restaurant in Iowa Falls, is what I want to do for people and what we can do together for the future of this country.

"Here is what else you need to know about me: If I decide to run, which I haven't yet, I will be the candidate who talks about the future. I will be the candidate who talks about universal healthcare using the systems we already have in place … Medicare, Medicaid, SCHIP for children's health in all 50 states…and expand them so that everyone has access to healthcare. There will be sacrifices to get there but we can do it together. I will be the candidate who talks about the underserved, the neglected, the forgotten. I will be the candidate talking about rebuilding our infrastructure across the country. I will be the candidate talking about a program I'm calling 'Schools Without Barriers.' They will be schools with before and after school programs, schools with early education programs, schools where no child is ever sent home hungry, schools open for after-hours tutoring and fitness and wellness opportunities, schools with adult learning and interaction so parents and grandparents can help their students at home. Schools with public computers so the neighborhoods are connected and people who live in the neighborhood have the same access to the web as everyone else. Schools where all barriers to learning are eliminated so that every student has the opportunity to thrive and become a valuable contributor to society.

"Now, everyone else you talk with before the Iowa Caucuses next February 1 will tell you I am the fantasy candidate. They will tell you we can't possibly do all these things, that they will cost trillions of dollars this country doesn't have. I believe they are wrong. We can do this because we are going to have an equitable tax system. The wealthy will pay their fair share. In my inaugural address, I will announce a 10 percent across-the-board reduction in every department in federal government. Now we know this could probably be 15 percent or even higher without any disruption of quality services, but we'll start at 5 percent and gradually go to 10 percent. Those funds will be redistributed to rebuild the infrastructure, provide health care access to all Americans. We already cover the most vulnerable Americans … the youngest, the poorest, the oldest Americans … we're going to fill in the remaining gaps with affordable, quality healthcare.

"I'm the candidate with vision. I want to do important things but it can't happen without your support. I don't care about the next election. I think this one is important enough. I see a different direction than the one the Jack Rushton administration sees. But none of this will work without your support. That's why I am here tonight. Next February 1 you will caucus here in Iowa. That starts the process of sending Jack Rushton back to Texas. We can do that.

"That isn't a negative thing. Texas is a wonderful, beautiful place. Not a bad place at all to retire. You can help the president retire if you share the vision I've described tonight.

"I am going to ask you to do something for me. I am going to ask you to participate. I'm going to ask you to help. I'm going to ask you to share the vision and share the responsibility. Knock on doors, register voters, volunteer. Together, we are going to do something life changing…country changing."

The reaction was a mix of first laughter at the thought of retiring Rushton, then applause and a couple of hoots as Buckman closed. The woman who asked the confrontational question was beaming. She moved across the room on her walker to hug the senator.

Buckman for President had a candidate. They didn't have money, they didn't have organization, they didn't have a campaign director, but Carl thought for damn sure that first day in Iowa they had a candidate, and the candidate had a message that would resonate with progressives.

About the time they left the Pie Ponderosa, Ryan Holton was out front with the motorhome. It only needed a battery. He was able to install it himself with the help of a couple of Ellington students. Cedar Falls and the North Iowa Teachers College were about an hour away. They were going to be at least 30 minutes late for a talk with college professors in a conference center in the education building.

"Beatrice. I'm naming her Beatrice," Ryan reported. "She can be cranky, like a grandma or a great aunt, but basically lovable."

"Beatrice…I like it," the senator said.

Beatrice rumbled toward Cedar Falls.

"This school has a very good reputation for educating educators," Buckman said of the next stop. He was apparently starting up the interview with Carl again.

Carl would understand that he needed to be ready when the senator had something to say.

"I almost enrolled there and could have gotten a scholarship for wrestling but my parents really thought I belonged at an Ivy League school. They thought I could handle it socially and academically. I visited Princeton and liked it.

"I was pretty independent by then. I'd had opportunities to see most of the country and many foreign countries on student tours my parents led every summer. I wasn't afraid of going across the country to college. And it was Ivy League. I always challenged myself academically."

"Do you think what you saw on those summer trips shaped who you are now?" Carl asked after flipping on the digital recorder.

"No question. We saw the best of foreign culture obviously, but we also went off the beaten path. I've been in rural areas of Mexico and Central America, Africa. I have been to China. I counted like 35 countries I had visited by the time I graduated from Princeton. When I was in high school on these tours with my parents, I'd go off on my own exploring. I definitely saw the need of these people and opportunities to help. We're blessed in this country but you know what, I see some of the identical needs and neglect I saw visiting other countries."

"Most of the countries you visited likely had socialized medicine. Is that where your thoughts about the need for single payer came from?" Carl asked.

"You know what happened? My father got very ill with a virus…a stomach thing… when we were touring England. We had to find a doctor for him. I think I was maybe going into

42

eighth grade. I remember my mom was concerned how that was going to happen and how expensive it was going to be. She was thinking about her U.S. experiences. It wasn't difficult at all. We found a clinic, he was checked over, he was given a diagnosis, medication and we reached the dreaded moment when she thought she would have to pay $100 or more, which was a lot then. No charge. Nothing. Not even a deductible. I don't know if they ever got a bill. We were not even part of their national health plan. I've never forgotten that. Neither has my mom. It was the moment when I figured out that maybe not everything was the biggest and best in the United States and maybe we had something to learn from other countries about values and taking care of their citizens. It was the same thing in other countries. We often have this tunnel vision that focuses only on ourselves. We have an arrogance sometimes as Americans. We often believe we have the best of lives. Rushton, unfortunately, has that narrow focus. This won't go in our book, but we don't have all the answers and we can learn from other countries. We need to be open-minded as a country. As a kid, I was lucky to have the parents I had. I saw other cultures and societies. A lot of Americans never experience much of the world outside our borders. Still, we often believe we are exceptional or different. That is Rushton's perspective."

"Senator, you need to add some of this to what you've been talking about to groups," Carl suggested.

In front of the educators, who the senator thought would understand what he was saying without believing he was critical of his own country, he did add the stories about traveling with his parents. He was still wearing jeans but he had pulled on a sport coat.

"I would tell you to challenge your students and challenge yourselves to look beyond your own biases, beyond your own borders, outside of your own comfort zone to understand the world around us and the occasional volatility of that world," the senator said. "I believe our focus in this country is too narrow and too parochial. There are other ideas and other perspectives around us. If we are inflexible to new ideas, if we believe the archaic logic that quote 'but we've always done it this way' we are imposing sanctions and limits on ourselves and diminishing our ability to work cooperatively with other nations. There are changes we can make together. Should I decide to seek the presidency, I will use my life experiences to open up communication with other countries and find common ground and common goals. It won't always be possible. There will always be conflict and seemingly unreachable solutions but in my administration, we will always have lines of communication. If I do open a campaign for president, I want your support. We can do big things together. I will be back to talk more but thanks for your time tonight."

The teachers were reluctant to leave. They asked the senator questions for another hour about everything from his plans for free college education, family-centric schools, volunteer service, universal healthcare, universal living wage and immigration reform. A group of political science instructors and professors asked Buckman to join them at a campus bar to further the discussion.

"We can't stay long. We're headed back to Des Moines yet tonight, but sure," the senator responded.

Buckman walked to the College Town district. The moment he entered the bar and grill he began introducing himself table-by-table. The dozen or so patrons, probably semi-lit already, treated him like he was already the president. They wanted photos and autographs. They wanted him to sit down and drink from their pitchers.

Carl had not seen the senator's transformation before. This was a guy who seemed to move effortlessly from a deep dive policy discussion with professors to a public house with students. He let one table pour him a glass from their pitcher but barely took a sip. It just seemed as though he did. It was a gift he had. He rarely drank the entire beer in front of him. He talked about being a professor himself and told them about his plan for two years of service in exchange for two years of tuition.

"Don't you think going into a city to help teach young children would be fulfilling? And you'll be paid a little for the experience and you'll receive two years to finish your education. It will be like a semester overseas except it will be for a year or two," he explained, talking over the din of the pub. "It will be like one of Franklin Roosevelt's programs like WPA or CCC, only for a new generation."

Ryan Holton and Susan Lyon had concluded they needed tablet computers or portable wireless kiosks to sign up potential volunteers and caucus voters more quickly and efficiently. For now, they were still going table-to-table with clipboards. Nearly every student in the place signed information cards.

They made it back to Des Moines by 12:45 a.m. At 6 a.m., the senator was back up and in the hotel's exercise room.

Team Buckman, such as it was, did a few more house parties and noon luncheons for two weeks before agreeing it was time to go back to Minnesota to write a candidacy statement, plan an announcement event and add staff to The Warehouse. The senator wanted to get Kim on the road with him.

CHAPTER 6
Jumping In

In the morning newspaper, the first Hawkeye State Poll results for the Iowa Caucuses nine months away were reported. Polling likely caucus goers based on past participation, the Democratic preferences were New York Governor Mike Clarke at 40 percent, former Virginia Governor Karla Foster, 32 percent, U.S. Senator Stanton Fuller of Florida with 12 percent, favorite son U.S. Senator from Iowa Lansing Landon, 11 percent, and Senator Pierce Buckman, 3 percent. Two percent of likely caucus goers were undecided.

"We apparently polled better than undecided so we have that going for us," Buckman said, smiling.

There was just enough money coming in, without having to dip into the newly formed PAC set up by the Holtons and their friends, to pay for some of the additions the campaign needed.

On the list were a campaign spokesperson in the field, another driver, a couple of advance kids for the road, another vehicle for the field staff, a paid campaign director, more staff in The Warehouse, and dozens of volunteers to make phone calls and provide content for social media sites. Direct mail to Iowa Democrats could be delayed. Ryan Holton and Susan Lyon broached the idea of wireless, portable kiosks where people could sign up for emails, commit to caucus, make contributions and register their willingness to volunteer.

"See if we can find something like that or at least laptops with the same capability," the senator said.

There was talk during the trip back to the Twin Cities about a luxury bus that would give the campaign some identity and comfort on the road. Buckman nixed that one himself. He claimed a $500,000 loaded luxury bus would be out of step with the grass roots campaign he wanted. He agreed to vinyl cling signs on the motorhome windows.

"We're keeping Beatrice. Now where and when are we going to announce we're moving forward?" the senator asked the group assembled in The Warehouse. "I'm thinking at the Capitol. Glen (Governor Glen McGrath) will support that. I think he'll endorse eventually. I'll talk with him personally. Carl, start working on an announcement. You've heard what I've been saying. Keep making the same points … moving forward, new ideas, universal health care … and talk with me more about our vision for family centric schools and how they can improve the future for millions of kids. And I might as well get it out there immediately; I support much more restrictive laws on access to guns, especially semi-automatic weapons, and I would support closing loopholes for gun shows and private sales by individuals. And if I am elected, I will push for much higher taxes on sales, sale of ammunition and replacement parts. Similar to how we tax tobacco sales now. A portion of revenue from sales taxes will support enhanced community-based mental health programs. Would a national buy-back of guns be effective in taking some guns off the streets? I will work on a date with the governor."

The boat house at the Holton mansion was the perfect place to start working on Senator Buckman's vision for the country. It was quiet with a view of Lake Minnetonka, which was showing the first signs of spring melt. Carl was comfortable being back in Minnesota with Susan. The Holtons were hospitable hosts. They invited the Lyons in for a meal at least once a day and wine at night. They had their run of the place, including the indoor pool, gym and wine cellar.

Three house parties for Senator Buckman were scheduled at the Holtons' home. The groups were larger than they had been so far in Iowa and the basket with the checks was deeper. The Holtons had friends with no reluctance to write four-figure checks to the political action committee funneling funds to the Buckman campaign.

Carl came up with a "Bowling with Buckman" exclusive fundraiser on the two lanes glowing with neon in the lower level of the Holtons' mansion. Twenty potential and likely supporters attended the first bowling fundraiser with the senator. Catered food and constantly flowing beer and mixed drinks helped open up wallets and checkbooks. Nearly $50,000 was raised.

"Senator, what if we tried 'Biking with Buckman' events in Iowa? Maybe a 10-mile or 90-minute ride and then drinks and snacks at the end. We could do them all over Iowa. End them with a pitch for volunteers and caucus votes," Carl suggested.

"Let's try it. We'll see how it goes," the senator said. "We'll make it an environmental message. Not so much a fundraiser. Invite families, kids, college students and we'll talk about our education priorities, too. Get those college students we met at Crossroads State involved. Order us campaign bikes, helmets, backpacks, that kind of stuff. Do you ride, Carl?"

"We did in Big River around the lake," Carl said.

"Biking with Buckman" would be a project the growing number of college students hanging out at The Warehouse would enjoy planning.

Overlooking the lake, Carl started working on the senator's announcement. The sun was setting on the horizon and it was a spectacular palette of pink, orange and purple.

"I wish everyone could see this," Carl said to Susan.

"Is that the theme of this campaign?" she asked. "A different, beautiful horizon that everyone should experience. Make it a message everyone can understand, whether they agree with the vision or not."

Vision, moving forward, healthcare, education, volunteerism, equitable taxation, across-the-board budget cuts, the environment ... they were subjects Carl thought would capture the attention of potential voters, donors and the media.

On a legal pad he started working on the talking points for an announcement.

McGrath agreed to every idea of his friend's plan except for his personal endorsement of the Buckman for President campaign.

"Pierce, you know that if you are the nominee, I will be the first to jump out there for you and I'll go out and do whatever I can to support you, but for now, let's keep it informal support. I won't endorse anyone else; it's just too early," McGrath explained.

On March 15, on the steps of the historic Minnesota State Capitol, U.S. Senator Pierce Morrison Buckman became the second Democrat – Karla Foster was first – to officially become a candidate for the presidency. On an unseasonably warm morning for Minnesota in March, Buckman laid out his plan for a different country. The basic backdrop was the Capitol building. There were about a dozen labor leaders, community activists and Democratic legislators behind the podium

Twenty minutes before the announcement, Jason Holton, senior reporter at the Minnesota Standard and the son of Buckman's most influential supporter so far, Carol Collier Holton, sat down for an exclusive interview with the senator, arranged by Carl.

"Jason, great to see you again," Carl said as he exchanged hugs.

"Hoodie," Holton corrected, laughing at the nickname he knew Carl preferred for him.

"Hooded sweatshirt to meet a presidential candidate. You didn't let us down today. How are my favorite reporters? How is Lisa? Is she here with you?" Carl asked. "How about Daniel? Is he your shooter today?"

"Not Lisa. She has other assignments. Yeah, Daniel is out setting up."

The senator, wearing khaki pants, a blue dress shirt and corduroy sports coat but no overcoat and no tie, came into the room where the interview would take place. He was 10 minutes late, which was pretty good by the senator's standards. Carl noticed Buckman was not wearing socks.

"Jason, how are you?" the senator said as he entered. "Your mom and dad tell me you are moving up at The Standard? Any chance you'll come and work with me? We need to talk."

"No sir, I think I belong on the outside looking in," Hoodie responded. "Besides, I'm a Rushton supporter."

They all laughed. His family was one of the most influential in Minnesota Democratic-Farmer-Labor (DFL) politics. Privately, Hoodie was a full-fledged progressive. He was careful readers couldn't determine his political leanings in his reporting, although it was no secret how his family leaned.

"Senator, what makes you think you can compete in a highly competitive field of Democrats? What will make you different?" was Hoodie's first question.

"Jason, if I accomplish one thing in this campaign effort, it will be to change the conversation and hopefully the direction of this country. We have just been going along for a long time as a country without any real vision. We don't take on the big things to improve this country and improve the lives of people. We don't rebuild highways, bridges, national parks. We don't come up with solutions to why too many people feel they have no future or path to success."

"We lack direction and ambition. We have become complacent as a county because our leadership is complacent."

"What will you talk about starting today?"

"Universal healthcare, an initiative I'm calling 'Schools Without Barriers;' free and reduced cost higher education; a plan to rebuild roads, bridges, sewer systems, water plants, parks, airports; volunteer opportunities to pay for college; equitable taxation and reducing government employment. I will talk about my plans to limit access to semi-auto handguns and rifles. I would push Congress for much higher taxes on sale of guns, on sale of ammunitions and parts replacement. We will consider the logistics and feasibility of a national gun 'buy back' initiative."

"How do you propose paying for all of this?" Hoodie asked.

"Equitable taxation will be necessary. By that, I mean big businesses and the wealthiest individuals and families have not been participating at the level they should be. I believe that if corporations want a skilled, educated and productive workforce in the future, they need to do more to make that happen. And Jason, I know this will not be popular with some of the unions in government, but I believe we can redirect our limited resources by reducing government budgets and employment. I will talk today about reducing government employment by 10 percent in my first term as president. I will ask for a phased-in 10 percent reduction in every department and 10 percent reduction in employment, and redirect those funds toward free and reduced college education, infrastructure improvements and providing quality healthcare to every person in this country."

"You know that doesn't sound like the stereotypical 'tax-and-spend' progressive?" Hoodie asked.

"I don't want anyone to tell us we can't do things differently because we don't have the funding. We will find the resources by doing things differently. We will ask for sacrifices by everyone, starting with big business, big banking, big insurance, big pharma and all the way down to the most vulnerable, who will have a brighter future if they are willing to participate in that future. I don't think any department of the federal government should be untouchable when it comes to budgets and employment levels. We will have a different vision and a vision that believes major initiatives can be accomplished. We will change our priorities. If you don't believe it can happen, I am not your candidate."

Media at the announcement appeared to nearly match the number of spectators at the event. Carl and Ryan both counted those in attendance – 97 to be exact. The senator didn't mention the sparseness of the crowd. He forged ahead from the start of the announcement.

"Last night here in Minnesota there was a spectacular sunset. It was God's incredible artistry. The horizon was splashed with pink, purple and red. Spectacular.

"I sat and experienced this wonder and I thought it was a shame that not everyone got to experience the sight.

"And I thought this: 'This is something we can all agree

upon.' It was a wonder. On this there would be no political debate. No one would complain about the cost. It was free. No one would say the spectacular sight was too progressive, or socialist, or impossible to accomplish. It was right there in front of me. Almost within reach it seemed.

"That is the horizon … the vision … we need to share. We need to find solutions we can work toward together. We need to share a vision of what can be done when we are together, not divided or polarized. I have a vision of quality, affordable health care.

"People will participate in the vision of a country where every child who wants education beyond high school will be able to afford college or trade school.

"People will gather together for a vision of fairness. The vision of a country where big business and the wealthiest individuals and families will be willing to support our future.

"I believe we can have better and safer roads, better and safer bridges, improved airport runways, schools with great environments for learning and young people scattered throughout the country and the globe making a contribution to society in order to help pay for their college education.

"If you share a vision where the United States looks ahead, not behind, isn't afraid of big projects and progress, isn't afraid of taking care of the most vulnerable, the forgotten, the neglected, the unhealthy, physically and mentally, and the most impoverished, then I ask you to join me.

"My campaign will be about vision and compassion, relentlessly focused on goals to improve this country and service to our country.

"I am Pierce Buckman and I am announcing today I will be a candidate for President of the United States. If you share this vision, please join us in our efforts."

Senator Buckman went on to talk in some detail about his ideas. He brought up his plans for reducing the number of guns in the country by half through buybacks and a ban on semi-automatic handguns and rifles.

Other than the small crowd, the day had gone well.

"Now find me some Iowans," the candidate said as they

headed back to the Holtons' manse on the lake.

Among the 97 in attendance was a young man who stood toward the back of the crowd. He was dressed in camouflage hunting jacket over a T-shirt with a happy face emoji. There was no reason to notice him. Throughout his life, he had been invisible.

CHAPTER 7

Jericho Adams Brooks

At 3 a.m., entering the bedroom incensed at hearing the distinctive clicking of keystrokes, Jericho Adams Brooks' stepfather, Michael Munger, grabbed the laptop computer from his stepson's hands. The 18-year-old Jericho tried to hold on but was overpowered. Michael smashed the computer against a bedpost. It wasn't destroyed with the first smash. The second time, Michael Munger brought it down, this time with two hands from over his head with additional force, smashing it into many pieces. He broke it into flying bits of plastic with a third attempt.

"You little fuck, I told you what would happen if you didn't get off the computer. Now you will get off, won't you? Fucking right you will, you faggot," Michael said. "You have to be the weirdest fucking kid I've ever knew. Can't wait until you get out of this house. You go to school and come home and you are up here all the time, or you are off with your faggot friends doing faggot things. You'll leave now. Your shit somehow got busted up.

"By the way, I am happy about one thing: Yeah, I'm damn near joyous you aren't really my son. I would hate it if I had a piece of shit little faggot as a son. You are just so weird. Hell, you are 18. When are you getting out?"

The one-sided rant went on for another 20 minutes. It wasn't the worst Jericho had experienced at the hands of his stepfather. Michael Munger had threatened to kill Jericho more than once. One night when he was wasted – Jericho believed Munger was an alcoholic -- he pulled a pistol out of a closet and pointed it at the young man's chest for the mortal sin of skipping classes.

"Like *you* are some scholar," Jericho wanted to say.

He didn't dare challenge his stepfather considering his likely drunken condition. A shaky trigger finger would kill Jericho. He didn't flinch at the threat or plead for his life. It wasn't that great a life anyway.

Munger was often unemployed and virtually unemployable because of his drinking. He married Jericho's mother after the overdose death of her husband and Jericho's father, Adams Brooks. The death wasn't considered a suicide although Adams Brooks had enough cocaine in his system to do the job adequately, even if it was "an accidental overdose," according to the coroner's report.

Harmony Brooks, Jericho's mother, was not abusive. She was also abused at the hands of Michael Munger. She had her own issues. She had struggled for years with depression. It was Jericho who took care of her most of the time. Jericho was devoted to his mother. He cooked for her and assisted with routine daily tasks. He sometimes helped her go to the bathroom.

His school career was patchy. Because they moved frequently from rental to rental, usually uprooting just before being evicted, Jericho attended four middle schools and was now a senior in his third high school in northern Minnesota. He was able to form relationships at every school with a few others who were avid gamers. They played video games together online. His limited network of friends introduced Jericho to ultraviolent games with realistic weaponry, modern warfare and disregard for human life. The images of figures being blown up, decapitated, run over by trucks, dropped in a heap by automatic weapons, were just part of the games. The farther a player advanced in the game, the greater the death threat he possessed.

Jericho and his small network of friends were binge gamers. He rarely invited friends to his own dysfunctional house. At friends' houses, though, with understanding, even loving parents, they would play all night, often against other socially isolated gamers all over the country. As they played, they talked trash and threatened each other through messaging. At school, Jericho was quiet, showing virtually no interest in school events or activities. He was considered by adults to be a bright kid who simply didn't care or pay much attention to classwork. But when the binge gaming started, he came out of his shell. He exceled at the games and the trash talk. He threatened opponents with disembowelment or decapitation. He was usually the first to advance to a new weapon.

His situation at home deteriorated when Michael destroyed his laptop. He was temporarily left out of his circle of friends until he was able to get enough money secretly from his mother and friends and applied for a credit card to buy another laptop. He got his life back. He hid the computer in his room. He had plans to steal one from school if he didn't get the money together.

Michael Munger's emotional and verbal abuse of Harmony Brooks sometimes became physical. Her worst beating resulted in a broken nose and a gash on her head where she fell. Munger threatened Jericho and Harmony with firearms he kept locked away in a floor-to-ceiling cabinet in the cluttered garage. He hit Harmony with his fists. She fought back and occasionally started the battle herself, purposely aggravating her husband.

Jericho stepfather would look for any way to intimidate and ridicule his stepson. He would suggest Jericho was gay, which he wasn't, and that he couldn't wait to "get you out of this fucked up house because you are the one fucking everything up around here."

CHAPTER 8

Hoops Campaigning

Carl Lyon knew where to find Iowans to court months before the caucuses. Thousands of them would be a few blocks away from The Warehouse headquarters.

"They will be coming here this weekend to watch the Crossroads State University basketball team in the opening rounds of the National University Union basketball tournament," Carl told the senator. "They have the top-ranked team in the country right now. Know anything about basketball?"

"Game played with a ball … and a basket?" the senator asked, grinning. "I know my alma mater, Princeton, has a really good team. I was too short for that game and don't know much about it. Wrestlers usually have no clue about hoops and generally no skills for the game. They would probably foul out every game. Every player would be on the bench wiping up blood if guys with a wrestler's mentality played. If the object of the game was to prevent the other team from ever scoring, by whatever means possible, that would be interesting. Thousands of people coming here? Can we get tickets?"

"With some help from the Holtons or the governor, maybe," Carl said. "You are a presidential candidate now. You can get a lot of perks. Sure, we can score tickets."

Carl was a sports reporter in a past life and was still a fan of college sports. He filled the senator in on the Crossroads State Explorers, favorites to win the school's first national basketball championship.

"No. 1 national rating all season. Very interesting bunch. Fans and media call them the League of Nations because of where the players are from. Kondo Kone is a 6-foot-10, 250-pound center from Nigeria. Fans started out calling him 'Big House' …you know, Kondo?... but that was soon deemed to be inappropriate. The Crossroads Foreign Students Association objected to the 'Big House' reference and the term's place in the history of slavery. Students then figured out that Kone is a global company making elevators and escalators. Kondo Kone became 'The Escalator.'

"Rico Arriaga is a 6-4 point guard from Puerto Rico who transferred from a junior college."

"They have a forward, Nigel Barton, from Quebec of all places. He is 6-8, maybe 170 pounds. They call him Sliver."

Now reading from the university's basketball website, Carl continued.

"Wilhelm Johann Wagner is a 6-7 swing player from Rotterdam, Germany, by way of Bettendorf High School in Iowa. His parents, both engineers, came to work for a global agriculture company based in the Quad Cities area of Western Illinois and Eastern Iowa. Everyone wanted Wagner. Pronounced like the composer … Vogner. He can shoot and score. A great passer. Couldn't defend a traffic cone but offensively, he is a brilliant player. Smart kid, too. Speaks German, French, English and Spanish. Give him any space at all and he is going to be making shots. He is in range, in his mind anyway, before the bus engine cools down. Shoots about 43 percent from 3-point range and 91 percent from the free throw line. But if he scores 30, whoever he is guarding will probably have at least 20. Had 47 one game and the guys he was guarding combined for 35. They call him 'The Kaiser.'"

"Kaiser, Escalator, possibly Sliver and probably the coach, James Jackson Webb … Jimmy Jack or J.J. to virtually everyone … will all be in professional basketball next season. They've got three or four more decent players. It says they have lost only three games this season … all on the road in overtime games."

Jimmy Jack Webb, a proud son of Texas, had repaired his image after his career was tarnished by indiscretions with an assistant football coach's wife while he was an assistant basketball coach at a college in his home state. He had moderated his drinking since then.

"League of Nations, huh? I like that. I'm better with college wrestling, though," the senator said.

"Well, the National University Union wrestling championships are in Des Moines this weekend, too. Tell you what, we'll go to basketball and still make it to Des Moines for the wrestling tournament on Saturday," Carl promised.

"I wrestled in it twice. Finished third as a senior. Got hosed in the semifinals," said the senator, now excited by the idea of being back at the national wrestling tournament.

Carl Lyon had not misjudged the situation. Thousands of Iowans had arrived in the Twin Cities starting two days before the Explorers opened play in the national tournament. The night before their tournament debut, there was a pep rally scheduled in a downtown Minneapolis convention center.

Carl drove the senator to the Iowans. What they found was a crowd of several thousand shoulder-to-shoulder drinking $7.50 beers and equally overpriced popcorn and hot dogs. The fans were whooping it up with the cheerleaders, dance team, Explorers mascot and the pep band. The mascot, named Meriwether, was a guy in a hat with a raccoon tail and a fringed leather coat and what appeared to be jeans with 5-inch permanent cuffs. The main event, which apparently would transpire after everyone had one too many $7.50 beers, would be the Explorers players and Coach J.J. Webb.

"Ok, how do we even start trying to get into this place?" asked the senator, who seemed slightly perturbed and uncomfortable with the mass of half-lucid people. "This place will be a mess if they run out of beers. Let's hope the supply holds out. These people could care less about who is running for president right now."

"Senator, give me a few minutes. Stay with me," Carl said.

"Call me Pierce."

"Absolutely not."

Carl knew a few things about gatherings of this nature. Somewhere there would be an entrance for the Explorers.

Preferably with a limited security presence. Or the live TV trucks from Iowa would have a door propped open with the cords they needed to feed the signal to the truck. Or there was one more nearly sure thing. Somewhere the kitchen staff would have a door they used to go outside and have a cigarette or a vape. Food service people are smokers. It was a cultural certainty, Carl believed.

On the back side of the convention center in an alley, three people who were dressed in white shirts, black slacks and aprons were outside taking a break. Another was bringing out the garbage from the kitchen. All were having a cigarette or a vape. About the time Carl was guiding the senator to the door, a luxury bus the Explorers were using for the trip from University City to the Twin Cities pulled up into the alley.

"It's the Explorers," Carl said, feeling brilliant about the timing.

J.J. Webb climbed down the bus steps from the first seat opposite the driver, "the coach's seat," and waited for the rest of the group. Kondo Kone, "The Escalator," was unmistakable.

"Oh my gosh, that is an immense young man," the almost 5-foot-8 tall senator said in an almost awed whisper as he walked toward Coach J.J.

"Coach, Carl Lyon. We've met. I covered a couple of tournaments your teams played in. This is United States Senator Pierce Buckman. He is running for president. I'm helping him out on his staff and he would love to meet you and your guys.".

They would laugh about what came next for weeks. Coach J.J. was very familiar with Rushton.

"So, you are going to beat that vile sonofabitch Jack Rushton? Pleased to meet you. No, ecstatic to meet you. Got to get him out of office. He's a drinker you know. Drinker, hell, he's a drunk," Webb said with a syrupy slow Texas drawl.

Coach J.J. used his pinky and pointer finger to demonstrate someone knocking back five or six drinks. He wore the typical garb for a practice, a coach's long pants, matching jacket and straight-out-of-the-box basketball shoes.

"Horrible drunk, too. Nasty and mean when he is sober, much worse when he is drunk. Oh, believe me, I know. When I was still drinking, we closed some bars down. That was before the sonofabitch had me fired at Texas Liberal Arts College as coach. He was on the board of trustees at the time and the governor. Still amazing to me he is president. What a country! How does that even happen? We had one bad season and he wants me out.

"But it worked out, didn't it? We're having a good run. Tell you what, you come in with us and I'll introduce you to all those crazy ass Explorers fans. Wait till you see this party. I can't endorse you but I can sure as hell introduce you to them. You stand by Sliver so people can see you. Kondo blocks everything around him for five feet. He is a human eclipse. And I will get you tickets right behind the bench tomorrow. How many you need? If I get a technical or two, I will make sure I have my fit in front of you. You'll get national air time. But with this team, I usually just give them a ball and yell if they get lazy on me. Sonofabitch Rushton will be watching from the White House. Bet your ass on that. He hates me and the feeling is mutual. It will make him nuts seeing you hanging out with us."

The senator would say later he had never met anyone like Jimmy Jack Webb.

"Because there aren't many of them," Carl said.

The crowd went crazy as the Explorers appeared on a stage. They were chanting "Escalator" and "Kaiser" and going through an entire routine with the pep band and Meriwether, the mascot, with the 5-inch cuffed pants. Carl knew his ears would be ringing for hours later, as they often were after he covered basketball in a noisy arena. Susan said he needed hearing aids. His response when she made the suggestion was always, "huh?" She didn't appreciate the humor. He speculated the injury to his hearing was permanent.

For the first time all night, the lines at the bars inside the convention center filled by thousands of Explorers fans were only two or three deep instead of a mob scene.

"Folks, this is amazing. The traffic was bumper-to-bumper from Iowa getting here. First traffic jams I've ever seen in Iowa. Thanks for coming tonight and we'll see you tomorrow," Webb finally drawled when he got the crowd quieted. "It has been a fantastic season but we've got lots of work to do starting in the morning. We can't stay long but I wanted to introduce you to U.S. Senator Pierce Buckman, who is running for president and will be in the Iowa Caucuses. Look at that hat he's wearing. He's an Explorers fan now and he'll be behind the bench tomorrow for moral support.

"When we're done here, I hope you do a little meet and greet with him."

The coach talked another five minutes or so, then introduced Escalator. In precise English, Escalator talked a bit about the opponent, suggesting that it didn't matter who they played if they played to their potential. It was something virtually every coach in the tournament would say at some point.

In no more than 20 minutes, the Explorers were headed back to the hotel.

Carl took the senator straight into the crowd as they finished beers and started thinning out.

"I'm Pierce Buckman. My parents are grads of Crossroads and I need your support next Feb. 1 for the Iowa Caucus," he said several dozen times.

Some of the Explorers fans made small talk. A few asked questions.

"Amazing," the senator said. "I've never been part of something like that. Not sure a one of them cared who they were meeting. Coach just told them to meet me. That is political power I'd like to have."

Carl took the senator out the same way they came in. They went through the kitchen. But before he left, Buckman struck up a conversation with the kitchen staff. He quickly realized only a couple of them understood English.

He finally said, ¿Qué hay para cenar?" (*What is for dinner?*). They laughed. He introduced himself in Spanish.

"Mis amigos, no olvide que quiero ser su president." (*My friends, don't forget I want to be your president.*)

They shook his hand and seemed impressed he at least attempted their first language.

Tip-off the next morning was 11:07 a.m. in downtown Power Arena in St. Paul. The first time Senator Pierce Buckman appeared on the national television coverage was at 11:08 a.m. when Wilhelm "Kaiser" Wagner lobbed a high pass into "The Escalator," who jammed the ball down with a roar. Buckman was on his feet behind the bench cheering.

In the White House, President Jack Rushton was pouring his first glass of the day. It was 12:09 after all in the East. Three knuckles of Dark Hills Bourbon with a splash of diet cola. The president had thick knuckles.

"Can you believe this crap? Jimmy Jack has a new frigging fan. It's Professor Pansy," Rushton shouted to no one because he was alone. "Can you believe it?"

One of the Secret Service detail opened the door to the study adjacent to the Oval Office with his hand by his sidearm, seeing what the commotion was all about.

"Look at that! Professor Daffodil at a basketball game," the president said as he swallowed, oblivious that someone else was in the room with the two massive screens tuned to basketball.

Rushton had started referring to Senator Buckman with the derisive floral nicknames for several weeks when it became apparent the senator would be seeking the nomination. His staff had followed along, trying to come up with new flower varieties to attach to the professor and senator. They thought the references were appropriate for a senator with a definite liberal persuasion. Every attempt caused Rushton to growl with laughter.

The Explorers were challenged only for a few minutes in a game they ended up winning by 35 points and passed the century mark with two minutes left. But in those few minutes, Coach J.J. was incensed when he yanked Wilhelm Wagner from the game for giving up a breakout defensively.

"Wil, I want defense like 1941 Germany, not 1945. You are a bright kid. You understand what I'm saying?" the coach fumed loud enough that everyone behind the Explorers' bench could hear. He then turned to the senator and winked at him.

Wil swore at either himself or his coach in German.

At least coach didn't refer to him as "that damn Hun," or "the kraut" as he had in the past before it was strongly suggested he never, ever, do it again, even jokingly, by the Explorers' athletic director. Usually, the coach just called him Wil or Wilhelm if he was really happy with him.

The Kaiser did his thing, floating around the entire game with devastating offensive results. He finished with 31 points and 8 assists. He was 5-of-6 from 3-point range and made 12 free throws without a miss. The opponent couldn't just guard him at the 3-point line because he was also just quick enough on the drive to create offense for himself and others. He had been compared to Larry Bird, although he was not nearly as physical as Bird. Creating your own offense is how you get to the line 12 times and make them all. At one point, the opposing player defending Kaiser just shook his head.

The Escalator had 18 points, 12 on dunks, and 14 rebounds.

Carl scouted out the building for media opportunities during the rout. He talked a couple of media people into doing interviews with the senator. He knocked on the doors of several suites filled by corporate types and asked if the senator could come up and introduce himself at halftime. The senator was shown on the national television coverage several times during the game, and he and the beaming, obviously pregnant Kim were on the "Kiss Cam," drawing a loud reaction from the sellout crowd dominated by Explorers fans in their green and white gear.

Carl and the senator were invited to the Explorers' locker room following the game. The senator went around the room shaking hands with every player,

"OK, we don't play tomorrow, but the next day we'll be back here. You have to come," Coach J.J. pleaded with the senator.

"We're going to Iowa for the wrestling tournament in Des Moines on Saturday. Lots of Iowans there, too," the senator said. "Tell you what, though, you make it to Las Vegas for the semifinals and we'll be there. Not a bad political stop either. We can beat Rushton in Nevada."

"Deal," Coach J.J. said. "Maybe we can get out to dinner. I'm buying. I know what U.S. senators make."

Coach J.J. made nearly 15 times the $174,000 annual salary of a U.S. senator.

Beatrice the campaign bus rattled toward Des Moines and

the Digital Bank Center where the National University Union wrestling tournament was being held. The University of Iowa Hawkeyes had gone through what were considered "down years" for the wrestling program but were back on top of the team standings heading into the final day.

The legendary Mack Daniels, winner of 15 NUU team titles, had been retired for 19 years and for the past eight of those, the Hawkeyes had not won the team title.

"You know, Mack Daniels thought about running for governor once in Iowa. It was like when Eisenhower was being recruited to run in 1952. No one knew what party he was," the senator explained as the bus rolled through North Iowa. "Both parties tried to recruit him. In the end, Coach Daniels decided he didn't really want to be governor and didn't know enough about the workings of government.

"No one in their right mind understands the workings of government. He should have run. Anyway, he is everyone's hero in wrestling. He didn't lose a match in high school and won every match in college except one; the last one of his college career. It's still considered one of the biggest upsets in the history of wrestling, maybe all of college sports. No one could fathom Mack Daniels losing to anyone. He won an Olympic gold. Maybe if he had won that last match in college, he wouldn't have been as motivated to win in the Olympics."

Carl had his recorder out but didn't really need to ask questions. It was the most excited he had heard the senator. The senator's voice quickened and got a bit higher when he was excited. This was in contrast to a conversation with Buckman about policy or politics or why he was running for president. Senator Buckman wanted to talk about wrestling, a sport Carl had discovered in the Olympics. He had met Daniels previously a couple of times when he was coaching in college and in the Olympics.

"I loved wrestling as a kid and still do," the senator continued. "When we moved to Minnesota, we lived next to a high school wrestling coach, Bob Jennings, and their four kids … three boys about my age. They were all good wrestlers.

"That's the thing about wrestling. It is passed down through generations more and better than other sports. If you'd skip a generation or two, the sport might not even exist but it just keeps going. Did you know it is one of the oldest sports known to mankind? Like 15,000 years old. There are ancient references. Abraham Lincoln was a wrestler.

"In the House and Senate there are several of us who wrestled in college. For some reason, they are on the other side of the aisle. Maybe brain damage from the sport is the explanation.

"It's also a very democratic sport with the lower-case d. It doesn't matter what size you are, there is a place for you in wrestling. I was the nerdy kid with glasses when I discovered what the Jennings boys were doing in their basement. Their dad put down old wrestling mats and let his sons and the neighborhood kids go at it. At first it was very humbling for me. Frustrating. I had no clue what I was doing, but Coach Jennings would come down and coach us when he had time, and his sons showed me some things. Really though, you just learn the sport by doing it for hours at a time, having the will to push yourself physically, risk having your ego damaged and working hard."

"It's the type of sport where things can get out of hand emotionally. We put a few holes in the wall over the years with punches, kicks and bodies being thrown off the mat. Coach would close the wrestling room for a while to make the point that the sport was about control and tactics, not anger.

"When it was hot in the summer, we'd take the mats out in the backyard and go at it. Then we'd go to the pool.

"Those were great summers. It was a sport I could be good at. I was competitive academically and wrestling was a sport where I could compete physically with guys my size. Coach Jennings was, and still is, an important influence in my life.

"I won a state championship as a senior and finished third in the nationals as a senior. Lost to a guy from Iowa that Coach Daniels had. To this day, I know I should have won that match. I should have at least made the championship match."

Carl scoped out the suites of the Digital Bank Center. He was looking for the suite occupied by the legendary coach. It didn't take long to find it. He looked inside the opened door of a prime location. On the floor were kids wrestling. The furniture had been shoved out of the way. Sweat dripped from the kids. Their heads were wet with perspiration.

This had to be the place. Carl didn't knock, he just walked in. Pacing around behind the seats at the front of the suite was Mack Daniels. He was intently watching the action, even though he had been retired from coaching for years. Everything he did he seemed to do with intensity.

When the match Daniels was watching was over, he said to the people around him, "Heck of a match for the Hawks ... they are going to win this thing."

Carl saw his opening.

"Coach, Carl Lyon with Senator Pierce Buckman's campaign staff," Lyon said, shaking hands with the coach.

"I remember Buckman from wrestling. Good kid. Have I met you before? You look familiar," Daniels said.

"I've talked to you before both when you were coaching in the Olympics and one year when the National University Union tournament was in Denver. You guys won, of course."

"Yeah, but that was a tough one. Is the Senator here with you? Where is he?"

"He'd like to come and meet you," Carl reported. "Can he come in and talk with you for a few minutes?"

"Of course, everyone else comes in here."

The senator didn't find anything unusual with the story Carl told him about the impromptu wrestling meet going on in the suite.

"That is the sport. Watch old wrestlers. They don't just shake hands. They will hug another wrestler and pretend they are going to throw the other guy for a five-point move or they'll act like they are shooting in for a single-leg takedown," the senator explained to Carl. "It's kind of a brotherhood."

Buckman walked around the impromptu matches of the Daniels grandchildren, which continued just inside the suite, and extended his hand to the legendary competitor and coach.

"Coach, I still think I should have beat your guy in the semifinals of the national tournament that year," the senator laughed. "I had that won."

"Well, that guy is here tonight. I saw him. Let's have a

rematch. We have room in here," Daniels said.

"Coach, I have arthritis in my neck and virtually every other joint because of wrestling. I had this heart thing a year ago. Look at these ears. I think I better sit this one out," the senator said.

They chatted more about the action in front of them and Buckman got to the point.

"Coach, I think you are a Republican but I need all the influential supporters I can get next February when we wrestle the Iowa Caucuses. I'm guessing the kids wrestling are grandchildren?"

"Twelve of them. Don't ask me all the names. I'd probably fail. I'm still excited about what the team is doing. Kind of distracted. I'd get them all eventually," Daniels said.

"I have some ideas about what the country should be doing for your grandchildren … my first child that will be born soon … all of our children and grandchildren."

The senator explained his "Schools Without Barriers" initiative, his idea to help young people who volunteer for two years of service pay for college and trade school educations. He talked about programs to prepare students for the next generation of jobs. He talked about universal health care but also about equitable taxation and reducing government spending.

"I like the voluntary service idea. College is so expensive. I'm not sure how our kids will pay for the educations of our grandchildren," Daniels said. "You consider me to be a Republican but I really don't have a party affiliation. I vote for people who have ideas I like. I like some of yours. Let me say this; you are a former wrestler and I know you are smart because you were at Princeton and I know you are an educator. That gives you some advantages in my mind. You call me during the summer and fall and I may come by a campaign event when you are in town. I'm retired now, I can do that. We have a fishing cabin in Minnesota. We'll go fishing."

"It would be great to have your support," the senator said.

"Want a beer?" Daniels asked.

"How about half a beer?"

They talked more about wrestling and the tournament while the informal Daniels Family Tournament continued on the floor of the suite. The senator met everyone and asked for their support. He and the coach got their photos taken. The senator put the beer down first out of the photo shot. Carl would make sure the photo was available to reporters at the tournament. In the concourse the senator was stopped several times and asked for a photo.

It was a good sign. They were in Iowa, and a few people noticed they were in Iowa.

CHAPTER 9
Vegas, Baby

The Crossroads State University Explorers of Coach James Jackson Webb had rolled through four opponents. None of the opponents had come within 15 points. The Explorers now headed to Las Vegas for the semifinals of the National University Union tournament.

The Kaiser, Wilhelm Wagner, was averaging 27 points per game in the tournament and The Escalator, Kondo Kone, was dominating around the basket.

J.J. Webb had the senator's cell number. Seemingly everyone did. He took Webb's call at 11:30 p.m. after the Explorers beat their fourth straight opponent to advance to the semifinals.

The senator, Ryan Holton, Gerald O'Malley and Carl Lyon were in the senator's suite in the extended stay hotel in Des Moines.

Buckman turned the speaker on his phone on.

"Senator, we're all going to Vegas," Webb said, with that drawl. "We need you. This next game will be tough. I hear Jack Rushton was pissed off when you were behind the bench with us in Minneapolis. I know some of his staffers. They talk. I can't think of much I'd rather do than win another basketball game with you behind our bench and piss Jack off again."

Webb didn't call Rushton the president. He called him Jack or "that son-of-a-bitch."

"Congratulations, coach. We said we'd be out there if you made it and we'll be there. You can get us tickets?" the senator asked.

"How about four? Good enough?" Coach Jimmy Jack suggested.

"Great. You know where you are staying yet?"

"Our team headquarters is the Mondelo. Want a couple rooms?"

The senator explained his group would need more room.

"My parents want to come and I'm bringing staff. We'll handle it," the senator said.

"OK, but remember that I'm buying dinner for everyone. I know some great places out there. And we'll have another fan rally somewhere. I'll call with details. Maybe you can threaten to deport Wil and he'll play some damn defense," Coach J.J. said, laughing at his joke and trusting the senator not to repeat it.

Besides, Wil Wagner was born in the U.S. but had lived all over the world, including his parents' native country.

The senator was no fan of Vegas, nor gambling. He did know the gaming industry. He understood the jobs the industry provided.

At least two of his staffers, Carl Lyon and Gerald O'Malley, had less rigid attitudes toward games of chance than the candidate. They expressed disappointment that no sports wagering would be allowed on the semifinal games because Las Vegas was hosting the events. No bets about how many points The Escalator or The Kaiser would score. No first half over-under bets, no bets on whether the Explorers could win the championship. No proposition bet on how many times The Kaiser would brush back his shoulder length hair.

Kim, the senator's parents, plus Carl and Susan, O'Malley, who was always in between relationships, Ryan and a couple of staffers from The Warehouse campaign headquarters were all making the trip. The senator said he considered it more of a campaign stop than a junket to Vegas. Las Vegas was full of people who would vote for the senator in a general election. He believed his positions about sensible immigration policy, an equitable taxation plan leveling the playing field for average workers, universal living wage and his volunteer service to help pay for secondary education would resonate with thousands of people who worked their behinds off in service industry jobs for

Las Vegas casinos.

"I want to do a big event for the Services International Union while we are out there. Where would we do that? You folks figure it out," the senator requested.

The semifinal games were on Friday night with the final on Sunday afternoon. O'Malley scrambled and called in favors at the last moment to secure the Celebrity Room at the Aurus Hotel and Casino. He was told it would hold 2,000 people. He figured 100 curious Democrats, progressives, socialists and hungover gamblers looking for the buffet might show up on a Saturday morning.

Ryan informed the senator they had found a large house – 8 bedrooms, 7 baths – that they could rent for $1,000 a night. It had its own pool, was on a golf course, and came with a golf cart.

"What do I look like, a Republican? I work for a living. I'm not Rushton," the senator said, only mildly protesting the idea of the rental home.

"But look at it this way, several rooms in a hotel would be very expensive and probably aren't even available," Ryan explained to the senator in what was agreed to be a strong defense of the cost and the extravagance. "Gerald had to pull a lot of strings to get this. It will be a bonding experience."

"Is this a donor's home?" the senator asked.

"We hope so," Ryan reported. "The guy owns the major restaurant supply company in Nevada and California. He is very tight with the Services International Union and with the people who run the casinos. He has good relations with both sides. His name is Frank Montez. He could help us later and solve this problem for us now."

"OK, but no special rates. We have to pay the full rate for this," the senator said. "I don't want someone finding out we got the place for a dollar a night. And I want to meet Mr. Montez if possible. Get him to the rally."

"Someone else wants to meet you in Las Vegas," reported O'Malley, who had quietly been listening, sometimes chuckling, at the exchange of the kid and the senator.

"Who is that?" the senator asked.

"Can't tell you now but he approached us, not the other way around. I'll just tell you it's a Hollywood couple," O'Malley said.

"Of course, it would be. Those people are even farther out to the left of the political spectrum than I am."

The younger staffers took O'Malley's cryptic news and ran off with speculation. As it turned out, they weren't thinking big enough on the stardom scale.

CHAPTER 10

The Powells

The Mondelo Hotel and Casino had a price tag of $1.15 billion when it opened just two years before the arrival of the Crossroads State Explorers and their fans, who had taken over like they were on the board of directors. They had done their part to fill up every one of the 2,172 rooms of The Mondelo. They were everywhere. The Explorers were rock stars. Even the practice session the day before the semifinals on Friday drew 17,000 fans of the four teams. Most of those 17,000 wanted to see the Explorers.

There were occasional sightings of The Escalator, Kondo Kone, and The Kaiser, Wilhelm Wagner, and the rest of the Explorers in the Mondelo's restaurants. Whether they were of age or not, the casino games and bars were off limits under Coach J.J.'s orders, as were the after-hours dance clubs and strip clubs. Coach J.J. had his team on a choke collar. The schedule of practice, media availability, meals, meetings, and a giant pep rally in the 12,000-seat Mondelo World Arena left little time in the Explorers' schedule for the usual distractions of Las Vegas.

Coach J.J. had decided he would take the senator and his contingent – Kim, the senator's parents, Gerald, Ryan Holton, Carl and Susan Lyon and the young staffers – to the most exclusive restaurant in The Mondelo after the pep rally the night before the semifinals game.

The pep rally was loud, and the beer was just as overpriced and just as vigorously pursued as it had been for the pep rally in the Twin Cities before the first-round game. Coach J.J. again invited the senator on stage.

"Let me tell you what I think is going to happen. I understand no one can bet on this game here in Las Vegas. That is a good thing because you folks are going to have to stay for the championship game on Sunday. You may have to sell more farmland to pay for this trip," the senator began. "Folks, now listen closely …"

He was doing it. The senator was grabbing the hands of thousands of people in the arena, most of them at least a bit loopy already. He had this way of making his most important points more quietly and deliberately. Kim Wakefield, now five months pregnant, was shaken by the moment and the memory.

"That…that… is the way he sounded just before his heart attack in Minnesota," she whispered to Susan Lyon with an obvious note of panic.

"No, no, he is fine. He is just doing that thing he does," Susan said, calming the senator's wife.

Buckman continued.

"You should be proud of this team but more importantly, you should be proud of this university you love. My parents are graduates … twice actually … of Crossroads State. I was born in University City while they were students. I've had the opportunity to spend time with Coach J.J. and his team.

"I'm a believer, too. They will win tomorrow and they will win Sunday. Forge on, Explorers!"

The Explorers fans were now in a frenzy. The pep band played "Forge on Explorers," the fight song, again.

The senator clapped along. He finally raised his hands after about 30 seconds, another of his speaking habits.

"The Crossroads State Explorers are going to give the state of Iowa its first National University Union basketball championship. You have the best players, the best coach, the best fans and folks, it is pretty much a moment of destiny," the senator said, now at medium intensity for the Orator from Owatonna.

He didn't drop the mic. He could have. He handed it to Coach J.J. and walked off the stage.

"And what the senator didn't tell you is that there is this guy in Washington, who I know pretty well, and he is hoping we'll lose," Coach J.J. told the crowd. "I think we're going to make him sick to his stomach."

Rushton was booed loudly, though he was about 2,500 miles away.

Coach J.J. knew what he was saying. Only he and the senator and Rushton himself would understand the very inside reference about Jack Rushton's gastrointestinal issues from years of heavy drinking. Coach J.J. could envision the President of the United States waking up with a throbbing hangover and finding out from staff what the coach he detested had said about him.

They moved from the pep rally to a private room in Glow, the featured upscale restaurant of The Mondelo. Chef Shriver Christopher's restaurant was considered one of the best in Las Vegas and he was considered one of the very best chefs in the country who had not yet sold out to become a "celebrity chef" with his own cable network show. Las Vegas was now filled with "celebrity" chefs. Shrive Christopher was a second-generation Vegas chef, although his father was actually the head chef of a Vegas buffet. Shrive started working in his father's hotel buffet as a 15-year-old bus boy. He moved up the ladder in the kitchen, attended culinary school, got a degree in business and built Glow from the opening designs to spectacular completion. He was a Vegas guy who usually sneered at celebrity chefs.

Glow was appropriately named. Located in half of the 45th through 48th floors of The Mondelo, the restaurant's 30-foot tall windows on three sides offered incredible views of the city. Chef Shrive prided himself on having one of the best wine selections in Vegas.

There were German, French and California wine selections on the 1,250-bottle wine list available. Glow was lit by the city and low hanging, subdued, lighting fixtures. The view of Las Vegas' strip was outstanding from the bar on the mezzanine level of the space. Chef Shrive stressed food and beverages, not décor. The walls were brick facade with thick, roughhewn wood accenting.

The senator rarely drank wine. He asked for The Mondelo's in-house microbrew, called Blonde Showgirl. Coach J.J. knew his way around a wine list and recommended several bottles to his guests.

"Y'all will enjoy the Rieslings from Germany and I favor the California Cabernets," Coach J.J. reported.

Chef Shrive – he said he preferred Shrive to Shriver or Chef Christopher -- arrived at the table and was greeted by Coach J.J. like they were great, old friends. It was obviously not the first time they had met.

"Coach J.J., it's been a while. What has it been, six months?" the chef asked. "If you hadn't arrived soon, The Mondelo might have entered bankruptcy."

"Last summer. Tough to get out here during the season," the coach said.

"Yeah, fantastic season, coach. I've got tickets if I can get out of here," Chef Shrive said. "Who are your friends?"

Coach introduced the senator. Buckman stood and introduced everyone else.

Ryan Holton was incredulous. The young, bright bus driver and campaign staffer caught the eye of other young staffers. He was a kid of family wealth but was still shocked that nothing on the list of entrees was less than $75, and the sides and appetizers were $15 to $20 each. What he didn't know was that the California Cabernet he was enjoying was $200 a bottle.

"Coach J.J., how did you arrive in Iowa?" the senator asked.

"Damn near by walking," he said, chuckling. "And begging. I needed a job and had some success but I ran into some issues and got fired with Rushton's help. I brought some of it on myself. I was drinking too much and doing stupid things and I recruited a couple of kids of questionable moral character. They got involved in a frat fight and one kid, not a basketball player, was seriously hurt. Severe brain injury when he fell or was pushed down steps. My guys didn't do the pushing. Everyone said that. It was a terrible accident. My guys shouldn't have been there. It was called an accident. No charges were filed but they didn't need charges. I was gone.

"Crossroads State needed a coach and they needed to win. The coach before me was losing and players weren't graduating. That double dip will get you fired quick in college basketball.

"I was willing to take the job and only asked for a three-year contract. We won 23 games and made the tournament my second year after I'd run off half the players and lost 20 games the first season. I signed for five years after two seasons and this is the third year of that contract."

Coach J.J. was now making $2.7 million a year and stood to pocket another $500,000 if the Explorers won it all. He could afford the wine, although he wasn't drinking a lot. What Coach J.J. wasn't drinking, Ryan Holton, O'Malley and the young staffers were. The senator's parents also made a hearty contribution by keeping their glasses full.

With little initial notice, a very large man in a black t-shirt, black jeans and basketball shoes, maybe 6-foot-4 and 300 pounds with thick biceps and chest, came into the private banquet room. He looked around with an intensity that was a bit frightening and slowly walked back out. In a few seconds he was followed by two of the best-known celebrities in the world and no one other than staff seemed to know they were even in the hotel.

Breckenridge Powell came into the room with dark glasses, a ball cap, scruffy gray beard and basketball shoes. He was holding hands with Brynn Jacobs Powell, who entered as discreetly and as well disguised in jeans, sweatshirt and floppy hat.

The Powells had won a combined five Best Actor and Best Actress awards – him three, her two, one each in the same movie that sparked their life together – and seven more nominations between them over the course of long careers. Three of their movies had won Best Picture. They had been married 27 years, an eon in Hollywood love affairs, and reveled in the art of acting and writing for other actors. They distanced themselves from the celebrity spotlight. They rarely distanced themselves from each other. Their longevity as a married couple was considered to one of Hollywood's great love story. They were in Las Vegas instead of at their ranch in Montana for one reason.

"That's … Ridge and Brynn Powell," the once-again amazed Ryan Holton whispered to Gerald O'Malley, who was seated next to him.

"Relax Ryan. They called. They want to meet the senator," O'Malley said.

"Why didn't you tell anyone?" Ryan asked.

"It should be pretty obvious. They didn't want anyone to know they were coming."

The senator was a fan of movies, especially older movies and classics. He stood and greeted the Powells by their first names. He introduced Kim, his parents and the rest of his staff at the table.

"Congratulations on the baby. You look spectacular," Brynn said, hugging Kim gently.

"You look pretty swell yourself, although I have to admit I didn't recognize you immediately," Kim said.

"I don't wear designer clothes except when required and as far as we're concerned, it is rarely required. We both enjoy trying to be what we are … normal," Brynn said. "When we make a rare red-carpet appearance and someone asks 'What are you wearing?' I usually say JC Penney. And sometimes I am."

"Senator, can we join you?" Ridge asked.

"Only if you call me Pierce," he said.

They all ordered, and with the exception of Kim and the senator, they went through more bottles of wine.

"Coach Jimmy Jack, how is it going, Hoss? Got the Explorers neatly bedded down in the barn?" Ridge asked with a voice that could out-Texas even the coach.

"I forgot you were from Texas," Coach J.J. said.

"Midland," Ridge responded.

"Permian Basin … home of oil wells, high school football and that son-of-a-bitch Rushton," J.J. said. "The stallions, I hope, are in their rooms playing video games and talking on their phones. I am hoping they are calling room service instead of escort services. They are good kids. I think they are ready."

"In honor of the Kaiser, will you suggest a couple bottles from Germany with what we've ordered?" J.J. asked when the sommelier stopped back by the table.

The Powells drank and ate with the group. They were comfortable being able to just talk without having the entire room fixated on them or interrupting meals for autographs and photos, which they usually agreed to when someone recognized them. Ridge Powell, who was talking Texas and trying to wrest the bill away from Coach J.J., got to the reason he had called Gerald O'Malley about meeting the senator.

"Brynn has a doctorate in psychology. Did it just for self-satisfaction and accomplishment. Very proud of her. Not a bullshit honorary doctorate you receive for delivering a graduation speech. A real doctorate. That's one of the reasons we wanted to meet you."

"We read about your concept of improving public schools … Schools Without Barriers I think you call it … and your ideas about serving to pay for college education or trade schools," Brynn said. "Those are great ideas. Are they affordable? Are they realistic?"

Senator Buckman was going to have to get used to the question about how to pay for his progressive agenda.

"It is realistic and is affordable. It is affordable by making sure taxation is equitable for everyone. It might mean you and Coach J.J., me, too, will pay more in taxes but by paying more, you will also be serving. You will be helping provide educations for at-risk kids who may spend their entire lives supported by government programs unless they have better opportunities. The idea of raising people up who have been near the bottom for generations will have to start with education.

"We will always need an educated, skilled workforce. We can also pay for the program by keeping more young people out of the prison system. I believe that if you work with all kids and their parents, grandparents, guardians, give them opportunities and provide them with the best education for their abilities and needs, we can reduce the costs of unemployment and all forms of assistance.

"We need to make sure we are doing the best we can to provide an education helping kids land jobs and careers. The public service idea will not only be attractive and exciting to young people, it will help them develop job skills."

"Corporations will come after you on the tax issue," Ridge told the senator.

"I don't know why. They need everything from production workers to executives," the senator said. "They will be investing in their own future workforces by paying equitable taxes."

"I guess I know a lot about your movies, together and separately, but I'm wondering how you got the name Breckenridge Powell?" the senator asked, now turning the conversation away from himself. "After William or Dick ... two pretty accomplished Powells in your world?"

Ridge flashed his distinctive grin, tilted upward only on the right side of his mouth.

"One, I didn't like the sound of Durango Powell and my agent at the time was suggesting first names of a Colorado city ... it was suggested I looked Western, whatever that means ... and second, my mother liked Jane Powell in Seven Brides for Seven Brothers. It was one of her favorite movies."

"Brynn should have become Eleanor," the senator said, referring to another Powell in the movie business.

They all laughed.

"No, true story. That is where Powell came from. A solid acting name I think. I've been interviewed a lot and I don't believe I've ever told anyone about my mom liking Jane Powell and Seven Brides."

Ridge Powell, who had not yet talked the check away from Coach J.J., had a few questions of his own about the Crossroads State University Explorers.

"I saw some of your guys downstairs. It's like they are rock stars right now. No one noticed Brynn and I were just walking around in the shops. They sure knew your guys. They must be kind of hard to control with women around."

"You call him Wil? He is a very impressive young man," Brynn Powell said, followed by feigned panting and patting of her chest.

"Brynn, that is exactly why we have to watch the Kaiser closely," Coach J.J. said. "It's not that he seeks women so much as he simply attracts them. His world is larger. The kid is very bright and he is wealthy because his parents are. Impressive people who have about 20 patents between them. Some of those patents they have made millions from. Kondo will be very rich once he plays a few years in the pros. Wil is rich now. He is worldly from following his parents around the world. Dresses the best of anyone on the team, certainly better than me … has a couple of custom suits … and speaks four or five languages. That means endless opportunities in a place like Las Vegas with all the foreign tourists. One of the team managers, who I threatened to make disappear if he screwed up, is spending every waking moment with Wil and is his roommate.

"Knowing them, they are probably somewhere having a beer and watching sports. But if you saw him with that long hair and his expensive, tight jeans, everyone will be watching him … women and men. Now if the damn kid could play some defense, he would be dangerous."

The check for the party of 16 was nearly $5,000 – Chef Shrive gave up the private room at no charge -- and didn't charge for the two bottles of wine for the road that Ryan Holton and Gerald O'Malley conspired to take along. They weren't driving. Or rather, they shouldn't have been.

The Powells told the senator they would be supporting him and when the time was right, they would make a day of stops with him in Iowa. As inconspicuously as they arrived, they also left after a phone call to the security guard. First, they left a tip of $3,000 and had photos taken with everyone. Everyone took menus from the memorable night and had them signed by the coach, the senator and the Powells.

The senator's group got into two large vans and headed back to the rental home with the golf cart and the golf course. Coach J.J. said he was headed to his suite to watch a couple of videos of the opponent again and make sure everyone was in their rooms.

O'Malley and Ryan Holton made the trip back to the rental home. But instead of ending the night, they made a decision that would nearly cost both of them their jobs on the senator's campaign staff.

They decided to take the golf cart out on the golf course running through the housing development. Their reasoning was that they had not seen much of the property. They had been too busy. They stayed on the cart path at first but then started swerving between slugs from the two expensive bottles of German wine they had with them.

Lights from an ATV came on behind the golf cart. Red ones, flashing ones, blue and yellow lights. Over a speaker attached to security's cart, they heard "stop the cart."

"We should have gone back to the Strip," O'Malley growled. "We would have been just two more drunk asshole tourists in town for the games."

The two security guards on the cart had questions. Fine questions, too.

Like, "what are you guys doing?" And, "have you been drinking?" And, "are you staying on the property somewhere?"

"We work for Senator Buckman. We're on his staff," O'Malley said when the questions stopped.

"Never heard of him, and considering you two, I doubt we ever will," said the smaller of the two officers, a chiseled specimen of about 250 pounds. "Where is the fine senator at this moment?"

"Umm…not sure," Ryan offered. "We've been out here for a while."

"Do you think you can get on this cart and not fall off?" the larger officer asked. "It would just ruin this night if two drunks fell off the back of this cart and got hurt."

When they moved off the cart, one of the empty bottles of very tasty German wine, carried out from Glow in honor of The Kaiser, fell out of the cart. The only thing that might have prevented private security from calling the police was a roll of luck. O'Malley would tell Carl Lyon at another time it was the best roll he had ever experienced in Las Vegas. The empty wine bottle fell into the grass and did not crash and break on the cart path, which would have required the already aggravated security guys to sweep it up.

Whatever thoughts the officers had of handling the incident without further intervention would likely have disappeared if they'd had to spend time in the dark cleaning up glass before the next golf day began in a few hours.

O'Malley and Ryan were not drunk enough that they couldn't stagger to the custom ATV, which actually had three rows of seats and a bunch of gear. It could double as an ambulance if they had to cart somebody in cardiac arrest off the course in the heat of the desert.

"We may need this AED at the house for the senator if we ever find the house," Ryan said, referring to Buckman's widely known heart issues.

"Any idea what hole the house is on?" one of the security guys asked.

"I think I saw the No. 7 tee behind the pool. Is that possible?" Ryan asked, slurring his words but with confidence that he sounded sober.

No response.

The drunk assholes held on tightly as the cart made its way on the cart path to the No. 6 fairway. Ryan recognized the house.

"This one I think," he said.

But the security guys were not going to just drop the two off at the back gate. They took a path to the street in front of the house. They rang the bell.

Carl and Susan Lyon, who knew the two were missing, answered the door.

O'Malley was standing on the stoop to the house. Ryan was sitting in the yard … singing.

"Forge on Explorers…

"O'er Mountain, Valley and Stream…

"Forge on Explorers…

"Through Peril Unforeseen…

He continued through the rest of the fight song. He reached the chant in the middle of the Crossroads State fight song…

"Zebulon Pike, Meriwether Lewis, William Clark, Saca… gawea …"

He fell to his back, laughing, in the yard. Then he threw up.

"My, my, my … Sue, oh look, this is a special, special sight. Two drunk dumb asses and two very large security guards. Not something you see every day … unless you are in Las Vegas. Gentlemen…umm … can we take them off your hands? Did they do any damage? Did you see a golf cart anywhere?"

"Is this where the senator is?"

"Yes, fortunately he is sleeping. Or he was until the doorbell rang," Carl said.

About that time Buckman arrived at the door in a Big River State University T-shirt, gym shorts and bare feet. He heard the story again from the security guards.

"Thank you for getting them back safely. If they are still here in the morning, they will be apologizing to your chief," the senator said. "*If* they are still here."

None of them had seen Senator Buckman as angry as he was at 3:35 a.m. with the two drunk staffers in front of him. His head and face were crimson. The guards shook hands with the senator and left. The professor lit into the two, as he would with an undergrad student who showed up hungover and fell asleep in his class.

"Listen. This cannot happen again. Is that clear? I depend on you to be ready every day. What if they had called the police and had you arrested? You are a vital part of this operation. We have too much to do to get our message out to the public."

"Gerald, I'm particularly upset with you. You are a professional. You are supposed to be the best in the business at what you do. I don't expect you not to drink. I know you drink. The entire political world knows you drink. But I expect you to be sober when I need you sober and that is a few hours from now.

"Tonight, was a good night. We got the endorsement of two of the best-known celebrities in the world. I understand being excited about that and having a few drinks. But you two appear to have been out of control.

"In the morning you will go to the management offices of this place and apologize. You will track down the golf cart and get it back here. You will pay for any damages. Go to bed. I will wake you in about three hours from now."

"Yes, Senator," Ryan said quietly.

"Senator, you are right," O'Malley said. "If you want my resignation, you will have it."

He did not. At that moment, the senator just wanted to go back to bed.

At 6:40, Buckman was on the treadmill. Susan Lyon and Kim Wakefield were swimming laps in the well-heated pool. The sound system in the house was on. Loudly. Ryan Holton and Gerald O'Malley ate breakfast in the kitchen … two extra-strength aspirin each and two sodas. They were quiet.

CHAPTER 11

Towel Boy

Wilhelm Johann Wagner, The Kaiser, went off in the semifinals like no one had seen in a National University Union game in 30 years. He dropped 44 on 9 3-pointers, four drives to the basket and nine free throws. He added 27 brushbacks of his shoulder-length hair. The Crossroads State fans had started charting hair brushbacks when he was a freshman. They counted in unison "one, two, three" all the way to 27.

It was a known fact that the higher number of hair brushbacks, the better game Kaiser was playing.

The Escalator, Kondo Kone, had 16 points and 14 rebounds. They pulled away and the Explorers were in the championship game.

Coach J.J. barely had to get off the bench during the last 10 minutes of the game. He only rose to welcome players to the bench when their night was done in the last couple of minutes.

Most of the senator's contingent was in the tenth row, the rest of them were up another row, behind the Explorers' bench. Every time the Explorers fight song was played, about 200 times it seemed, the senator tried to keep from chuckling at the thought of Ryan Holton on his back singing the song at 3:35 in the morning. He liked the kid.

Sitting one row behind the senator was Jericho Adams Brooks, now an unemployed and unhappy 20-year-old who said he was from Minnesota himself when he introduced himself with his full name to the senator at halftime. Jericho Adams Brooks had shaggy bleached blond hair with thick black glasses and wore a

Crossroads State T-shirt with the sleeves cut off. He didn't look out of place considering the way some of the Crossroads State students were dressed. The fans had fur caps, calf-high animal skin boots and for no identifiable reason, some of them had painted faces. Jericho Adams Brooks looked like just another fan of the Explorers.

Gerald O'Malley made it through the game with some difficulty. This was not his first cruise through Hangover Town. He was functioning. He got the senator into several suites to meet with Las Vegas corporate types. At halftime, he had the senator in front of a few sportswriters Carl found talking about the Explorers. One of the suites was occupied by Frank Montez, who owned the house they were renting and had been working to organize the morning campaign event the next day.

Gerald and Montez talked about the campaign event the next day.

"Shit! Again?" President Jack Rushton said as he watched the television coverage from the Oval Office. "Professor Begonia! What is he, the honorary towel boy now? The freaking manager of the team?"

It was midnight in Washington, D.C. Rushton had lost count of his tumblers of Dark Hills Bourbon.

On Saturday morning at 10 a.m. the ballroom at the Aurus Casino was jammed and people were in the hallways. Montez had come through. Gerald had figured maybe 100 people would show up. Montez had rounded up hundreds of service union members, culinary union members and teamsters. They mingled with their bosses, mid-level and senior casino executives to listen to the senator.

Montez had promised he would be there himself. He was in the front row.

The turnout was unexpected by O'Malley and Carl Lyon, although they had done what they could to get the media out to their event. For the first time in the young campaign, they had a media section on risers at the back of the room.

"Did we expect this?" the senator asked O'Malley just minutes before taking the stage.

Buckman took several deep breaths, kissed Kim, and bounced

out quickly from behind the podium. There weren't 30 flags behind him. There were two; a Nevada flag and a U.S. flag. There was one large banner that simply said "Senator Buckman for President."

O'Malley had arranged to have 400 signs printed with the messages "A Shared Vision" and "Buckman." The big crowd waved the signs as the senator came out. There were also signs featuring a caricature of Buckman with a perfectly round head, no hair, a big smile and large black glasses.

Kim Wakefield, who had called Pierce Buckman "Cue Ball" since their relationship began to get serious, had a huge grin. She had personally been responsible for the caricature signs.

Jericho Adams Brooks stood near the back of the room with a sign someone had placed in his hand when he entered. He held it, but didn't wave the sign.

"My name is Pierce Buckman and I am a candidate for president because I think we can be much better as a people and country if we share a vision. A vision of better education, better jobs, fairer taxes, better healthcare and better roads, highways and airports. A country where everyone has a chance to succeed. That is my vision. If this is your hope and your vision, we ask for your support.

"Thank you very much for coming out this morning. This is a big weekend in Las Vegas and we're happy to be here. My parents, who are with me today here on the stage … mom, dad, wave … both have two degrees from Crossroads State University and I was born in University City, Iowa, so you understand why I'm kind of a fan this weekend.

"Wait, I must say something before telling you what I'd like to do as president.

"I'm going to run a different campaign … I hope, anyway … than you are accustomed to seeing. So, as of today, media people way back there can escape the corral. Is that how you refer to it? I respect your roles in the process. To me, you represent the public. I may disagree with you. Some of you I will never agree with. But hopefully we'll stumble across something we agree upon. As of now, go wherever you want in the room, talk with whomever you want to talk with. We're not going to put you in a corral. Get up here closer if you'd like."

The senator's reprieve for the media was a surprise to the two hotel security people in the room. They scrambled from the back to the front as several reporters moved forward. They called for assistance.

For 35 minutes the senator laid out his plan for Schools Without Barriers, voluntary service in exchange for college or trade school tuition, equitable taxation, a universal living wage, infrastructure investment and an immediate reduction of 10 percent in the budgets of every department of the federal government.

"Now you and I both know that we probably could reduce the cost of government by much more than 10 percent," he said.

"I believe in service. I've never looked at the political world as my career. I have a career. I am an educator, like my parents. I will teach again someday."

He then touched on thoughts that not even his own staff knew he supported.

"Government does not work when it is bloated by excess ... excess employment, excess spending, excess regulation, and, most certainly, excess campaigning.

"How can we expect our Congress to be effective when the next campaign essentially starts the day following election day? Virtually every move a representative makes, every vote they take, can jeopardize their career in Washington. We can fix that issue with term limits. I believe two terms are enough for presidents and should be enough for Congress. Term limits would mean we would see a regular turnover of public servants with fresh ideas coming to Washington.

"But understand what that means. Two terms in Congress, two in the Senate and possibly two more as vice president and president. That is still a long time.

"I have to tell you that most of my colleagues in the Senate will think term limits are the worst idea since the Volstead Act of 1919; the one banning the manufacture and distribution of alcoholic drinks. They like those Washington jobs. They like them so much they just keep running and running to keep their jobs.

"Some of my colleagues in the Senate might even be tired of being there but because they can still be elected, the entire process becomes nothing more than politics. The party wants to protect that position so the person holding it just keeps running.

"It becomes all about running, not governing. Because of the system, we are not doing visionary work that benefits Americans."

Senator Buckman was interrupted several times by applause, especially when he talked about a comprehensive public schools plan and equitable taxation.

"One more thing I want to talk about. Listen now, this is important," he said, quieting the crowd. "The president believes in rounding up undocumented immigrants and sending them out of the country, even if they are productive, have a job, buy cars, houses, goods and services, pay taxes, have loving family structures and have committed no crime. The raids will end on the day I am elected. We are not going to target people and deport them simply because they look different or speak a different language.

"I promise you today ... hold me to this ... there will be no more raids on good people who came to this country for commendable, understandable reasons. We are a country shaped by immigrants and because we are the greatest country in the world, immigrants will continue coming to this country. They make us a better country, not a worse country. If I am elected, I will ask Congress to put a comprehensive, reasonable immigration reform bill, including an expedited path to citizenship, on my desk and I will sign it with no hesitation. Because it's the right thing to do.

"Our country's history is a wonderful, colorful quilt of inclusion. We are white, black, brown, European, African, Asian and yes, Hispanic. You can be man, woman, straight, gay or transgender and there is a place for you in the United States of America.

"Thank you all for coming and I will see you again."

The reaction to the speech, especially in a melting pot like Las Vegas, was energetic. Dozens of people moved toward the stage to meet the senator.

Buckman waved for about 30 seconds as Kim and his parents came on stage to join him. The senator walked down the five steps from the stage and shook hands with people in the crowd. Four Las Vegas Police Department officers surrounded him and his wife. Reporters asked questions about term limits and about President Rushton's raids on undocumented immigrants.

"Some of what you said today is unlikely to be embraced by either party ... term limits and the across-the-board budget cuts ... are two examples," one reporter suggested.

"But are those ideas that would be good for the country?" the senator countered. "I think we can do many things differently. It's not about me or my ideas, or my party or the opposing party, it's about doing something for the nation."

"Are you sure you are a Democrat?" the reporter followed up.

"I am a Democrat. Maybe a little different version of one, though," the senator conceded. "Eisenhower wasn't sure he was a Democrat or a Republican. He seemed to do pretty well with what today would be considered a liberal agenda by the right. The Interstate Highway System was a pretty progressive idea, don't you think? Eisenhower warned of the Military-Industrial Complex and its possible power. That was prophetic, don't you think? Today, the president and his party would consider the great highways crossing the country an unaffordable government project. We have a president who wants inaction. He wants limited participation. He doesn't want to hear every voice. We can do big things if we share the will to do them."

The senator continued to shake hands and listen to people for another 20 minutes and took more questions from the media before leaving. Now waiting on the rope and stanchions creating distance between the crowd and candidate was a young man with dark glasses, a fedora-style hat and dark long hair, dyed black. He wore a T-shirt with a "sad face with tears" emoji on the front.

One question caused Gerald O'Malley to move forward to end the impromptu news conference.

"Do you believe in the legalization of marijuana?" a reporter asked.

"I think the states are pretty much handling that issue

themselves. Nevada is one of those states. I personally would favor fewer restrictions on use and I would consider growth and production as cash crops with high taxes for distribution and purchase like we now have with tobacco cigarettes.

"And I certainly don't want to spend billions of dollars investigating and then incarcerating people arrested for distributing relatively small amounts or being in possession of marijuana. And, I do believe there are likely medical uses that should be studied more thoroughly."

O'Malley asked Carl to move in after the marijuana question. His immediate assessment was that the senator may have tried to say too much in one event, but what he said seemed to capture the crowd. O'Malley thought moving the media out from a designated area might work now but not for long if the senator could gather any momentum.

Buckman made his feelings clear on the matter.

"Oh no, we're doing it for as long as I am a candidate. No more media corral at my events."

CHAPTER 12
Forge on Explorers

The Crossroads State Explorers fans arrived hours early for the national championship game against Northern California University. It was a warm day for early April in Las Vegas. The fans, thousands of them, attended a pep rally and tailgate party hosted by Crossroads State.

They were already singing the fight song:

"Forge on Explorers...

"O'er Mountain, Valley and Stream...

"Forge on Explorers...

"Through Peril Unforeseen...

"Forge on Explorers...

"Until the Trail May End...

"Forge on Explorers...

"Win the Game Again."

It was followed by the chant before a repeat of the fight song:

"Zebulon Pike, Meriwether Lewis, William Clark, Marquette and Joliet, Saca (pause) gawea."

The Explorers fans had long been considered among the most creative fans in college basketball. An online poll at mid-season also determined that they were among the most annoying. The Explorers fans were ranked No. 2 with a bullet. This only served to make them even more determined to step up their annoyance level.

Over the years, the students at Crossroads State had very unofficially added a name to honor explorers of the West as part of their fight song.

When the whole fight song process had been completed, they shouted in unison "Eat Their Livers."

"Eat Their Livers" was repeated at opportune moments like after every first down in football and nearly every stoppage in basketball, especially when the action was favoring their team. There weren't as many opportunities in football. In 120 years of games, Explorers fans had never grown hoarse yelling after first downs. There weren't that many.

Liver-Eatin' Johnson was not an explorer in the same category with Pike or Lewis and Clark. Jeremiah Johnson was more of mountain man. The legend was that in retribution for taking the life of his American Indian wife, he personally murdered many American Indians, took their scalps and showed total disregard for humanity and good taste by eating their livers.

The first time the senator figured out what the Explorers fans were chanting, he was incredulous.

"They are celebrating a ruthless murderer who was not even an Explorer," Buckman said.

"They have been doing it for years," Carl reported to the senator, who was seated beside him before the tip-off of the championship game. "Have you heard some of the other stuff they are saying?"

"It's basketball. I barely understand any of it except I like Coach J.J. and he can sure draw a crowd," the senator responded.

"You haven't heard the fans yelling 'blitzkrieg' when Wil scores on a 3-pointer? Not exactly politically correct."

"Missed that," the senator said.

"Nigel Barton … you know the kid from Quebec they call 'Sliver'? When he scores they shout 'ferme ta gueule.' I think that is what I heard. That's what I thought but I couldn't remember all the swear words we looked up in high school French class. I could be wrong, though, because I was terrible in high school French and I was never paying much attention, except to the swear words."

"That is shut the f up, right? Or shut your mouth," the senator said quickly.

"I think so."

"Someone needs to have their mouth washed out with soap," the senator said.

"Yeah, like every fan of the Explorers," Carl responded. It was the first time he'd heard the senator come close to dropping an "f bomb."

Some of the routine was just for laughs. Like the long-hair wigs meant to honor the shoulder-length hair of the Kaiser. And the big images of Escalator and Kaiser on bouncing poles. And the continuing count of Kaiser hair brushbacks. Kaiser didn't brush his hair back as often on the opponents' offensive half of the court. He was too focused on running back down the court to score.

The Explorers pep band was not left out of annoying opponents. When Kaiser scored, they played the highly recognizable bars of the German composer Wilhelm Richard Wagner's "Ride of the Valkyries." Wilhelm's family pronounced their name the same way … Vogner. And when they finished the bars, that's when the crowd shouted "Blitzkrieg."

The name Wagner in German is a derivative of wagonmaker or wagon driver. So, the students also chanted "carry the load" when the Explorers needed a boost, and they urged The Kaiser to provide the spark.

Creative, funny and the polling was spot on: The Exporters fans were damned annoying for opposing teams.

The championship game of the National University Union basketball tournament would be considered an instant classic. The Explorers finally had their hands full with a team just as quick and just as physical.

Coach J.J. had told the senator on Saturday night in a quick phone conversation that it would be a tight game for his team.

"They have a big guy who may be able to match up with Escalator. Maybe not over a season, but in one game…yes. They also have a couple of very good 3-point shooters. Kind of like watching us on film," J.J. said.

From the start, Escalator had to work hard to get his shots and rebounds. The Northern California big guy was quicker running the floor and was beating Escalator to prime scoring positions down low. He was matching Escalator point-for-point, rebound-for-rebound.

Kaiser could beat the Northern California guards off the dribble but he had also turned the ball over several times.

The lead went back and forth eight times. A brief flurry put Northern California up four in the last minute.

The Kaiser was dribbling quickly to the 3-point line but instead of pulling up to shoot, he slashed inside the line and spotted Escalator under the basket for a soaring dunk.

Northern was still in a great position for what would be considered a huge upset. Coach J.J. was up bellowing, gesturing wildly, to urge his team to defend. Northern had the ball and the lead in the last 16 seconds when Kaiser did the most improbable thing.

He defended.

He got right up on the Northern guard, who had played him point-for-point the entire way. Coach J.J. was now screaming at Kaiser to foul. Instead, he slashed at the ball with his fingers on his right hand extended and got a piece of the dribble with a fingertip, batting the ball out to half court. He won the race to the ball with :03 left, took two dribbles toward the sideline, rather than toward the middle of the court and lofted a 25-foot shot. The ball barely riffled the net. Kaiser had one hand high in the air as the ball dropped through.

The game officials didn't look at the video replay to see if the shot beat the buzzer. They were convinced it did. The video replay confirmed it was good. Crossroads State teammates ran to Kaiser and piled on him. Coach J.J. had both arms in the air at first, then calmly sat down on the bench, leaving the celebration to players, assistant coaches, cheerleaders and the Explorers mascot.

Crossroads State fans started several chants simultaneously, starting with "Blitzkrieg" after the band played that section of "Ride of the Valkyries." Fans sang the fight song several times, followed by chants of "We Ate Their Livers." Walking around in the crush of Explorers fans in his cut-off T-shirt was Jericho Adams Brooks. He wasn't celebrating, just wandering around.

Northern California players were despondent. Several sat on the floor in tears.

After a couple minutes of celebration, Coach James Jackson Webb gathered his players around him.

"I am so proud of every one of you and all you have accomplished. You don't get here, to this moment, to this position, without going through a lot. We've gone through a lot together ... but through whatever adversity we faced, including tonight against a great team ... you were winners and you've made me very proud. You will never forget this moment. Enjoy it. It probably won't come around again.

"Now bring it in one more time..."1-2-3, Explorers."

The Explorers fans continued to sing, chant and wave the big signs with the players' images.

"Go be with them," J.J. finished.

The Explorers ran to the sections where the band, cheerleaders and students celebrated. Coach J.J. was walking to the media room when he looked up at the senator and Kim and raised both arms.

The senator and Kim made only a brief appearance at Mondelo to join the championship celebration. Coach J.J. brought both of them together in a hug at the same time. Carl took photos and asked the coach for an interview on the phone soon.

"Coach, you should be very proud of this team. It was a great game," the senator said. "I heard some people saying it was the best championship game they had ever seen. Your team has a flair for the dramatic."

"Too much drama for me," Coach J.J. said, promising he would do what he could to help the senator before the Iowa Caucuses.

The senator, his parents, Kim, Carl and Susan Lyon and Gerald O'Malley, carrying drinks in both hands, got a van back to the house.

Ryan Holton stayed to party with Crossroads State fans. He showed up the next morning in time to make the flight back to Des Moines.

Four days after the championship game, Coach J.J., Escalator and Kaiser all announced in a tear-filled joint news conference they would be leaving Crossroads State for The Pro League the following season. J.J. had been offered a $750,000 salary bump and millions more in incentives to stay at Crossroads State.

"It's not only about the money," the coach told the senator when he called him hours before the news conference. "The Pro League is the highest level in my profession. You don't have to worry about making sure guys are academically eligible and going to class. You don't have to recruit all year. And there is the money. There is that."

He was going to be the new coach of the Las Vegas Royals at $5 million per year, according to media reports. The Royals were going to have the second player in the draft. It was possible Escalator would be available at No. 2 and Kaiser was projected as a high first-rounder.

The senator and Kim, Carl and Susan were headed back to their Iowa base in Des Moines to get back out on the road. Gerald was headed for The Warehouse to expand the headquarters operation and interview interns for the road. Las Vegas had been a boost to the campaign with a very successful rally and now the campaign had an association with the national champions and the hottest coaching commodity in basketball. They also could call on one of the most famous couples in entertainment for help. O'Malley knew the campaign operation was going to need more kids and an advance team.

In the White House, President Jack Rushton was beginning to take the professor from Minnesota seriously.

"What have we got on Professor Petunia?" Rushton asked political advisors on his staff.

He was drunk.

CHAPTER 13
Raid

At nearly every campaign stop so far in his brief campaign, Senator Buckman had emphasized his disagreement with the Rushton administration about raids of workplaces believed most likely to have undocumented immigrants.

With Rushton's blessing, the U.S. Immigration and Customs Enforcement (ICE) and Homeland Security were carrying out raids in various parts of the country on employers suspected of hiring undocumented workers. Rushton was running for re-election and he was pressuring the agencies to crack down. It was what his party faithful wanted.

Raids required extensive planning weeks in advance. They were expensive to carry out depending on the scope of the raid, but they were effective. The raids were good visually and politically for the president.

Raids took place in Nevada, Minnesota and Illinois. There was no irony at all that so far, the raids were in states that lean or are fully vested in the Democratic Party. The raids were pulled off during the day when the largest number of production employees were on the job. On the day of the actual raids, ICE and Homeland Security agents, along with city, county and state law enforcement willing to participate, would stage the actions 20 or 30 miles from the target. They had the final staging of the raid down to a few hours. They would then head toward the target site in heavily armored vehicles, helicopters, white buses with Homeland Security markings, along with a long line of marked and unmarked cars. A string of command vehicles, specially equipped motorhomes, would take the lead.

In recent months, the immigration raids moved to the Midwest. Targets were increasingly meat processing plants. There had been no raids of this kind in the first three years of Rushton's presidency. He was giving his base of support the "red meat" it wanted.

The raids were disturbing to witness. The execution of the raids had a look of the country's forces turning against their own citizens.

Dozens of agents of the two federal enforcement agencies, with assistance of other law enforcement departments, rolled to the site and methodically deployed. Local law enforcement in some areas refused to participate. The routine was to enter the plant and order it shut down. Every employee working, including company foremen and management, was escorted out. By the time the plant was cleared, large tent shelters had been set up to start the initial process of determining the citizenship and legal status of every employee. Liberals like Buckman had come to the defense of the employees who often were gathered without cause or due process.

Employees were asked for driver's licenses and Social Security numbers. If they were fraudulent numbers not matching the information available in the government database, the employee being questioned would have thick, plastic cable ties placed on their wrists and they were taken to another area to wait.

The waiting buses were loaded with the alleged offenders. Those detained were often a mix of Hispanics, Central Americans, Eastern Europeans and Africans, although the stereotype encouraged by the Rushton administration was that they were illegals from Mexico.

It never took long for the residents of the communities where these plants were located to hear what was taking place. Families gathered on the perimeter and were prevented from getting closer. Family members of those being detained would express shock and audible grief as they watched a husband, father, brother or uncle be walked to a bus.

When buses were full, they would head to a secret staging area to begin the next step of deportation, maybe a plea offer, a quick appearance before a judge and finally, a sentence, and later, deportation out of the country. Family members didn't know where their loved one was headed or when they would see them again. They understood it might be months before they would reunite.

Only Rushton's most ardent supporters, plus the suppliers of all the vehicles, security systems and law enforcement hardware needed to pull the raids off seemed to favor the raids. Rushton understood well that the suppliers would write checks to keep him in office if his administration was a financial boost to the businesses.

Senator Buckman had called the raids cruel and inhumane. At every campaign stop he made in Iowa, Buckman harshly condemned Rushton and the raids. In these moments on the campaign trail, he became the Orator from Owatonna again, but with a notably angrier tone than usual.

In Iowa City on May 12, the day of a raid in Austin, Minn., only miles away from Buckman's hometown of Owatonna, the senator made an impassioned plea to stop the raids.

"Again today, the administration demonstrated its disregard for human dignity," the senator started quietly. "Again today, the administration deliberately, with military-like presence and precision, separated children from parents, husbands from wives, and for what purpose other than obvious pandering to the angry mob on the right?

"Again today, people who were working, earning a living, paying taxes, producing a product that the country needs, had their lives disrupted for no reason other than the ridiculous claim that these are jobs not available to Americans. Get in line for these jobs because this president is determined to separate and disrupt families. These are hard-working people who are just trying to do the right thing for their families.

"Again today, the president will talk about the need for immigration reform and that is why these raids are necessary. Well, we'll get him real reform legislation and personally deliver it to him. We can make the borders more secure … I favor that

… but at the same time we can make it easier for people from all over the world to come to this country. If they can contribute to the workforce and have not committed a crime, they should be allowed to stay. If they maintain those requirements, there should be a less cumbersome path to citizenship.

"Again today, I am outraged by this administration and its disregard for people who don't look like they do, sound like they do, or have the same color of skin.

"I ask the president to end these inhumane assaults on families. All of our families were at one point immigrants. This is a great, diverse country because of our history. I again ask the president to demonstrate compassion and understand the values we share.

"Stop the raids."

It was the first time Senator Buckman had gone so directly after Jack Rushton. He still didn't mention him by name.

Within 15 minutes, every cable news program was calling to talk with Buckman. His comments were breaking news on the news networks, repeated dozens of times in the next 24 hours. His comments ran with the video of the raid in Austin.

The National News Network, 3N, had reporters on the campaign trail in Iowa. Carl Lyon set up a live interview for the early morning show.

"I didn't do it for votes, Carl," Buckman said. "As you might have detected, I'm pissed off. But you know what, I think by raiding the plant in Austin, this guy (Rushton) was jabbing me. Maybe he is taking us seriously. He will be if he isn't yet. I won't let this continue without fighting back for these people."

Jack Rushton was aware of Buckman's comments. He was not happy. He worked on a statement with his communications director.

"These efforts are not about politics. They are about the safety and security of our borders and our country," communications director Jess Edwards said in a White House media briefing. "They are about our security as a country. They will continue as needed."

Edwards was asked specifically about the content of Senator Buckman's comments.

"Politics," Edwards said. "Professor Pansy is running for president. He and his socialist crowd are out of touch with Americans. If people aren't in this country legally, we're going to track them down and kick them out."

Edwards' media briefing was the first condescending public reference connecting Buckman to flowers.

CHAPTER 14

MegaPack Revolt

The raids increased in frequency until one effort went unexpectedly badly for the agencies involved and for Jack Rushton.

In a school parking lot, another raid was being staged. The target was MegaPack, a pork and beef processing plant in Tama. This raid would be larger than most. There were 300 employees in the plant at midday.

This time there was a problem that could have led to disaster. A native of Honduras who lived in the neighborhood of the high school saw the staging and understood what was going on. She had family members who worked at the plant. A text message to one of them tipped off employees about the impending raid. At 11:40 a.m., the production lines at MegaPack shut down. In Spanish, a MegaPack shift boss explained to production workers that the raid was coming. It was a possibility they had talked about many times and feared. They had read the reports of similar raids and the splitting of families.

They had decided in the past they would not run if a raid came. They believed they would be tracked down regardless.

"¿Qué quieres hacer?" asked the leader

(What do you want to do?)

"¡Apágalo!

(Shut it down!)

"¡Tómalo!" shouted another worker.

(Take it over!)

Management and administrative employees on the kill floor

were led calmly and safely out of the plant. The multi-lingual group led management to the doors. Security officers were armed with pepper spray and tasers. No guns. They were in no mood to be heroic with a group of a dozen employees around them. The officers' less-than-lethal weapons were confiscated from security officers. Some in the group in charge of clearing management from the plant had picked up knives used in their processing work. They also had the stun guns used on the kill floor to propel lethal bolts into the skulls of animals before processing.

Once managers were escorted out of the building, the doors were secured. Every entry to the building was closed and either locked, or heavy storage racks were placed behind the doors to prevent entry.

Long before the line of command vehicles, troop carriers, transport buses and two helicopters and drones arrived, local police and county sheriff deputies had been called and were on the scene. They didn't know how to assess the threat. The information was inconclusive from the managers about whether this was a serious threat and whether the workers were armed. Several officers with shotguns and handguns tried to enter the building through the doors. They couldn't get in and were told by to back off by the employees holding the plant. Officers on the scene started to create a perimeter about 100 yards away from the plant, not knowing what to expect next.

The radio traffic was ominous.

"The situation is that employees have taken over the MegaPack plant in Tama. They were tipped off to the raid," said a local police chief to the commander of the raid that was still, the chief was told, going on as scheduled.

"Could they be armed?" the commander said.

"Yes…knives, pepper spray, tasers the security guards carried, and the stun guns used on the kill floor," the chief reported.

"Security! What happened to those people? Why didn't they prevent this? Is this a hostage event? No one gets near the building. Move the perimeter to 200 yards from the plant."

"No sir, no indication hostages were taken. Just the production workers doing this themselves."

There was no immediate line of communication with the MegaPack employees. As far as the employees were concerned, they were there for the long run. They had food, water, restrooms, electricity and they had a cause. Some workers had gathered in the cafeteria. The cafeteria employees were cooking food and giving it away.

Complicating an increasingly tense situation on the perimeter established by city and county officers was the fact that Tama is also the home of the Meskwaki American Indian Settlement. Some of the employees now holding the building were not Hispanic, African or Caucasian, they were Meskwaki, certainly legally in the country, and their families were beginning to show up in large groups.

Inside, the workers were united. ICE and Homeland Security may have been after the undocumented immigrants but the American Indians and Caucasians worked side-by-side with them. They were sympathetic and supported the occupation of the plant.

Meat processing jobs are difficult, potentially dangerous, and workers are at high risk for injuries. Permanent repetitive use injuries in hands and shoulders are not unusual. The positions are notoriously transient. Meat processing companies are nearly always hiring. There is always pressure to have enough production workers to meet the country's appetite for meat and fulfill the profit expectations of the company stockholders or owners. The qualifications for employment are not rigorous. The processors need able bodies to keep production moving. Someone who shows up, keeps up with the production and can handle the unpleasant environment could become a valued employee and earn a decent living for themselves and their family. Word got around in tight families when the plant was hiring. It was a self-perpetuating, never-ending career fair.

From the moment the production workers were tipped off about the raid, they knew they were likely to lose their jobs, be bused away and unless they could prove they were in the country legally, they were going to be deported and probably separated from loved ones. There wasn't a great deal of tension inside the plant. It was still an unorganized, but determined, movement. There was some fear among occupiers about the gathering law enforcement efforts.

Would this gathering force storm the building, risking their own lives and the lives of the workers? No one believed that would happen. But they knew ICE and Homeland Security weren't going to call off the raid. Not after spending so much time and taxpayer money in planning.

Would they shut down power and water to the plant and wait the workers out? That seemed to be a possibility.

Would law enforcement and government be willing to negotiate some sort of solution short of a mass deportation? Workers agreed that avoiding deportation was their best hope. That was the goal. If they couldn't keep their jobs, avoiding being separated from their loved ones would be the next-best solution.

At 1:50 p.m., armored vehicles, secured transport vans, white Homeland Security buses and helicopters arrived on site. The chants, jeers and threats started immediately from the diverse group of spectators. There was outrage in several languages.

Law enforcement couldn't deal with the unknown threat inside the building until they got the crowd under control. They moved the perimeter back further. They moved angry spectators across the frontage road from the site. They were now nearly a quarter of a mile away from the plant entrances. The crowd was warned they would be moved forcibly if they didn't move voluntarily. The spectators were increasingly abusive toward the authorities, shouting epithets at them.

The national media, roaming around the state on a daily basis in the months before the Iowa Caucuses, now had a real breaking news story to cover instead of campaign appearances in diners and luncheon meetings. The media trucks began pulling up and reporters talked with the spectators.

"The government has created this mess themselves by continuing these raids. This is no longer only outrageous. Now the situation has become dangerous," said a woman who identified herself as an executive with a faith-based social services agency called Central Iowa All Faiths. She explained that the agency offered immigrants and poor a list of services, including a food pantry, career counseling, a health clinic, addiction counseling, transitional housing and legal services.

"This is a volatile situation and the president's administration is responsible. This is on his desk and on his watch. It is his policy. He must live with the outcome. He owns this," she continued.

CHAPTER 15

MegaPack Negotiations

Senator Buckman was in the Des Moines area speaking at a noon Rotary Club luncheon in Johnston. His crowds were still small unless you counted the Crossroads State basketball rallies and Las Vegas event, and most of those people cared only about the Explorers and the bar. He was barely a blip in the polling of Democrats. He was consistently polling at less than 5 percent, about 30 percentage points behind New York Governor Mike Clarke and 28 percentage points behind former Virginia Governor Karla Foster. But Buckman's message was attracting enthusiastic reaction, even if those crowds were small. At least local reporters were showing up, and occasionally, like on this day, one of the networks would appear. They needed each other. Buckman needed free media. The media needed to fill every minute of news time every day.

Carl was at the Johnston event when Kim Wakefield reached him.

"Carl, you need to get to a television. There is an employee takeover at a meat processing plant in Tama. The employees knew a raid was coming and they have taken over the plant. Pierce needs to know. He may be asked about it."

A reporter from Traditions and Values News, which Carl referred to as "unfair and unbalanced," stopped Senator Buckman after his luncheon speech. Carl was not able to get to the senator before the reporter did.

"Senator Buckman, you have made it clear you want the government to end or suspend the raids on illegal immigrants.

Do you have any reaction to what is happening in Tama, Iowa?"

"First, you mean undocumented people, right?" Buckman said to the reporter, making an obvious point with his tone. "Second, I haven't heard about this. I've been here for the last couple hours. I don't want to say more until I know more."

Carl filled the senator in from what he knew from Kim.

"You have other events scheduled. Do you want to postpone them and go to Tama?"

"That would be political grandstanding. No. I will comment if asked, but that sounds like a volatile situation and I'm not going to change our plans. Meskwaki Indians? Wow. I'm kind of glad I'm not Rushton right now. No way this looks good. I hope no one does anything dangerous to escalate this."

Jack Rushton was given the details of the planned raid and informed about the plant takeover by the director of Homeland Security. Communications director Edwards briefed the president that the story had gone viral. The cable news stations, 3N, Traditions and Values Network, and Century were broadcasting live from Tama.

Rushton was livid. He had downed a couple of three knucklers of Dark Hills in a tumbler embossed with the presidential seal. It was his lunch. His immediate response was that the raid should be carried out as planned and the plant should be cleared out, forcibly if necessary. Not responding could make him look weak on illegal immigration.

"Mr. President, the optics of this are very bad," Edwards told his boss. "It's Iowa. All of the media is there. Politically…"

"Stop right there Jess. Don't try to tell me about fucking politics. We are going to get these people out of there and if they are not in the country legally, we're going to fast track their asses in front of judges and get them out of this country as quickly as possible," Rushton fumed, now out from behind his executive office desk and on his feet, pacing angrily and a bit awkwardly around the office. He was still carrying his tumbler.

His rant continued.

"Shit, I know the politics. We have said we will crack down on people in the country illegally and we will do it, no matter what Professor Tulip or any of the other Democratic crybabies say in Iowa."

The condescending references to the senator were becoming more common but Rushton religiously avoided mentioning the name of any of his possible opponents.

"Sir, at least give us a few hours to try to develop lines of communication with the workers," Homeland Security Director Morris Banks pleaded. "We don't even know what they want. Let us develop some options short of going in there with force. We'd like that to be the last option. If we have to, we can clear the plant forcibly but there could be injuries or worse involved in using force. It could look like the last day of Waco."

Rushton sat back down behind the desk. He was quietly seething. He poured another tumbler of Dark Hills. He turned on the non-stop cable television coverage. He could see that the crowd of spectators was getting larger and noisier.

The reporter Rushton was tuned into said, "This is potentially a volatile situation. Law enforcement has the force here to end the situation at any time but would be risking serious injuries or deaths with any plan to retake the meat processing plant."

"This is a real urinal mint isn't it?" Rushton said.

Rushton's image was that he was a tough-talking Texan, a former governor, who was in the third year of his first term after slipping into office by grabbing the 13 electoral votes from highly contested Virginia in the early morning hours of the day after the election. This was despite Karla Foster sitting in the governor's chair at the time. He beat New York Governor Mike Clarke by a single percentage point, 48-47, in popular vote. The same election-day matchup was being projected in 18 months.

Rushton was elected with a message of conservatism, bluster, braggadocio, political pandering to the far right and tough talk about "Traditional American Values," which had become code in his administration for anti-immigrant, anti-gay marriage, anti-entitlements, anti-poor, pro-military, pro-Wall Street, pro-big health insurance, and big pharma. His policies on those issues got him elected as governor in Texas and got him elected to the Oval Office. He won the "Angry American" vote easily and there were millions of angry Americans. He gave voice to those who would report in polling they didn't like the direction of the country. A portion of Rushton's support didn't like those whom they considered to be lazy, entitled and didn't seem to like anyone who didn't look like them. Rushton had basically swept the South except for Florida, picked up every one-party red state like Oklahoma, Kansas, Nebraska, the Dakotas, Wyoming, Montana … all the states he had to win. Then he picked off Virginia, a shocker in Wisconsin and the swing state of Iowa, and he was in the White House.

His approval rating had slipped precipitously since. In fact, he began losing support nationally on his first day in office when he crudely said in his inaugural address that "we will take back America from those who are here illegally, taking the jobs of Americans and violating our laws.

"Mexico is not sending us their finest. That is not who is coming into the country illegally. They are not only allowing but are encouraging their drug dealers, murderers, rapists to stream across the border, and I am promising that we will send those people back. We won't allow them into our courts and we won't pay to keep them in our jails. We'll send them back.

"We will take America back for real Americans."

His 33-minute disjointed, barely lucid discourse called an inaugural address was immediately critiqued by historians as among the worst and most polarizing in the history of the presidency. And, if you have ever read some of the inaugural addresses, the bar is not that high. Not everyone did it like Kennedy or Obama. It was a frigid inauguration day and thought was given to moving the event inside. Rushton's team declined. The day might have been more palatable to everyone had that decision been made.

His speech was purposeful in widening divides on many issues: immigration, entitlement reform, gun rights, health care reform, foreign policy among them. Rushton also gave observers the impression he was uncomfortable and out of place with the formality and expectations of a new president on Inauguration Day. It should have been a magnificent celebration of a coalition that had voted him into office. Instead, it was a horrible start to his presidency.

The new first lady appeared sluggish and fatigued. Two pain

killers and several drinks will do that. She was rumored to have a more severe problem with substances than her husband, who relied on booze to make it through the day.

Rushton's resoluteness to look strong had gotten him into the disturbing situation he was watching play out on television from Tama, Iowa. He was too far down the road of meeting the conservative expectations of the people who voted for him to turn back. They expected him to run illegal immigrants out of the country and to prevent others from penetrating the borders. It was one of the reasons they voted him into the office.

He could barely get the words out of his mouth. It was painful for him, but he finally conceded, "Wait them out. Talk with them if you can. But damn, make it a show of force and make it clear they are getting out and they are getting out of this country, going to jail, or both."

Rushton didn't need to worry about any appearance that there was a lack of force available. Later into the afternoon and evening on the first day of the takeover of MegaPack, additional federal and regional law enforcement arrived. There was really nothing for them to do at the time but they still showed up. There were attempts at communicating with the workers inside. Several of the plant employees answered the ringing phones in the administrative offices.

Drones were used for surveillance of the plant and also were directed at the growing crowd of agitated spectators.

The media became the initial contact between the occupiers of the plant and the outside.

"What do you hope to accomplish?" asked a reporter in Spanish who got through to the offices.

"We want to know what the plans are. We aren't coming out and no one is coming in until we have guarantees," was the response, in English. "We are not coming out just to be jailed and sent in front of a judge like they were in Postville and other places. Some of us, probably many more than half, are American citizens who are just trying to make a living for our families."

"We can guarantee one thing; we are together now and we're coming out together and I don't think that is happening any time soon. We are unified and I believe we'll stay unified. This isn't about MegaPack. We want to keep working here. We are making a living. This is about the raid."

The employee declined to identify himself.

The May 2008 raid on Agriprocessors Inc., in Postville, Iowa, was the most extensive and expensive domestic workplace raid ever. Nearly 400 plant workers were rounded up. They were charged with having fraudulent work documents and stolen Social Security numbers. They were transported off the site, handcuffed together and generally offered plea agreements that would still mean jail sentences and deportation. They faced expedited or "fast track" appearances before a judge. After serving their sentences, they were deported or jailed.

This raid was different if the first contact on the inside was credible. Occupiers weren't unhappy with poor or unfair work conditions. They were closing ranks to avoid what those arrested in Postville faced, including criminal charge and disrupted families. Rushton had knowingly chosen the eighth anniversary of the Postville raid to execute the raid in Senator Buckman's home area of Austin, Minn.

In the early evening on the first day of the MegaPack occupation, Homeland Security officers unloaded a six-wheeled, all-terrain vehicle from a black trailer. The utility vehicle was also midnight black. Twenty minutes later the vehicle moved slowly in darkness toward the plant. There was no driver at the wheel. There were cameras mounted on the front and the back. From the perimeter, the well-lit six-by-six was guided slowly around the building scoping out and mapping possible entry points. From a computer screen, operators and agents could see the "night vision" video being sent from the ATV. The occupiers watched television coverage in the cafeteria. They saw the vehicle moving along the side of the plant. Media cameras could focus on the ATV from a distance.

"It's a robot. Can they arm that thing? What are they doing?" asked one of the women employees watching on television.

They were good questions. The specifications for the ATV said it could be operated as an explosive sweeper but mentioned nothing about it being weaponized. Just a convenient omission in the operating manual, it seemed. The U.S. Army had worked with the manufacturer to arm the robot ATV with weapons that could be operated or detonated remotely. The problem with arming the robotic ATV is that then it could become an expensive, single-use robot. At a cost of several hundred thousand dollars per vehicle, it had better be important to weaponize the ATV and detonate the weapon. The 62-horsepower vehicle was equipped with a 3,500-pound winch on the front.

This particular use of the ATV appeared to be a surveillance mission to collect information should it be necessary to break in and end the occupation of the plant. It was also an effort at intimidating the occupiers. If intimidation was a goal, it was working.

"See that winch. They could open one of the big garage doors like a can of pork and beans any time they want. We may need to start talking," said one of the workers. "I don't want to be deported but I don't want to die either."

Senator Buckman was among the millions of Americans watching in offices and homes. He was keeping abreast of what was going on 75 miles away from a town hall appearance for a United Food Workers group of about 50 people in the Des Moines union hall. It was the right audience for what he was about to say.

"You by now have heard or have watched what is happening in Tama at this moment. I want to say something about this volatile situation," Buckman said as he wrapped up his remarks. "I also believe in immigration reform, but my plan does not include these inhumane raids by federal authorities that prevent good people from earning a living. The raids result in the cruel separation of families when these people are arrested and deported. These raids will come to an end if I am president."

The crowd in the room was on its feet cheering and hooting.

Buckman quieted them by holding up both hands.

"Now listen, this is important," he said. "In my administration, we will not expedite deportations like this president. We will expedite citizenship for people who leave their native countries with their families for something better.

They are willing to risk jail, deportation and possibly worse to get to the United States where the opportunities are available. If you are able to make a living, support your family and not commit a crime, we will clear a path to work visas and eventually, citizenship. And it will be good for your union and for owners of the businesses you work with. What the president's administration is doing now is expensive, and more importantly, it is inhumane and cruel.

"It needs to stop ... today. Thank you for your time, your attention, and next February 1, Iowa Caucus night, we will take this country in a new direction with your support. There is a new horizon out there and nowhere on that horizon do I envision deploying all the military hardware within our grasp to break up families. Our movement toward that horizon is not just for the wealthiest, or the privileged, but for all Americans."

Union members were back on their feet. They spontaneously moved toward the stage to shake hands with the candidate and have photos taken. Ryan Holton and Susan Lyon collected the cards and reminded everyone to stay involved.

Senator Buckman stayed another 30 minutes with the group. They left in Beatrice back to the extended stay hotel outside of Des Moines after the crowd signed the motorhome.

Walking past the small bar area of the hotel, Gerald O'Malley jumped up to get the senator's attention. O'Malley wanted an update on where they perceived the campaign was at this early stage. The answer, the senator said, was that he had no idea. He knew he needed more people in "The Warehouse" headquarters in the Twin Cities. He wanted more diversity throughout the campaign staff. He wanted a staff matching the message of inclusion. He was taking advantage of every opportunity to speak before groups but had no idea if it was making a difference. The poll results were abysmal.

He had a website, social media and an apparatus for online donations, but incoming funds were still a trickle. Clarke and Foster, one of them the most likely Democratic nominee at this point, had millions of dollars already banked for the next eight months.

"We need more help on the road, too. We can't get to everyone at our events to get their contact information," the senator told O'Malley. "Wait, is it because off a lack of field volunteers, or are the crowds growing?"

The senator, sipping a diet cola, looked straight ahead, thinking about the question.

"Both I think. Yeah, people are listening. The people who show up want to tell me their stories and there seem to be a few more of them. Doesn't it seem that way to you?"

"Yes, I'm seeing that, too. You are talking policy with them, not generalities," O'Malley said.

"Always policy. Always what I would and wouldn't do as president," the senator said.

"We have policy statements on the website. People don't know you so they need to know about you," O'Malley said. "Keep telling them where you stand every opportunity you get. Media coverage seems to be good. Media is free. We're doing a good job of using the media interest. You are interesting and different to them compared to other candidates and campaigns. You are giving them time at events."

"Yes, and we're not confining them to a pen like Clarke and Foster are," the senator said. "I like to think they have good access to me."

O'Malley had ideas he shared with Buckman. He wanted better coordination between the field and The Warehouse. The staff in Minneapolis needed to make sure the senator's events were prominent every day on the home page of the website and in every social media platform. O'Malley said he would work with Carl to take advantage of local, state and national requests for interviews. He believed the senator would succeed or fail with specifics, not just "feel good" generalities. He promised to add diversity to the campaign, starting with openly gay campaign spokesman Curt Jaslow, whom the senator had moved from his Washington office to the campaign.

One of the best media opportunities of the entire campaign was about to cause the first serious internal conflict.

At 1 a.m. the senator was asleep. Carl was at the bar talking with O'Malley and O'Malley's young drinking buddy, Ryan Holton. Carl's phone rang from a number he couldn't identify.

"Is this Senator Buckman?"

"No, this is Carl Lyon with the senator's staff. Who is this?"

"We don't want to say right now. I'm calling from MegaPack in Tama."

"From the outside or inside?"

"Inside," the MegaPack caller reported.

"Everything going OK? The senator is sleeping."

"Well, there is a big show of force outside. Dozens of officers and vehicles, including a robotic ATV. We don't know what to think. We don't know what to do."

"How could the senator help with this?" Carl asked.

"We want him to come and negotiate some sort of deal for us. We saw what he said the last few days about these raids. We know we're going to have to give this up. We're trying to at least stay in the country and maybe we can keep our jobs here with temporary visas. These are good jobs for us. We're doing well. The company is better than others some of us have worked with."

"Just a minute." Carl said. "Let me explain this to the senator's campaign manager. Stay with me."

After explaining the call, O'Malley took the phone.

"We don't think the senator will come to Tama. We don't think he would want to be involved because of the scope of this. You could be considered to be illegal occupiers of a private business by most people. We know he is sympathetic to your cause and he doesn't believe in these raids, but interfering with law enforcement would be an awkward position to put him into."

"Will you talk with him? We need help," said the caller inside MegaPack. "Will he do more than just talk about supporting us?"

"Are you communicating with the people outside?" O'Malley asked. "You need to start talking if you want to work something out. Call us in the morning."

The senator was up and on the treadmill in the hotel's exercise room by 5 a.m. By 7, he was wired and ready to go. He wanted to start his campaign day at another factory gate. Ryan had disappeared in Beatrice at midnight and didn't return until 3 a.m. He wasn't alone. There had been speculation he was finding companionship on the road.

"Ryan, let's go to the tire plant here. Let's go meet some people. We don't have anything scheduled until noon otherwise. Bring your friend."

"Sir, not a good idea. I'll get her back and come right back."

Carl and Susan Lyon were awake next. O'Malley was last.

"Senator, we have something important to talk about," O'Malley said when he arrived in the breakfast room of the hotel. "We got a call last night."

O'Malley explained the call and the request.

"No," the senator responded flatly. "I can't do that. I can't interfere. The president has screwed this up. He has to find a way out. It's a law enforcement matter. He owns this. Suppose I get involved in some way and something tragic happens. As sympathetic as I am for these people, this was probably the worst thing they could do. Besides, anything I could do would likely be rejected by ICE and Homeland Security. Is FBI there, too? That is what it looked like in media coverage I saw."

"What if the people in the plant start talking with ICE and Homeland on their own? Would you act as an intermediary?" O'Malley asked.

Buckman said he was still reluctant.

"What would the best solution be?" he asked in between bites of a toasted bagel spread with peanut butter.

They agreed that the optimal solution would be to get the workers out of the plant and maybe get them off with misdemeanor trespassing charges and fines. There would have to be some repercussions. They occupied the plant illegally. Already there was a divide developing between those who, like Rushton, wanted them out of the place immediately, regardless of how it was accomplished, and the sympathizers who, like the senator, looked at the occupation as a possible catalyst to discuss real immigration reform.

"They want to stay in the country and keep their jobs," Carl said. "Any way that is possible in this scenario? The company would probably agree to that. They need these workers to keep the plant open and producing."

"If the workers start talking with ICE, Homeland Security or FBI, I'll agree to mediate," the senator finally decided. "Personally, no way I believe Rushton will allow that. He may think he'll look weak by negotiating. But maybe he isn't taking me seriously as a candidate. He is much more concerned with Mike Clarke and Karla Foster as opponents. He should be at this point. He might want me to give Clarke and Foster some heat by letting me into the spotlight for a few minutes. The workers have to start talking first."

The incident commander tried again to reach someone in the plant who could speak for the occupiers. The phone call was picked up by a male voice who identified himself as Ron. He didn't share a last name.

"Ron, you have to get out of there. You know we can make that happen forcibly but that isn't what either of us want. We would be risking injuries and possibly lives on our side and yours. So, your call, Ron. How can we end this peacefully?" the commander asked.

"We want Senator Buckman to negotiate a solution. We want him to come in here and help open the communications. Will you agree to that? He understands our situation and we think your people can respect him. We've talked with his staff. We think he'll come here."

"Ron, you don't have much of a position here," the incident commander said. "We know some of the people, probably a lot of them, are in the country illegally. That is why we are here. Our mission here is to identify the workers who are illegal, charge them, and we'll see what happens then."

"You want to deport them," Ron snapped back angrily. "That is why we are in here. We're together on that one. No deportations. We're good employees. This is a good operation. Leave us alone."

"We won't promise that. I'm not in any position to say there won't be deportations. That is for others to decide," the still unidentified commander said.

"Then we aren't coming out," Ron said. "You need to get to the right person. That is what we want … no deportations. We aren't criminals."

"Right now, yes, you are."

The phone went silent. Ron had hung up.

The commander was inclined to sit and wait. He wanted to end the standoff with no injuries or casualties. The visual image of breaking into the facility and taking people out forcibly would damage the reputation of ICE and Homeland Security. He was convinced that it would be an ugly, historic moment, like the Branch Davidian siege and final deadly conclusion. He escalated the discussion to his supervisor, who was not on site but was being updated frequently.

"Sir, they want Senator Pierce Buckman, who is in the Des Moines area right now, to come here and negotiate a settlement. They want no deportations. So, two things: would you approve Buckman getting involved and second, what about taking deportations off the table?" the commander said.

"You know this is political, too. It isn't just law enforcement now," the Homeland Security supervisor said. "This will go far above me. It may take a while and the answer is likely to be 'no' on both questions."

At 11 a.m., Eastern Daylight Time, Homeland Security Director Morris Banks and the president's communications director, Jess Edwards, entered the Oval Office to update Rushton.

They relayed the conversation about Buckman and taking deportation off the table to end the occupation.

"Mr. President, we think taking the plant forcibly could result in injuries and possibly worse, and it would happen live on television. It could look horrible," Banks reported. "We can do it quickly but there is some access to weapons ... knives mostly ... on the inside. And the stun guns used in the kill process. We doubt they would use weapons and would likely come out easily but there is always risk and possible volatility in a situation like this. These things can be unpredictable."

Rushton was calm. He thought about the possible images of a forcible takeover and leading the workers out. On their feet hopefully, but it could be in ambulances or on gurneys. And that would just be the start of a long, drawn-out story for the media as the workers were transported away from the families.

"Let Professor Geranium see what he can do. I will approve that," Rushton said of Senator Buckman. "Give him a day or two to get this done. You have my approval to negotiate a settlement. But if we find any drugs in this plant or on any of these occupiers, they will be deported. That is not off the table. If they have criminal records and are not here legally, they will be deported. If they resist in any way, they will be deported. And criminal charges are not off the table. There have to be repercussions to this mess. But let Professor Chrysanthemum do what he can."

Rushton did not talk about the political ramifications during the update. But they were in his head. Buckman was right. Rushton felt he would have a much better chance of being re-elected if somehow Buckman was the nominee. Buckman was not even at 10 percent name recognition, let alone 10 percent in polling of probable Iowa Caucus voters. He was harmless at this point. And he was considered by Rushton to be a crazed socialist. If the occupiers were looking for help from Mike Clarke or Karla Foster, Rushton said he would have rejected the idea immediately.

President Rushton's approval of Senator Buckman attempting to mediate a solution was passed down to the incident commander. He tried the phone to the administrative offices again.

"I want to speak to Ron. We have news," said the commander, who now identified himself as James.

"This is Ron. James … first name or last name?"

"First. This went all the way to the president and he has agreed to allow the senator to come here to try to end this. Ron, we can come to an agreement, can't we?" the commander asked. "We will let the senator come in.

"It will probably take a couple hours to get him here. Let's get this over today. We'll give you 48 hours before we're going to have to come in and get everyone out. Two days, preferably much faster. Neither of us wants a forcible extraction but you've seen what is going on outside. We're mobilized. We certainly have the capability to force everyone out. If we have to do that, there are no promises about what happens to everyone,"

James said.

Buckman was at a noon lunch with an Optimist Club group of about 30 people. There was no media and there appeared to be more interest in the chicken sandwiches than what Buckman was saying. The senator was glad the event was coming to an end. He wasn't alone, apparently. The club members applauded politely and started for the door. Only a few members approached the senator to talk further and thank him for coming.

O'Malley's phone rang as the event wrapped up. The caller ID said MegaPack.

"This is O'Malley, who is this?"

"It's Ron inside the plant in Tama. We want to talk with the senator."

"You mean right now?" O'Malley asked.

"No, we want him to come and work out a deal for us with the government before this gets out of control," Ron said.

"He won't do that unless the president approves. This isn't going to happen," O'Malley said.

"It did happen. He gave us 48 hours to end this. We need the senator here. We think he can help us. We've followed what he has been saying. We need someone who understands us and is sympathetic."

O'Malley ended the conversation by telling Ron he would ask.

Beatrice the ugly motorhome was on the road within 10 minutes. The senator changed into jeans, a T-shirt, worn sweater, equally worn sport coat, walking shoes with no socks and his new Crossroads State National Champions cap.

"Senator, what are you going to try to accomplish? What is the goal here?" O'Malley asked.

"End this with no violence is the first goal. My goal is to have these people back returning to work in a few days with no deportations. This is an opportunity to change the tone of the conversation about immigration. Rushton is doing two things here: Avoiding a potentially violent showdown and indicating he would be willing to look at a real solution to immigration. I hope we can turn this into a discussion about real immigration reform instead of polarizing rhetoric.

"These are people who are trying to find a better life for

themselves and their families. They should not be considered enemies. They are hard-working people who buy cars, pay taxes … they pay more taxes by percentage of income than the wealthiest Americans in many cases … support businesses and produce a product Americans want. I want to find common ground. We can create a new, quicker path to citizenship."

There was still little indication who was riding in Beatrice when it pulled up to a temporary security checkpoint about a mile on the road leading to MegaPack. The motorhome seemed to throw off security at the checkpoint and the guy in a sweater and jeans and Crossroads State cap didn't look like a U.S. Senator either. Buckman started fishing IDs out of his wallet to convince the county sheriff deputies he was expected. They checked with incident command.

Two dogs and handlers arrived 10 minutes later at the checkpoint. Five heavily armed federal agents wearing protective vests followed in an armored transport and boarded Beatrice before anyone was allowed to get off.

"Excuse us, sir, but we have to check out the vehicle," one of the agents explained. "The dogs will be coming on as soon as they are done on the outside. Please be patient for a few minutes."

The few minutes turned into 25 minutes. The senator was back on the stationary bike by the bedroom in back. He was angry and was pounding the pedals.

"OK, we're clear. You can get off. You'll meet the incident commanders in the tent there," one of the agents said. "You will be briefed."

At incident command, it was clear that the U.S. Department of Homeland Security, with help from its friends at ICE, the ATF and FBI, were taking this event seriously. They had to do something with those annual budgets in the billions.

"Do you guys have any clue what this operation is costing?" the senator said to the assembled detail.

There was stony silence and glares from the officers. Not a good first impression for the senator. He was not one to care about first impressions of himself.

Helicopters circled overhead, and various armed vehicles,

additional teams of K-9 officers and bomb sniffers, and several teams of sharp shooters were in various stages of readiness. There were three large tents set up, a fleet of white buses waiting to carry away everyone inside the plant and several vehicles that appeared to be capable of simply crashing through the walls of the building at any second to end the occupation.

"They've got all the toys out, haven't they? Remind me to cut Homeland Security's budget if I become president," Buckman said loudly to Carl as the senator was finally escorted from the briefing, surrounded by men and women with semi-automatic weapons, helmets with dark face shields and bulletproof vests. "This is ridiculous."

James W. Martin introduced himself as the incident commander.

"Former military, James?" the senator asked.

"Yes sir. U.S. Navy," he said, and continued, "When you go in, we will take you in a robotic ATV. We can monitor the exercise from here. Senator, we want to end this quickly and without using any force. You will go in alone."

"No sir. I will take my media director, Carl Lyon, with me."

"We can't allow that."

"He is going with me."

"This is our exercise and our decisions." Martin said.

"I am a U.S. Senator and this is my decision, or we turn around and drive out of here. We'll leave this nightmare to you. I will be happy to call the president to tell him it didn't work out."

"That won't be necessary. Let's go."

A call had been made into the plant to tell the occupiers that the senator and a staff member were headed to the building. They agreed on a door by the offices as the entry point.

Carl had his cellphone in his pocket. He gave an iPro camera from inside the motorhome to the senator, sensing correctly that no one would dare confront the already annoyed Buckman further.

"Put it in your pocket, sir," Carl instructed.

The robot ATV moved slowly toward the agreed upon door. The senator had now lost his escorts.

"Ok, this is weird," Buckman said of the ATV plodding along toward the entry point. "What do you suppose happens if I pull this?"

"Sir, I believe that would take it out of remote mode. You could drive it."

"Next time," the senator said.

The door was opened and two men and a woman were waiting. There was no indication they were armed in any way. Incident command could also see the greeters were unarmed as the senator and Carl Lyon walked in and the door was slammed quickly behind them. They were led through the administrative offices to the cafeteria.

The robot lingered at the door providing remote video to incident command.

The senator would say later it was one of the most intense moments of his life. Scarier than the time he and his parents, the Old Hippies, somehow got mixed up in an anti-U.S. demonstration in Paris -- the one in France, not Kentucky or Missouri.

"Two men, one woman, appear to be unarmed. We have video and photos of the entry," the incident commander reported. "Let's see if we can identify the three from the plant."

What the senator and Carl found in the cafeteria was not raw emotion, tension or anger. It was the cafeteria of a production plant. They found food and card games and televisions dialed into media coverage. The two new people in the room were immediately noticed.

"Amigos y Amigas, este es Senador Pierce Buckman," was the introduction.

There were hoots and applause. Carl was getting video from the iPro that had been hidden in the senator's pocket.

"Listen now," Buckman said in English. "I'm here to help you but I need to know what you want. We all know this can't go on for long. At any moment they can come in and take everyone out. You need to assure me that if this reaches that point, you will go out peacefully. No one is going to be hurt here. So where are your heads at?"

"Senator, we can keep our jobs?" asked one of the occupiers.

"We have no problem with MegaPack. This is all about the raid."

"And we don't want to be deported. We have families. That has to be off the table," said a black man with what sounded like a Caribbean accent.

"They won't go for that," the senator said. "If you only have false or fraudulent paperwork, maybe we can avoid deportation. If you have false documents or Social Security numbers and you have committed a crime in this country, you will probably face trial, jail and deportation. Anyone here with that situation?"

A couple of people in the group of about 50 in the cafeteria raised their hands sheepishly.

"We'll do what we can. This is only part of the group. Where is everyone else?"

The senator was told the remaining workers were scattered around in the offices, at each possible entry point as security. Others were sleeping or passing time in the plant.

"Can we get everyone together in one place?" the senator asked.

"Yes sir," said the woman who had met him at the door. "How about in 20 minutes on the kill floor?"

"That will work," Buckman said.

He sat down at one of the tables. Without asking, they dealt him in.

"What's the game?"

"Hand and foot," he was told. "You are my partner and it's a penny a point. We win by a couple thousand points, well, you get it."

"I know the game," the senator said.

It took an hour to get everyone together. Buckman and his partner had lost by 2,300 points. He fished around for his wallet. Carl knew the senator rarely carried cash. Carl paid the $23 to the winners.

There were 325 production workers in the building at the time of the takeover. Only foremen and management staff had left. The workers were spread out around Buckman, who stood on a metal table. Carl was at his side shooting video. MegaPack employees were standing on equipment, chairs, and seated on the floor in front of him. They were quiet and attentive.

"Folks, I'm here on your behalf not only because you asked me to come, but because I am with you philosophically. I'm on your side and will advocate for you. The solution to immigration reform is not deportations. The solution isn't jail. The solution isn't separating families."

He was interrupted by applause and unidentified reaction in about four different languages. He knew there was no way everyone understood what he was saying.

"Tearing apart families as a solution to a problem Congress has not had the resolve, the compassion, nor the new ideas to solve, is cruel. I am running for president. If I am elected, we will push for real reform. I believe you want to work, right? This isn't about your jobs. It is about your families, your desire for a better life, your dreams."

The crowd shouted and moved closer, snapping photos with their phones.

"Listen now, here is what is going to happen. I'm going to call the commander outside. I'm going to ask for no deportations and no jail sentences. Fines only for trespassing, not for being here illegally. I want to warn you, they may want jail terms, and if you have illegal IDs and have committed a crime in this country, they will want to deport. I'll do what I can but I have to tell you, in that situation you will likely be sent out of the country and could face jail for more than a few days.

"We're going to do this in a democratic way. We're going to vote. If you are good with fines, no jail, back to work quickly but deportations if you've committed a crime, raise your hands."

Hands went up but there was an obvious reluctance from some in the group.

"I'm sorry we don't have an amnesty agreement, and there won't be one. I understand. I have to tell you, though, that committing a crime when you are not a citizen of this country is not something I would approve of either. I will make the path to citizenship less restrictive, but you cannot commit crimes and expect to avoid any penalty. There must be some penalty."

"It is time, people," said one of the men who seemed to be leading the group. "Let's show those hands again. I think the senator is trying to get us a good deal. Let's give him our full support."

This time nearly every hand went up. The workers rose to their feet and cheered again.

"OK, I'm going to make the call, but how about I wait until the morning. I need to get my $23 back from Judd and Jesse," the senator joked with that big grin. "Besides, I'm hungry. What's on the menu in that cafeteria?"

"Whose $23?" Carl muttered.

Buckman lacked the ego he was told he would need in a campaign for president. He did not lack intellect or political astuteness. If he was going to lead the group out, he was going to do it live on the morning cable news programs when millions would be watching and would have been waiting for something to happen for hours.

Buckman sat back down to play cards and eat a sandwich.

At 3 a.m., the senator sat down in the offices and made the call.

"Commander Martin, please. This is Pierce Buckman inside."

"Here is how we can end this," the senator said when Martin took the call.

Buckman talked about the employees asking for fines, no jail terms and that they wanted to go back to work quickly.

"No deportations unless you find out the workers who have fraudulent paperwork have also committed crimes. They understand the repercussions of that. I've explained that deportations are possible in those circumstances."

"Trespassing and obstruction of justice ... five days for everyone?" James Martin asked. "There has to be some penalty. This has cost a lot of taxpayer money."

"Kind of a waste, too," the senator said. "Couldn't this have been a bit more restrained?"

"Too far along now," Martin said.

They went back and forth for more than 30 minutes. Martin finally agreed that workers would be processed, would be transported to jail and would spend a night. Those with fraudulent papers and a criminal record in the U.S. would face a judge and would likely be deported quickly. They agreed that those with fraudulent papers and no crimes would spend two nights in jail, would be offered a plea and if they pleaded guilty, would be fined $500, the fine suspended, and be sentenced to year in jail, all of it suspended as long as they did not commit a crime during a year of probation. If any drugs were found on the employees or drugs were found in the plant, there would be further charges.

"I'm not a lawyer. How do we know federal prosecutors will approve this deal?" the senator asked.

"We'll call the federal prosecutor for this district. Give us an hour or two. Senator, we have an agreement, correct?" Martin said.

Carl Lyon had taken over the card game for the senator. This time the senator and his partner lost by 1,500 points. The night had cost Carl $38 for the senator's losses. He was satisfied he didn't have to pay for Buckman's dinner.

Martin called the senator and assured him the federal prosecutor would agree to their negotiated plea agreement. They talked about how the workers would leave the building.

"We'll come out to you. They understand they will be processed," the senator said.

"We will meet you as the group comes out. We can't risk anyone trying to run. They will not be allowed to see their families at this time. Agreed?" Martin asked.

"Yes sir, that makes sense. I will tell them not to go to their families. How about at 6:45 a.m.? Will your people have everything in place by then?"

"We'll be ready, Senator."

There was one more mass meeting on the inside. The senator stood on the table to speak with the group.

"We're going out at 6:45 folks," he reported. "I'm told that at about 6:30 there will be two teams of Tactical Emergency Medical Support, they are called TEMS, coming into the building. They are special teams that are activated for high-risk law enforcement operations to provide medical support. I've told them we don't need these teams and everyone is doing fine physically but they were insistent. They want to assess the situation from the inside.

"When we go out, there will be a large presence of ICE, ATF and Homeland Security, the FBI, and state and county law enforcement. It may be kind of unnerving but you will be safe. I will walk out with you. You will be asked to hold up your hands and place them on your head so they know no weapons are being carried out. Your families are probably here. They will be quite a distance away. You may hear or see them. Don't go to them. The officers may think you are leaving or trying to run. How are you feeling?"

Several of the workers expressed they were nervous about what would happen to them.

"They will keep their word," the senator said. "I'll make sure they do. Let me just say I have been impressed by your resolve. Sometimes resistance is the only real solution. I wish Congress was as sensible as this group. Good luck to all of you. I believe you may have changed the discussion about immigrating to this great country. You may have opened doors for others and hopefully, you have, through your actions these last couple days, prevented others from being victims of raids like this."

At 6:30, Carl Lyon posted videos and photos on the Buckman for President website and the site's social media platform. He had set up two interviews for the senator from the inside with 3N and Century Network. In both interviews, the senator said he hoped the incident would raise awareness about immigration, he emphasized the idea that these were people striving for better lives, and he said he was hopeful there would be compassion instead of anger and resentment for the people who occupied the plant.

The TEMS teams, armed, outfitted in tactical protective gear and carrying supplies a paramedic might carry, found only what Senator Buckman had told them they would find. There were no injured workers nor anyone who required medical attention. The teams had been told about Buckman's heart attack. A TEMS team member took Buckman's blood pressure and pulse with his consent. His blood pressure was only slightly above the normal range.

When the workers opened the door at 6:45, they were led out by the TEMS teams. The senator lingered inside shaking hands with workers, wishing them well in English and Spanish and taking photos with groups and individuals.

Lined up on both sides were armed officers holding a thick rope line, creating an alley between the ropes. There were cheers and scattered taunts and boos as the workers walked out to the tents where processing would take place before transport to a pre-arranged holding area in a building at the Iowa Agricultural Exposition grounds in Des Moines.

The senator was the last person out of the building. Carl Lyon was in front of him, walking backward at times, recording video. Carl asked a few questions.

"These are good people who are trying to give their families a better life. I am hopeful that this event and the peaceful way it ended will be the starting point to begin a serious conversation about immigration reform," the senator told Carl. "I want to thank President Rushton for his role in negotiating a sensible settlement. I would now ask for a moratorium on these raids until we can work out a real reform package. I will spend all the time we need to spend in Washington to make this happen.

"I thank all of the law enforcement people for handling this with restraint and professionalism.

"I am hopeful that MegaPack will be open again quickly with the same good employees who are walking out right now. That is what these employees want."

Senator Buckman and incident commander James Martin conducted an informal news briefing. The senator, Carl would recall later, did not want to embarrass the president. He again mentioned the role of Rushton in reaching a settlement. Carl counted 15 Iowa and national cameras focused on the senator.

Several cameras followed Buckman as he went to the perimeter where families and friends of the workers waited. The crowd estimated by the media at 500 waved printed "Sensible Reform Now" signs in English, Spanish and French, courtesy of the United Food Workers. They cheered the senator, who was flanked by two county sheriff deputies, as he first walked in front of the roped-off area, then lifted the rope and went under to mingle with the crowd.

"Senator, please!" one of the deputies pleaded to keep him

outside the perimeter.

The deputy urgently talked into a radio on his collar. Four more county and Tama Police Department officers trotted to the senator. They nearly circled him as he met families of workers and had more photos taken. Reporters, Carl among them, were getting jostled trying to get the videos and photos they wanted of the senator with his new fans, who were now pressing forward shouting, "Buckman, Buckman, Buckman" and "El Profesor."

Watching the impromptu rally with the families was Jericho Adams Brooks in a camo jacket and sunglasses. He wasn't cheering.

Ignoring security and the possible threat within large crowds would become a habit of the senator in his unconventional campaign.

Buckman suggested to Ryan Holton that everyone in the crowd who would pledge to support him in the Iowa Caucus sign Beatrice in permanent marker.

"I love that idea," said Ryan, who had purchased a cheap, battery-powered megaphone at a novelty store and had been messing with it on the motorhome as he drove.

The senator entertained his staff, such as it was, by singing '60s, '70s and '80s hits through the megaphone backed by a karaoke CD. Considering his personal story, it wasn't surprising that The Doors were one of his favorites. His voice wasn't bad.

Ryan produced the red plastic megaphone for the senator.

"OK, they are going to want you to disperse," the senator told the crowd through the megaphone. "Here is what we are going to do. We want you to come over to the Beatrice, our beloved bus, and sign voter information cards. If you do that, we want you to sign Beatrice in markers. Write messages to our campaign. This will be our memento of this unusual day."

"I'm asking for your support on caucus night. And I am asking for your support of sensible immigration reform. Raids are not sensible reform."

The offer to sign the bus assisted law enforcement toward a

goal of dispersing the crowd gathered to watch the conclusion of the MegaPack occupation.

In the White House, Jack Rushton was watching the media's coverage, which to him seemed endless. The senator kept showing up on the screen talking with the big, enthusiastic crowd waiting out the takeover. It seemed to Rushton that there was nothing on the screen but a potential political rival whose campaign was going nowhere fast until this very moment.,

"Oh, shit. What have I done? Professor fucking Posey!" Rushton said out loud to no one but himself.

The president poured himself another tumbler of Dark Hills bourbon. It was his third blast in two hours. The president was usually drunk by 5 p.m. His staff kept the secret and another. They knew the most powerful man in the free world washed down a sleeping pill or two each night with one more tumbler full. He was a functioning alcoholic usually. At least once a week, though, he drank a couple extras and became a stumbling, pants-peeing, full-fledged drunk.

First Lady Anna Lynae Johnson-Rushton didn't really care how much her husband drank and wasn't around him enough to know how much he was drinking. That was by choice. She was out of it most of the time herself. She was dependent on pain medications to treat chronic pain from a back injury acquired falling off a horse. It was a real, debilitating injury she had never really gotten relief from. In fact, the pain was chronic even after three surgeries. She wasn't coping well with the back pain and she wasn't coping at all with life as the first lady.

They had a political understanding. They would tolerate each other and keep their distance. They had separate bedrooms and separate lives.

The first lady detested her closely scrutinized responsibilities. She hated the job. She hated Washington, D.C.

A beauty who was born into great wealth in a prominent Texas family, she was uncomfortable in her role. It hadn't always been this way. She enjoyed being the wife of the governor of Texas. That was status in her home state. She considered being the first lady of the country to be a miserable existence by comparison. She blamed the president for dragging her into this. She wanted to disappear back to Texas, where the couple's children and grandchildren still lived. She did often spend time in Texas while the president remained in Washington or was out of the country. She was in a dark, desperate battle with what she felt was a miserable life.

CHAPTER 16

After the Raid

For two hours, the diverse group that had waited out their friends and loved ones during the occupation of MegaPack signed voter information cards and signed Beatrice in permanent green, orange, purple, red and black markers. There were a lot of "thank you" messages and best wishes from the families of the occupiers. Some of the messages were written in Spanish, French, Haitian Creole and several other languages. There were many "God bless you" messages.

Carl invited newspaper reporters from Des Moines, Marshalltown and the Tama weekly paper into the motorhome to talk with the senator.

"Senator, what was it like inside during this event?" asked a reporter from Des Moines.

"Resolute. Their focus was on a standing together against the president's policy of deporting undocumented people. But it was the president who agreed to this solution. Maybe we transformed the conversation today about how we can expedite some form of citizenship or an easier process to obtain a work visa. The people inside MegaPack are people trying to better their lives for themselves and their families."

"The president, I hope, opened a door to discussion and negotiation today. This could have ended very differently and possibly violently had it not been for the president's leadership today."

O'Malley and Carl were both listening to the interview. They looked at each other immediately and grimaced when their candidate again mentioned the leadership of the president. They hoped he would stop that very quickly.

"What was going on while you waited this out?" another reporter asked.

"It was calm. We talked about families, our backgrounds, played cards, ate, napped," Buckman reported. "Not exactly revolutionary activities, but maybe this was the start of a revolution of immigration reform. These are proud, ambitious people who want to contribute and make a living for their families."

It was a noisy, jubilant trip back to Des Moines. O'Malley and Carl talked about raiding the cabinet in the galley kitchen where they knew the wine bottles were stashed out of sight of media visitors to the motorhome. There was also beer in the refrigerator.

"Wonder what Mike Clarke and Karla Foster thought of this?" said O'Malley, who had been working his cellphone constantly talking with media outlets. "The Warehouse people say they raised half a million in small donations the last two days. Maybe we can get a real bus. How about it, Senator?"

"Beatrice has charm. We're keeping her. Every place we go, I want people signing her."

"Yeah, Beatrice has charm if you think charm is a rolling tenement the color of the stuff in a baby's diaper," O'Malley said.

"Baby! I haven't talked to Kim in two days. Give me the room please."

Carl closed the door to the bedroom.

Averting the crisis at Tama was not on the schedule. The senator needed rest but events were still on the schedule.

"What are we going to do? Our guy needs sleep," Carl asked O'Malley. "We all do."

"Well, that's life out here," O'Malley responded. "He knows the routine. He'll find some time. I think we better get another driver, though. We need so many things right now, including money, but today was really something special. This guy is different, that's for sure. He may be just crazy enough to at least make it to caucus night. Did he really mention Rushton's leadership? Let's try to keep him from doing that again anytime soon."

The senator slept most of the way back to Des Moines after talking with Kim, who mentioned that his magnanimous gesture to credit Rushton might have been a bit over-the-top.

"What did you do in there with the workers?" Kim asked.

"Talked. Played cards. It wasn't all that tense," he admitted.

"Glad you didn't tell the media that."

"I just did about 20 minutes ago," the senator said, chuckling.

Late in the afternoon in the Warehouse in the Twin Cities, the college students acting as IT and social media managers were convinced the website, Buckman for President, had crashed. Buckman for President wasn't down, it was overwhelmed by traffic. Several hundred thousand people across the country were trying to get on the site at the same time. They wanted to look at the videos, trying to find out more about the senator from Minnesota with the shaved head who appeared to lack fashion sense but not common sense.

"Just guessing, but I think we're going to need more capacity," one of the IT kids reported.

By the time the site was fully functional again, the campaign had taken in $1.5 million in 24 hours. The video of the senator walking out of the building with the occupants and the video of him mingling with families and friends outside with a large group of law enforcement officers was being watched approximately every three seconds. The presence of law enforcement gave the senator a new level of credibility. He was now a real candidate who was worthy of grim-faced security, even if they were local law enforcement. The Warehouse phone lines were jammed. Within hours of the end of the "Occupation at MegaPack," as one network was now referring it, the senator had invitations for events in Iowa and New Hampshire, again in Nevada and South Carolina, the earliest states in the nomination process. For now, O'Malley declined them all outside of Iowa, although a return to Las Vegas sounded attractive to staff. Iowa was the only focus of this campaign and would remain so through caucus night.

O'Malley was making sure the media knew what was going

on in Tama, Iowa, and who was responsible for bringing a potentially dangerous situation to a calm, peaceful conclusion. He talked to reporters, union officials, immigration reformers and potential donors. He was committing to Iowa events where the senator was invited to appear.

O'Malley had spoken several times with the chief marketing officer of a health system in Davenport who was promising a big crowd, a tour of a new hospital and lots of media attention.

"How many people do you think would come to a town hall type of event … 200, 300?" O'Malley asked Kenny Kroeger, whom he discovered to be a highly confident, brash transplant from New Jersey with a trail of life experiences, including a stint as a congressional aide.

"O'Malley, my staff can get that many people in a phone booth," Kroeger said. "I think we can fill the RiverFront."

"What is that?" O'Malley asked.

"A 2,000-seat theater that used to be an RKO Orpheum and has been renovated into a very nice traditional venue for plays, concerts, that kind of thing. I think we can fill it considering what you have been up to this week. I suggest you take advantage of his momentum by getting over here. When can you do it?"

They agreed that Monday, only five days away, would be the day.

"We'll be there Sunday night," O'Malley said. "Tell you what, you get 2,000 people in that theatre and I'll hire your staff on the spot. Where do we stay?"

"They will do it. You are dreaming about hiring them away. They are loyal to me," Kroeger said. "There are several very nice hotels within walking distance of the theatre."

They talked more about the hospital tour, the time of the town hall event, and some general ideas about what the senator would talk about in Davenport.

"We've been talking about doing these events called Biking with Buckman. The idea is to get a bunch of bike riders together for a ride with the senator. Maybe a few miles. Then a Q and A session for a few minutes after the ride. We think it would be a good event to build a database of voters and the type of voters who would support the senator in the caucus."

"There are great bike paths here. Only a few blocks from the theater," Kroeger said. "So, we're doing the hospital tour, the town hall, and the short bike ride. We can do this. We've got a lot of contacts with people who would likely support the senator. We'll start working on everything."

"A few more things," O'Malley said. "The senator wants the media to have access to him. He isn't afraid of defending his policies. We'll be driving a big, ugly bus we're calling Beatrice.

"And don't overdo the theater setup. No flag waving. The senator isn't into a bunch of flags behind him on the stage. At this point, he just walks out and talks and takes questions. Our events don't look like the typical, flag-waving campaign events with a bunch of people behind him. He thinks the so-called patriotism looks fake.

"Hey, will the senator talk about public service?" Kroeger asked.

"He usually does."

"That will be a good message for the hospital visit," Kroeger added. "We encourage employees to live our mission of compassionate care outside of their work. Imagine that on a national scale with every company participating."

"That's what he is talking about," O'Malley finished.

The conversation convinced O'Malley the campaign needed help on the road. If they were going to reach the point they wanted to reach, they were going to need an advance person or two to set up what O'Malley and the hospital marketing guy in Davenport had talked about.

"Senator, we need to talk about a few things," O'Malley said when they met in Buckman's room back at the hotel. "They are kind of frantic at The Warehouse. They need people and they need a real IT crew. They need to get the place wired better to handle the incoming calls and web traffic. I'm going there for a few days to help them get the people they need. Senator, you definitely won the day at MegaPack and probably the week. The Sunday morning news shows all want you.

"We've got the stage at least temporarily. Now we need to figure out what to do with it. You need another strategy guy who knows Iowa. Someone who knows the landscape. There are counties in Iowa where you won't have a chance in a general election. Any county represented by Congressman Monte Dumas, you can write off."

Montgomery Dumas of Shingles, Iowa in the far Northwest part of the state is one of the most radical of the radical right. He is sometimes considered an embarrassment to Iowa in counties outside of his district, but in his district, he is "their guy" and his supporters had a remarkable ability to explain away even his most extreme statement, some of them borderline racist and homophobic by just claiming "that's just Monte being Monte."

O'Malley said, "You might as well forget just about everything west of Des Moines, too, except for Council Bluffs. The counties south of Des Moines won't be much better for you. The cities are your sweet spot."

"O'Malley, we're going to every county. On caucus night, we just need to get the most Dems. Republicans won't matter," the senator countered. "We aren't giving up any of them. I'm going to Sioux County, Appanoose, Lyon, Plymouth, Cherokee … all of them. Get a map and start marking them off. The full Grassley."

Long-time U.S. Senator Chuck Grassley kept his promise to visit all 99 Iowa counties every year.

"Works well for him," Buckman added. "He is unbeatable in Iowa."

"How in the hell do you know those counties?" the incredulous O'Malley asked. "No Democrat wins in those counties in a general election. No Democrat I know even knows where those places are. I think you will be wasting time and money. Those counties not only won't go to a Democrat in a general, they detest them deep within their souls. Don't waste your breath on them. What will you possibly say to these people? If you get 30 people to show up at an event, that will be fantastic because in some of these counties, 30 people are the entire base of Democratic support."

"We'll get them to sign Beatrice and I will speak on college campuses and organize bike rides," the senator said. "They have colleges, right? I'll make the diner circuit. We can do Bike with Buckman events in college towns. I will talk to them about ethanol subsidies, which I support, and making the government more efficient … which I also believe we need to do. We'll talk about wind power. I won't hide from these people or avoid talking about the issues with them. Remember, it's only Dems who get to participate in the Democratic caucus unless they change parties for the night. I will win these counties on caucus night and I think I can win one if I am the nominee. More than one."

"You only have that stationary bike if you are going to Bike with Buckman, which by the way, isn't a bad idea. Environmentally friendly and a good health and wellness message," O'Malley finally said, giving up the fight about going to the reddest Iowa counties. "We're going to Davenport and do the first Bike with Buckman there."

"I have five bikes. We'll get a couple later this week in the Cities," the senator said.

House parties are a traditional way to meet Iowans face-to-face during caucus season. Small groups are invited by the hosts to meet the candidate. Maybe they attract 15 people in a living room and kitchen. The candidate basically makes an introduction and takes a few questions. The people attending, if the candidate makes an impression, might become precinct captains on caucus night. Or maybe they agree to show up at party headquarters to make phone calls and take a list of addresses and knock on doors for the candidate before caucus night. The attendees do one more thing, write checks. The hosts make "the ask," not the candidate.

As Beatrice rumbled onto the street in Marshalltown later in the same day the crisis ended in Tama, there were police cars, bumper-to-bumper vehicles parked on the street and maybe two dozen people outside the front of the house. Two TV station live trucks blocked the street. There was nowhere to park Beatrice.

"Wow. Did anyone expect this?" Ryan asked. "Are these people here for a pancake breakfast or a fish fry? I don't smell fried food."

The senator stopped a few minutes in the street to talk with reporters. He was asked if he thought his support would be higher in polls.

"Polling is meaningless at this point. We're nearly nine months away from caucus night and another ten months after that to election night. I'm trying to introduce myself to people and talk about what I believe in at this point," the senator said.

"What *do* you believe in?" a reporter asked.

A hanging curve ball for the senator.

"You saw it today in Tama. I believe in families, fairness, future. They are all related. If you think about those three things, and everything that can fit in one of those categories, what we're talking about begins to coordinate and overlap. We'll focus on those three."

There was applause as the senator entered the house. It was jammed and so was the backyard where the food and drink were. There were kids with their parents and grandparents. These were the party faithful … the activists … the caucus night regulars … and they were energized.

Buckman talked for 20 minutes about the events of the past few days.

"Here is what I want you to know about myself," he began after meeting everyone. "I am going to be on the side of the men and women who work hard for a living making products Americans want and need. Look at those folks at MegaPack who felt so strongly that they took over their workplace because they thought they had a job worth fighting for. It is a rugged, physical line of work but they are willing to do it every day because Americans need fresh meat. These are productive employees. We were able to stay united and reach a compromise. There will be penalties for the workers who occupied the plant but we have been promised they will not be deported unless they have committed a crime.

"They weren't only thinking about themselves. They were thinking of their families and their children and grandchildren. They were thinking about their futures. Taking over a plant is not going to be the solution to comprehensive immigration reform. It won't work and it's bad for business. What will work is finding common ground as we were able to do today to diffuse the situation in Tama. I am confident that we can find a solution so productive people who are making contributions to the economy can remain in the country with some sort of expedited work visa. I don't believe in wide-open borders. In my administration, secure borders will be part of the solution. And if you come to this country and break our laws, you will be sent home permanently.

"But we are going to also be compassionate. If you are here working, making a better life for yourself and family, contributing to society, buying goods and services, purchasing homes and cars and supporting schools, you are going to be welcomed. We can find a solution by showing some flexibility."

The schedule said he would stay 30 minutes. He stayed twice as long, guaranteeing he would be late once again for the last stop of the day, another house party in Des Moines. Every person at the Marshalltown event wanted to shake the senator's hand or get a photo with the smiling man in the baseball cap.

CHAPTER 17

Davenport Rally

Kenny Kroeger, the marketing guy for the health system in Davenport, called a special huddle of his corporate communications staff. On an erasable white board in their meeting room, they came up with a list of tasks.

"We need help. Top of the list is call the county Democratic Party and call Richard at the RiverFront. First things first. Secure the venue and start generating interest. Hand this off to the regular cast of characters in the Democratic Party here.

"The campaign already has the events on their website so they will handle media, but I want media on the senator's tour of the hospital. That's what is in this for us, along with having the ear of the campaign for a few minutes to talk about issues important to the health system.

"We have the best event planner in the business right in this room. Do your thing. Set up the events … RiverFront town hall meeting, a meet and greet before that event, and the bike ride. I'm thinking the ride can start at LeClaire Park and head to Bettendorf, not across the bridges to Illinois."

Kroeger continued with a steady stream of ideas about how his staff could help make this visit by a senator who was relatively unknown nationally until two days ago, a success. The staff was accustomed to the staccato ideas of a demanding boss.

"Who is that kid from Bettendorf who played on the national championship team?" asked Kroeger, who knew little about Wil Wagner. "Anyone know the family? See if he might happen to be home. It's a Monday, he might stay home for this. Maybe he'd get on a bike for the ride."

"Can I ask why we are doing so much for this particular candidate? Aren't we kind of out of our scope here?" asked the health system's internal communications specialist, who happened to be a Rushton supporter.

"We won't support or oppose any candidate as an organization, but there is benefit to our organization if we can be part of a presidential candidate's visit. I promise that if Rushton wanted to visit Davenport, which he likely will before the election, we'll try to worm our way into that event, too. We're the largest employer in Scott County; we should have a role."

Ryan Holton was the driver of Beatrice, the beat-up campaign bus. O'Malley was trying to find him to ask him to start working on the stop coming up in Davenport. He was having a difficult time tracking his protégé down

Holton finally showed up at the Des Moines extended stay headquarters at 9 a.m. the morning after the Marshalltown house party.

"It's probably none of my business where you have been or what you've been doing but I'm perplexed about what kind of impression you could possibly be making driving Beatrice around the streets of Des Moines. Not exactly a chick magnet is it?" O'Malley said. "That being said ... answer your damn phone!"

O'Malley filled Ryan in on the upcoming trip to Davenport and what they needed.

"Find a bike shop and get us three or four bikes and helmets and how about polo shirts that just say Buckman for President? We have a logo. Get it from The Warehouse for the shirts. Same with caps. The senator wears them pretty much all the time. Kind of his thing now. The media is mentioning the caps and all the different ones he seems to have. Order about 100 Biking with Buckman hats and we'll give them to everyone who goes on the first biking event in Davenport. But only at the end of the ride. No one is riding without a helmet, including the senator.

"One more thing. Lease us an SUV for campaign trips and those times when Beatrice breaks down. Can you get all that done today? I'll give you a credit card. Let's get it done."

Holton and O'Malley, who both nearly blew their futures with the campaign on that night with the expensive wine in Las Vegas, were becoming close. The kid was O'Malley's most dependable drinking buddy. The candidate wasn't a very good companion when someone needed a snootful. The kid could keep up with O'Malley for a while, although his disappearances were becoming more frequent.

"You aren't driving Beatrice when you are drinking, I hope," O'Malley said. "That's all we would need is for a campaign staffer to get busted for DUI on the campaign bus. I am in charge of the stupidity department."

The team made a quick trip to the Twin Cities before heading to Davenport. The Warehouse wasn't at quite the level of disarray O'Malley anticipated. It was clear more staff and a management level was needed. The donations were still coming in primarily small amounts, but there had been calls from representatives of big donors wondering if they could meet or talk with the candidate or his top staff.

"I understand that I need to raise lots of money but you've heard me. I am not going to say everything they want to hear," the senator said to Carl in an extended interview on the trip from Des Moines to the Twin Cities. "I won't compromise my values just to be elected, but you set up meetings and I'll talk with these mega-money people. They may not like the fact that I want to make them pay their fair share of taxes, but I'll meet with them."

Carl and O'Malley worked with the senator on several additional policy statements for the Buckman for President website. They ignored very predictable and often contentious and vile social media exchanges between the senator's supporters and some individuals who certainly weren't supportive.

"They are calling Pierce Professor Marigold and Professor Sunflower," reported the expanding Kim. "There have been suggestions that Pierce isn't the father of our baby. Someone suggested the baby was somehow the offspring of Karl Marx. Che Guevera was another suggestion. Those made us laugh."

"And Bob Marley," one of the online interns said. "I had to

look up who Bob Marley was. Pretty funny."

"We think the incoming messages are coming from Rushton's campaign staff and supporters," Kim added.

"Now that wouldn't surprise me. Can we reciprocate in some way?" the senator asked. "Not too personal. More policy than personal."

"Not too personal? Anyone ever tell you don't have the toughness for this political thing," O'Malley asked.

"Pretty much every day," the senator responded.

The campaign's online operation was a concern to O'Malley. These were mostly volunteer kids. He decided they needed the leadership of a full-time supervisor who had worked on campaigns. He also decided to hire a vendor for online fundraising. It would still appear that the campaign was a low-budget operation, which it was, but the vendor would be able to take and process contributions better and faster than they could in The Warehouse.

O'Malley stayed in the Twin Cities as Beatrice rolled to Davenport on Sunday morning. A new volunteer, a recently graduated American Indian from Minnesota, was at the wheel of the black, full-sized SUV leaving from Des Moines. The candidate preferred Beatrice. He had made that clear to his staff.

"Keep her going. Have you read the messages on her?" the senator asked Ryan Holton, who was behind the wheel of the bus.

Carl and Susan Lyon, and Kim joined the senator on Beatrice. Ryan was at the wheel. Four young volunteers Ryan had rounded up in Des Moines were already in Davenport planning the events the next day.

CHAPTER 18

"The Recycler"

William "Willie" Canton was familiar to people who lived and worked in downtown Davenport. He was nicknamed by some as "The Recycler." He got the nickname because of his obsession with free publications. He could frequently be seen removing the numerous copies of free publications from racks in office buildings, hotels and restaurants. He would grab every copy and put them in a plastic bag. He would mutter and swear for no apparent reason as he left each stop. No one knew what he did with the copies.

Those familiar with The Recycler speculated that he was homeless and needed the paper either as toilet paper or to pile up around himself to fight off the cold. The joke was he recycled the papers.

The senator entered a downtown Davenport hotel, Placid, on Sunday night before the tour of the hospital, town hall and the first-ever Bike with Buckman event. They were surprised that about 100 possible supporters and two Davenport police officers were waiting for them.

In the group was Willie Canton. He had months of growth of black and grey facial hair and had gone at least that long without a haircut. His long, scraggly hair also had patches and speckles of grey and white. He was wearing a sweatshirt, heavily worn jeans and boots with holes on the toes of each boot.

"Cunt! I told that bitch not to eat all the food. Gets a restraining against me. There sure are a lot of assholes in this world. Bitch! She thinks she is just going to leave me out here.

Son-of-a-bitch. Whore. Screwing around with everyone behind my back.

"They keep leaving these magazines all over the place."

Willie was oblivious to what was going around him. He didn't know anything about a U.S. Senator and presidential candidate standing only several feet away from him. He wasn't even looking at Buckman. As always, Willie was in his own hazy world. He continued to rant.

"I should kill...."

That was it. Willie didn't finish the sentence. Ryan Holton stepped between Willie and the senator, who were separated by only a couple of feet, and he was ready to take the unarmed Willie down. The Davenport officers quickly grabbed Willie, whom they knew, and restrained him.

Willie was still yelling about some affront that may or may not have actually happened to him. He was always mumbling about something.

Virtually everything that happens during a presidential campaign is available on video. This situation was tense enough visually that even though Willie was harmless, Ryan wasn't certain. The video of an obviously disturbed person possibly threatening a presidential candidate was enough to make every local newscast.

Several people waiting for the senator shouted "stop him!" or they screamed.

A young man in a long coat and stocking hat was looking on. He didn't flinch during the brief chaos.

Local television reporters were still recording when the senator forcefully said, "Ryan, no! It's OK," as the campaign aide got his hands on Willie's torso, apparently preparing to throw him to the floor of a hotel lobby.

One of the local stations sent a live truck out when their reporter quickly called in about the incident.

Within an hour the video was breaking news on various national media and social media sites. Other people waiting in the lobby for Buckman also had their phone cameras recording. The video was being watched nationwide on social media platforms.

Willie was still muttering as he was escorted in handcuffs out of Placid by the two officers. Three more police cars arrived with sirens on. Willie was placed in one of the cars. The other officers gathered at the door and inside the lobby.

"Ryan, thanks for stepping in. I think he probably has a mental health condition," the senator explained. "I don't believe he intends to harm me or anyone else."

Reporters on the scene asked the senator to comment once the incident was over.

"Do you want the short answer or the long answer to the crisis we all must face eventually?" he asked "Short answer is, I wasn't too concerned. This person didn't have an obvious weapon. Every city in the country has people like this gentleman who are struggling day-by-day with mental health conditions.

"But the longer answer is much more complex. That question is, 'What can we do as a nation about mental health?' Mental health still carries baggage which I believe makes it easier for all of us, me included, to turn away from the issue. There is still a stigma when we admit we struggle with mental health. There is much more we could and should be doing that isn't being done now, at least not everywhere. We can start as a nation by considering mental health conditions to be an illness, just as cancer or heart disease are considered illnesses."

A reporter asked, "You have been part of two incidents requiring intervention of security or police this week … MegaPack when you met with families … and today. Is your campaign at a point it requires security on a permanent basis?"

"Well, it sure looked to me that our driver and campaign aide, Ryan Holton, was ready to step in to my defense. And I remember from wrestling to shoot a double-leg takedown. Seriously, this is a campaign of inclusion.

"We have a vision of an administration that will every day believe it can do more to benefit all people. That includes the mentally impaired. We're going to do what we can for our former military who have served us admirably and courageously and now have elevated rates of PTSD, depression, addictions and other mental health issues. We will consider all health and health care to be a right for everyone. Not only for those fortunate to have health insurance through an employer or privately because they have the resources to pay for the treatment.

"This campaign is open to the public and the media. I will take comments, suggestions and yes, critiques, from anyone who believes their voice is not being heard. Silence and fear are not democracy."

Another reporter asked, "Did you ask the police not to charge this man?"

"At my suggestion, one of my staff people did. What purpose would jail have served for this man? He doesn't belong in jail. He belongs in a community-based behavioral health program. We need more of those programs across the country.

"Got to go. Thank you all for coming out. Despite the brief, harmless drama, this was a pleasant surprise for us."

The senator grabbed Kim's hand, which he noticed was still shaking.

The incident with Willie and the media interview was the top story on the local network affiliates, which had also made sure their networks had the video.

The senator and Kim spent the evening relaxing after he met with local Democrats in a hotel suite. The senator also met with a group of business leaders from the region.

Hundreds of people of all ages were already waiting outside the RiverFront 90 minutes before the town hall meeting in the morning when the senator and Kim left Placid to take a tour of PrimeCare Health System's Davenport hospital.

Kenny Kroeger, the chief marketing officer of PrimeCare, and its CEO, Jordan Douglas, conducted the hospital tour. They took the senator, his wife, and the media following them to the Emergency Department and to a new behavioral health unit. Kim asked to see the birth center and the sick and premature babies being cared for in PrimeCare's highly regarded neonatal intensive care unit.

"I can't imagine what it's like for parents who have a child in the NICU," Kim said as they met staff and parents of babies in the unit. Kim looked into a couple of rooms with names like Lullaby Lane and Teddy Bear Place to glance from a distance at the tiny humans struggling to survive.

As the senator and Kim walked through an atrium, staff watched from above. The senator waved and answered shouted questions. Some of the staff rushed down steps to get their photo taken with the senator.

"Get everyone in here," the senator said to one group of staff from the orthopedic unit.

He also stopped to greet the hospital's customer service representatives.

"Now if I come back here later, treat me well," the senator said. "Come sign Beatrice the Bus."

Hospital staffers were unlikely to know of the senator's past heart issue. He was at the stage of recovery now that he made dark jokes about his medical history.

Scott County's Democratic Party and Kroeger, the PrimeCare marketing guy, had done their job of turning people out. Hundreds of them. It took a while to get everyone registered on mobile devices by the heroic Ryan Holton, Susan Lyon and local volunteers. The database of names, addresses, cellphone numbers and email addresses would be readily accessible to the staff back in The Warehouse. Before the Iowa Caucuses, some of them would be contacted several times.

They were late, as always, when Beatrice was pulled into an alley behind RiverFront Theatre.

"Someone needs to say, 'Kenny was right again.' I told you we would turn people out," Kroeger said.

"How many?" asked Carl Lyon, who had joined the hospital tour.

"More than 1,000. The lower level is full," the beaming Kroeger reported.

"Good job. We're going on a bike ride after this, right?" Carl asked.

"Only a couple blocks away," Kroeger said.

The staging of the event was basic. One U.S flag and one Iowa flag behind the podium, which the senator was unlikely to use. He usually wandered the stage as he spoke. There was no teleprompter and no one else on stage.

Democratic Congressman Marion Jackson, former Iowa

City mayor and now the only Iowa Democrat holding a house seat, was warming up the crowd for Senator Buckman. The two were close friends and on the same pages politically. Both were considered progressives and radicals by the other party. Jackson was prominent in Iowa and Washington as the first-ever minority to be elected congressman from Iowa.

"Senator Pierce Buckman is a voice for all Americans," Jackson said, his voice rising with emotion. "Pierce Buckman will get big things done to help people.

"I am pleased today to announce my support of Pierce Buckman for president. Now it is my pleasure to introduce you all to my friend, the next president of the United States, Pierce Morrison Buckman of our great neighbor to the north, Minnesota."

Buckman kissed Kim, took off his Crossroads State University National Championship cap and handed it to Kroeger, fist-bumped him and walked quickly onto the stage. He was wearing one of his standard campaign stop outfits of jeans, a shirt with no tie, a corduroy jacket and although no one could likely tell, no socks under his sneakers. His bald, shaved head was shiny in the lights of RiverFront Theatre. He wasn't wearing his black, horn-rimmed glasses, although he routinely did. He didn't care what political consultants relentlessly suggested, that the glasses made him appear older than his years. He did what he wanted.

"Thank you very much. Thank you so much. Thank you. Thank you for coming out on a Monday morning."

The environmental advocates, single-payer health advocates, social service agency staff, mental health advocates, progressives ... true believers ... were conspicuously placed in the first three rows. They were on their feet cheering.

In the crowd in front was a young man in a fedora and thick glasses. He was wearing a "pile of poo" emoji T-shirt.

After 30 seconds or so, Buckman raised his hand to quiet the crowd.

"I want to thank my friend Congressman Jackson for his great introduction and for his support. We hadn't talked about that. What a great surprise. I have great respect for your congressman in this district and I hope there are many more occasions like this.

"I want to start by saying a few things about our vision and our campaign. We've heard it called the people's campaign. I kind of like that.

"I believe Washington very often lacks vision so we forget why we are there. It's because of people that we are there. The problem is that we don't do big things that benefit Americans, like Social Security, Medicare, Medicaid, interstate highways, saving the auto industry, progress toward universal health care, which I would sign the minute it was placed on my desk if I am elected president. But we are so politically polarized that our politics prevent us from doing important work.

"We started this campaign with a pledge to talk about the issues impacting all of us. We will talk about quality, compassionate healthcare that is affordable for everyone. You know what? Those words are the mission statement of our new friends at PrimeCare Health System. I like that. I'm borrowing their mission today whenever I talk about health care in this campaign. We just visited your hospital this morning and were awed by the work the caregivers do every day of the year.

"They don't make judgments based on race, or gender, or where someone was born. They just provide quality, compassionate healthcare to every single person who needs it. Every single one. They don't ask anyone about their legal status or citizenship. We can have that kind of an America … bringing us together instead of separating us.

"Now, I'm going to ask you to do something. If you share our vision of big ideas, big projects and making them possible, I'm going to ask for your support in the Iowa Caucuses in February. It seems like a long time from now but it really isn't, and it's important.

"We have a president who divides much better than he brings together. He worries more about his party faithful than he worries about the daily struggles of any one of you. He wants to exclude, we want to include. He listens to his advisors based on ideology. We will listen to everyday Americans. We'll listen to every one of you."

He was on a roll emotionally and had the crowd's attention.

Then, he got much quieter. Carl was starting to call it "the knockout punch."

"Some of you feel as if you have no voice and maybe even no future. You worry about paying for healthcare. You wonder if you'll ever be able to retire. You worry about the future and safety and security of your children and grandchildren.

"I have to tell you … I'm not sure this president cares about your concerns.

"We care," he said, gesturing with his hand and now at full volume. "You all can be part of the revolution that changes the path of this country. We can provide quality, compassionate healthcare to everyone. We can provide educations that help everyone prepare for a career with all the skills they need. We can provide that education tuition-free if you are willing to serve in some capacity. We can rebuild roads, bridges, airports. We can have equitable taxation.

"We can reform our criminal system and stop wasting money incarcerating people who can be reformed. I support decriminalization of marijuana so no one spends even a single night in jail only for recreational use of marijuana. But unless we fix our education system we will never be able to build enough jail cells to put everyone away. It starts there. Education leads to opportunities to make a living and live a different life than one of despair, desperation and detachment from society.

"We can limit access to guns designed to kill people with common sense change. The semi-automatic weapons often used in the mass shootings in this country and others are human-killing machines. They are not needed for hunting, target shooting or home defense.

"We must do the big things. We must share the vision that we can accomplish the big things if we direct our efforts toward people and away from politics."

He was winding up and he still had the attention of the crowd.

"Come with us on this journey. If you believe that you can make a difference in people's lives, join us. We can create the America we want, an America for everyone, if we believe we all can make a difference. Come with us."

The senator waved as he walked down the steps from the stage to meet people. Considering the incident at the hotel the night before, security was now on edge. There was a line and stanchions separating the senator from the people in the theater and the media representatives. He stopped every few feet to have photos taken, shake hands, listen to a story, and take media questions.

"Can you explain more about what you would do with decriminalization of marijuana?" a local television reporter asked, sensing the liberal senator's views might be the story of the day on the campaign trail.

"Not only decriminalize it, but open it for medical use. There is plenty of anecdotal evidence that the use of cannabis products is beneficial for some conditions, including post-traumatic stress disorder and some behavioral health issues. Let's see scientifically if that is true. We need to allow credible, science-based research into appropriate uses. As president, I would support turning marijuana into a cash crop. And we would tax the purchase appropriately the way we now tax tobacco and alcohol. The tax revenue would help us support healthcare for everyone and mental health programs.

"States are already doing on their own what I'm suggesting. Ten states now allow recreational use of marijuana and the number is increasing, not decreasing. Members of Congress can legally possess and use marijuana in Washington, D.C., and I happen to know fine representatives who do smoke marijuana legally when they are in Washington."

"How about the senator from Minnesota?" the reporter pressed.

"I won't share," the senator said cryptically, grinning.

Anyone around him knew he didn't smoke anything. Kim and Susan Lyon would freak if he did, not because of the legality, but because of his cardiac condition.

The walk to the first-ever Bike with Buckman event was only two blocks. A block away, Carl could see the banner for the start. As they walked, he counted the bikes going past. He quit at two dozen. Waiting for them were maybe 100 people on bikes.

One of the people getting ready to ride stood out.

"Looks like a Great Blue Heron riding a bike," Carl told the senator as they got closer and he recognized an unmistakable figure.

Wilhelm Wagner, The Kaiser, was surrounded by reporters who didn't have any problem recognizing him. The biking helmet he was wearing only covered a small section of the tied-back mane now even longer than when he led the Crossroads State Explorers to the national basketball championship. He and his parents had ridden from their estate to the riverfront to join the ride and support Senator Buckman.

"We were all around Senator Buckman quite a bit during the tournament. He was very supportive of us then and I wanted to be here to support him today. It's also a great day for a ride with my parents," Kaiser said.

"Do you support his positions?" a local newspaper reporter asked.

"Probably not all of them, but our family has lived in Europe and experienced universal healthcare. I'm, of course, in favor of every American having access to good health care," Kaiser said.

"Keep going. If this professional basketball thing doesn't work out for you, we'll hire you," Senator Buckman said as he walked up to the attentive media huddle around Kaiser.

Kaiser uncoiled himself off the bike. It was the least coordinated anyone had ever seen him. He shook hands with the senator and Carl and hugged the senator's wife.

"Introduce me to your parents, Wil," the senator said. "Coach J.J. has told us a lot about them."

Ryan Holton had the cheap, red plastic bull horn from Beatrice the Bus and handed it to the senator to get the ride started.

"We didn't know what to expect today. This is the first time we've done this. We'll probably do a lot of them if we can get this kind of turnout every time," the senator said. "It's a beautiful day for a ride but first I want to tell you that I'd like to create bike friendly and walker friendly areas within every city like this bike path we are riding today.

"I understand we could start here today and ride all the way to our condo in the Twin Cities if we all had the inclination and Wil's athleticism. Maybe another time. Before we take off, have fun, be safe, make sure you are wearing a helmet. We have a few with us and we want you all to have a Biking with Buckman hat. We're going to ride out a few miles and back.

"Along the way you can shout questions at me if you want to ask or we'll hang around after the ride, too."

Two of Davenport's officers on their own police-issued bikes rode out first. The senator thanked everyone as he pulled out at the rear with two more Davenport officers. Davenport's police chief had made it clear to his top officers they would step up security while the senator was in town after the hotel incident the day before. There were also two Scott County Sheriff deputies staying back at the start and finish line to prevent anyone riding out from behind the group.

After the ride the senator talked and took questions from riders for 20 minutes. There was one more unplanned stop in Davenport before Beatrice the Bus headed back to the campaign headquarters in Des Moines. Senator Buckman yelled out from the bedroom of the bus just seconds after they got moving.

"Ryan, we're stopping at the brewery about a block up the street," the senator said as he and Kim stretched out on the bed.

"Cool. You got it."

They ordered flights of local brew and appetizers. The Kaiser and his parents were among the patrons in the downtown Davenport establishment called Catfish Brew.

The senator carried around a 4-ounce brew called Bodacious Blonde and stopped at every table. He finished it, called it "very worthy" and sat down with the Wagner family. He didn't elaborate on the "very worthy" comment, but bought five growlers of Bodacious Blonde for the trip back to Des Moines.

"Seriously Wil, why don't you come on the road with us for two or three months this summer? It would be a great internship for you," Buckman said.

"I would love that but can't. I'm spending the summer in Las Vegas playing in a summer league before I report to camp in late

September. Kind of required," Kaiser explained as he knocked back his own Bodacious Blonde.

Within five minutes of starting toward Des Moines, listening to a Moody Blues recording, the senator and Kim both fell asleep. They slept the rest of the way back to Des Moines.

CHAPTER 19

Senator Hemp

Top political advisors were anxious to show their boss, the President of the United States, Jack Rushton, a video from the campaign rally of Senator Pierce Buckman in Davenport.

The video was from the rope line after his speech on the stage of the RiverFront Theatre. As he walked the line talking with people who attended, they had video of the local television reporter asking the senator to explain further his thoughts on decriminalization of marijuana. The president's advisors had watched the response more than a dozen times trying to determine how they could use the response against Buckman. Not that they were particularly concerned about the senator at the time. There were more serious, credible candidates with much better funding. But the president's staff was happy to find and use whatever they could find against any of them. They were not playing favorites. If anything, their boss might have an easier path to re-election if the radical lefty senator from Minnesota was his party's nominee.

When Buckman was asked if he had taken advantage of relaxed marijuana use laws in Washington, D.C., the senator said, "I won't share" with a grin.

Did he mean he wouldn't talk about his personal use? Or, was he saying, "I smoke but I don't share when I do." Or, most likely, it was a weak attempt at humor.

Whatever the intent, it didn't matter to the president's advisors. They would find a way to use the comment against the senator.

"How do you want us to use this?" asked Brock Baffleman, chief political advisor to the president. "As far as we know, he is saying 'Yes, I smoke marijuana and I don't share when I do.'"

Rushton took a deep pull out of a tumbler of Dark Hills and ice. It was his second tumbler of the day, and the day was young. He offered his advisors their own tumblers with the presidential seal embossed on the glasses. They all declined for the time being.

Rushton liked playing the game with his staff referring to Senator Buckman using floral references. Today it was Professor Begonia.

"Begonia is going to regret he ever stumbled down this path," Rushton said, slightly slurring the words. "What can we do with this and how quickly can we do it?"

"We can get it up on social media in a couple hours but let's think about this," Baffleman said. "Instead of referring to Buckman as a flower, how about Senator Weed this time? Or Senator Reefer? Senator Joint? Senator Blunt could work nicely. We'd have to explain that to our base, though. It's kind of street slang still, isn't it?"

Rushton was apparently in deep thought or an approaching deep stupor. He kind of grunted, paused, and said "Senator Hemp."

"I like that." Baffleman said. "We can work with that. We need a graphic with a cloud of smoke around the senator and maybe a bunch of people behind him smoking joints. There needs to be a couple dangerous looking minority guys behind him, maybe looking like they are making a drug deal. A couple people with sunglasses smoking and Senator Hemp big in front of them."

"Put a cap on him with a green marijuana leaf on it," the president said. "Have the social media folks work up several options for us to get this out there in the morning. And we need to use that line, 'when I smoke, I don't share.' It's not exactly a direct quote but close enough."

Rushton was feeling brilliant but was fading with each swig from the tumbler. He leaned back. His feet were on the coffee table in front of the couch where he was spreading out.

Rushton rallied with "how about another graphic with a big smile on Senator Hemp's face surrounded by smoke that indicates he supports relaxed marijuana laws across the country?"

The president's political advisors continued to hash out, so to speak, the details and brought in one of the lead people on the social media staff for another short brainstorming session. They had access to 27 million followers on Facebook and 22 million on Twitter. Rushton didn't know much about the details of either medium, although he could post messages and did post regularly himself.

Advisors were used to seeing the president nod off noisily with gasping breaths. They paid no attention to the sight after seeing it so frequently and finally went back to their offices, leaving him on the couch of the study adjacent to the Oval Office. If only those millions of social media supporters could see him now, drunk, asleep and snoring loudly.

Early the next morning, the Senator Hemp campaign was launched. Within minutes, the crew in The Warehouse in downtown Minneapolis had noticed.

"Oh, geez, I don't think this is good," one of the college kids in The Warehouse reported. "Do we need to call Gerald to prepare the Senator for this? It will probably be the b.s. story of the day on the campaign trail."

Gerald O'Malley wasn't 100 percent sober himself in his Twin Cities apartment when the cellphone woke him up.

"Senator Hemp or Professor Hemp?" asked O'Malley, who wasn't shocked or angry with what he was hearing. "This is kind of childish, but you know what, I think we can use this favorably. The fact is, Senator Buckman favors decriminalization of marijuana laws. So do a lot of states and more are moving in this direction.

"I want you to get us research on the medical benefits of marijuana, the cost of prosecuting marijuana laws and the financial benefits of allowing marijuana as a cash crop and heavily taxing its use the way we do tobacco. He has been talking about this. Let's own it and turn this to our benefit. We have a different candidate. He will have a different message than voters are accustomed to hearing or considering. He is comfortable with this, and we need to help craft messages based on fact and polling. This can benefit him."

O'Malley's only concern was that the senator's support of decriminalization of marijuana would now dominate the campaign temporarily and undermine other messages. He thought Buckman would handle it well, quickly and move forward.

"Is this Senator Hemp?" O'Malley joked when he reached Buckman's phone.

"No, this is Mrs. Hemp. The senator is in the shower. There is smoke pouring out of the bathroom. Well, maybe steam. He just got off the treadmill. Next, he will have his morning joint. He knows," Kim said when she picked up the phone.

"Tell him we'll get him talking points quickly this morning. By not prosecuting and enforcing marijuana laws, billions of dollars could be redirected to much more useful purposes. We could empty some jail and prison cells all over the country. He knows all this but we'll help him out before he goes to the events he has on his schedule today."

Rushton's social media staff had been very thorough getting the message out to the millions of their base. It was a blanket blitz of social media, traditional media and the websites and news sites leaning right. The morning news shows were offered interviews with law-and-order types.

Canyon Rivers, Chief of the Texas Rangers -- the law enforcement agency, not the baseball team -- was a panelist and source offered to the morning shows to talk about the scourge of marijuana in his home state and across the country. Chief Rivers just happened to be a good friend of the former Governor of Texas, who was watching the shows from his bedroom in the White House, trying to recover from those three tumblers of bourbon the night before.

Rivers hit all the right messages to appeal to the right people; the people on the right.

"Marijuana is not a harmless recreational drug. It is a serious problem across the country, and especially in the home state of our president," said Chief Rivers, who was a career law

165

enforcement administrator with a law degree. "Marijuana is a factor in thousands of crimes in our state every year. Multiply that by 50 states and you begin to understand the scope of the problem.

"The opioid crisis can be directly traced to the use of marijuana as a gateway drug. Talk with opioid users and they will tell you about their use of marijuana. It isn't coincidence that as more states decriminalize marijuana, the opioid crisis becomes more serious.

"Senator Buckman is on the wrong side of this issue and many other issues, as far as I am concerned.

"In Texas, we still believe marijuana is a dangerous drug and we enforce our laws."

The hosts of the shows tried to get Rivers to refer to the senator as Senator Hemp. Rivers was thinking about his own possible political future in Austin or Washington. He didn't oblige, which was only slightly frustrating to the president's staff.

"That is President Rushton's reference to someone he disagrees with when it comes to decriminalization of marijuana. I believe those who support decriminalization as the senator does are misguided, misinformed and just flat wrong on this issue."

Rushton's staff had still accomplished the goal. The social media staffers had reached out to their supporters in an instantaneous message from Rivers that those supporters would pick up and run with. They had targeted a potential rival, although it seemed unlikely to them Senator Buckman's progressive message would ever find enough support to even get his candidacy out of Iowa. But maybe this would be his knockout punch.

Media calls to Carl Lyon and Gerald O'Malley asked when the senator would be available for comment. The best opportunity, they were told, was a noon meeting in Ankeny, a north suburb of Des Moines.

Club members in Ankeny may not have known who the speaker was that day until arriving at a local hotel conference center. Local and national television trucks were in the parking lot. Reporters were setting up in the conference center as the 40 or 50 regulars entered the room gazing around at the commotion. The National News Network, 3N, had its team waiting, as did Rushton's favorite network, Traditions and Values Network. TVN was the operation Carl Lyon referred to as "unfair, unbalanced and unhinged." Traditions was on 24 hours a day throughout the White House. It was one of the outlets offered an interview with Texas Rangers Chief Canyon Rivers, who obliged with what Rushton's supporters would want to hear.

There were bloggers from internet political sites, reporters from major newspapers and television reporters from stations throughout Iowa.

Senator Buckman, Kim, Carl, Ryan Holton and Curt Jaslow, who had just been transferred from the senator's Washington staff to the campaign road staff as media spokesman, showed up a few minutes after they started serving the lunch of chicken breasts with gravy to the service club members. Jaslow was becoming the public face of the campaign and supervised the set-up of events.

Jaslow had not done much set-up for this event. The senator had insisted on only an American flag and an Iowa flag flanking him. He also wanted the introduction to be understated.

"Joining us today is Senator Pierce Buckman of Minnesota. He was born in University City. He is a candidate for president of the United States, and we're glad he is joining us today," said Manly Forest, the member in charge of the day's program.

Buckman kissed Kim, which he was now doing before every speaking engagement, and got up in front of the audience of 100, about half representing the media, which was now sensing blood in the water. He didn't waste any time getting to what the media had gathered to hear.

"Good afternoon. Glad to be here with you today. And thanks, Manly, for the introduction, but you kind of botched it," the senator said, smiling at the surprised host. "Yes, botched the introduction. In some quarters, I am now apparently referred to as Senator Hemp or Professor Hemp."

The club members probably already wondered about a

presidential candidate in front of them wearing jeans, a Buckman for President polo, a Buckman for President baseball cap and no socks with his loafers. Now he was talking about marijuana use.

"You may have heard this ... gosh, it has been all over, how could you not? ... but I will reiterate today my support of decriminalization of marijuana for several reasons, and if the president wants to come out of the White House and talk about this on the same stage in a debate, I'm available. I'm ready anytime, anywhere and we'll talk about this subject or any other."

Buckman continued, talking about universal healthcare, his plan for family-centric schools without barriers, gun reform, college tuition in exchange for service, immigration reform, and a massive infrastructure rebuild. Then he got back to the reform of marijuana laws.

"If the president wants to talk about the states already decriminalizing marijuana, I'm ready. If he wants to talk about his state, Texas, which has some of the most punitive laws in the country regarding marijuana, here I am. He should frankly be embarrassed by the Texas record of arrests, the minority disparities in who is treated most harshly for marijuana possession and the exorbitant cost to Texas taxpayers. We can talk about the thousands of marijuana arrests in Texas. If he wants to talk about healthcare, great, here I am. If he wants to talk about equitable taxation, we're ready."

With those words alone, the issue of marijuana regulations, and several others, had been thrown back at the president. Buckman was just getting started.

"I'll be happy to tell you why I support decriminalization of marijuana. First, the cost of enforcement of the patchwork of laws across the country is billions of dollars. That is with a capital B. Does that make sense? I don't believe it does. Polling indicates that most Americans agree with me. Imagine what positive programs we could have benefiting people with a redirect of those funds. We are perpetuating the jail and prison industry. Did you know there are companies whose business it is to build more jail cells and provide temporary lockups?

Business is good, too, because of Jack Rushton and others who believe the appropriate way to deal with small-time drug offenders and undocumented immigrants is to lock them up at great cost.

"We spend a lot of time, energy, manpower chasing people around and locking them up for minor offenses. We separate families, children from parents. If I am elected, we will redirect those resources to positive programs truly helping people.

"I have a vision sharply different than Jack Rushton's. I would be happy to explain to him our great philosophical differences face-to-face if he would like to come out here to Iowa. This is where he will find us and where he will find people who want to make a positive difference in the lives of all Americans, those with different names, those who were born in different countries, those with broken spirits and understandable skepticism, those who have been underserved and those who have been forgotten.

"Come out to Iowa, Mr. President, and we'll talk. I am Senator Pierce Buckman of Minnesota. I am the one with a vision and a plan."

Many in the crowd were cheering and on their feet, even the members, contradicting the unofficial non-partisan nature of the service organization.

Before leaving the stage, the senator asked everyone to sign Beatrice and to provide contact information. Most of the club members did sign the bus and thanked the senator for showing up for the meeting. Buckman shook hands and had photos taken. He took a few more questions from the media.

Lake Northwood, the reporter from Traditions and Values Network, asked the question the senator was expecting.

"Have you smoked marijuana before?"

"Of course. I haven't smoked in about 30 years. I would hope you would ask the president the same question. I was making a joke that didn't work."

"How about cocaine? Have you used cocaine?" Northwood continued.

"No. How many drugs, legal or illegal, do you plan to ask about?" Buckman shot back. "Provide me with a list and I'll go through my medical records and figure it all out. But … now understand … that is another example how I differ from the president. You can go to the Buckman for President website and find out plenty about my health history. There is information about my heart attack. It's right there with bio information. The president didn't share information about a hang nail or hemorrhoids, let alone any semblance of a real health history traditionally made public by candidates, especially by presidents."

When he was running for president, Rushton had provided only a one-page statement of highly questionable validity about his health history. Nowhere in the statement was any mention that Rushton, even then, drank a lot and nearly three full years into his term, drank more than ever.

"That's it, no more questions," Curt Jaslow interrupted, sensing the exchange was headed in an unfavorable direction.

"Senator, rethinking that open campaign with the media?" Carl asked when they had fired up Beatrice.

"No, but I will only play along up to a point with biased reporters. That reporter was biased and had an agenda," the Senator said.

"Senator, now you understand why I believe objectivity is a myth in the media. Reporters may spout some sanctimonious crap about being objective but this old reporter ain't buying it. Everyone has an opinion on virtually everything these days," Carl said. "Most reporters don't even bother to hide their biases any longer. They take sides like anyone else, although in general the media still leans to the liberal side of the scale.

"This guy didn't care that you could see his bias. This guy will take sides on any number of issues and on every one … I virtually guarantee it … it will be a side opposite of yourself, or any Democrat for that matter.

"I will remember this guy and we already know the unfairness of the network he represents. Unfair, Unbalanced. Unhinged. TVN destroys the concept of objective journalism. What a joke!"

The senator didn't take the discussion further.

CHAPTER 20
Moral Dilemma

The service club luncheon put the senator in the local spotlight again. His "Come to Iowa Mr. President" challenge to Rushton was airing every few minutes on the 24-hour news stations as panels of so-called experts desperately sought deeper meaning to what Buckman had said.

TVN focused its coverage on questions asked by their reporter in Iowa, Lake Northwood, and the response from the senator. There was outrage from the more conservative on-air hosts about the senator's "cavalier attitude toward the national epidemic of opioid abuse."

"He wasn't even asked about opioid use," Lyon fumed as he watched TVN with Susan on the television in their room in Des Moines. "Marijuana is a little different than oxy or heroin."

"How about a beer, big boy?" Susan said, changing the subject.

About the time Carl and Susan headed for the bar in the extended stay hotel, a room full of college kids was paid $10.50 an hour each to ask a scripted set of questions to Iowans. The Hawkeye Poll was focusing this evening on likely voters in the Democratic Caucus in Iowa. They were asked qualifying questions about age, party affiliation and where they lived.

They were asked about how likely they were to participate in the Iowa Caucuses still months away. The choices were very likely, likely, possible, not likely, will not participate.

Participants were asked about their preference at that time if they responded they were very likely, likely and possibly would participate in the Iowa Caucuses. Participants responding "not likely" or "will not participate" were allowed to escape the early evening intrusion. Republicans were also discarded from this particular poll. Rushton was a lock for the nomination anyway. There would be a Republican caucus in Iowa on Feb. 1, it just wouldn't be competitive.

The college kids were instructed to poll only Democrats or independents.

There were measurements sought in the poll so many months away from the caucuses -- name recognition and preference -- if the poll participants expressed any preference.

"Have you heard of Mike Clarke, governor of New York?"

"Have you heard of Karla Foster, former governor of Virginia?"

"Have you heard of Pierce Buckman, U.S. Senator of Minnesota?"

"Have you heard of George Kaplan, U.S. Senator of Illinois?"

"Have you heard of Lansing Landon, U.S. Senator of Iowa?"

"Have you heard of Stanton Fuller, U.S. Senator of Florida?"

There were more questions about issues … immigration reform, healthcare and taxes.

Landon had not officially announced he was running. He was spending most of his time at home in Des Moines with his wife, Elizabeth, who was fighting end stage breast and ovarian cancers. The cancer had spread to her brain and lungs. After returning to Des Moines from the trip to Davenport, Senator Buckman and Kim, who knew the popular liberal Iowa Democrat and his wife, visited the Landon home. The two senators had been roommates in a small Washington, D.C., apartment when both were freshmen. They all sat together in the living room and talked. Elizabeth Landon, who had stopped chemotherapy and radiation treatments, appeared to the Buckmans to be gravely ill. She was in a wheelchair.

The Lansings shared a secret plan with the Buckmans and explained how important it was to keep their secret.

"God bless you both," Senator Buckman said, tears in his eyes, as they said goodbye. Kim was trying not to cry.

They rode silently back to the hotel in the rented SUV driven this time by Curt Jaslow. No one was quite sure where Ryan Holton was. He had been AWOL quite often recently.

Senator Buckman broke the silence in the SUV.

"That would be so difficult. Promise me I get to go first because I'm not sure I could do what Lansing is doing, and I would be lost without you."

"What did you think about what they told us?" Kim said.

"I'm not surprised. Faced with the same circumstances, is that what you would want? I would."

Three days later, Landon Lansing said he would not be campaigning for president of the United States. He cited undisclosed personal reasons. In a news release, he announced his support of "my good friend and colleague Senator Pierce Buckman of Minnesota."

"Senator Buckman will make a fine president who will represent the interests of all Americans and will not fear change or progress. I look forward to campaigning with Pierce all the way to election day. It isn't my time. It is Pierce Buckman's time. I am proud to offer my support."

Elizabeth and Lansing Landon had agreed that she would make a valiant attempt to survive. But if the condition was irreversible, she asked her husband to provide her with pain relief patches to end her life. Lansing resisted vehemently at first. He worried about their two adult children and what they would think about the plan. Would they feel their mother had quit or let them down? What if the patches only made her sick and she survived?

As his wife continued to slip away, she persisted. She didn't want to extend her life when it was impossible she would survive, and the quality of her life was miserable. The Lansing children accepted their mother's wishes.

A United States senator essentially agreed to help his wife end her life. He was anguished by the thought of assisting in the suicide of the woman he had been with for 27 years. He kept imagining the love of his life growing progressively weaker and then awakening confused and still fighting pain. If she needed medical assistance, he would possibly be charged with a crime.

The alternative was to watch Elizabeth fade.

On the day following his announcement that he would not be a candidate for president, Elizabeth Landon said goodbye. She slipped into a coma without any assistance from her husband. Over several hours her breathing was at first labored, then there were quieter breaths with more time between breaths. The final breaths were shallow, quiet and peaceful. In a few minutes, her breathing stopped. For several hours he had held her hand. Now Lansing Landon hugged his wife and sobbed.

The Buckmans attended the memorial service for Elizabeth Landon, who was cremated. Lansing Landon hugged his Washington colleague at the end of the service. Tears dripped down his cheeks.

"Pierce, I couldn't do it," he whispered into his friend's ear as they hugged. "I couldn't. I think she just willed her own end. She was ready. She was at peace. I said I would always love her. I held her hand. She nodded and drifted away. I didn't do what she wanted. I was too afraid. I was afraid she would just be nauseous. I was afraid she would still hang on. I was afraid she would suffer for hours. We had read it can take time, even with enough of the fentanyl patches. I was terrified someone would find out.

"It's a terrible position to be in when someone you love makes it clear what they want at the end of life and you can't fulfill their wishes. She deserved better from me. She didn't suffer, though."

"You made the right decision. I'm certain," Senator Buckman said, also whispering. "I'm not sure I would have the courage to even consider what you two did. I would have the same concerns when the time came. I'm sure a lot of people with Elizabeth's prognosis find a way to go out on their own terms. Probably thousands every year."

"Something else, Pierce. Until it really got bad, Lizzy was smoking marijuana and she believed it was helping. If she believed it, I believed it. I smoked with her. We bought marijuana cigarettes illegally. Or, I should say our kids did. Iowa doesn't allow use even for all terminally ill patients. We can do something in Washington. We need to at least make it possible to do medical research about the benefits. You know that federal law doesn't even allow most medical research because of how marijuana is classified. The states are doing it on their own. Professor Hemp, we need to do something."

"That is Senator Hemp, although I kind of like Professor Hemp better."

They laughed.

CHAPTER 21

Jericho's Rage

Jericho Adams Brooks was consumed by anger, depression and deepening despair about his bleak life and future. He was angry with his stepfather, his mother, and now, a new thorn in his side, Senator Pierce Buckman. Buckman seemed to Jericho to be gaining momentum with a disturbing anti-Second Amendment campaign message. Jericho considered Buckman to be a frightening candidate who would welcome immigrants from all over the world and make them citizens.

Jericho had followed the campaign of his home-state senator and had attended several events, including the National University Union championship game won by Crossroads State University and the event in Davenport. He had become obsessed with "Bullshit Buckman" and the senator's anti-gun messages. As president, Buckman had said he would restrict access to certain guns and make them even more expensive. He would require registration of all guns and restrict sales from gun shows and person-to-person and internet sales. With a Democratic Congress, which seemed to Jericho to be a possibility, President Buckman might be able to act on his plans just short of totally dismantling the Second Amendment.

Guns were the one link of normalcy in the relationship between Jericho and his stepfather, Michael Munger. Jericho rarely received a shred of approval or emotional support from Michael. But the one experience they shared was a fascination with the guns in the floor-to-ceiling gun cabinet in the cluttered garage. Jericho was allowed to take guns from the case.

In the wild, heavily timbered and remote areas of Northern Minnesota, Michael had introduced Jericho to the weapons that were usually locked away. Jericho felt connected with his stepfather in a positive way on these excursions. Over the years, Michael had acquired shotguns, rifles, hunting knives, traditional bows and crossbows, and weapons better suited for killing humans than animals. He had two AR-style rifles, semi-auto pistols and a sawed-off 12-gauge shotgun. The AR rifles were Jericho's favorites to shoot. He also liked the power and fast action of the pistols, which he thought were similar to the weapons in his favorite video games.

Jericho was allowed to use the weapons and take them out with friends in his stepfather's high mileage 1996 pickup. They loaded the guns into the covered bed of the truck and headed deep into the woods. The day Michael Munger allowed Jericho and his friends to use the truck and take out the guns was the best day Jericho could remember in his life.

They took the guns out lacking any particular purpose except shooting and burning up ammo. They shot everything in sight, including signs, junk cars, abandoned buildings and animals. They would have contests for accuracy shooting cans and bottles. Jericho had discovered a personal skill. He was better at "plinking" targets than his friends. The thousands of hours spent with video games had apparently helped him develop his skills.

"I love all this," Jericho said to his friends.

"You know, that ass wipe senator wants to control or stop everything we love," said Dylan Doyle, one of Jericho's friends, during one of their outings. "He doesn't believe in peoples' gun rights. He would take all of these guns."

"He is a fuck up. He is the dangerous one, not us. I'd like to see him come and get this gun," Jericho said, waving a semi-auto pistol.

He unloaded the pistol to make his point.

"I could do it to protect our Second Amendment freedoms," Jericho said.

"Do what?"

"Him. Do him. Or others like him. Gun owners would like us for doing it," Jericho said.

Dylan wasn't surprised by his friend's threat. He'd heard the whole spiel about the Second Amendment and the threat of society to gun rights in past conversations and rants by Jericho. He'd heard similar rants in the video game trash talking.

"He won't be president," Jericho said of Senator Buckman. "I can't believe the guy is even from Minnesota."

Dylan didn't take the threats of his friend seriously. He passed it off as bluster from a kid who was usually quiet, but came out of his shell around guns and ammunition. He had no idea how fanatical his friend had become about Senator Pierce Buckman.

Two years earlier, as Jericho prepared to graduate with a senior class of 53, his plan was to enlist in the Marine Corps or Army. He rarely told Michael Munger anything that might get him beaten up, but told him of his plan.

"I think that could be good for you," Munger responded.

"I think so, too. I shoot well. I usually dominate our shooting contests."

He walked across the stage to receive his diploma on a Saturday. Under his graduation gown he wore a T-shirt with an emoji with half its head apparently blown away on the front. He woke early on the Monday following graduation. He headed to the recruiting station in Duluth. He had decided on the Marine Corps. He didn't need the standard sales pitch. The recruiter in his dress uniform represented what Jericho thought he wanted. The recruiter carefully explained the process, including the background check and testing starting with the Armed Services Vocational Aptitude Battery and a physical examination. Jericho knew he would score well on the aptitude test. He had tested well enough on standardized college admission tests to be admitted to colleges, despite his lackluster grade point average and lack of participation in high school organizations or clubs.

He didn't care about high school and didn't have any desire to stay in school. He wanted to do what he was good at -- shoot weapons available to him in the military.

When the recruiter explained the physical, he mentioned drug testing. Jericho thought about the prescriptions he took for his chronic anxiety condition and the depression he had frequently experienced. Jericho believed he would be rejected, just as he had been rejected by his stepfather and the other students in the long list of schools he had attended since the eighth grade. Rejection was a feeling he was familiar with.

Finding out he would likely not pass the physical drove Jericho even deeper into himself. He knew he couldn't rely on anyone else for anything positive. He was desperately adrift now that the Marines were not an option. At least he still had the gun cabinet and shooting.

Jericho needed help again. He was sleeping less than four hours most nights. His mother noticed he was getting thinner. He was becoming more agitated than usual. He admitted he was no longer taking his medications, which he blamed for stealing his dream of enlisting. He thought that if he got off the meds, he could go back to the Marine recruiting station and try again.

"I think you are just fucking nuts," said the ever-insensitive Michael Munger, offering his twisted diagnosis.

Jericho's rants about anything he considered to be a threat to his guns from the garage were more frequent.

"No one is trying to take them away," Dylan said during a video gaming session.

"Ass wipe would if he could," Jericho said of Buckman.

"He can't if he isn't elected," Dylan said.

Jericho smiled.

CHAPTER 22

Campaign Love

The campaigns of Mike Clarke and Karla Foster occasionally crisscrossed Iowa at the same time the campaign of Pierce Buckman still spent most of its time around Des Moines with occasional ventures outside, including the eventful trip to Davenport. These were vastly different operations. Clarke and Foster had everything Pierce Buckman did not on the campaign trail. They had prominent nationally known advisors on issues, communications, social media, political strategists and their own polling operations. They flew luxury charter jets with comfortable sleeping cubicles from their homes to Iowa and back. They would arrive in Iowa for a few days, make the rounds of events and meeting people in diners, homes and noon luncheons before going home. They were recruiting caucus operatives in Iowa, the activists vital to winning the quirky caucus event kicking off the presidential campaign. And there was the money. They had most of that, too. They benefited much more than Buckman from the Democratic Party's most generous, traditional donors. They already had extensive direct mail and robocall operations.

But the one area where Clarke and Foster lagged behind the Buckman operation was in media coverage. The series of events experienced by the Buckman campaign had attracted major media attention, including the MegaPack takeover, the coverage of the Crossroads State University national basketball championship, the Willie Canton incident in Davenport, and the outrageous revelation … outrageous to the Traditions Network anyway … a presidential candidate supported decriminalization of marijuana.

Clarke and Foster appeared to have virtually every advantage over Buckman's overmatched operation.

Those advantages tempered the expectations when Susan Lyon monitored national news on the internet and saw the results of the Hawkeye State Poll. She was jogging to the convenience store next door to the Iowa extended-day hotel headquarters. She wanted the print versions. She grabbed two copies of five different newspapers, although each had virtually the same story about the Hawkeye State Poll. She jogged back to the hotel.

She stood over Carl, shaking the newspapers loudly enough to wake him. She had a huge smile.

"This is going to make our day," she said, waving the morning newspapers.

Carl read the graphic first.

"Holy shit. Holy shit," he said loudly. "We're in this."

The top of the story read:

New York Governor Mike Clarke, who was nearly elected as president less than three years ago, is the early leader in polling of Democrats who intend to participate in the Iowa Caucuses next February.

Clarke was the top choice of 18 percent of the 1,400 likely Democratic caucus participants in the polling completed June 8-9 by the Iowa-based poll organization sponsored by the University of Iowa, Drake University and Crossroads State University.

Former Virginia Governor Karla Foster was the second preference, polling at 16 percent. U.S. Senator Pierce Buckman of Minnesota, who announced his candidacy for president in March, is a rising and surprising third and gaining at 15 percent. In the first polling of caucus preference in March, Buckman was at 3 percent.

U.S. Senator Lansing Landon of Iowa, a "favorite son" possible candidate who has announced since polling he would not pursue the office following the recent death of his wife, was at 11 percent. U.S. Senator of Illinois George Kaplan is at 8 percent. Florida Senator Stanton Fuller is at 7 percent. The plurality of individuals polled, 24 percent, reported they were undecided.

"Not bad. We've caught up. We've got a shot now," Carl said after reading the story. "If we get even half of the people who like Landon, we're in front. Comparing what we have right now to the operations Clarke and Foster have, we shouldn't even be close. We have one thing they don't have. We have the best candidate."

Lansing Landon called Pierce Buckman, who was on the treadmill. His phone in the cup holder was buzzing. The senator had not seen the polling results.

"Senator Hemp, did you see the Hawkeye State Poll results? You are right there with Clarke and Karla Foster. If the few folks who were supporting me come over, you are going to shake some shit up, pardon my Iowa barnyard slang. What are you doing today? Let's go out and talk to some voters. I can't hang around the house … I miss Lizzy too much … and we're not doing much in Washington as long as Rushton is in office. Let's go work on getting him out of there."

Candidates who are polling in single digits will downplay the significance of polls.

They will question the accuracy of the poll.

They will talk instead anecdotally about a mysterious groundswell of support no other observers have noticed.

They will talk about how early it is in the process. After all, the Iowa Caucuses were months away.

It is the mantra of candidates who may not make it to caucus night. The campaigns of Kaplan and Fuller might be on life support.

Senator Buckman now had an even stronger message. He had good polling numbers.

It was not unusual in the months prior to the Iowa Caucuses for candidates and their teams to schedule events in the same cities or towns on the same day. Sometimes at the same time, same town, different locations. The staffs became familiar with each other. Sometimes they put their competitive natures aside and became tenuous friends. When they did talk about campaigns and politics, they had more agreements than disagreements unless the topic was whose candidate was more suited to run the country.

Ryan Holton, the senator's aide and bus driver, had gone the next step with a staffer for former Virginia Governor Karla Foster. They had begun an intimate relationship. They started slipping away from their candidates almost from the time they announced they would run. The couple would get away to meet in restaurants, night clubs, parks and motel rooms. Their colleagues on campaign staffs knew only that they were disappearing for hours at a time. No one had discovered they were gone at the same times. It was all very discreet.

Ryan's liaison was with a Foster staffer who was a recent graduate of the University of Virginia with degrees in social work and early childhood education. She was petite with a vivacious personality like her mother. She had strong opinions she wasn't afraid to share; also, like her mother. People said she looked like her mother. Kassidy Foster was the daughter of the candidate and her companion and confidante as they traveled around Iowa. Kassidy roomed with her mother and remained in Iowa when her mother returned to Virginia after a day or two on the campaign trail. Unlike Senator Buckman, Mike Clarke and Karla Foster did a lot of commuting between their home states and Iowa. Buckman was putting everything into Iowa. It was the campaign's entire focus. Buckman did make occasional trips to Washington for key votes and to spend time in the office. Kim had been with the Senator most of the time in Iowa but was now back in Minnesota preparing for the birth of their baby, who they now knew was a boy.

Ryan Holton and Kassidy Foster spent every minute they could together. No one else with either campaign knew the seriousness of the relationship until the day when they could have brought down both campaigns and cleared an easier path for Jack Rushton to be re-elected president.

Ryan Holton asked for a few minutes privately with Senator Buckman. He stressed the importance of the meeting. Gerald O'Malley was the only other person in the room.

"Senator, I have something very important that I have to talk with you about," Ryan said, looking Buckman in the eyes. "For a few months I have been spending a lot of time with Kassie Foster, who is Karla's daughter. We didn't think it was anyone's business but our own. No one else needed to know. Now they will know. We fell in love."

"Happy for you, Ryan. Kind of explains where you have been going, but you are right, none of our business. You are adults," the senator said.

"There is more," Ryan said.

There was a long pause as Ryan appeared to struggle with the words. O'Malley understood immediately where the pause was leading.

"Ryan, she is knocked up, right?" O'Malley asked, demonstrating the frankness he was known for within the campaign.

"She is going to have a baby. Yes," Ryan said. "We are going to have a baby together."

"Well, at least it's the daughter you are having the affair with, not the candidate herself. That would have been slightly worse news," O'Malley said.

"There is more. Kassie has told her mother. They are very close. I was there when she told Governor Foster. Kassie's mother was fantastic about it. At first, she may have been a bit angry but she is excited now about being a grandmother. She hugged us both and kissed me on the cheek. We all had tears but it wasn't negative."

"She is a good woman," the senator said.

"No, wait. Let me get through all of this. Somehow, the Traditions Network found out. I think the governor may have shared with her top advisors. One of them must have shared the news with the wrong person. You know how secrets are out here. The last couple days, Traditions and Values people have been calling their campaign manager, Gil Grimes. They are trying to put off talking with the network. That won't last long. I needed to tell you."

"I know Gil. Smart guy," O'Malley said. "OK, Ryan, thanks for being honest about this. Congratulations by the way. You are having the baby, right?"

"Absolutely. We love each other. We plan to be married sometime next year."

"Ryan, it isn't the best news for the campaign but life isn't about campaigns and being elected," the senator said. "I think I need to call Governor Foster. Gerald, what about a joint news event to get ahead of Traditions? I don't want them to break this huge story and spin it all over the air before we announce ourselves."

"Ryan, stay around. We'll set something up quickly if we can," O'Malley said.

Ryan shared Karla Foster's cellphone number before leaving the senator's hotel room. He left believing it was one of the most difficult conversations he'd ever had with anyone, especially a candidate for president of the United States.

"I'm going to try to get the governor right now. Stay here with me," the senator said to O'Malley.

The Foster campaign was headed to Cedar Rapids on a leased $500,000 campaign bus with a king bed in the suite at the back. Karla Foster was talking with staff about her planned remarks for the day. Nowhere in those planned remarks was any mention of the pregnancy of her daughter, Kassie, who was also on the bus.

"Governor … Pierce. I think we need to talk. First, give your daughter a hug from Kim and I and our best wishes for a healthy pregnancy," the senator began. "Those crazy kids. How do you want to handle this?"

"Pierce, congratulations on your own baby. About seven months now, right? I have to tell you, I really like Ryan. We talked for a long time and I've seen him since…"

"Probably more than I have," the senator said. "We wondered where he had been going."

"Pierce, he seems like a good kid. And he comes from a good family. My staff did some research," Foster said.

"Also, a very prominent and successful family in Minnesota. His father is a partner in a major Twin Cities law firm with his brother. I think you will like them," Buckman said.

"I think we should get ahead of the media by announcing this in a joint news release. We both know we'll still get questions but maybe we can head TVN off from going crazy with this. Ryan told you they have been calling me, right?" Karla Foster said.

"He mentioned it. I think you are right about the joint news release," the senator said. "Probably better than a news conference. I think that would only create more questions. It might go on for days after that. Carl Lyon on our staff would be able to write this. Would you like me to have him draft a release and send it to you for approval?"

"Works for me," Karla Foster said. "Let's do this as quickly as possible and I'd keep it brief. One more thing, Pierce … when a producer from Traditions Network called my communications person they mentioned they were also working on a story about your relationship with Kim while she was still a student. Welcome to Jack Rushton's world."

O'Malley had not seen the senator angry when a day was not going well or overly excited on a good day for the campaign. He didn't know what to expect when the call ended. He had listened to the conversation.

"You will be asked about this … both the pregnancy of a candidate's daughter and your and Kim's relationship when she was still a student. You have to know that some people will believe a college professor having a sexual relationship with one of his students is inappropriate," O'Malley said.

"Of course, there will be the narrow-minded and simple-minded. You know, Republicans. First, Kim was not a freshman. She was a graduate student. She was an adult. Second, we fell in love and have been together since. She has been my wife for 10 years. We are having a child. If people still want to pass judgment on our relationship, they need to find another candidate to support. I'm not the right candidate for them," the senator said, his bald head now crimson. "Holier-than-thou bullshit."

It was one of first times O'Malley had heard the senator curse.

CHAPTER 23
Pink Revolution

Carl Lyon looked forward to his assignment. It meant he would be able to sit down at a computer and create news reaching millions of people. It would be part of the history of the election. And, he had a deadline of a couple of hours. He could feel the rush of adrenaline building. It was like being a real reporter again.

He chose the phrasing carefully. He struggled with a headline after working on the body of the statement. He ended up with this:

Joint Statement from Presidential Campaigns
Cedar Rapids, Iowa – July 18 – Virginia Governor Karla Foster announced today the governor's daughter and campaign assistant, Kassidy, 22, is expecting a child.

Ryan Holton, 23, from Chanhassen, Minn., who is on the campaign staff of U.S. Senator and presidential candidate Pierce Buckman of Minnesota, is Kassidy Foster's partner.

"We are young adults who met each other at campaign events. We found that we had a great deal in common. We had great conversations. We both believe we are working on the campaigns of people who would make a fine president of the United States. We fell deeply in love. We are excited about the news of the baby and we intend to be married next year," said Kassidy Foster. "We want to thank mom and Senator Buckman for being so totally supportive."

Governor Foster said the couple told her about their

relationship in recent days.

"They were very honest and open. Kassidy and Ryan will be very good parents and are very good for each other," the Governor said.

"We wish these impressive young adults all the best. In the meantime, they will continue being valued by our separate campaign organizations," Senator Buckman of Minnesota said.

Carl had O'Malley look over the draft of the statement for any changes. He made none. Governor Foster wanted to change impressive to wonderful in the last paragraph. Once the change was made, the release was sent to media contacts, including Traditions and Values Network.

Sending out the statements was intended to moderate the reaction of the media, particularly TVN, which would likely turn it into a breaking story rehashed for days if the network broke the story as an exclusive.

O'Malley believed Traditions would still try to find every conservative voice it could round up as a panel to criticize the moral values of Kassidy Foster and Ryan Holton, who they would remind audiences, were not married.

It didn't take long for TVN reporter Lake Northwood to track down Senator Buckman at a campaign visit to Iowa City hours after the statement was released. Senator Buckman was already pleased by the reaction of members of the Iowa Education Group, the union of school teachers in the state. As he was doing at every stop, the senator made himself available for questions from the media. Northwood was back to confront the senator.

"Senator, one of your campaign staff people is in a relationship with Kassidy Foster and she is pregnant. Is this situation reflective of lax moral values of yourself of your campaign?" Northwood asked. "Does your campaign have a different moral compass than most people in this country? Following up on that, did you have an inappropriate professor and student relationship when you were a college professor in Minnesota?"

Buckman was angry but controlled, like he was wrestling again.

"I'd like to expand on the statement today and answer your question.

"Let me start by saying Kassidy Foster and Ryan Holton of our campaign staff have my total support and will continue to be out working for myself and for Governor Foster. These are high quality young people with great futures. They will also make fine parents.

"About 15 years ago I had a graduate political science student named Kim Wakefield when I was a professor at Big River State University in northern Minnesota. Our relationship started as student and professor but grew into to something much more, much deeper and much better. I was amazed she was interested in kind of a wonky professor who was older than she was. We began to socialize casually. I would cook for her. We understood some people, even in a college environment, would not approve. We didn't care what anyone's reaction was. We were adults and we needed to be with each other.

"We began to date more formally with full knowledge and love and support from our families and friends, just as we are now supporting Ryan and Kassidy. We are in love, just as these young people are. We are having a child, just as these young people are. Loving Kim and being with her is the best thing I have ever done in my life. My life would not be the same, would not be as rewarding, nor exciting, nor balanced had I not met Kim and fallen in love with her.

"Not for one second have I regretted my relationship with my fantastic wife. The mistake would have been to not pursue this wonderful person. That would have been inexcusable. Unimaginable at this point in my life.

"So, if someone at Traditions and Values Network or anywhere else wants to be critical of the relationship of these young people or the relationship between my wife and myself they are welcome to voice their opinion. I will continue to love my life and my wife."

There were several more questions about the relationship between the senator and his wife. He swatted each away. Carl called them "hanging curve balls" for the senator.

Buckman walked away after several minutes, gently grasping

Kim's hand as they walked to Beatrice and went up the steps. Once inside, he kissed her.

"Sorry to put you through this. Intrusion into private lives is part of politics, unfortunately," the senator told Kim.

"Asshole," Kim said of the reporter.

"Well put."

Carl Lyon was frantically taking notes from memory. He sensed this would be "a moment" in the campaign. The confirmation was outside. About 30 people who had heard the senator's comments in front of the teachers, then his impromptu press conference, were outside Beatrice cheering and chanting "Buckman, Buckman, Buckman."

"It's a curtain call," Carl reported, referring to callbacks in baseball to the dugout steps after a key moment in a big game. "You have to open the door before they start rocking Beatrice. The bus might tip over."

The senator, wearing sunglasses and his bald head now uncovered, opened the door. Kim stepped out in front of him. He had a huge grin and waved to the cheering crowd. The cameras of the networks and bloggers, maybe hoping for an ambush of the Buckman campaign – at least Traditions was – were still recording in the midst of the chanting crowd outside the bus. Carl captured photos, too. He was thinking cover photo for the senator's biography he was working on.

Ryan Holton wasn't in hiding. His image would now be on the screen on every network and news channel for at least an hour or two. He was signing up possible supporters on the PoliPad, the campaign's new device manufactured specifically for remote registration of supporters and instant polling. Two of the online millennials back in The Warehouse had worked out the secure software for PoliPad over the past two years waiting for an opportunity to launch the device in a sort of trial. Their patent application was being processed. Holton, who was congratulated by many of the supporters cheering the senator, tried to get all of them to sign Beatrice with thick, permanent markers in a variety of colors. Pink seemed to Ryan to be the most popular choice.

"We've got a pink revolution going on with the people signing Beatrice," he reported as he climbed into the driver's seat.

"That figures. Maybe that's what this is. Yeah, a pink revolution," Carl said. "We're not a red campaign, which certainly has its own connotations, considering the buffoon's policies. We're not exclusively a blue campaign. Not many mainstream candidates of either party would admit they favor relaxation of marijuana laws. Our candidate does," Carl said. "Who else campaigns in a piece-of-crap bus and encourages people to write messages on it? Our guy does. Who else talks about higher taxing of guns, ammo and replacement parts. Only one candidate is actively embracing the LBGTQ community. Our guy does."

"Yeah, we've got a pot-smoking, gun-banning, college girl-chasin', bus-defacing, baby-makin' campaign. We're definitely pink," Ryan said.

"Ryan, don't press your luck today," the senator said from the back of the bus. "Pink, huh?"

The last noise from the back bedroom of Beatrice was loud laughter from the senator and Kim. They fell asleep with Crosby, Stills, Nash and Young on the sound system.

Carl went online as the boss slept. He wanted to know more about the color pink. Colors are considered to have different impacts and different meanings.

"I once knew a big-time college football coach who insisted on painting the visitor locker room pink. He said it was a mellowing color which would distract the opposing team and make them softer," Carl said to Ryan, passing the time. "He won a whole bunch of football games. Maybe he was right about the pink thing and maybe our campaign truly is pink."

Carl looked up "the meaning of pink" online. He read to Ryan straight from the website color-meanings.com.

"Pink represents caring, compassion and love. The pink color stands for unconditional love and understanding, and is associated with giving and receiving care. Since pink is a combination of red and white, both colors add a little to its characteristics. It gets the lust for action from the red color, and the white color gives it an opportunity to achieve success and insight. Passion and power from the color red, softened with the purity and openness of the white color completes pink color meaning. The deeper the pink color, the more passion and energy it radiates.

"Pink is romantic and intimate, feminine, loving, caring and extremely considerate. The color pink is insightful and intuitive and it shows tenderness and kindness from its empathetic and sensitive nature.

"In color psychology, pink is a sign of hope. It is a positive color that inspires warm and comforting feelings. The color pink gives the feeling that everything will go well or be okay. Most people have heard of the saying 'everything is rosy.' It may also indicate good health and success."

Ryan was listening intently.

"Caring, compassion, love, hope, passionate…oh, hell yes, our guy, our campaign is pink," he said. "I certainly have benefited from his caring, compassion and love."

Carl made a mental note to check out the messages and graffiti on Beatrice. Especially the messages written with the pink markers. Might make a chapter in the book he was working on.

CHAPTER 24

The Project

There was no reason Jericho Brooks' mission he called "The Project" would draw any attention. He didn't have to purchase what he needed to accomplish his plan. He already had access to what he needed. His deteriorating mental health wouldn't stop him. Instead, his condition would empower him. He had never been hospitalized for his severe mental health issues. He had never been arrested or even stopped for a traffic violation.

He was a ghost. There was no reason he would show up on any list of possible terrorists.

He had tried twice to enlist in the Marine Corps but was rejected when he failed the physical because of his anti-anxiety and anti-depression medications. He was not allowed to take the physical again. His condition had been identified and he was "red flagged."

After high school, he had bounced around several jobs. He worked in a customer service call center for a couple of months. He worked for a tree service and landscaping company for nearly six months but was laid off in the winter.

He had moved out of his mom and stepfather's house. It was made very clear he was leaving voluntarily or otherwise.

"You have to get out of here. We can't afford to continue supporting you. Go get a job," Michael Munger had said matter-of-factly to his stepson. "Don't let the door hit you in the ass. You have keys to the cabinet. Just come over when you want them."

Jericho wanted out anyway. He had a new girlfriend, Marin

Gabbard, whose own life experiences mirrored Jericho's in some ways. The most negative experiences were among those they shared. She had experienced a broken relationship with her parents after they divorced. She had bounced around between their homes, and like Jericho, between schools. With her preference for alternative, drug-themed music and rap, also like Jericho, she was considered weird and well outside the norm by classmates, no matter what school she attended. She was small and had hair dyed regularly in bright colors. She introduced Jericho to consensual sex, marijuana, painkillers and techno music. They both battled periods of depression, sometimes together, which they agreed helped each of them cope.

Jericho introduced Marin to guns and shooting.

Jericho nicknamed his girlfriend Magda after Magda Goebbels, the "First Lady of the Third Reich." They looked up Magda Goebbels together on the Internet. They discovered she poisoned six of seven children – an older child was a German soldier who was a prisoner of war – then took her own life in the final hours of the doomed Third Reich.

"She was very close to Hitler and she suffered from depression, like both of us," Jericho said. "You and I are the new Goebbels of our generation, except it isn't the Jews we hate, it's the anti-gun fucks like Buckman."

Magda thought she was in love with Jericho. It was her first loving sexual relationship. She had been abused … raped … several times as a young teen by a group of males in one of her middle schools. She was living with Jericho in a drafty farmhouse owned by an elderly couple who had moved to a nursing home. Magda was supporting them with her cashier job in a "big box" store. Jericho was looking for another job.

They smoked grass, used painkillers and shot up a lot of ammo on the farmland and along the narrow, quiet creek running through the land. The land was rented to a farmer for cropland by the owners in the nursing home. They enjoyed what seemed to them to be a very normal relationship. More "normal" than any of the relationships they had ever known growing up in dysfunctional families.

Jericho was becoming more outspoken and enraged about

what he called "the gun control nuts." He had heard about the Minnesota Gun Rights Association, a fringe organization with a position there should never be, nor could there ever possibly be, common ground with any infringement on gun rights.

"No compromise. Not ever," Jericho told Magda on one of their shooting trips along the creek. "That's the stand of Minnesota Gun Rights Association. NGL (National Gun Lobby) is weak. Pussies. They will give in eventually to Buckman and his crowd. The NGL only cares about memberships and money members bring in to pay the big salaries of the NGL executives and those payoffs to politicians.

"Buckman and the politicians like him are attacking our way of life. We can never give up our liberties. The NGL doesn't understand people like me."

In the three months they had been together, Magda had never seen Jericho as excited as he was before the event of the year sponsored by the Minnesota Gun Rights Association. On a beautiful summer weekend, they planned a trip to Gun Fest. The event was held every summer in a remote location in Minnesota. Gun Fest honors Second Amendment freedoms, which this group believed were untouchable and without limits. After all, if government ever did turn on its own citizens, those citizens would need more than pistols or shotguns. Jericho and Magda borrowed a tent and cooler to camp at the festival. They went to Jericho's mother's house and loaded up the guns they wanted, including the semi-auto pistols Jericho planned to teach Magda to use.

Events at Gun Fest included gun range shooting of high-powered rifles and handguns, shooting competitions and firebrand speakers and entertainers who espoused their beliefs. There was also a huge gun sale, music and paintball. The speeches followed a pattern. The speakers warned of the gathering storm of the enemies who would come for their guns.

"No compromise," Jericho shouted in a quiet moment in one speech.

"No compromise," echoed someone else in the crowd of about 250.

Jericho shouted out the phrase again and within seconds

everyone in the crowd was joining in like it was a pep rally for pistols and all other weapons, from black powder antiques to semi-auto rifles easily adaptable to be full auto.

They chanted "No Compromise" in sync for a minute or so.

Jericho was exhilarated. He had started this wave of fervor sweeping through the crowd. He had never felt so normal and so much a part of something so exciting, so righteous in his dark mind, in his entire life. He was shouting "No Compromise" the loudest. He was accepted by those around him. He thought some people at the event may have even considered him to be a leader at this moment. He had a cause shared by others. No one hassled him about how he looked, or talked, or ridiculed his obsession with weapons. In this crowd, everyone seemed to be obsessed by weapons.

He wasn't being abused by his stepfather or anyone else. He had found himself and found his people. He knew his plan was going to earn him even greater respect from the people he cared about and who seemed to care about him.

Jericho had talked to Magda only in very general terms about "The Project."

He said "The Project" would protect the Second Amendment "from the socialists who want to infringe on the freedoms of gun owners."

"When the government of Pierce Buckman and the other socialists come after our guns, they better bring guns with them," Jericho had told Magda. "They'll need them."

Jericho worked on convincing Magda to help with "The Project."

"It will be monumental. I'm prepared to give my life if necessary to protect the civil liberties of millions of others. My life is a mess anyway. But I want you to survive," Jericho explained as they enjoyed a flickering, warm campfire at their Gun Fest campsite. "I want you to be the witness. I want you to create a record of "The Project." Video, photos, writing. You are good at those things."

Magda thought he was maybe talking about a video game or was joking. He assured her he was serious. Magda was shocked. She stammered for several seconds before saying, "you think you are going to die?"

"Maybe not. I said I'm prepared to die to protect the rights of others. We will be heroes. We will have books written about us. People will remember 'The Project.' You will be famous."

"Will I get in trouble?"

"You won't die. I promise you that."

"That is not helpful," Magda said, still incredulous about where the conversation had turned.

"You will be someone. You will be the main character in a movie. We will disrupt something millions of people value. They will be terrified such a thing could happen."

Jericho was manipulating Magda, who he understood to be as detached from "normal" as he was.

No one knew the detailed plan of "The Project" other than Jericho, who had worked out the plan over months. At first, he tried out a number of ideas in his head. He began to focus in on a plan. He had written down the details in a notebook he had hidden. He assured Magda that he would tell her everything and share the location of the notebook.

"It is really a simple plan. You can have a great impact if you have a plan, passion and commitment," Jericho said.

Deadly Heat

No candidate campaigns in an Iowa Caucuses year without going to the Iowa Agricultural Exposition. Senator Pierce Buckman made the expected appearance on the hottest day in Iowa history.

"Oh yeah, we're predicting the hottest day in Iowa history today when we report from the Iowa Agricultural Exposition, which people around here generally refer to as The Expo," said reporter-anchor and noted eccentric Teddy Thermal to viewers of Rapid Response Weather. "By 10 a.m. we are predicting 92 degrees. By noon, 102. At 2 p.m., 107 degrees and after that we're predicting damn hot for the Midwest. The high could reach 111, which would be the all-time record high in Des Moines. Council Bluffs, Waterloo, Cedar Rapids, Davenport … from border to border…records could fall today."

"The heat will be dangerous in Iowa and in the Midwest. About 104,000 visitors are expected today at The Expo. If you are in the Midwest today please follow these tips: Drink plenty of water and sports drinks. Avoid caffeine and alcohol, which are diuretics and flush fluids out of the system quickly. The elderly and the young and those with chronic health conditions are at higher risk for heat-related illnesses. If you are not feeling well, for example, you are nauseous, vomiting or have a headache or cramping, seek medical attention."

"Oh yeah, this will be serious heat today at The Expo. We will be providing updates all day on Rapid Response Weather. From The Expo in Des Moines, Iowa, this is Teddy Thermal on Rapid

Response Weather."

Thermal was well known by Carl and Susan Lyon. He had made his first visit to Big River, Minn., to report on the coldest day in the history of the city in north central Minnesota. Thermal also reported on a huge fire that threatened to destroy downtown Big River in the record cold. He returned months later and stayed in the lake house with Carl and Susan Lyon after Big River was hit by a devastating and deadly summer storm. Carl was the editor of the Big River Beacon when the events converged, including Senator Buckman's heart attack during a speaking engagement at Big River State University on the day of a winter storm ahead of the record cold. The staff he directed won a coveted First Freedoms Award, the highest recognition of excellence in community newspapers.

Teddy Thermal's given name was Theodore Cline Jr. He grew up fascinated by weather and weather statistics. Teddy gained a reputation as an eccentric student of Meteorology and Journalism when he enrolled in college. Even then he was recognized for his delivery of weather on university radio. People liked his unusual delivery. A producer at the campus radio station initially thought Teddy Thermocline fit as a "television name." From that, he became Teddy Thermal and was now nationally recognized for his newsy, insightful reporting and analysis of weather. He was a senior field reporter and anchor of Rapid Response Weather.

"Hey, Teddy is in town. Oh yeah, going to the Iowa Agricultural Exposition," Carl Lyon said, imitating Thermal's delivery and quirky "Oh yeah," which always made it sound as if Teddy was only at that precise moment remembering some other newsworthy bit of information to share with viewers of Rapid Response Weather.

Carl loved Rapid Response Weather and Teddy Thermal. Susan thought their "Bromance" was humorous, although she also was fascinated by Teddy. Carl and Teddy Thermal had talked at least once a week since they met when Teddy showed up in Big River to report on the severe weather outbreaks.

Carl and Susan walked to the convenient store next door for breakfast and their personal choices of caffeine, soda for Carl, heavily flavored coffee for Susan.

"It's like walking into an oven and it's 8 a.m.," Carl said. "Oh yeah, going to be a hot one."

The Expo, a highlight of the Iowa summer calendar in the steamy days of August when the fields of corn and beans and the family gardens are growing by the day, has been around since 1862. It has a number of traditions. As it has across the country, the population distribution of Iowa has changed from primarily rural to more urban. It doesn't matter at The Expo. Whether they live in a city or the country, they show up. More than a million people attend the 10-day run.

As Expos go, it is one of the best, although if you wanted to get under Pierce Buckman's skin, you suggested it was better than the Minnesota State Expo. "No one with any real understanding of state Expos believes that," he would say to such sacrilege.

"They never made a movie about the Minnesota State Expo," Carl would jab.

One thing Iowa's version of The Expo had that the Minnesota State Expo didn't usually have was a trail of presidential candidates showing up every four years. The Iowa version also regularly attracted sitting presidents who were approaching re-election. President Rushton had attended four years ago when he was trying to win the nomination and started his campaign for the presidency.

Rushton showed up very much looking the part of a Texan running for president. He wore alligator skin boots, jeans and a long-sleeved bright, white shirt with the sleeves rolled up. On the Street Corner Soapbox, sponsored by the Iowa Media Association of newspapers, television and radio stations and online sites, he outlined his conservative values before a crowd of hundreds.

"On my first day in office I will sign any legislation I believe will stop the flood of illegal aliens not only coming into the country from Mexico but going back and forth unrestricted. Better than any other candidate, as a former governor of Texas, I know the cost of unrestricted flow of illegals into our country. A large majority of the crimes committed in Texas are committed by illegal aliens. No Democrat has ever proposed strong efforts to shut down our borders."

"I guarantee you we will stop the flow and if they somehow get over the border, we'll round them up and send them back. And we'll keep sending them back every time. I support building a wall to stop this illegal movement threatening our security and society by bringing drugs into the country."

The part about illegals committing "a large majority" of crimes was not even within sight of truth but that day, no one seemed to care. There was a new political star appealing to conservatives on the horizon. The only thing missing was a cowboy hat. He bought an expensive one during his day at The Expo and wore it the rest of the day.

Rushton was followed around by media as he checked out 4-H projects and talked with kids about their projects. He visited a couple of barns. He ate a pork chop on a stick, a bag full of mini-donuts and signed dozens of autographs and had hundreds of photos taken. Photos and video of him with 4-H kids ran on newscasts and in newspapers all over the country. When the media produced retrospectives about the path of Jack Rushton to the White House, his appearance at the Iowa Agricultural Exposition was considered a pivotal moment. It appeared to be the day Iowans, many seeing and hearing him for the first time, started to consider him as a viable Republican candidate that day.

In one day, Rushton went from invisibility to viability. He won the Iowa Caucuses and won the tight general election in the early morning hours after voting.

"We have a couple surprises for them this year at the Expo," O'Malley said, without explaining when the topic came up as they headed toward the expansive, hilly Expogrounds just outside of Des Moines.

"Gerald, have you been hitting the wine stash? We don't need surprises today. We can only hope the air conditioning keeps working in Beatrice," Carl asked.

"Wait and see," Gerald said. "Folks are going to forget all about Rushton's day at the Expo four years ago. You'll know in a little bit. Ryan, we're going to The Principal Hotel downtown.

Pull up right in front. You probably know where that is. I think the Fosters stayed there. Heck, you probably conceived a baby there. You've at least seen the rooms. Now you know how those campaigns roll. Right? Different than ours."

Ryan just grinned.

At 10 a.m., it was already 93 degrees, one degree higher than Teddy Thermal's prediction.

Ryan pulled Beatrice up in front of the hotel. Coming toward the bus first was the burly bodyguard they had first met on the night in Las Vegas when they dined with Crossroads State University basketball coach J.J. Webb on the weekend the Explorers won the national championship.

"Holy shit," Ryan said.

The senator, aware of who was joining the campaign for the day, laughed from the back of the bus.

Breckenridge Powell and Brynn Powell climbed on the now very colorful Beatrice the Bus. Unlike their meeting with the senator over dinner in Vegas, they were not incognito. They were very much identifiable as two of the best-known movie stars in the world. No hats and no sunglasses. They appeared as their screen personas. The burly black bodyguard, who Ridge Powell introduced as Lincoln Zion, followed his clients onto the bus. Lincoln wore black jeans, a black T-shirt and what appeared to be right-out-of-the-box sneakers. He didn't appear to be armed but was menacing just the same.

"Don't let the look fool you. He's a teddy bear," Ridge said of Lincoln as they boarded Beatrice. "Unless you piss him off. Then he doesn't react well. That's why we like him."

The senator shook hands with Ridge and hugged Brynn. Kim hugged both. The senator's hand disappeared when he shook hands with Lincoln.

"Kim, you will take it easy today, right?" Brynn asked, hugging her again. "I think it's supposed to be one of the hottest days ever in Des Moines. That's what Teddy Thermal said."

"Teddy is a good friend," Carl piped up.

Susan Lyon was fascinated that her husband had met virtually every big sports icon of the past 60 years and was now working for a man who might be president. During his time on Beatrice,

202

he wrote the candidate's biography for release in a couple of months. It could be a historic campaign and a historic book if the senator was elected. And Carl was name dropping Teddy Thermal.

"Oh Lord," Susan Lyon said, mocking her apparently excited husband.

There were now 10 of them on the bus, and two black SUVs behind them, for the trip of only a few miles through downtown Des Moines to the Expogrounds. They also had two Des Moines officers on motorcycles in front of Beatrice.

Ryan was able to get the bus approved for a special parking spot inside the Expogrounds, although it wasn't easy. The security at the gate looked at the RV with the oddly defaced body and figured there was no way a candidate for president was onboard. The two officers leading the group assured them there was. Lincoln also got off the bus to make sure this was all straightened out.

"Can we borrow Lincoln for a few months?" Gerald O'Malley asked. He was serious.

"No, but he has an identical twin ... Zeke ... in the private security business," Ridge Powell said.

"Zeke Zion? We need that guy's phone number by the end of the day," O'Malley said.

The bus stopped. Lincoln had walked from the gate to the parking spot. There was a stream of already steaming Iowans walking past Beatrice. Some of them who had heard about the colorful campaign bus stopped to sign.

"How do you want to do this? Would you introduce the senator and talk about your support of him?" O'Malley asked the Powells. "We'd like both of you to introduce him and after this soapbox event, we'd like you to join us. We're going to meet some of the kids competing in a talent contest, some 4-H kids in a sheep showing contest and probably make a couple food stops, although the senator doesn't want to be photographed or recorded gnawing on any meats on a stick."

"We're with you wherever you want to go today," Brynn said.

"Ryan, we want you with us to get people signed up on the PoliPad but have one of the staff keep Beatrice cooled down if

Kim or anyone else wants to come and cool down and escape," Gerald instructed.

Gerald had arranged for golf cart transportation. He hoped it wouldn't be necessary to walk the couple of blocks to the Street Corner Soapbox stage.

Almost immediately, the thousands of fans coming in the gates on Main Street of the Expogrounds noticed the Powells, the senator and Kim. The group was stopped every few feet by Expogoers who wanted autographs or photos. Gerald had not known what to expect from one of the most recognized celebrity couples in the world. They were totally into their roles. They posed for photos, signed autographs and greeted fans. They were fan friendly. They asked people to support the senator in the Iowa Caucuses. Buckman wore his standard summer attire … a Buckman for President polo, matching baseball cap, khaki pants and sneakers with no socks. Kim started walking but switched to a golf cart to reach the speaker's stage. Lincoln and the two Des Moines police officers walked on the perimeter of the group.

The senator smiled widely as he walked and asked people for their support along the way. He shook hands and signed scraps of paper, Expo programs and Expo updates from the morning newspaper.

Still a block away from the stage, the entourage was totally stalled and engulfed by the crowd. They were going to be late. The crowd was becoming overwhelming. The officers radioed for assistance. They were concerned about the close quarters, the heat and the security of the candidate. They told the senator they were uncomfortable with the crowd attracted by the Powells.

Expo security showed up with two thick ropes to create an alley for the group. It did help but what happened next was inevitable. At 11:03 a.m., two older people fell to the street. One appeared to simply fall. The other fainted, possibly from the extreme heat. Both needed medical assistance quickly. In rapid succession, seven other people asked for help. They couldn't escape the crowd to cool off.

"This is becoming a crisis," Carl told the officers. "We need ambulances and anything to cool these people down."

The rope line helped, although the Powells and the candidate continued to stroll along the line talking with fans and supporters. The celebrity couple made it clear this day was about Buckman. They stayed close to him to create better video and photos for the media following them. Carl and Ryan were also taking photos and video.

Susan Lyon, a Master's trained nurse, tried to do what she could for the people in the crowd. She advised the officers, "Please get these people water. Lots of it."

She was also concerned about the senator's health. She asked repeatedly how he was feeling. She quickly took his pulse.

The group finally made it to the stage about 20 minutes late, which wasn't bad even on a good day for the senator. This was not a good day. A total of 15 people had been transported either to the medical facility on the Expogrounds or off site to a hospital, and they continued to drop.

At 11:30 when the Powells began speaking, the temperature was 102. Police estimated that 3,000 people were crowded around the stage.

Just before they began to speak, a 6-foot-5 man in jeans, T-shirt and cowboy hat was escorted to the stage. Scheduled to appear in the grandstand at The Expo that evening was four-time country music Artist of the Year Beau Cole. He had now joined fellow Texan Ridge Powell on stage with Brynn, the senator and Kim.

"Folks, I am Ridge Powell, this is Brynn, this is our Texas pal Beau Cole and we're all here to tell you we are supporting Senator Pierce Buckman for president."

Packed into the street in front of the stage, most of the people were doing fine. Others were not. Susan Lyon was now in the middle of them, trying to help. She was able to reach the office of the Expo on her cellphone.

"This is a mass-casualty disaster. Call the All Saints Hospital and give them those exact words so they can staff up for patients," Susan told the person who answered. "This is extremely important. There could be fatalities if we don't respond. We need ambulances, and can you have people bring water here somehow?"

Police responded, and within minutes a caravan of ambulances arrived.

On the stage, the Powells and Beau Cole kept the introduction brief.

"We believe in Senator Pierce Buckman and his vision for our great country. We're not from Iowa so we can't vote in the Iowa Caucuses in February, but if we could we would stand with Senator Buckman," Ridge Powell said. "Here is our friend and another Buckman supporter … Beau."

"I saw Senator Buckman's compassion and ability to get things done after the terrible storm last summer about this time in northern Minnesota," Cole said slowly with his deep, distinctive voice. "It was a horrible storm and his response was compassionate and powerful. He listened to people and asked what they needed. Then he got it. He cares."

"Folks, I am not usually a Democrat. I am a Pierce Buckman supporter. I support the Pierce Buckman Party. We won't agree on everything but I know he would be a great president for y'all."

Brynn Powell voiced her support and said, "We're honored to be here today to support Senator Pierce Buckman for President. Here is Senator Buckman and his wife, Kim."

Senator Buckman kissed Kim and asked one of the police officers to get her back to Beatrice. The overheated crowd was still enthusiastic with its applause and reaction. Some of the people in front of the stage had been waiting for nearly two hours.

"Folks, thanks for coming out to The Expo and coming to listen to us. I'm concerned about all of you being out in this heat. We're not used to anything like this in Minnesota but I understand the heat is about the same up there. We'll keep this very short. Kim, as you may know, is about eight months pregnant and I insisted she get out of the heat."

"Here is why we need a change in the White House. As long as Jack Rushton is in the White House we are going to be a country lacking vision. We will be a country lacking empathy. We will be a country lacking a long-range plan for my child, your children and grandchildren."

"We will be a country that believes global warming is some sort of conspiracy theory. Where are the deniers today?"

"So here is what I want to do if I am elected …"

He talked about immigration reform and his experience at MegaPack during the takeover of the plant. He talked about free college tuition in exchange for public service. He talked about family-centric Schools Without Barriers. There was one twist to what was becoming a standard stump speech, although there always seemed to be something new.

"No one understands the role of agriculture better than you people who are around it every day. We can feed this country. We can feed more of the world, but we will not do it in my presidency by abusing land, water and air. We will not allow pollution in the name of progress. We will re-engage with the world on climate change. Climate change is real, regardless of what you hear from the current administration.

"Iowans also know about clean energy. You see it every day in the hundreds of wind turbines scattered across the state. Iowa is a leader in clean energy. Iowa is a leader in ethanol-based fuel and will continue to be a leader in my administration.

"Iowa is a leader in education. We're not going to trust your great Iowa public schools to for-profit organizations. They are interested more in profit than student outcomes. We will support local public schools. You have some of the best in Iowa. We want more states to have schools like Iowa. We will ask for sacrifices because as a country we do need to create a better future for more of our students, particularly the impoverished, forgotten and underserved.

"Now listen … our best path to a bright future and thriving economy for everyone is education. We will create a program called Schools Without Barriers and we will dismantle the barriers keeping too many American kids from receiving the education they need to become productive employees, leaders and entrepreneurs.

"We can do these things and many more if you share our vision. We want you to join us."

Near the front, in the large group of spectators who had arrived early, was a heavily tattooed young man with a cowboy hat and sunglasses. He was able to get close enough to shake hands with the candidate. Hundreds, of people, so close their wet shirts nearly stuck to each other, tried to get close enough to shake hands or get a photo with Buckman.

Twenty-seven people in the crowd to see the senator and his celebrity friends were in the process of being taken away for medical treatment when the truck arrived. The senator, Beau Cole and Ridge Powell all began handing out bottles of water from the truck bed. The water was warm. No one seemed to care.

The temperature was 106 by 1 p.m.

One of the dozen or so print, television and political and entertainment website reporters following the group to a livestock show arena was Teddy Thermal. He knew how to get the attention of his friend, Carl Lyon.

"Oh yeah, hot one today. So hot Jack Rushton begged to be waterboarded," Teddy said.

Carl laughed and immediately glanced around looking for the voice he recognized.

"Oh yeah, so hot the dairy cows at The Expo are giving powdered milk," Carl shot back, mocking Teddy's eccentricity as he spotted the forecaster, his shoulder-length hair soaking wet with perspiration.

Carl lifted the rope slightly so Teddy Thermal could join them. They fist-bumped each other and hugged. Their shirts were both drenched. They talked as they walked in front of the rest of the group. As they walked, Carl tried to introduce Teddy to the Powells. He didn't need to. Ridge Powell took over.

"Teddy Thermal, we watch you all the time," Ridge Powell said, offering his hand. "We were watching when that storm first hit Minnesota last year. That was when we first saw the senator and were impressed with how he handled the disaster. Hang out with us. I think we're going to see 4-H kids showing animals and I don't think it's air-conditioned."

"Will there be beer?" Teddy asked with a grin.

"Pretty sure there will be later. If you are hanging out with me, you can count on it," Ridge said. "The senator is on a short leash. A beer to him is a few sips."

The group met with startled kids grooming their livestock before a show. One girl, a 13-year-old from Osage, Iowa, shrieked when she realized Ridge Powell had one of the combs used to groom her sheep and was combing the ewe she was showing later in the afternoon. Several teenage boys in jeans, cowboy hats and boots had surrounded Brynn Powell and talked all at once about their favorite Brynn Powell movies. The senator asked questions about how meticulously the animals were groomed before shows. Large fans in the barn were at least keeping the air moving.

Reporters, held back by the rope line, shouted questions. After visiting the kids and signing autographs and having photos taken for about 15 minutes, Ridge Powell and the senator went to the rope and talked with the reporters. Brynn Powell continued to be surrounded by teenage boys. She appeared to be enjoying the attention.

"Ridge ... Mr. Powell ... um, will you be campaigning for Senator Buckman more ... um ... leading up to the caucus night?" a star struck reporter managed to finally get out.

"Whenever and wherever he needs us. The more Brynn and I hear what the senator has to say, the stronger our support becomes for him. He'll make a great president. He cares about the future. Instead of leading a country moving from crisis to crisis, Senator Buckman will return foresight and sense of future to the presidency. We don't have that now. He calls it vision. I know he has it. I think the thousands of people here to see him today would agree.

"We started by being very interested in the idea of Schools Without Barriers. Brynn and I, like the senator, believe this country needs to improve our student outcomes to make every student able to be a productive employee, employer or manager in the future. We can do that through education."

Lake Northwood, the reporter from Traditions Network who was now following the Buckman campaign on a regular basis, apparently was trying to find the most negative story today to confront the senator with. He found his story in the line of ambulances headed to the hospital with lights and sirens on, filled with victims of the steaming, drenching heat.

"Lake Northwood, Traditions Network ... should you have canceled today's speech considering the number of people overcome by the heat? A lot of people went down. Is this on you personally and your campaign staff?"

The senator didn't hesitate before saying, "We kept the remarks brief because of the heat. On any day like this, with so many people in one place, there are likely to be people who get sick, are injured or overcome by the heat. My understanding is that there are more than 100,000 people expected today. Of course, we are concerned with everyone who needed medical attention. My staff was out there taking care of people, too. The Expo staff I believe is doing a great job under these conditions. They have my respect."

Northwood kept on. "If I can follow up, are you concerned you will now be tied to the Hollywood community with its well-deserved reputation for being out of touch with the traditional values of Americans?"

Ridge Powell flashed a crooked smile and said, "I think you are right about Hollywood being detached from the rest of the country politically. That's why we live in Montana. People are capable of forming their own opinions there, as they are in Iowa."

There was more news from the Expo. The Grand Champion 4-H steer, worth thousands of dollars to the young owner, had died. It was natural to blame the torrid heat.

Senator Buckman and his celebrity entourage headed for concession stands. He was sensitive, one of his apparent idiosyncrasies, about being photographed or recorded chewing on a hunk of grilled mammal flesh or dripping meat juice or something down the front of his shirt. He also had made it clear that there would be little flag waving or flags at all on his campaign. And there would be no photo opportunities of Buckman climbing around military vehicles or holding weapons.

"That isn't me at all. I've hunted but never served in the military. I will reduce the budgets of the military and federal law enforcement agencies. I don't want it to appear I support the incredible amount of money spent by the country on military and law enforcement gadgets and vehicles and weaponry," Buckman had explained to Gerald O'Malley in one of their first conversations.

"It's part of who I am. Go ahead and include it in the book," the senator told Carl, who had also heard the candidate's admonition.

The media continued to follow the senator and the Powells as the candidate downed a freshly squeezed lemonade.

They also stopped at a bar and grill concession in a large, air-conditioned tent on the Expogrounds. The senator and Ridge Powell waited in line personally for their locally brewed beers, talking with people in the jammed tent. The people approaching them were as attracted by Teddy as they were the Powells. They may have been in disbelief the Powells were at their Expo. They went almost table to table together talking with surprised Expogoers. The Powells and the senator were doing the Expo with a flair, unlike numerous candidates who had visited before. The reporters following them shot photos and video of the senator mingling with the Powells. All the national networks had video of the senator's campaign event at the Expo.

"Kim is back in Beatrice. Let's get out of here. Who wants a beer?" the senator asked.

Teddy had one more live report before he could join them. He did the report from a show barn.

"Des Moines experienced the hottest day in the city's history today when the temperature hit 112 degrees, breaking the previous record, set twice, of 110 degrees. We have spent the day at The Expo in Des Moines with more than 100,00 people who turned out even on his horribly hot day.

"The day did take a toll, as we suggested earlier it might. By the time the temperature began to slowly drop, a total of 272 people had been treated or transported from The Expo because of heat-related illness. Sadly, two people, ages 86 and 77, both reportedly with chronic health issues, died at The Expo. Rapid Response Weather wants to share our condolences with the family and friends of the victims. Teddy Thermal from The Expo in Des Moines, Iowa."

By the time the Beau Cole concert started, six more Expogoers, all attending the show in the grandstand, were transported to the hospital for symptoms of hyperthermia.

Iowa Brews

Teddy followed the rest of the group about an hour later to 100 Iowa Brews and Buns, which featured more than 100 Iowa craft beers on tap. Beers from major national brewers were not available. The owners were reverse beer snobs. They wouldn't offer anything not made in Iowa or the Midwest. If anyone asked for a national brand, they were booed and ridiculed.

"Oh yeah, what a day. Who wants beer? I got it," Teddy announced not only to their group but on the overhead P.A. system to about 200 people. Everyone was parched if Teddy was buying.

"*Ted-dy, Ted-dy, Ted-dy*," chanting was initiated by Ridge Powell. In seconds, the whole place showed its appreciation by chanting for the weatherman they all knew.

One entire wall of the old warehouse building in downtown Des Moines held 105 taps. The number of brews changed often. Two new Iowa craft beers had been added just this day. The building with high ceilings and exposed HVAC ducts covered an entire block. It was like a traditional German beer hall. There was nothing on the menu except burgers and about every form of hot dog and sausage you could imagine, in addition to beer. If you wanted a mixed drink or a vegan wrap, salmon or anything fried, this wasn't the place. But if you wanted an Iowa Bun Bash two-pound cheeseburger with a half-pound of Iowa bacon or smoked pulled pork as a side, covered in an Iowa barbeque sauce called Smokin' Butt, this was the place. Or if you wanted knockwurst with kraut, a bison brat, a duck brat or liver sausage, they had you covered.

The senator's crew had tried about 50 of the 105 Iowa craft beers, passing the pints around their table and to people around them. They were owning the music system when the first semi-sober guy with enough testosterone and urged on by his buddies, got the courage to ask Brynn Powell to dance. She didn't hesitate. She didn't even look at Ridge, who was engaged in a serious conversation with Teddy, Carl and Ryan about how the craft beers were named. Brynn got up and danced. Ridge was used to men being attracted to his movie star wife, who was, he knew better than anyone, spectacularly attractive. She was short for an actress at 5-foot-4 with dark hair cut very short. She was smart and approachable. She was more welcoming than intimidating and didn't seem to be surrounded by a thick shell of ego. Ridge didn't think anything about others fantasizing about his wife. He was busy anyway. The only person who paid any attention to Brynn leaving the table for the small dance floor was Lincoln. He stayed close by, on the edge of the floor. Lincoln was an imposing chaperone.

Teddy Thermal had the next dance.

"Oh yeah, one for the book. I'm dancing with Brynn Powell. Someone better have a photo of this. Oh yeah, nobody will believe me unless I have a photo or video."

At their table, Ridge, Carl, Gerald and Ryan named new brews while sipping their Cherry Bomb Blondes from Davenport.

"Homely Hooker Hefeweizen," Ridge offered.

"Rabid Bat Bock might not be a big seller," Gerald said.

"How about Angry Animal Amber?" Ryan offered.

"Brynn Baby Ale," Carl said.

"I love that one," Ridge said. "I'm going to start that one when I get home. I may just open a place like this in Montana. Only beers and anything in a bun."

"Big Bitch Brown," Ridge said.

"Rushton Stinking Stout," Carl said.

"Rushton Dubbel Trouble," Gerald said.

"Big Pimp Pumpkin Spice Pilsner," Ryan contributed.

"Past Due Rent Pale Ale," added Ryan, now on a roll.

He quickly named a few more: "Undocumented Immigrant

Stout," "Marci Maximum Malt," and "Loose Lexi Lager."

The senator and Kim flitted around the bar doing "table touches" as they call it in the restaurant biz. He wasn't drinking himself, he just made it seem as though he was. Mostly he was listening and pitching his campaign in brief stops at each table.

"Remember us in the Iowa Caucuses. Be there for us on Feb. 1. We're asking for your support and we'll ask for your involvement in the process," the senator said to a large group at one of the 30-foot-long tables. "No matter what the weather is that night, we need you. We can do a lot together, but it starts here in Iowa."

Across the room, the beer name game continued.

"Bald Buckman Lager," Ryan said.

"Obnoxious Houseguest Hops," Carl said.

"First Lady Pass out Pale," Gerald said.

"Drunk POTUS Pilsner," Ridge said.

What they couldn't know was that at an adjoining table, a cellphone camera had been recording the entire session of craft beer christening. The young man doing the recording may have been apolitical … he claimed later he was … but he was an entrepreneur. When he offered the video and audio file to Traditions Network and the National Republican Party, the bidding began.

There were rumors about what the young man had pocketed. All parties in the auction denied their involvement. The guesses of the windfall to the young man ranged from $7,500 to nearly ten times that figure.

On the night the video was made, the senator's group was more interested in another social media blast.

"Hey look at this. Look what the president posted," Ryan Holton said, showing his phone to O'Malley and Carl.

The video was from The Expo. It showed spectators, several of them elderly and looking very distressed, their arms and legs dangling from wheelchairs being pushed to waiting ambulances by concerned EMTs. Several of the patients appeared to be unconscious as they were shown being transported out of the crowd at Street Corner Soapbox. In the background on the stage were Ridge and the senator. The video also had closeups of the senator speaking.

The social media video closed with ***"Hollywood Hack and Senator Hemp ... Always Out of Touch."***

"So now the guy is a drunk, a shitty president, *and* a movie critic," Ridge fumed. "Screw him. He must have seen Desperation Depot. I was only in it for 20 seconds when I was 23. I did suck in it."

The senator was more stricken than Ridge by the video. His concern wasn't about the optics of the incident. He shared his thoughts, saying, "Maybe I didn't pay enough attention to the people who were sick." He thanked Ridge and hugged Brynn. He told them they were welcome to join him anywhere, anytime.

"Are you leaving?" Ridge said. "You need to get Kim back to the hotel? Tell her we love her and best wishes for the baby."

"Yeah, I need to get her back. Thanks for everything today. You guys were great out there," the senator said, hugging Ridge.

He motioned for Carl to follow him away from the table.

"Carl, can you figure out if any of the people from today are seriously ill? Were any of them hospitalized?" Senator Buckman asked. "Kim and I are going to the hospital. No media. Let's use one of the SUVs, not Beatrice."

At 11:05 p.m., the black SUV with the darkened windows drove through downtown Des Moines to All Saints Hospital, the only Level One trauma center in Des Moines, and one of only two in the state. Ryan Holton drove the senator with Kassie Foster in the passenger seat. The senator and Kim rode quietly in the back seat. They entered through the emergency department. Senator Buckman introduced himself and asked about patients who had been transported from The Expo. He was told he would not be allowed to talk with patients unless they approved a visit from him. Besides, he didn't even have their names. It would be a major violation of federal patient privacy law to share their names, even with a U.S. Senator.

"I understand. We'll wait. Please ask if we can visit any or all of them," the senator said.

Twenty minutes later the senator and Kim were escorted by hospital security to the fifth-floor intensive care unit. Ryan and

Kassie waited in the emergency department. Senator Buckman was familiar with the look of this setting from his heart attack. He had an uneasy feeling around the lights, noise and bustle of the unit. This one was much busier than the one in Big River, Minn. He remembered being awake all night watching bad television, interrupted often by nursing staff and stressful alarms on the various machines. He recalled worrying about his future. At the time, the baby he was about to share with Kim was only a dream.

He went room by room meeting people who had been at the Expo. He talked quietly with each patient, asking how they felt and what happened. Family members took photos of the senator leaning over their loved one, holding hands with them.

"I am sorry this happened. It was just so hot today. I don't know, maybe we should have canceled," Buckman said to every patient he visited.

"No, Senator, this was a highlight of her year," said the daughter of 86-year-old Melvina "Mel" Mora. "Mom was a teacher for 53 years in elementary school here in Iowa. She wanted to meet you so badly. It was just one of those things. She has diabetes and she just got too hot."

"I will be there every time I can when you come to town," Mel said. "Maybe not outdoor events, though. I will be there in February for you, too. I hope to meet that baby, too."

"You are a sweetheart," the senator said, the darkness of his mood improving. "You call my campaign staff in Minnesota and we'll make sure you have a prime spot when we come to Iowa."

They hugged as he left the room. He kissed her on the cheek. He wrote a note to himself about Mel Mora.

He spent just more than an hour in the unit. He had his photo taken with the ICU staff working the third shift.

"I know very well how important you all are. People like yourselves saved my life last year. I admire you for all you do. Somebody send our campaign a photo and thank you for setting this up so Kim and I could come visit."

There was no mention of the senator's late-night hospital visit in the media. His staff didn't know. He didn't make the visit for attention. He made the visit because he was concerned and felt guilty about the appearance at the Expo in the record heat. The only notice of the visit were the photos loaded several days later to the campaign website by employees of the hospital.

As they drifted off back at the hotel, Kim said, "I don't care what Rushton says, you are a good man who would make a great president and will make an even better dad. I love you, Cue Ball."

The campaign of Pierce Buckman had absorbed fierce criticism from several fronts since midsummer. He was now considered a legitimate contender for the Iowa Caucuses. He was still written off as far too progressive to win a national election. For those reasons, he was the subject of criticism not only from Rushton, who wanted to stop any Buckman momentum before it moved from Iowa, but from his own party activists and big dollar donors who believed Mike Clarke and Karla Foster were much more viable and better positioned to beat Rushton in a general election.

Two people had died at the Iowa Agricultural Exposition. The video compiled by the National Republican Party and posted to social media made it look like everyone transported was saved only through the valiant efforts of medical teams. In reality, even a body temperature of 105 can be regulated fairly routinely and the suffering person usually recovers quickly.

It had been suggested that Buckman should have canceled the campaign event. He was being criticized for drawing too large a crowd on a day when most people with a lick of sense would have stayed home in the air conditioning. The candidate had second-guessed himself about the day. Karla Foster and Mike Clarke, the leading Democratic candidates in Iowa Caucus polling had both said they would have canceled or insisted the event be moved to an air-conditioned building. It was harshly suggested by Rushton's people the deaths were an indication Buckman lacked leadership.

On the morning after The Expo appearance, as he read newspaper coverage of the event, Buckman wasn't angry. He was hurt.

"What have we done? Are we responsible for these two deaths?" Buckman asked O'Malley.

O'Malley believed Buckman was about to break down.

"Senator, it was the hottest day ever in Iowa. It wouldn't have mattered what was going on ... if we were there or not ... people were likely to die. Do you know there were 213 deaths in the Midwest from heat-related illnesses yesterday? Two of them happened to be at The Expo when you were. There were five other deaths in Des Moines alone. All of the victims were at least 77 years old, all of them reported by the newspapers to be frail or already sick with chronic conditions. Two of them were on oxygen for COPD, one had an early stage of dementia, and the air conditioning went out. It was 126 degrees in that apartment. The woman didn't know what to do. It was a horrible day, and I'm sorry two people died when we were at The Expo. You were not responsible."

The Buckman campaign was rocked further several days after The Expo when the young man's video of the senator's staff naming beers first appeared on the morning news shows. The video had been purchased by the National Republican Party. It didn't matter the video was shot without the knowledge of the senator's staff or that the young man who shot the video was paid well for its release.

Traditions and Values Network neglected mentioning how the video was recorded or the fact that they had acquired the video from the White House itself. Maybe not directly from Rushton, but certainly indirectly on his behalf. For hours, TVN ran the video on almost a constant loop. The loop was interrupted only by outraged Republicans and conservatives talking about "insensitive and inappropriate" comments from the paid staff of a presidential candidate."

"I don't know we've seen anything so vile and repugnant from a presidential campaign in a very long time," said the pompous Lake Northwood, who was still following the Buckman campaign Iowa, looking for the most negative stories he could come up with. "The language ... bitch, whore, pimp ... horribly disrespectful references, is considered by many who have seen the video as inexcusable from a United States Senator.

"For a campaign which talks about being the voice of all people, this campaign showed a disregard for virtually all groups of the very people they are trying to attract as supporters. They disrespected women, poor people and minorities."

The fact that Northwood was a reporter, but was no longer worried about objectivity, changed how the Buckman campaign would react to him in the future.

"We will not talk with that son-of-a-bitch," Gerald O'Malley fumed.

The senator hadn't participated in the beer naming banter and wasn't on the video. That didn't stop Traditions from linking the senator personally to the video. The network mixed in video from earlier in the day at The Expo with its commentary on the video shot in the bar.

Buckman called Gerald, Carl and Ryan into a private meeting.

"I understand this was an outrageous violation of our privacy. Unfortunately, we probably would have reacted the same way Rushton's campaign staff did. We would have used video like this against them," the senator said. "I think this is really slimy politics but that is the way this is played now. I am not unhappy with you. You had spent a long day in the heat and were cooling off. You were having fun. But from now on, be aware this can happen and there are people out there who would think nothing about destroying us this way."

"Notice Traditions didn't use the references to POTUS or the First Lady. Those were some of the best names we came up with," Carl told the senator with a slight smile.

"I can think of a bunch more myself. I particularly like Bald Buckman Lager," the senator said, now in a lighter mood. "Don't worry about this too much. We'll get through it. Every day is an adventure."

CHAPTER 26

Owen Morrison Buckman

Kim Wakefield was the attentive blonde regularly seated in the third row on the center aisle of Professor Pierce Buckman's History of the Presidency (PoliSci 460) at Big River State University. Same place every class. The professor had noticed she listened to his sometimes rambling, gossipy stories about the often flawed, often troubled leaders of the free world. She laughed at the right places in his lectures. He was flattered when she would stop him after lectures to ask questions. He was her graduate advisor.

Buckman was in his mid-30s with a Ed.D and doing what he believed he was destined to do for the rest of his working life. He loved history and politics and especially where the two fields intersected. He enjoyed the interaction with young minds. He encouraged them to dissent from his opinions when he expressed them. There was something different, though, about Kim Wakefield.

Buckman was already owlish looking with shaved head and black-framed glasses. He wore sweaters and khakis most days with an occasional sport coat thrown in. He rarely wore socks, Kim had noticed, not even on days when the temperature didn't come close to the single digits below zero. When he did wear socks, they tended to be bright and themed, like with super heroes and cartoon characters.

About midway through the semester, Kim Wakefield stuck around after class. It was one of those northern Minnesota days when the blue sky and bright sunlight belied how the day felt. It was 15 degrees below zero at 1:30 p.m.

"Professor, it's about a trillion below zero. Aren't you cold with no socks?" she asked. "How about if I warm you up with coffee or hot chocolate? I'm buying."

The professor was not unfamiliar with the female form. He had been in long-term and short-term relationships, committed relationships, and casual flings. Never, though, with a student. Such relationships were taboo then and remain so today. In high school or middle school, relationships with students would get you fired with three years of jail tossed in for good measure, followed by permanent unemployable status as an educator.

Buckman had often told the story of the casual start to their relationship with a story teller's flair.

"Kim was wearing a hooded sweatshirt, a heavy parka, floppy hat. She had all these layers on. What could go wrong? We talked about FDR's final months and his full knowledge he would not survive his fourth term, but he was a war president and wanted to see it through. The country also wanted him to finish the war effort. When the war was over, he thought he would resign and turn the presidency over to Harry Truman, whom he barely knew personally.

"We talked for three hours in the coffee shop. She was funny and lively. She challenged me. I was really wired by all of the caffeine by the time we parted. It was odd leaving. Shake hands? Hug?"

"We just kind of said goodbye and walked away."

They were both smitten.

When the senator entered the birthing room after leaving for a few minutes for a break, he sensed the tension.

"What's going on?"

"Senator, we're concerned about the baby's vital signs … his respiration especially. We're going to take him immediately," the doctor said. "I think it would be better if you leave the room. We'll see you in a few minutes and your baby boy will be ready to meet you and Kim."

"Relax Cue Ball, we'll be fine," Kim said.

The senator asked with his typical naivete about women if

Kim was in pain.

"This kid probably has a melon like yours. Of course, I'm in pain. I'll be fine," she said. "Get out now. They are about to give me a scar. Love you."

The minutes were agonizing for the senator. Buckman had his head bowed. He grabbed Susan's hands. She had helped save his life once; maybe she could help in this situation. Maybe he thought he needed the good karma of his own lifesaver. He whispered a prayer.

After the "Amen," they sat quietly for a few more minutes.

"When did your relationship become more than professor and student?" Susan Lyon asked, breaking the silence and possibly avoiding the onset of panic she thought she detected in the senator's big, green eyes.

"It wasn't quick. I think we both understood the possible public and university reactions to a student-professor relationship," he said. "I finally just thought, 'she is an adult, she can do what she wants.' I hoped she would want me."

"Who was responsible for taking it further? Let me guess … Kim was," Carl said.

"No, it was pretty much mutual. She started calling me Cue Ball, like she did tonight. She does it a lot but usually not in front of others. I didn't care as long as she was spending time with me. I thought she was smart, funny and absolutely gorgeous," the senator said. "We started hanging out more. We were careful about being together in public. We started watching movies together and ordering food or I'd cook. I can cook you know."

"How long before … oh, you know … you became intimate?" Susan asked.

"Made love? Hooked up? Got lucky? Oh, whatever … Carl, this doesn't go in the book. Off (the record) right? Maybe the third or fourth night when we were hanging out in my apartment. We were drinking a little and watched a movie. Pot may have been a factor. It was very natural. It was just right there on the couch. Then in the bedroom. After that, we were inseparable."

"College towns are usually pretty liberal bastions. Even in

Big River, Minnesota. I was a DFL activist, had been a national convention delegate for Al Gore and was a known socialist-leaning crazy professor. Maybe people were just shocked I found someone as perfect and beautiful as Kim. Maybe they didn't believe I could be with her. Like it was some sort of optical illusion.

"We started going out in public and were together on campus. You know, no one ever said a word. I think people were just happy for us. It was just right. Our parents approved. That was enough for me."

A nurse came out of the room and asked the senator if he wanted to meet his son.

"He is going to the Neonatal Intensive Care Unit but everything looks good. Just precautionary. We want to watch his breathing. It's kind of labored," the nurse said.

"But he will be fine, right?" the senator asked.

"We believe he will be fine," the nurse said, making no assurances.

The senator gently hugged Kim, who was still groggy from pain relief during the C-section delivery.

"We have a baby boy," he said, again through tears. "You did fantastic."

They had decided he would be named Owen Morrison Buckman.

Kim and little Owen would spend several days in the hospital. The senator was spending hours at a time in the hospital. His parents were getting the townhouse ready for the new addition.

Minnesota Standard senior reporter Jason Holton, now commonly known as "Hoodie" for his choice of apparel, was shadowing the senator for a few days. Buckman was beginning to look like a viable, or at least possible contender in the Iowa Caucuses. The senator and Hoodie made a circuit of several of the large number of colleges in the immediate Twin Cities or within easy driving distance. His campaign was starting to recruit precinct captains and surrogates who would represent the senator at 1,681 precincts in Iowa.

"The goal is to have a captain or a representative in every one of them," the senator told Hoodie. "We need about everything

224

but we're spending less than everyone else because we can. We've put the entire campaign into Iowa. Win we go on, lose and I go back to the Senate or maybe back to a university with my family.

"We don't need as much money because we will outwork everyone else out there and we have a different message. We're pulling everyone to the left. We'll have money for television in the last month or so but we're relying on people who are getting the message and agree with our vision."

"How is Big O (Owen) doing?" Hoodie asked.

"Well, he has hair. He is terrific. He's out of the NICU most of the time now in the room with Kim."

The senator, still an educator at heart, went into a lesson plan he couldn't recall using when he was a professor.

"You know how neonatology became a specialty field? JFK and Jackie had a baby boy born while he was in office. Patrick Bouvier Kennedy. He was born prematurely by 5 1/2 weeks. He only lived 39 hours before he died.

"The baby weighed nearly 5 pounds even that early. Today, that baby would have a high survival rate because of the advancements of neonatal intensive care since then. The Kennedy baby ... no baby has been born to a sitting president since ... is now considered a milestone in the development of the care of sick babies."

Hoodie put the story away in a notebook for an extended profile he was writing about the senator.

CHAPTER 27

Montgomery Dumas Territory

The campaign, at O'Malley's urging, had given up the senator's idea of a "Full Grassley" visit to every county in Iowa before caucus night.

"We shouldn't waste our time in counties Republicans dominate even when the Republican candidates are pathetically unqualified, which they often are," O'Malley said.

"I didn't say we aren't going to any of those blood red counties. I just agreed that it doesn't make sense to go to all of them," the senator said. "How about a tour of colleges in northwest Iowa? I want to go to Montgomery Dumas country. We'll do a couple Biking with Buckmans up there."

"Senator, can I talk you out of it?" O'Malley asked.

"Nope. Listen, so far Rushton has done very little of what he promised during the campaign. We might get a few people to listen to us about improving schools, an infrastructure rebuild and public service in exchange for college or trade school tuition," the senator said. "Focus on college campuses."

"Sir, you are a Democrat. They will hate you no matter what you have to say," Gerald pressed.

"Who hates a guy on a bicycle ride?" the senator asked.

"Just don't pull out in front of any farm implements. They won't hesitate to hit you," O'Malley said. "And don't make us go to Shingles, Iowa. That is where Dumas actually lives. In a cave, I believe."

The Warehouse staff in the Twin Cities arranged a series of college events and two Biking with Buckmans. The itinerary called for stops at Storm Lake College, and colleges in Orange City, Sioux Center and LeMars.

Beatrice the Bus and a growing caravan of SUVs headed for Storm Lake. The bus had been signed by what Ryan Holton estimated to be 3,500 names. Many also wrote short messages of support. And there were more than a few "Fuck Buck," types of messages. Beatrice, though, was becoming increasingly unreliable, though at least the air conditioning still worked. In early September on the trip to northwest Iowa, the projected high temperature was 93 degrees, according to Teddy Thermal on Rapid Response Weather.

Only 1 hour, 20 minutes after leaving Des Moines, Beatrice was acting up again. The accelerator had a kind of dead spot, driver and campaign spokesman Curt Jaslow reported. He would push to a certain point on the accelerator and the engine would seem to flood.

Beatrice was drivable, Jaslow reported, "but we're going to be real late at this rate."

"Buckman time," Carl Lyon muttered.

They had an afternoon speaking engagement at Storm Lake College. They were more than an hour late when they arrived on the college campus.

"This should be interesting. Wonder if anyone will be there?" Carl mused.

"Maybe 20 people. That would be good," Gerald said.

There were 240 waiting. The advance people who set up the auditorium had counted them several times and were as surprised as O'Malley they had stayed listening to local Democrats, none of them elected to anything.

The senator, smiling as usual at the start of events, walked on stage and grabbed the young audience immediately.

"When you leave college, you will leave with a degree or multiple degrees. You will leave with satisfaction of your accomplishment. You will leave with friends and great memories. And, you will leave with something else ... you will leave with $30,000 to $100,000 in debt."

"Right? Think about that. That debt is yours. You re-elect this president, you may still be paying it down 10, 15 or even 20 years after graduation. If you go on to an advanced education, maybe medical school or law school, those numbers will skyrocket.

"Together, we can do something about this situation. Don't count on this president to do anything about it. He is too busy doing nothing. If I am elected president, we will offer an opportunity to earn college tuition through public service. First, what an honorable thing to do. Serving your country. It doesn't have to be military service, although it could be.

"It could also be service to the underserved, the disenfranchised, the disrespected, the forgotten segments of society who Republicans always want to leave behind.

"If I am elected, we won't leave anyone behind. The silent will have a voice. Can you imagine the power of a force of hundreds of thousands of our best and brightest young people going out across the country and the globe to make lives better for infants, children, the poor? Maybe you will work as a paraeducator in a school, a host in a National Park, or help build adequate housing or clean water systems in developing African nations. Maybe you will be involved in introducing wind power to new areas across the globe. Or maybe you will serve in the military to keep our country secure.

"Imagine the benefits of this service, not only to those being served, but to you personally. You are bound to become more engaged students, probably better students, and enter college with incredible experiences. It will be like a G.I. Bill for volunteerism. Service won't be required but why would you not want to serve in exchange for affordable education?

"This will only happen if as a country we make a change in the White House. Next February, you will have the chance to make a difference in your own life and in the lives of others. It may be raining, it may be snowing, you may not have a baby sitter. No excuses. Take the baby with you. Take an elderly person who can't drive themselves with you. By then you may not even have to attend. There may be a process to caucus remotely … from your own home or any computer. I'm asking for your support in the Iowa Caucuses.

"The path to a more compassionate nation, a nation that leaves no one behind, a nation willing to serve and sacrifice for the benefit of all, starts in Iowa."

The senator was getting wound up as the crowd did.

"Listen now, this is important," Buckman said, his hands up to regain the focus of the audience. "Our president would not like Storm Lake, Iowa. Do you know why?

"Too many foreigners," someone shouted, drawing laughter and applause.

"Blunt and true. Exactly. You may have noticed that the president and I have vastly different views on immigration. He wants to deport people who have come to this country for all the right reasons. They came for family and jobs. They are productive, tax-paying workers who purchase cars, homes, groceries and help drive our economy.

"I know you have a meat processing plant in Storm Lake. Did you see what happened in Tama when one of the president's raids failed miserably? He would have deported dozens of workers at a processing plant with an overzealous display of military force. On our own soil he had all the military toys out. I'm in the Senate and I didn't know we had all that hardware. He would have separated families. He would have separated children from their fathers. He would have deported people even with no criminal background at all. Had he been successful, Storm Lake might have been next."

"We can do things differently. We must do things differently as a nation. That is my promise. We will have a greater level of compassion. We will leave no one behind. We need your help on Iowa Caucus night."

It was the first time anyone on his campaign could remember his using his role in Tama at MegaPack as a political tool.

Buckman was not through with surprises. While voicing his support of foreign workers in the meat processing industry, he struck at industry owners for being neglectful environmentally.

"If I am elected, we will not allow the agricultural industry, including meat processing, to pollute our land, water or air.

Owners will be required to act responsibly or they will face the repercussions of their inaction. We will enforce environmental standards and not look the other way as this president has. We will be vigilant and we will prosecute offenders vigorously, no matter what excuse they believe they have. We will strengthen the EPA, not decimate it or threaten to eliminate the agency. Our message will always be, 'make good products the country and world needs, but don't pollute the Earth in the process.' We'll be watching the agricultural industry closely and will be working with the industry to promote practices protecting air, water and earth.

"I am pro-business but I am also pro-environment. We cannot be one without being both. We are being held accountable, and should be, for how we treat the Earth and how we leave it for our children and grandchildren and for the generations to follow."

The senator, sensing the enthusiasm of an audience made up primarily of students, their instructors and university staff, switched on that emotional, deliberate delivery that his campaign staff was hearing more often at campaign stops.

"The president doesn't agree with me. He calls me Senator Hemp, Senator Gladiola, Senator Tulip. That's fine. Flowers are beautiful. We are that kind of campaign. Everyone is welcome in this effort … white, black, brown, Asian, Hispanic, gay, straight, transgender, the underserved, the impoverished, the forgotten, the hidden, the voiceless, the disenfranchised, students, professors … everyone has a place in this effort. This is a pink revolution of inclusiveness. That's why I don't care what the president, the Divider-in-Chief of this country, the president who wants to deport, disregard and divide, thinks about our campaign.

"This isn't just a campaign, it is a collection of people who want to make a difference. So, I'm going to ask for your help. Today I want you to commit to participate on February 1 when the Iowa Caucuses are held. We want you to be part of our pink revolution. Our campaign is made up of many who not only want a better life, they expect it, and if I am elected, they will demand a better life.

"My name is Pierce Buckman and I am running for president."

The crowd was standing and applauding as the excited Senator, earning the Orator from Owatonna label on this day, in ruby red northwest Iowa of all places, pressed forward to the rope and stanchions in front of the stage. He stepped off the stage and stopped at every person on the other side.

Along the rope line was a young man wearing a Storm Lake College football cap. He was dressed in a camo jacket, which certainly wasn't unusual in Iowa in the fall. He didn't say anything. He reached from behind someone in front of him to shake hands with the senator.

From Storm Lake, Beatrice was directed toward Orange City, where the senator was scheduled to speak at 7 p.m. in an auditorium there, meet with Democrats at a house party, and spend the night. Senator Buckman followed the same themes of the speech at Storm Lake College. The crowd was smaller and younger.

The next morning, after a breakfast with supporters at a local diner, a Bike with Buckman 13-mile ride from Orange City to Sioux Center was planned. No one knew if there would be only campaign staff on the ride, or if a few people would actually show up.

"Ryan, what is this restaurant we are looking for?" asked the senator, who was sitting up front in Beatrice's passenger seat.

"You'll know it when you see it," Ryan said with a chuckle.

"How is that poss…" the senator asked, his question cut mid-sentence when he saw the sign. He broke out in laughter.

The parking lot of Hermosos Tulipanes was jammed with pickup trucks and cars. Beatrice would have to be parked on a side street.

"Beautiful Tulips. My deep respect for our schedulers. I love their research, and sense of humor, on this one," the senator said.

Dressed in a jogging suit, tennis shoes and a Buckman for President cap, the senator was ready for the bike ride from

Orange City to Sioux Center after the breakfast event. Gerald O'Malley and the political staff in the Warehouse in the Twin Cities thought this trip to Northwest Iowa was a waste of time and resources. The upbeat Buckman had insisted that he would find common ground with some people even in the most Republican towns and counties in all of Iowa.

They had compromised. Buckman gave up the idea of visiting all 99 counties in Iowa prior to caucus night voting if he was allowed to make a trip to northwest Iowa and another to southwest Iowa. Both areas were Republican strongholds.

O'Malley had informed Ryan of the restaurant stop, saying, "maybe there will at least be a friendly crowd in a place called Beautiful Tulips."

The senator sat down at a table where a place had been reserved for him with two leaders in the Hispanic community, a prominent area farmer and two women who were active in the Sioux County Democratic Party. Or maybe they were the entire Democratic Party in Sioux County.

"Good morning, folks, what's on the menu? I'm Pierce, or I'm sometimes called Senator Tulip by the president. We thought this was a good place for me," the senator said, breaking up the table.

Buckman talked about expediting citizenship for undocumented immigrants if they were productive and didn't commit a crime.

"The president wants to build a wall. We want to build families. He wants to deport people and break up families. We want them to stay and contribute to the economy. His immigration policies are inhumane and unacceptable. Whenever possible, I want to keep families together, but if you commit a felony crime, I also will advocate for deportation. Where we differ is on the issue of rounding up people who came to this country for better opportunities for themselves and their families. They are productive workers who pay taxes, buy homes and cars and make products for not only our country, but globally.

"I know you have experienced the growth of the Hispanic population in Northwest Iowa. The issue should not divide us. It should be an issue where we can find a sensible solution benefiting our economy and benefiting us as the diverse country we have always been. It is not only people from Mexico, Cuba, Central America, South America who are coming to the United States for a better life. It is Europeans, also Africans and … and, it is our rich history as a nation."

CHAPTER 28

27 Misunderstood Words

"A well regulated Militia, being necessary to the security of a free State, the right of the people to keep and bear Arms, shall not be infringed."

The Second Amendment to the Constitution of the United States, ratified with the rest of the Bill of Rights amendments on Dec. 15, 1791, was written in only 27 words. As amendments to the Constitution go, the Second is one of the shortest. Only the Eighth, 16 words, the "cruel and unusual punishment" amendment, and the Ninth with 21 words were written more tightly.

Most Americans it seems, don't care what the Ninth says or does. When was the last time someone said, "what about that Ninth Amendment?" in between sips of a pitcher of beer?

The Second though, everyone believes they understand. To gun owners, it is perfectly constructed and crystal clear in its intent: "The right of the people to keep and bear Arms, shall not be infringed."

But it isn't perfect. For one thing, well-regulated should be hyphenated. And what did founders mean by "well-regulated" anyway? "Well-regulated" would be acceptable to most people. Gun advocates somehow seem to read those words as never regulated. And why did the smart guys who wrote the Bill of Rights capitalize the M in militia, the S in state and the A in arms?

That's the thing about the Second Amendment. It may be only 27 words, but millions of words have been written and spoken about it since. The Second may be one of the most analyzed amendments. Also, one of the most adjudicated and interpreted.

People like Jericho believe the Second Amendment is untouchably clear. It is all right there; the right to keep and bear Arms cannot be infringed. They believe it is that simple. It is not. Weapons available in 1791 were incredibly primitive compared to the array of killing hardware available now. At that time, the weapons were single shot, short-ranged and not very accurate. They could be five-feet long, weigh 10 pounds or more, have an effective range of maybe 75 yards, or three-quarters of the length of a football field, and were loaded by muzzle.

 In the gun cabinet in Jericho's stepfather's garage were weapons like the semi-auto pistol with limited range, maybe half the length of a football field, but with the power of a round drum loaded with as many as 72 9-millimeter bullets. A semi-auto pistol might weigh less than a pound fully loaded. Jericho had several 32-round clips. Jericho also had access to two gas-operated semi-auto rifles constructed with lightweight aluminum and synthetics. Range of the semi-auto rifles is nearly six football fields and they can be made more lethal with the repetitive force of 10-, 20-, and 30-round magazines or clips.

Also, in the gun cabinet were assorted other pistols and shotguns. The only gun considered "off limits" for Jericho was a sawed-off shotgun. Jericho had shot it, though, and liked the way it felt and shot.

Three days before Jericho's mission, he went to the house of his mother and stepfather and removed two semi-automatic pistols, the two semi-auto rifles, two other pistols and the sawed-off shotgun. He also removed several clips and boxes of ammunition. He put them under the tarp in the bed of the old but reliable truck he had purchased with Magda. The bed was covered by an aluminum topper.

Magda still didn't understand exactly where they were going or what their plan was. She didn't understand "The Project" until she and Jericho were ready to leave their farm house on a Thursday afternoon in early November. It was cold and dark earlier after the change to Central Standard Time.

Jericho, trusting his girlfriend's discretion and loyalty, shared his plans.

"Lots of people have done terrorist acts. They have used airplanes, bombs, guns, trucks, cars … anything to make people afraid. We're going to do something that will shake up the entire country and create chaos for weeks or years. And we're going to make a point. We'll make the gun grabbers back off. People will be so scared they will make guns more legal, not less. Everyone will be afraid to go anywhere without protection."

Jericho had considered several options. He thought about driving his truck into a Bike with Buckman event. In seconds, he could kill or injure dozens of people, including the senator. He thought about a bombing. He thought about assassinating just Buckman, whom he had stalked since his announcement he would be a candidate for president. Jericho had attended seven Buckman events in various disguises, including prominent and realistic looking fake tattoos.

"I knew I wanted to use guns," Jericho explained to Magda. "That is the entire point. Fucking Buckman is a gun grabber. He has even favored getting rid of the Second Amendment and rewriting it. He and the others will do what they can to restrict us from guns. They always think they can get away with changing the Second Amendment. The National Gun Lobby won't stop people like Buckman. They aren't tough enough.

"You and I will stop it by stopping Buckman."

Jericho said he had a simple plan. He and Magda would drive to Iowa. Buckman was scheduled to participate in a rally of Young Iowa Democrats at Crossroads State University. Jericho had been following the senator's schedule of events on the campaign's website. He would be at Crossroads State on Nov. 5. It was the Crossroads State homecoming game with a crowd of 71,000 expected. The Young Iowa Democrats had invited the local and state candidates to a tailgate party and rally in a parking lot at Explorers Stadium. Buckman was the only one of the three leading Democratic presidential candidates who had committed to attend.

There would be limited security. It was early in the Iowa Caucuses campaign.

Jericho and Magda would stay the night before and be in line when the parking lots opened to tailgaters seven hours before the 11:05 a.m. kickoff. The early start of the game would be perfect for the plan. If they pulled it off, they would disrupt the remaining schedule of games for the day and maybe for months or years into the future. Other colleges would fear the attack at Crossroads State was part of a coordinated effort.

Jericho dreamed others would follow his example and show just how vulnerable all these colleges campuses were on game days. If one motivated activist could pull this off, what could 50 scattered across the country do with a truck, a car, guns or a bomb?

Jericho's plan was to appear to be "Joe College" like any other college football fan. He would wear his Crossroads State University cap and hooded sweatshirt. In the covered bed of the truck with the weapons were two bicycles, two backpacks, and a small gas grill, cooler and plates and utensils. In the hours before the Young Iowa Democrats tailgate event, Jericho and Magda would fit in as others filled up the parking lots with their trucks, RVs and cars. Thousands of fans would set up their tents, grills and generators to power big screen televisions and sound systems. Jericho knew exactly where the Young Iowa Democrats were planning their party in two long party tents. He knew that in addition to Buckman, liberal U.S. Senator Lansing Landon, Buckman's friend and supporter from Iowa, and Congressman Marion Jackson, whom Jericho had heard offer his support of Buckman in Davenport, were also scheduled to join Buckman at the tailgate party.

Jericho and Magda would tailgate in a prime spot close to the Young Iowa Democrats event, he said. They had burgers and hot dogs and a couple of bag chairs they bought before their weekend at Gun Fest. They would not draw any attention and they would stop over at the open-to-the-public rally after they ate. When the time was right, Jericho would pull out his backpack and ride his bike closer to the target. Magda would put on her backpack. A digital video camera was all she was carrying inside. There was little chance they could get their plan past the security checkpoints at the stadium. In the parking lots though, neither the backpacks nor the bikes would attract any attention. Crossroads State and other colleges outsource the security and parking lot detail on game days. The companies providing the security often sign on college students to direct vehicles to parking, check bags at the stadium gates and process tickets. Their primary job was to move traffic effectively and efficiently and get everyone into the stadium before kickoff.

Bikes weren't unusual outside of college football stadiums. Ticket scalpers who moved tickets used bikes at remote parking lots to find and sell the tickets.

Jericho had researched online how to possibly poison the food and drink of the Young Iowa Democrats event. His choice would be carfentanil, a horrifically potent opioid. Even the dust of the stuff could kill. So could direct contact. Just a small amount mixed into the food at the rally might kill the people he was targeting. The problem he considered was that was he wouldn't know the source of the food and drink. He would have to dump the drug into the food himself. He had no idea what would be served. If he pulled it off, though, he might escape.

To make the point he wanted to make and orchestrate the chaos he envisioned, it had to be an assassination of Buckman and mass shooting. The weapons Buckman and others like him wanted to take away would be Jericho's choice. He understood he was then unlikely to survive. Most of the security available would be unarmed college kids. Some of them, somewhat ironically, would be international students often stereotyped as more likely to be associated with what Jericho was planning. They wouldn't be armed, but campus police, city police and state troopers would all be close by on foot, in ATV vehicles, or on bikes. They would be armed. Jericho knew he would only have a couple of minutes, if that, before any of those officers arrived on the scene.

Jericho kept telling Magda, "No one has done anything like this. This will shake up the entire country."

They lit the small gas grill and cooked their hot dogs and hamburgers. They had a bag of chips and sodas in the cooler. They appeared to be just two young Crossroads State Explorers football fans tailgating with thousands of others. They were able to park about 200 feet from the rally site of the Young Iowa Democrats, who were already drinking beer and having a buffet brunch at 9 a.m. The guests of honor – two U.S. Senators, one of them a possible president, plus a congressman – were expected to arrive at 9:45 separately in golf carts.

CHAPTER 29

Terror at Crossroads State

The "Project" was working as Jericho had planned. The plan had become an obsession. He studied it and revised it numerous times over the past few months.

It was a gorgeous November morning with bluebird skies and a predicted afternoon high temperature of 53 degrees. About 1,000 people were expected at the Young Democrats event.

Jericho and Magda had left their farm house in northeast Minnesota on Thursday. They camped on Thursday night and made a few stops on Friday. That night they stopped for two hours to nap at a rest stop. There was no problem parking close to the three large tents set up in the parking lot for the Young Democrats rally. At 7 a.m., nearly three hours before the special guests were expected to speak, Jericho and Magda were waved directly through by the rental parking attendants. He had a parking pass he had purchased online for the right section.

Jericho casually wandered over to the rally tents. The special guests – U.S. Senator Lansing Landon of Iowa, Congressman Marion Jackson and U.S. Senator and presidential candidate Pierce Buckman of Minnesota – had not yet arrived.

Jericho asked when the featured guests were expected.

From their bag chairs, Jericho and Magda watched dozens of people begin to arrive at the rally. It was a mixed crowd of young, enthusiastic party faithful, families with kids decked out in Crossroads State football clothes, young and older. They saw the golf carts approaching carrying Senator Landon and

Congressman Jackson. They were greeted with applause. It was a casual, carefree gathering of left-leaning activists and others, most appearing to Jericho to be college students who showed up for free lunch and beer.

Jericho had done nothing to draw attention to himself. Magda had been instructed by Jericho to stay on the periphery and be ready to record video.

Jericho was not wearing body armor. He believed the protection might be obvious under his sweatshirt.

His primary target was late. Jericho knew that was not unusual for the Buckman campaign.

Buckman and his Iowa staff, such as it was, were stalled.

Three miles away from the rally and already 20 minutes late, the aged motorhome was sputtering again. Ryan Holton was at the wheel in heavy traffic of cars and trucks headed to the game.

"Ryan, are we walking again?" Senator Buckman yelled from the back.

"Sir … I think we are. Sorry. Right now, I'm just trying to get us off the road and out of traffic," Ryan said.

Jericho was concerned his primary target was not going to get to the rally. Maybe Buckman had canceled.

"Now Magda. We're going ahead. Now," Jericho said. "I love you. You are the best thing that ever happened in my life."

"I love you. If you can, walk away," Magda said.

The senator, and Carl and Susan Lyon were off Beatrice intending to walk and jog the rest of the way to the rally. Ryan had gotten Beatrice off to a side street.

Jericho didn't use the bike. He casually walked toward the rally tents. He stopped and pulled off his backpack. He was close enough for accuracy with the semi-auto pistol. Out of his backpack he pulled a device called a pellet grenade. The grenade was packed with 125 rubber pellets. The device would explode and send the plastic shrapnel from the outer core and the rubber pellets into whatever was in their path. It was a less-than-lethal device intended to confuse and incapacitate victims. There were two armed county sheriff deputies in the tent.

The senator was still a mile away from the rally, slowed by fans headed to the game. When they recognized him, he smiled and talked and shook hands.

"Carl, we are going to be really late," the senator said.

"Sir, what else is new?"

Jericho pulled the pin on the pellet device and tossed it into the crowd at the rally. Seconds later, he pulled a semi-auto assault pistol.

The pellet grenade served its intended purpose. It exploded not with an overpowering noise or concussion, but the tiny rubber pellets created confusion.

Magda was already recording. There were screams. People were injured.

Jericho discharged the pistol. He didn't wait for his intended target. His new primary targets were Landon and Jackson. One of the shots struck Landon on the right temple. Jackson was shot in the chest. Two more shots also struck Landon, both in the chest.

Jericho discharged the rest of the bullets from the pistol indiscriminately. He pulled out a second assault pistol and unloaded. He was able to change magazines and fire the second assault pistol again. This had taken no longer than 30 seconds.

One of the deputies drew his weapon and fired back. The first shot missed Jericho. A second did not, striking him in the abdomen. The other deputy was down. Jericho no longer had a weapon with ammunition. The deputy who had fired, fired four more rounds at Jericho. He was dead. The other sheriff's deputy had been mortally wounded but also managed to fire back at Jericho. One of his shots also struck Jericho.

Senator Pierce Buckman was still trying to get to the rally.

Within seconds, a stream of police vehicles and ambulances sped past Buckman and his staff. In the heavy traffic, the vehicles drove on the wide sidewalks, their drivers desperately looking for ways to get through the pedestrian and vehicle traffic headed to the game.

Two of the police vehicles had been assigned to find Senator Buckman. There were unconfirmed reports the senator had not been at the event as scheduled. He had to be somewhere. A university officer was the first to find him. He pulled his squad onto the sidewalk and with his weapon drawn, pushed the senator into a bar and grill. The door was locked behind them. The 15 people in the bar getting lubricated before heading to kickoff were not allowed to leave.

The tense university officer asked everyone in the bar to stand with their hands on the bar. He still had his sidearm in his hand and was prepared to shoot.

"Senator, there has been a mass shooting at a political tailgate party. I think you were supposed to be at a rally. Is that correct?" the officer asked, still holding his weapon in front of him.

"Yes. What happened?" the senator asked.

"Too early to know exactly. Shots were fired and exchanged. We believe there have been fatalities. Unconfirmed."

A black SUV pulled up in front of the bar. Two men in suits with earpieces pounded on the door. The university officer unlocked it, never turning his back on the bar crowd.

"Senator, we are leaving immediately for your campaign headquarters in Des Moines. We need to get you to a secure location," said one of the suited guys, who identified himself as a special agent of the FBI. "Just the senator, and we are leaving now."

"What's happened?" the senator asked again.

"There has been an assassination attempt. We're not sure if it was successful. Others were shot. There are fatalities," the same agent said.

The senator didn't need more information. He understood he would have been a target also had their transportation not failed again.

"Oh God, no … Senator Landon, Congressman Jackson?" the senator asked.

"Yes sir. Both were reportedly targeted," the agent said.

Buckman, feeling very alone in the back of the SUV headed to Des Moines, had tears rolling down his cheeks.

The football teams were already on the field when the shooting started. They were immediately raced into the tunnels leaving the stadium and leaving sight should there be other shooters.

An ominous announcement was made to the thousands in the stadium awaiting kickoff.

"There has been an incident on campus today. The game has been postponed. Umm...We are going to ask fans to clear the stadium through the south, east and west entrances. The north exits will be closed. Please be patient. There may be long delays before you are able to leave campus."

"We are asking for your patience and cooperation. We do not believe there is a risk to the stadium. Again, please leave through south, east and west entrances."

A further announcement minutes later said, *To avoid traffic congestion, you may stay in the stadium. The incident is believed to be over."*

On the giant screens in Explorers Stadium, the live news coverage was constant. It was the same across every college football stadium in the country. Fans lingered to watch the coverage from Crossroads State. Each minute of coverage seemed to calm fears there was a further threat.

Traditions and Values Network ran coverage under a banner of "Breaking News: College Football Terrorism."

Another 24/7 news network used the banner "Terrorism at Tailgate Party." Not exactly accurate because of the political nature of this particular tailgate event, but certainly threatening enough to frighten anyone who had ever attended a large tailgate party.

The news anchor at 3N was the first to suggest the assassination was the result of "a single actor" or "rogue terrorist." One of the terrorism experts brought into the 3N studio for analysis termed the attack a "a lone wolf act by a highly motivated person."

"What we are going to show now is disturbing," the weekend anchorwoman reported. "This video was posted minutes after the mass shooting at Crossroads State University in Iowa. The video suggests that the shooter, who has not yet been identified, may not have acted entirely alone. We have not confirmed the source of this video."

The video showed the chaos of the moment when the pellet device was tossed by Jericho. Quickly, there were pops of gunfire. Magda had focused mostly on the rally and captured the last breaths of several of the victims. She also recorded the exchange between the county deputies and Jericho taking a deputy's life. She had video of Jericho falling and the ensuing shots.

At the National University Union headquarters in St. Louis, the chief executive made the decision to ask all universities to postpone scheduled football games. No one from administration at Crossroads State University could assure the chief executive that this incident was not part of a larger, coordinated threat against college football.

Games had kicked off at 11 a.m. (CST) and noon (EST) but they were all halted. Not one point had been scored in any college game.

The scene of the rally and Jericho's mass shooting was chaotic. Standing close to the tents before a perimeter was established, Magda was still using her camera to record the rush of law enforcement officers, paramedics and bystanders who were doing what they could to assist. She had already posted videos to social media when two city police officers noticed her and approached with sidearms drawn. She was searched and asked if she knew the shooter.

"Jericho Adams Brooks is my boyfriend," she confessed.

She was cuffed and taken away.

Searching Jericho's bag was a mistake. He had carfentanil somehow purchased online in the bag. There was enough found to kill dozens more. A university security officer made the mistake of opening the bag and finding the tiny grains. He went into respiratory failure and collapsed. A quick-reacting paramedic was one of the heroes of the day. She reversed the effect of the still unidentified drug with injections of Naloxone. One shot wasn't enough. It took five injections from three paramedics to save the life of the officer. A perimeter inside the perimeter was established around the backpack until specialists in drug identification and mitigation joined the dozens of other university, county, state and federal officers already at the site.

Officers who first talked with Magda were the first to learn the shooter's identity.

She shared other information as she was transported to an undisclosed county jail. She shared their address, the street and town address of Jericho's mother and stepfather, his age (23), his possible motivation (gun rights) and additional details.

Public information officers for the county, university and city police briefed the media for the first time approximately 90 minutes after the shooting during a news conference in a Crossroads State athletic department building. Details were sparse. They knew more than they would share in the first briefing. They explained it was an active investigation and would be for some time. They did not share the shooter's name, the weapons of choice and said only "there had been fatalities."

On social media platforms, Jericho Adams Brooks was being named as the shooter. His friends in the gun rights world identified him and the weapons involved. They were especially interested, bordering on excitement, with the pellet grenade.

"If you want to have any chance to escape you got to distract anyone who might shoot back," said a poster identifying himself as "Jericho's Team." "RIP Jericho Adams Brooks. No Compromise."

"Are you fucking kidding me Jericho's Team. People died," responded someone with what appeared to be a fake social media page. "Buckman survived. Ban assault weapons."

CHAPTER 30
Manifesto

Only 52 minutes following the assassination of a U.S. Senator and a congressman, and the deaths of 12 others and injuries to 16 at the Young Democrats Get Out The Vote rally, members of a combined task force arrived at the farm house shared by Jericho Adams Brooks and Marin Anne Gabbard and at the homes of their parents and step-parents.

In constant contact with the FBI in the Twin Cities and Duluth and Homeland Security, the joint force of county, state and local officers arrived at the locations with the responsibility to close down access to the sites and create wide perimeters in advance of the arrival of federal authorities. The joint task force arrived with the full inventory of response vehicles, including armed carriers, bomb robots, drones and dozens of officers in full protective gear and weaponry.

It would be a couple more hours before federal officers arrived. By then, Jericho and Marin's parents had already been transported from their homes surrounded by officers. Startled residents were evacuated from the neighborhood around the homes of the Jericho's parents. The perimeter around the farm home was established at half a mile.

No one knew what to expect from the three sites the joint task force raided. They didn't know if Jericho Adams Brooks and Marin Anne Gabbard, who had survived but was now secured in Des Moines, had co-conspirators or had rigged the sites with explosives or some other methods to create mass casualties.

When federal officers arrived at the three sites, they first used the drones and robots for surveillance inside the structures. The FBI special agents, part of a terrorism task force deployed from the Twin Cities, entered with precision. They didn't lose sight of their responsibility. They searched first for any risks and then for evidence related to the attack on the rally more than 400 miles away.

It didn't take long to find the floor-to-ceiling gun cabinet in the garage of the house Jericho used to live in with his mother and stepfather. His mother and stepfather expressed their regret that Jericho was involved. His mother was sobbing as questioning continued about Jericho's motivation. His stepfather, physically and mentally abusive throughout his relationship with Jericho, suggested a search of Jericho's room and computer. Those were basic tasks rising to the top of investigations. Jericho's mother and stepfather turned over their mobile phones. Computers were carried out. A cyber FBI team took down Jericho and Magda's social media pages.

Michael Munger provided access to the gun cabinet. In the cabinet was a folded document of pages of bold, italic print written on a computer. On the outside was a handwritten message … A Manifesto of Mayhem.

Written Nov. 1
By Jericho and Magda (Marin),

If you are reading this I have probly been successful. May be greatly. Walls came tumbling down and Jericho Adams Brooks was responsable. The world is a better place though I probly amd not around to enjoy it. Peoples who believe in the Second Amendment rights can thank me for my service. OK with me if I am gone. This was more important than me or my pathetical existance.

Senator Pansy … I like when the Presideant calls him that. So perfect. The Pansy could not be elected presideant. Think we solved that. He was the worst kind of gun grabber. Liberal who probly never shot a gun in his life. He was an enemy to everyone who beleeves in a right to own guns. He said he would make guns and shooting so expensive people wouldn't shoot. Moron.

People will always have guns and will allways have money to shoot them. People still by cigarettes don't they.

Since the day said he would run for preisdeant I started planning how to end the campaign. I knowed he would destroy our rights under the Second Amendment of the Constitution. Maybe Rushton would beat him. Maybe not. I diddn't want to take that chance. The country could not be in Senator Pansy's hands. He would do everything to weaken our right to bare arms.

I called this "The Project" because others in the past have made mistakes in there plan by talking about it to much before. Dylan Kleebold and Eric Harris, Timothy McVay and Dylan Roof couldn't shut the fuck up. They did stupid thins like take selfies with guns and they told their plans to different people they bearly knew. The government can pick up on anything like that. You won't see shit about what I planned by myself until its over. All that matters is results. Ask Buckman if my plan was good. Thats a good one. Wait. He is dead. Don't try to ask him. I dint buy guns. I had the guns already. I dint register the guns. I already had them. I had never been arrested, Not even a traffic stop. I was in no one;s system. Only Magda, who u probly lerned about by now, knew what was up.

You may wonder about some things.

Why Buckman? Simple. Because he was the biggest threat to fun owners. He would have done everything to take away our rights. He would have been the Gungrabber in Chief. Let's face it, he could maybe beat Rushton. If I hadn't done this someone else would have. I wanted it to be me. And he was out in the open a lot. I shook hands with him several times at different events in Iowa. I was at a lot of places when was talking his gun crap. He was an anti-gun radical. He dint have security. He refused it. I usually weared some stupid disguise at each event. Thought about just doing it at The Expo in Iowa but I though there would be a better chance somewhere else. I was a few feet away that day. Who do they think killed the champion stear that day at Expo? Look at photos. I'm the one with thet emoji Pile of Poop t-shirt. That is how clouse I was that day. I could have taken him out any time. I could have got him on the first bike ride in Davenport. I was right there. I choosed the time to create the most chaos. That was the point. Create so much fear everyone woud carry guns and no one would be trying to take guns from us.

Why at a football game? He was supposed to be there and college football games from what I seen dint have very good security. I checked it out earlier. Millions of people go to these stupid games across the country every Saturday without thinking they could be easy targets. The Young Assholes from the Crossroads State Democrats and Gun Grabbers had a big rally planned I read about. Buckman was there. I decided to take all I could get. The game starts at 11. By 11:15 every game in the country will be posotponed. It will be beautiful. People will be running over each other panic to get away from those stadiums. Maybe for several weeks there won't be games.

Americans will be terrified instently. There great fall tradition turned upside down. There will be momentus terror. No one will attend a game for a long time without thinking about the massacred at Crossroads State University. People will want to be armed in all public places. Everyone will carry and the people who want to destroy guns will lose. Not a school, not a movie theater, not like that lowlife Dylan Roof in a church. A football game. By the way, when the liberal media picks this up my middle name is Adams ... with an s ... Media will want to know. They will always call me Jericho Adams Brooks. That is what they do when this happens. I earned all three of my names in the history book. Like John Wilkes Booth, Lee Harvey, whatever. This was an assassination and a mass terrorism event comibined. Oh, call it whatever you want. I don't give a shit ... I'm probably gone. It will be historic. I could have driven over people with a truck or built a bomb or somehow got inside the game with a semi-auto. Could have been done and I know how but I decided against it. I might have gotten stopped. I wanted to do something I knew would be successfully. I wanted to make a point and I sure as hell did, didn't I?

Who knew? Magda and me. That;s it. I only feel bad because I finally had someone who loved me and understood me. We had great times. She understood I might not get away. I didn't figure

250

I would. Hope someone looked carefully at my back pack. I had enough carfentanil to kill a herd of elephants. For you media idiots, it's a Parade of Elephants. (I may not have even been shot. Might of just taken the 'serial killer' myself. Thought about blowing a little dust around the rally). Hope the law was very cfcareful around that shit after the mayhem. The dust of carf will kill you if you breath it in. Police have all sorts of weapons. I approve and admire them. They weren;t my target. Sorry if I got any of them. My bad. I could have killed the young radicals with the serial killer dust. I was prepared to do that.

Let me tell you that until I met Magda, my life was shit. I got beat up or bullyed about every other day at school and sometimes it was a doublehitter. I'd get beat up at school and again at home by my asshole step father. What an ass that guy is. I didn't have many friends other than Magda and the gunners I hung out with. I was teased about every day for being weird. I had thoughts about leaving my shitty life permanently since I was about 12. I should have just shot my asshole step father instead. I could have shot im with his own sawed off 12 gauge. Magda understood this was important to people wyo believe in the right to bear arms. When we went to Gun Fest for the weekend in summer, it was the greatest time of my life. Magda was with me. I was still deciding about Buckman then. Gun Fest was so exciting. People like me were there and we were considered normal for the first time for some of us. When I started a chant of No Compromise and dozens of people started chanting to, it was the greatest momen of my life. I was finaly excepted by people. I wanted to kill Buckman for all these great people. And like I say my life was shit anyway other than Magda.

By now you liberal media assholes who support gun control have probably started posting this letter or portions of it even before you get this deep in the letter. Maybe the FBI or whomever released it when they raided my mom's place or our farm house. The liberal reporters are puppets for the gun grabbers and are pretty ignorant. You are going to analyze and critique this letter. You'll point out all of the grammatical errors and how disjointed this document is. You'll put panels of pseudo psychological experts on the air to talk about my mental health. They will talk about my dissociative disorder and my extreme depression and label me as a sociopath. You'll call this letter chilling and disturbing. The rent-an-expert psychoanalysis will be laughable. You won't be able to stereotype me because I'm a new type of mass murderer ... someone willing to die for cause can create a lot of mayhem. If you don't understand anything else about me, understand that. I was willing to die for a cause so I could pretty much accomplish anything. The discussion will go on for days. Eventually, the discussion will turn to how someone like me had a semi-auto carbine, assault pistol and a sawed-off 12 gauge. Easy. They were my weapons, or at least they belonged to my ass wipe step father. People like Buckman will continue trying to grab guns from people like me. It will never, ever happen. We're stronger and more motivated than the gun Nazis.

By the way, your analysis will be way off. I didn't throw cats off train bridges. I didn't skin them and put them in the freezer. I didn't hire out as a clown at parties and kidnap and rape the kiddos. I always scored well in standardized testing. No one could figure me out. Don't try. There is more than one of me. There is the loving boyfriend who was well-read and believed in a cause. And there is my personality capable of what happened. By the way, I put the grammatical errors in this deliberately. Just for kicks, thinking about how stupid the analysis of the fake psychiatrists would sound. Wish I was there to hear the pitiful attempt at analysis of how twisted I am. If you got this far, maybe you aren't as stupid as I believe you are. One more thing. I'll be a good guy and save you morons a step. When you report on this, it's 1,806 words.

I just want to close by asking that you take it easy on Magda. She had very little to do with this. Although there may be video. I love her and hope she truly understands the right, moral and just act at Crossroads State.

NO COMPROMISE! NOT EVER!

Jericho Adams Brooks

The suggestion of carfentanil in the manifesto of Jericho Adams Brooks and the officer who found the drug in Brooks' backpack instantly elevated and slowed the investigations of the houses. Both home investigations were suspended. Jericho's mother and stepfather were still alive. Their home would not need the scrutiny of the farm house where Jericho and Magda had been living.

The farm house investigation was abandoned following discovery of the manifesto. Any contact with even a minute amount of carfentanil, by skin or through respiration, could be deadly. Carfentanil is 100 times as potent as the same amount of fentanyl and 10,000 times as potent as a similar amount of morphine. The FBI investigators inside the farm house were not wearing personal protective equipment. No one would enter the house again for hours. Not until the FBI's Hazardous Evidence Response Team (HERT) from the field office in Brooklyn, Minnesota, could be deployed, along with bomb and drug-detecting canine teams.

Every surface would have to decontaminated. Every piece of furniture would have to be handled by another specialized team. There would also have to be an investigation and mitigation of possible hazards in the barn a few hundred feet from the house.

It would have been easier to just destroy both structures but also extremely dangerous should there be explosives or toxic, airborne particles of carfentanil carried by any wind or draft created by demolition activity. Considering the contents of the letter, there were any number of possible hazards on the sites.

Marin Anne Gabbard, aka Magda, gave up her phone, which had the minutes of video footage of the assassination and massacre. The video was criminal evidence. It had been taken down from Magda's social media pages but not before it had been viewed and shared globally via social media. FBI agents on the sites of the homes were in close contact with Magda's interrogators. She was assuring the questioners the farm house was not a trap and was not dangerous. She told agents talking with her about every weapon she could recall in the house. Jericho Adams Brooks was not to be trusted. The farm house was searched with extreme caution.

Taking down the social media platforms of Jericho and Magda didn't stop the reaction to their carnage. It ranged from outrage about the cancellation of football games across the country, to debates about the courage of Jericho's support of gun rights, to debate about whether Magda should receive the death penalty for her role as co-conspirator. Lethal injection was within the federal penalty guidelines for assassination, kidnapping and assault of elected officials, even if she wasn't the shooter. She could have stopped her boyfriend. Not stopping Jericho made her a co-conspirator, according to the experts sitting on television panels filling the uninterrupted news coverage.

CHAPTER 31

Edge of Darkness

Riding in the black government SUV, surrounded by Iowa State Trooper cars and SUVs, the senator was taken back to Des Moines to the campaign headquarters. At several points in the trip he wept loudly. The senator's first social media post after the incident, made during the trip to Des Moines, said: "It has been a tragic day in this country. I have lost great friends today and the country has lost great leaders. We cannot yield to extremism. In honor of the lives of these great representatives of the voters, we will not yield. God bless these great men, these young people and their families and friends. I am heartbroken."

He posted nothing about his own health. Carl and Susan had returned to Des Moines in another government SUV. Carl talked briefly with the senator, who shocked Carl by saying, "we're shutting down the campaign ... maybe permanently." Carl didn't know how to respond.

Carl took over the senator's social media and posted, "The senator was unharmed. The campaign will be suspended temporarily in respect for those who were the victims of this senseless act. We ask for your thoughts and prayers for the families and friends of the victims."

Gerald O'Malley had stayed in Des Moines, skipping the tragic campaign event.

"If we aren't going to the game, I'm not going," Gerald said, explaining he had work in Des Moines anyway.

The response to the senator's first social media posts following the assassination and mass shooting were not all positive.

"Jericho, RIP. Good effort but also a fail. He didn't get Buckman. There'll be another day," said one poster with what appeared to be a fake page.

"It's a great day for gun advocates. Two anti-gun politicians gone, one scarred forever, many more to go. No Compromise," said another poster.

Senator Buckman's closest associates met with him in the mini suite that now seemed very small and overpopulated. There was a female FBI agent with a semi-auto firearm in the room. Their phones and emails and social media pages were all lit up by people who needed to know the senator was well.

"Sir, we're going to be asked about these next few days." Carl started. "We probably need to come up with a plan."

"While I know we will be very much in the media and I know the campaign will change with a security presence I still don't want, these were my friends and I want the campaign to go dark at least until their funerals," the senator said. "No campaign events. No stops. No speeches. If I am offered the opportunity, I want to speak at the memorial service. I probably won't be invited; I understand if I'm not."

He then quietly repeated what he had told Carl. He was considering quitting the campaign. He was having trouble getting out the words.

"I was happy being a professor. I would be happy returning to a university. Right now, I'm thinking about withdrawing. I can't put my family through this. My mom and dad are terrified.

"Carl, start working on a speech. I think I want to end my campaign."

The room went quiet. While everyone would understand if he withdrew, considering the circumstances, no one in the room wanted him to quit. They looked at each other wondering who would step out to redirect the senator from his obvious and understandable emotional distress.

"Sir, I understand and I don't want to minimize how you feel right now, but I firmly believe this country needs you. People need you," Gerald said after what seemed like a long silence but was actually only 30 seconds or so of staring at each other.

No one wanted to protest if the senator did truly want to quit.

"Sir, have you talked with Kim?" Gerald asked.

"I have but only for a minute to assure her I was fine. About the same with my parents. If I can have the room please …"

"Senator, I have to stay," the agent, quiet before, insisted.

"I understand. Our campaign has lost some of the innocence and spirit today. I hate that already."

Buckman changed from his polo and khakis into a sweat suit in the bathroom. He emerged wearing his glasses again. They had fallen off as he ran to the site of the rally before the shots were fired. He stopped and stuffed them into a pocket before the trip to Des Moines. The glasses may have been hiding his tears.

The agent could hear both sides of the conversation on the speaker phone.

"Sweetheart? Sorry I couldn't talk more. I am devastated. I'm thinking about withdrawing. I want to just come home with you and the little guy. What do you think?"

"Cue Ball, you can't do that. People need you. The people you care about … The people you want to have a better life. You can't."

"I know … but."

"But what? I hate what happened today. We lost friends and all those innocent kids … Imagine their parents seeing that video. Damn her."

They both were crying again. There was a minute of silence in the conversation.

"What are your people saying there?" Kim asked.

"The same as you. Am I really that vital? I don't think so. I could endorse Karla Foster today and be perfectly happy."

"What? You would never be happy. You were made to do this. You are important to the future of this country," Kim said. "I would love to spend the rest of my life having you all to us. But it wouldn't be fair."

"What do you mean?"

"It would not be fair to this country. See what happens in February when they vote in Iowa. I think you will win the Iowa Caucuses but it's still a long road after that," Kim added.

"How is my little buddy?"

"He is sleeping quietly. Your mom and dad were here. They were so sweet making sure I was OK. We could have ..."

"I know. I can't get the thought of not seeing ..."

He cried again.

"Pierce, we can get through this because we need to," she told him. "It's a path we have chosen to take. It's a path we must walk. I saw your post. We can't let zealous gun owners win."

"I'm coming home tomorrow for a couple days. We'll talk more then."

"Your head still looks like a cue ball, you know. Love you."

She ended the call believing he might need counseling to overcome the thoughts he was expressing.

Carl Lyon and Gerald O'Malley were getting calls every few minutes asking for comment and interviews with the senator. They explained that Buckman would likely not be available for several days.

They were having second thoughts about commenting.

"What about a Facebook Live with our own campaign page?" Carl said.

"If we do that, we might as well invite 3N in for a brief interview. It would run all weekend everywhere and it will assure everyone the senator is fine," Gerald responded. "Let's see if he'll go for it. But I'm afraid he may tell them he is going to withdraw. We need to know that before we set something up."

They reassembled in the senator's suite, which had an increasingly large security presence.

"Sir, we think it might be a good idea to do an interview with 3N, not those bastards from Traditions and Values Network. There is already speculation you will withdraw. If you are still thinking about that, let's wait. We can give it a couple days," Carl said.

"What did Kim think?" Gerald asked.

"I think she is with you guys. We've still got a long road just to get out of the Iowa Caucuses," he said.

He took another long pause.

"OK, make the offer to 3N. Set it up but do it quietly. The ground rules are that they can do the interview live but they then have to share the video with everyone, including Traditions and

Values," the senator said.

Two county sheriff deputies escorted 3N reporter Alex Davis through the employee entrance to the third floor where the senator's suite was located. The floor had been cleared of guests other than the senator and his staff.

The senator still wore his workout suit and glasses. He had no intention of wearing anything different during the interview. No makeup. He had socks on for once but not shoes.

The FBI agents outside the senator's room asked for identification from Alex Davis and the videographer with him. The videographer wore a backpack allowing her to transmit live to a truck outside the hotel. The agents examined the backpack and camera closely. They asked questions about how it worked. They called a 3N producer in Atlanta to verify the two were employees and how the backpack functioned. The check took about 20 minutes.

It was nearly 10 p.m. when the senator sat at the small kitchen table in his suite.

"First, Senator, how are you?" Davis asked.

"Physically I am fine. In every other way it has been a horrible day for this country and for Kim and myself. We lost friends who were great public servants. We've shed a lot of tears today thinking of families and friends of young people who will not be allowed to live their dreams and do great things. Like so many others, we're devastated. It sounds cliched, but we offer our condolences to the families"

"Senator, it is believed now you were the target of this plan. That has to be a terrible feeling but also a relief."

"I guess it is understandable that I feel some relief … I am a son, husband, father. People rely on me … but it is outweighed by a survivor's remorse. Why not me instead of these college students with productive lives ahead of them? Why not me instead of my great friend Lansing Landon? Why not me instead of a great congressman and friend Marion Jackson? Those are questions … (his voice was shaking) … questions I will live with … (tears began to fall down his cheek)…for the rest of my life. There is no answer, you just continue and hope you can honor them through your actions."

"You weren't there on time. What happened?" Davis asked.

"The bus broke down again."

"That is your unique RV bus your campaign calls Beatrice?"

"Yes. We were headed to the event and the fuel pump went out. We were still about three miles away so we got out and started jogging to the event. We were trying to get there. A university police officer stopped me and took me into a restaurant. He said 'something has happened at the stadium.' He kept us there. He was able to get updates. He told me shots had been fired. Seconds later he told me people had been hit by the gunfire. More officers showed up in the restaurant. I wanted to leave and go to the site, especially when I heard it was at the rally I was supposed to be attending. They made me stay. The officer kept getting updates but he stopped updating me. I knew it must be bad."

"Will you continue as a candidate for president?" the reporter asked.

O'Malley and Carl Lyon were not certain how Buckman would answer.

"It is too early to talk about that. I'm going home to see my wife and son," the senator responded.

"Would you consider this to be a period of mourning?"

"Our campaign will be suspended as we remember our friends and loved ones."

"You've had a very open campaign thus far, but security is now very tight around you. Will this tragedy affect your campaign?" the reporter asked.

"I hope not," the senator replied. "I think I need to listen to people, talk with them about issues face-to-face. That is the campaign I want to run. Our campaign is all about people and how we can make their lives better. I hope we don't lose that ability."

"Did gun control advocates win or lose today?"

"I won't discuss our gun policy at this time. I assure you we will talk about what made today's tragedy possible. No, nobody won today. People … good people, public servants, young people with great dreams … are now gone. I assure you, we must talk about this country's incredible access to weapons.

Today isn't the day, but the day will come when we will have a sensible policy discussion of the gun culture of this country."

"Last question," Carl said.

"Let me repeat. Today isn't the day, but the day is coming," the senator reiterated.

Alex Davis didn't want to risk asking another question. He also had sensed the senator's growing anger.

"Sir, thank you. We wish your family well and we're very sorry for your loss today."

"Thank you. God bless the families and friends of the victims today."

The senator considered himself a Christian but was not religious. The Religious Right had mentioned the fact about a million times already. He listed no church affiliation in his biography. To them, it indicated he was a non-believer. They didn't believe it was possible for the senator to believe in the teachings of the Bible and believe in a higher power but not belong to a church and not be pro-life.

The senator had explained repeatedly he was pro-choice but he did not favor late-term -- 20 weeks or later – abortions and he supported making adoption an easier, less cumbersome, less costly process. He was accurate when he said on the campaign trail when explaining he personally opposed abortion as a form of birth control that abortion rates were already the lowest in decades, as was teenage pregnancy. He believed the Religious Right didn't want to hear facts other than their version of them. It served them no purpose for the senator to equivocate on the subject of abortions. True liberals never did that.

After Alex Davis left the room, the senator dropped to his knees in tears and prayed outloud for the victims and asked for comfort to families of the victims. He prayed for strength, guidance and asked God to "help us with this burden and incredible sadness."

Only once before, on the night his son was born and developed early breathing issues, had the staff seen the senator pray.

When the senator finished his prayer with "Amen," Carl and Susan Lyon, Gerald O'Malley and the FBI agent all said

"Amen."

"Where is Ryan?" the senator asked of his driver, whom he hadn't seen since Beatrice broke down again. He stayed with the bus to await a tow truck.

"Probably hitchhiking here," Gerald announced as he left the room with Carl and Susan.

Gerald wanted a bar.

The senator lay down on top of the bedcovers, his glasses still on his face. He was sleeping within minutes. The agent, who still hadn't introduced herself, gently removed his glasses.

CHAPTER 32

Memorial Planning

Throughout the first night, the senator slept fitfully. Others faced a sleepless night.

Agents at the Minnesota sites connected to Jericho Adams Brooks continued to secure the farm house using portable lighting. Jericho's father-in-law and mother were no longer being interrogated, but they weren't back in public either. They were in an undisclosed location under FBI protection.

Magda was in the Polk County Jail in Des Moines. Her interrogation was over for the night.

The administrative and athletic offices at Crossroads State University were brightly lit. Solemnly and meticulously, plans were being made for an on-campus memorial service for a U.S. Senator, a congressman, a county sheriff's deputy and 11 other people, five of them students. Administrators making the plans talked with parents and siblings of the students nearly every hour to update them and get ideas about how they would like their children remembered and what they envisioned for the memorial service. The president of the university, Dr. Dana Moore, made many of the calls herself. She had a list of questions and talking points prepared by the university's communications staff.

She personalized the calls by frequently using the name of the student who was killed.

"Tell me about your (son/daughter)," the university president would begin the follow-up contacts after an initial call of condolences and updates about the investigation. She tried to draw personal stories about the students. The calls were on speaker phone so others could listen and take notes.

Plans for the memorial service at the university came together as the first night went on. It was decided there would be a public memorial service at Explorers Arena, located about a quarter-mile from the site of the shootings. It had the largest capacity on an indoor site on campus and the FBI made it clear it preferred the arena for security reasons. Everyone would be required to go through a full security check at a limited number of access points.

There was extended, sometimes tense debate about whether Senator Pierce Buckman, clearly the primary target of what was now being referred to as "assassination and domestic terrorism," should be invited to participate. If he was invited to participate, what role would he have?

"Can we safely get him into the arena, safely have him speak, and safely get him back off campus?" Moore asked. "Will we be risking the safety of others by having him speak? The terrorist may have targeted the senator partly because he was so accessible. He had essentially stalked the senator for several months, according to media reports."

"How can we be positive there aren't others? No question the senator will want to be at this service. He should be, don't we agree with that? So, we need to start thinking about his role."

It was suggested he would want to meet with the stricken families.

"Maybe they won't want to meet him considering the circumstances. Their children died but they apparently weren't the actual targets. The senator was," said the vice president in charge of facilities and security.

"OK, we prepare as if Senator Buckman will be at the service and will want to meet with families," Moore finally said decisively, ending the debate. "Start coming up with an action plan to safely execute this event."

The moment the word left her mouth, she regretted it.

"Umm, let's not use that word again in the planning of this," Moore said.

The media coverage was endless.

Sports network programming focused on details of the massacre. The greater focus was on the oddity of a fall Saturday without football. Not one game was finished. The Crossroads State game was an early start. Within 30 minutes of the brief, deadly act, teams were taken off the field. Fans streamed to the exits. Some football fans the network talked with believed the games should have been played as scheduled. The same sentiment was a common thread on the social media forums of the sports networks.

Senator Buckman's interview with 3N was playing every minute or so somewhere. The news networks assembled panels of terrorism experts, psychologists, political experts and a few college football analysts mixed in to discuss the day and what it would mean to the political landscape.

More than one of the experts on Traditions and Values Network expressed the opinion Senator Buckman would or should withdraw from the race in the next 24 hours and resign his Senate seat.

"He was the target of the attack. I think that will be very difficult for the campaign to overcome from a political perspective," said Lake Northwood in an update from Crossroads State. Although he was several hundred feet away from the site, the bright lights of the ongoing investigation in the background were visible. "Imagine the survivor guilt Senator Buckman must be experiencing tonight."

For once, Northwood was right. The senator fell asleep quickly but only for brief periods. He awoke after three hours and turned on the television news. The FBI special agent, who said her name was Kianna Curtis, was still his roommate, at least for the night. She sat in the small kitchen of the suite with her pistol on the table when he awoke.

"Senator, what can I do for you?" she asked.

"Tell me it didn't happen," the senator said.

"I'm very sorry sir," she said.

"How come the FBI, not Secret Service, is watching over me?" he asked.

"They will take over probably tomorrow?"

There was a statement from the White House soon after the

event. It wasn't Rushton's work. He was drunk by 2 p.m. when it was issued. He was maybe the first Texan since Sam Houston to have little interest in college football. He was informed about the tragedy as it was happening.

"Was the guy after Buckman?" Rushton asked.

Rushton called the FBI director several times for updates. He was especially interested in whether Buckman was the target and where the senator was.

"It has been a tragic day for our country. We lost innocent college students, two representatives of the people of Iowa and a courageous law enforcement officer who died a hero. We are asking flags be lowered to half-staff in memorial and admiration for Senator Lansing Landon and Congressman Marion Jackson. The thoughts of the nation are with the families of the victims of this act of violence today."

Not one mention of a troubled young man with access to automatic weapons, a sawed-off shotgun, the pellet grenade and enough carfentanil to kill another 20 people had the officers not taken so much care with the backpack of Jericho Adams Brooks.

CHAPTER 33

Day After

The senator dozed off a couple more times with the television on when he finally got up for the day at 4:30 a.m.

"Can you get the gym open? I want to get on the bike," Buckman asked the FBI agent.

"I don't think you can do that," she said.

"Make it happen. I am going to exercise," Buckman insisted.

"Let me check," she responded. "You're going to be difficult, aren't you?"

"You just met me. Hang around."

Flanked by Kianna Curtis and one of the agents still posted outside his door, Senator Buckman got on the treadmill at 4:55 a.m. They locked and guarded the door to the gym.

He was more determined than usual. He was still riding hard at 6 a.m. when he remembered he was heading back to the Twin Cities on a 9 a.m. flight.

"We're not going to let you do that. We'll take you on the plane we came here on," Kianna said. "The Twin Cities is my field station. The faster you are ready, the faster we can get you home. You understand that we are going to be with you 24/7 for a while, probably permanently, don't you?"

"I kind of figured. Can you be part of the detail?" he asked.

"Different details. I can't stay. You will have Secret Service protection," she explained.

At 7 a.m., the senator and two FBI vehicles headed to the airport with Gerald O'Malley and Ryan Holton, who had shown up in the middle of the night with a rejuvenated Beatrice.

Governor Karla Foster called the senator during his ride to the airport.

"I'm fine. I feel horrible about this. I keep thinking I would have rather it been me than all those kids."

"I'm headed home to see Kim and the little guy for a couple days."

"Yeah, driving me crazy already. I understand, but I don't like it."

There was a long pause from the senator's side of the conversation. He was listening intently. So was O'Malley.

"I have to tell you that I have thought about withdrawing. I could be happy just going home with Kim and Owen. But if I do that, the extremists win. There must be changes made, or these horrible mass killings will continue. We have to limit access to the weapons this young man had. Apparently, this was a troubled young man. Who else plans something so horrendous, knowing they will probably die themselves?"

"Thank you, Governor, we'll talk again."

"Did she just ask if you are going to withdraw?" Gerald asked.

"No, she suggested we run in the caucuses as a team with her in the top spot. She thought that might appeal to me personally. I think it is an interesting concept. No one has ever done it in the Iowa Caucuses to my knowledge," the senator explained.

"You didn't say 'no.'"

"I did not."

There were benefits to the sudden security entourage. From wheels up to walking in the door of the Buckman townhouse took 1 hour, 45 minutes.

The only delay was the media staking out the townhouse. The senator kept walking as reporters asked him about the need for new gun control measures.

"I think it would be inappropriate for me to talk about that now. The day will come soon to have this discussion," he said as he walked into the front door.

Just before he shut the door, he added, "Right now, I would just ask God to comfort and shoulder this incredible burden of the parents dealing with the loss of their children."

Kim held Owen Morrison Buckman as the Senator entered. He hadn't seen his son or wife in a week. He embraced and kissed both of them.

"I can't tell you how good it is to see you and to be home," he said.

"Don't get too comfortable. Carol Ann and Jack have invited us over this afternoon. Hoodie and Lisa will be there and want to see you and Carl," Kim reported. "It will be a nice break from the media coverage. Have you been watching?"

"Kind of hard to not see some of the coverage. It's been on for 24 hours now. I've died a thousand deaths," the senator said.

'Still feeling guilty about surviving?" Kim asked.

"I think I always will … for as long as I live," he replied. "I keep thinking about what those families are going through today. I don't feel like I should call them. I don't know how they would react to hearing from me. Will they resent that I survived when their child didn't? I would feel that way. The officer who died had a wife and three children…"

"Hey, I'm reading your book. Carl called and said it would require a rewrite of the first chapter. I like the title, 'A Progressive's View … Where We Are, Where We Could Be'."

"Better I guess than Professor Petunia... A Socialist's View," Buckman said, smiling for the first time in 24 hours. "I've read most of the draft. I think it has to start with Crossroads State University. Otherwise, I think it's a pretty good reflection of where we have been and where I hope we are going as a country. It is well done. What do you think about starting the book with yesterday?"

"I think it has to start with Crossroads State and your thoughts about continuing the campaign. Carl is concerned. It is going to print very soon. He wants the assurance you are going forward. He is afraid to ask, I think," Kim said.

"He hasn't asked. Some of the media is convinced I will end my campaign. Some want that to happen. Kim, I need to know how you truly feel," the senator said.

"I believe you owe it to the country. You can make this country a better place for millions of people who have been powerless, neglected, left behind. I have always understood the risk. I personally want you to continue," Kim said. "I don't care about being first lady. I care about helping people and so do you. You truly have a progressive's heart and vision and that is a good thing."

The senator and Kim were not able to leave the townhouse alone for the trip to the Holton family's mansion. The Secret Service took over for the FBI, as Kianna Curtis had explained. As the FBI's criminal investigation continued into the massacre, it was now the Secret Service's role to protect the candidate.

Rushton's staff had made calls to start the process of providing security for the senator.

"Sorry about all this," the senator said to Kim, referring to the new security detail.

The Holtons were waiting at the arched entry under the portico of their mansion. Carol Ann Collier Holton and Jack were dressed casually. Carl and Susan Lyon, back in the boat house apartment on Lake Minnetonka, walked to the back entry of the main house about 10 minutes later.

Jason Holton, Carol and Jack's son and a senior reporter for the Minnesota Standard, was in the dining room with his wife, Lisa Fitzpatrick. They had quietly eloped only weeks before. The senator greeted Jason and Lisa. Jason's hoodie of choice for the day was an obviously new Buckman for President issue.

Carl and Susan walked into the formal dining room with the massive table, adjoined by an equally large kitchen. It was a warm reunion of the Big River Beacon staff that had a great year-long run covering news and winning awards. Jason and Lisa both hugged Carl and Susan.

Several conversations went on simultaneously at the table. Senator Buckman and Kim were talking with the Holtons about little Owen, who had stayed home with the senator's parents. Carl and his former reporters at the Beacon talked about the Senator's biography about ready to go to print.

"I read the draft of your book, Carl. Mom had a copy. Very well written and reported and as you made clear to us in Big River, there is a difference in the two ... writing and reporting. When you can do both, you have something," Hoodie said.

"How are you going to handle yesterday and the memorial

service?" Lisa asked.

"I think I'll have to rewrite the first chapter, don't you?" Carl asked.

"I think so. You have some great personal stories to tell. And some really funny stuff. Even if it wasn't a campaign biography I think people would be interested in the senator's story. I found out a lot," Hoodie said. "Is the senator going to the memorial service?"

Now, Buckman was paying attention to this second conversation. He was getting bored and slightly discouraged with the discussion of campaign finances. He knew money was coming in but the donations were typically $100 or less. Gerald O'Malley was trying to get the candidate to "play nice" with the well-known big money donors. Breckenridge and Brynn Powell were doing their part among celebrity circles, but Buckman himself was not meeting with the management of major political action committees. Their money seemed to be going to Karla Foster and Mike Clarke.

"I want to be at the memorial service if I am welcomed," the senator interjected into the new conversation now grabbing his interest. "I don't think I will be allowed to go to funerals."

"What will you say? What can be said?" Carol Ann Holton asked.

"I want to talk about the young people and the great price this country continues to pay in lost potential and the noticeable decline of our soul as a country every time a mass shooting occurs," the senator said. "I want to talk about how we somehow are only able to focus on these incidents for a few days because they occur so regularly. We have become complacent, almost accepting and anticipatory about the next tragedy. They have happened so often that we expect, no, we know, there will be another soon. We are constantly on high alert. Meanwhile, we do nothing as a country to stop these tragedies. We are frozen as legislators by outside forces who don't want any changes. Jericho Adams Brooks was not the last gun culture radical. This will not be the last tragedy. We need to do more to prevent the next, and the next, and the next.

"I won't talk policy change or new laws in a specific way,

although I have ideas and have been talking about those ideas on the campaign.

"Mostly, I'll talk about people and our responsibility as a nation to change our laws in a sensible way allowing sportsmen and sportswomen to have guns but keeping them away from the Jerichos of the country. It may take small steps and a progression of steps. We can take them."

Carl Lyon and Jason Holton took notes as Senator Buckman talked about what he would say at the memorial service.

"Jason, I should have asked. We're off the record until the day of the service," the senator said. "Ok with that?"

"Yes sir. Can I ask a few more questions though?"

"Sure, as long as you don't use anything until the day of the service. We owe it to the families of these kids to not have any appearance we're politicizing this horrible event," the senator said.

As they ate lunch, Lisa and Hoodie both asked Buckman questions about the day of "Tailgate Terrorism," as it was now being referred to quite often by the media and on social media.

"Do you feel relief that you weren't there? That old bus saved your life by breaking down again," Lisa said.

"Not relief as much as guilt. I am experiencing terrible grief and guilt about those students and the lives lost. I would have been there and maybe Jericho Brooks would have focused on me and the killing would have been minimalized. In that crowd, he probably could have shot me and got away, at least temporarily," the senator said. "I'm not sure he planned to take out others. He snapped possibly when he saw I wasn't there. At least that is my theory. But who knows what he was thinking at the time? We only know what his plan was from his manifesto. He was targeting me."

"Will you continue to campaign?" Hoodie asked.

"I had not come to a definitive decision until I talked to Kim and came here today. Immediately, I just wanted to come home, maybe get another teaching position and live out my life as a husband, father and educator," the senator explained. "I started this for a reason. We can be a better country and we can do much more for people … provide universal health care, a

272

universal fair wage, educate our population so they are prepared for the workforce, tax fairness so the middle class is treated the same way at tax time as the wealthiest Americans, and rebuild our roads, bridges, sewers, airports ... there is so much we can do."

"How do you feel about your chances to win the Iowa Caucuses?" Hoodie asked.

"We seem to be hanging in there in the polling. We're trailing Mike Clarke and Karla Foster by a few points. We have a huge disadvantage financially. It's simple ... they have more money. Much more. They are tapping into the traditional Democratic donors. We're relying on the people who believe in us and are making small donations. We're doing well for a grassroots campaign. We have a better digital team and social media team than they do. We will be able to afford some television closer to the caucuses. They are both already running television. We have to rely on free TV and frankly, with 24-hour news, we're making the newscasts regularly, thanks to Carl and just all the circumstances and events we've already experienced. We have to rely on our message. That's what it comes down to. Enough people have to believe what we believe."

They talked another hour over dinner about issues, voters, Iowa and the shootings.

The senator had slipped away from the table toward the lake before anyone, except his new Secret Service detail, noticed. It was thought he was in the bathroom. He sat on a bench on the lakefront. The sky was glowing. He sat reflecting on the past 30 hours.

After maybe 20 minutes, Kim found him.

"You OK?" she asked.

"Not really," he said.

"Pierce, this may be serious. Do you believe you need counseling? Umm, are you having ... you know, thoughts ... about harming yourself.'

Kim felt relief the moment she asked. She had been thinking about the seriousness of the senator's emotional condition.

"No, not that. I'm struggling with what everyone is going through and what they lost. Those families," he said, tears welling up again.

His Secret Service agent was nearby but not within listening distance.

"Did this really only happen yesterday. Everything seems to be moving so slowly. It's like a nightmare that doesn't end. You just keep thinking about it and you feel powerless," the senator said. "I'm a candidate for what people consider to be one of the most powerful positions in the world but I am powerless. There was nothing I could do yesterday. There is nothing I can do today to change what happened. There will be nothing I can do tomorrow."

"But maybe weeks from now or months from now, or when you become president, you can move people on some sort of sensible gun control," Kim said.

The conversation continued inside the Holtons in the ornate dining room.

"Why don't you get the Standard to send you out with us as embedded reporters?" Carl asked Hoodie. "It will be like old times at the Beacon and frankly, we're getting really tired of Lake Northwood and the Unfair, Unbalanced, Unhinged Network."

"Daniel Fallsfeather and I are coming to the memorial service and it's pretty open ended. As long as you're still a factor in the race, we'll hang out," Hoodie reported.

"Umm, I'd suggest not wearing that particular sweatshirt when you are out with us," Carl said of the Buckman for President hoodie. "Hope you bought it, by the way. We make a few bucks on each one. Who knows, you may have just helped cover Gerald's bar bill for an hour or two."

The senator and Kim were gone for about 45 minutes.

Parents of the students murdered by Jericho Adams Brooks generally voiced support for the idea Senator Buckman should be one of the speakers during the memorial program. Several noted the unusual circumstances ... he was the target, not their children ... but none wanted to exclude him.

Acting on the consensus of the parents, university president Dr. Dana Moore called the Buckman for President headquarters in The Warehouse to invite the senator. She wanted to ask personally on the phone. Campaign spokesman Curt Jaslow called the senator to arrange a time to talk with Dr. Moore.

Moore, a doctor of veterinary medicine and a Ph.D. in education, called the senator's cellphone on Sunday afternoon when he and Kim were still at the Holtons' home.

"Frankly, I'm devastated. I can't stop thinking about the horror of these parents. I can't imagine what they are going through," the senator said.

The others at the ornate wooden table could only hear the senator's side of the conversation.

"Initially, I didn't think I wanted this or that anyone would want me at the service. I wasn't sure I could respond adequately or thoughtfully considering the situation. What could I possibly say that could make anyone feel better when I myself feel great loss?

"Thank you for saying that. If you talk to any of the parents again, tell them my prayers are with them. I haven't reached out because I didn't feel it was appropriate.

"I'd like that. I would like to meet with them privately before the service and I'd like to speak during the service.

"I have to warn you that I have a new security detail. I don't like it but I understand it. Security may be cumbersome for people planning to come. I hope I'm not a distraction. I survived …. (his voice broke and there was a long pause as he tried to stay composed) … my friends and all these innocent young people didn't. I don't want this to be about me in any way or to be political in any way.

"Thank you and I look forward to meeting you."

The senator ended the call. He hugged Kim, possibly to hide his tears from the others.

"I … I … don't know … what I can say," he said.

He was quiet for a moment. Carl thought he was saying a prayer.

"The memorial service is Wednesday at noon. I'll be able to meet with families before the service," the senator finally broke the silence. "I'll be able to meet Lansing's adult children and Marion Jackson's kids. They are in their teens."

"Do you want us to try to write something for this?" Carl

asked.

"I could probably use some help. Thanks," the senator said. The candidate did daily live videos about a variety of issues. He posted short messages once or twice a day; usually about conversations he had with voters and their ideas.

In the boathouse apartment where he had written the senator's speech to announce his campaign and had been working on the Buckman biography, Carl stood at the window looking out over the lake. After 10 or 15 quiet minutes, Susan asked what he was thinking about.

"I'm thinking about our sons and how we would feel in this situation. What could the senator say to make us feel better? Would I personally resent him saying anything considering the circumstances? He asked the question of himself, what can he possibly say?"

Carl picked up a yellow legal pad and a pen.

The senator was still wavering about continuing the campaign until he committed to speaking at the memorial service at Crossroads State. His thought was that if he didn't continue, the focus would be on him, not those who died.

On Monday following the Saturday mass shooting, Traditions and Values Network reporter Lake Northwood had "Breaking News." That's what Gerald O'Malley saw on the big screens in The Warehouse as the chyron came up.

"Someone turn this shit up!" O'Malley bellowed at startled young staffers scrambled to find the right remote.

Running across the screen instantly was a graphic saying "Senator Pierce Buckman, the surviving target of a massacre at Crossroads State University, is considering withdrawing as a candidate for president."

Northwood, standing as close as he could to the site of the massacre with the yellow perimeter tape, investigation activity and the tents still visible, reported the story about Buckman possibly giving up his campaign and his Senate seat.

"Well, it's not a steaming pile of shit lie at least. Unusual for this guy," O'Malley said. "He (Buckman) has seriously considered the possibility. We all know that. The news would be that he decided to keep going. But I don't care what the guy is saying, he is still a pompous pretty boy. And a puppet for Rushton's drunk ass."

There was one more news item in the report from Northwood, who added, "We also understand the campaign of Governor Karla Foster has reached out to Senator Buckman about forming a team with the governor at the top of the ticket prior to the Iowa Caucuses. That would be an unprecedented partnership matching Democratic candidates prior to the Iowa Caucuses. The partnership would also match a liberal outsider with Governor Foster, a more traditional and established Democratic candidate. We're told the discussion has gone no further than an initial contact. The idea of a Foster-Buckman merger would, if it was worked out, dramatically change the campaign."

O'Malley was now quietly fuming. He knew Northwood was, again, accurate.

"He said no by the way," O'Malley told staff about the offer from Karla Foster.

Predictably in a 24-hour news world, Traditions and Values hammered their reporter's exclusive "Breaking News" for the next 12 hours and gathered "expert panels" to talk about whether Buckman should withdraw or join a Foster ticket. The consensus seemed to be that under the circumstances, it might be better for the Democratic Party and the senator's own well-being if he withdrew.

"Yeah, of course they want him out. He has these people worried about Rushton's chance of being re-elected," O'Malley said to no one but himself as he shook himself awake at 6 a.m., four hours after his last pull from a bottle of wine he found in the office. He spent the night at The Warehouse on a couch in his office.

His office consisted of three temporary walls and a missing wall that said "door" on the floor. The fourth wall had disappeared after O'Malley pushed it down in anger one late night.

The other networks wanted comment from someone high in the campaign about the Traditions and Values story. O'Malley gave it to them via email.

"The Senator remains a candidate for President of the United

States and will remain a candidate until Tuesday, Nov. 4, of next year when he becomes president-elect."

O'Malley also confirmed that the senator would be speaking at the memorial service at Crossroads State University.

O'Malley was spending the next couple of days in The Warehouse operation. Staff organization and coordination was a continuous issue with all the people walking in the door to volunteer. The volunteers and paid staff were not just idealistic millennials. It was becoming a diverse operation that could speak at least five languages with callers and donors. The operation needed additional clarification of the senator's policy statements on the website.

The social media operation was outstanding, as the candidate professed. The digital team handled dozens of outside posts to their pages every day. The campaign on Facebook had soared past 500,000 followers and was about to double that number. The Twitter team posted an average of 20 times a day. The team had been instructed to allow an open forum. Only posts threatening violence against the candidate or the source of a post were taken down.

After the shooting at Crossroads State, there were a number of inflammatory, reckless and frightening posts supporting Jericho Adams Brooks' terrorist act. Supporters of the senator responded accordingly, voicing their support of Buckman's ideas of a better national database of sales and owners, restricted access to certain weapons, national gun buyback, no internet sales, no gun show sales and heavy taxes on gun sales and ammunition.

Twitter was used primarily for campaign news. There were updates about where the candidate was, what he was saying and what others were saying about him.

The campaign's video platform now had 273 videos posted from the campaign trail. The most responses resulted from the 3N interview with the senator hours after the tragedy at Crossroads State University. The interview had been viewed 2,581,072 times in less than 24 hours

CHAPTER 34
The Service

Explorers Arena holds 12,500 for basketball games and more for events where the floor could be used for additional seating. Crossroads State officials had said they expected as many as 8,000 to attend the memorial service following the mass shooting on campus.

The plan was to script a memorial service to begin the healing process. Classes had been canceled for three days. They were scheduled to resume the following day. Crossroads State had already said it would play a scheduled home game one week following the tragedy and would reschedule the postponed game in late December. No National University Union football games were completed on the day of the shootings. Only a few kicked off.

In two heavy duty black SUVs owned by the federal government the senator, Kim, Carl and Susan Lyon, Ryan Holton and campaign spokesman Curt Jaslow made the trip from the Twin Cities to University City on the afternoon before the memorial service. The senator's security task force and advance team had reserved an entire motel floor several miles away from Explorers Arena at an undisclosed location. It was suggested for the first time the senator wear a lightweight ballistic protective vest. It took him about two seconds to reject the idea.

"This campaign is not going to cower in the shadows," Buckman immediately responded. "Don't ask again."

At 5:05 a.m., the senator was on the hotel's treadmill with 3N on the screen on the wall. Nearly six hours before the service, there was already extensive coverage. A reporter was doing a live report from the steps of Explorers Arena in darkness and talking about "a massive security effort planned to protect the senator, although there have been no credible threats."

The senator, Kim, Carl, Susan and Curt Jaslow were driven directly into the service entrance of the arena. The garage door was closed behind them. They were behind the stage at the east end of the arena. From there they were escorted to a windowless meeting room in the lower concourse. The senator kissed Kim and opened the door. The Secret Service detail waited outside but had looked over the room and approved it for the meeting. There would be only one entry point, which was guarded by two Secret Service agents. Waiting for the senator were the families of the students and the two friends – Senator Lansing Landon and Congressman Marion Jackson -- who had also been killed. Their deaths were being called assassinations.

It was quiet when Buckman entered. He would later admit he was terrified how the families might react.

"I don't know what to say except that I am terribly sorry for your loss," he said quietly. "I want to know about your loved ones. Maybe if we share their stories, we can begin to see the light beyond this dark moment.

"I have to tell you I have asked, 'why not me?' I will never get over the thought … not in my lifetime … not as long as I have any memory of past events … that I was the target. I wasn't there but your children, your fathers, your grandchildren were. I grieve with you."

"You are still here for a reason," said Lawrence Landon, the grown son of Senator Lansing Landon. "You are here to carry on for my father and for the father of the Jackson children. You are here to try to make life better for millions of neglected people. It was what my father wanted to do."

The senator, growing emotional again, walked over and hugged Lawrence. Others gathered around him.

One by one, loved ones of the 14 who were killed, shared stories. Carl wrote down details of names and memories.

"Kathryn wanted to be a teacher, like yourself. She wanted

to get her degree and teach first in a foreign country. She was an idealist and a progressive. She thought we should do better. She supported you and talked about you all the time," said the mother of Kathryn Kimball.

"Alan planned to go to medical school," said the father of Alan Jordan.

After about 40 minutes, the senator asked if someone had a prayer.

"God bless you all and I pray He relieves this burden you all share and leaves you only with great memories," the senator said before he left.

He stayed backstage at the request of security. He would not be seated on the stage, he was told, and when on stage, he was told he would have Secret Service agents on each side of him. He would not be allowed to leave the stage to shake hands or hug anyone in the crowd.

"Everything has to be different now," the agent in charge of his detail informed him.

"We'll see," the senator said.

"We would like you to wear body protection," the agent in charge suggested.

"That is not acceptable to me," the senator said.

It took two hours to get everyone through security and seated. The crowd appeared to be somewhere around the 8,000 predicted. There was music and an invocation, speeches by several people, including the university president.

Lawrence Landon spoke eloquently on behalf of his father.

From what Buckman saw from the live television coverage he watched from backstage, the event was generally upbeat. He was the last scheduled speaker. There were occasional humorous stories, drawing laughs from the crowd.

Senator Buckman wore black slacks, a white dress shirt, no tie and black jacket. He wore his glasses, which political consultants continued to tell him not to do. He didn't care. His shaved head glowed under the bright lights.

What started out as seemingly scattered applause escalated to general applause and finally, a standing ovation. He was embarrassed by the response. He didn't want to seem political.

This was a memorial service for the victims and their families. He considered himself to be a guilty survivor.

"Thank you. Thank you. Please sit. Sit please … but thank you for the warm greeting," he finally said.

"Last Saturday I was coming to Crossroads State University to a rally of Young Democrats. I looked forward to a great day with young people and my wonderful friends Lansing Landon and Marion Jackson. It was a gorgeous day as only the Midwest can produce at this time of year. I wanted to tell the students what I hoped we could do to make college more affordable for them and talk about public service in exchange for tuition reimbursement.

"Our lives changed in an instant. I lost my friends. These great idealistic kids with dreams and fantastic futures ahead of them were stricken by a senseless act. We lost so much in a matter of seconds.

"I should have been there. Through a twist of fate, I wasn't. For that reason, I will forever question why I am still here. I now can only honor their memories and all they had already accomplished and what they would have accomplished.

"My friend, Senator Lansing Landon, will not be a grandfather to Lawrence's children or the other Landon grandchildren to come.

"My friend Marion Jackson will still be a force in the life of Marion Junior but will not be there physically for his sports events or to see him graduate from high school and college.

"Sheriff's Deputy Ron Royster courageously saved the lives of others while giving up his own. He was a veteran of the Army and was a non-traditional student earning a law enforcement degree, which would have allowed him to advance in his career.

"Kathryn Kimball wanted to be a teacher overseas. I happen to believe teaching is an admirable, wonderful profession.

"Alan Jordan wanted to be a doctor."

The senator mentioned every individual who was killed. He shared a story about each one.

"That is what we lost. We lost potential, we lost people who would have done wonderful things. We lost great public servants. We lost people who would have made a difference. We lost so much, not just individually, but as a country.

"Each violent event like this reminds us we live in a dangerous, changing world where acts like this are no longer rare. They are global in scope.

"But, they will never be acceptable. We cannot now, nor will we ever, accept senseless acts of the zealous as something we think about for a few days and then our thoughts fade away until the next similar tragedy.

"We cannot just go on with our lives until the next act of terror. We cannot just move on. We are losing too much because we have not reacted forcefully enough or quickly enough. I blame myself for that, too.

"So, I ask on the behalf of the parents, grandparents, children, brothers, sisters, loved ones and friends, including myself, to never accept or promote violence to make a political point or to support a political view.

"And we will never forget.

"I heard your prayers. I want to add my own …"

"I ask God to wrap his loving, healing arms around us all at this moment. Lift this horrible burden of grief from our shoulders. Bless us as we grieve. Amen."

Thousands in the crowd responded with "Amen."

That was how he ended his tribute to the victims.

There was restrained applause to the senator's message.

As the service ended, the senator did not immediately walk off the back of the stage as he had been instructed. He spotted the family members of the victims in the front row and went down the stairs to the stage to greet them. To the relief of his grim-faced security, he did stop at the stanchion and rope line. Agents scrambled to surround him. He continued along the line for 20 minutes, shaking hands, hugging, talking little and listening a lot. Music continued as the crowd slowly filed out after the 1-hour, 15-minute service.

"For a supposed agnostic, he sure does pray a lot," Carl said to Susan Lyon as they watched from behind the stage. "He is not following the script of the evangelicals, who can't imagine a progressive who is a Christian."

"A heart attack … your own mortality … has a way of doing

that. It can also make people fearless and compassionate. I think that has happened to the senator," Susan said. "He is very aware of his mortality, much more so than others, and he sure seems fearless to me."

In the minutes following the memorial service, with the crowd still making its way out, there were polarizing media reactions to the service and to Senator Buckman's role.

"In what sounded very much like a return to the campaign trail, appropriate or not, Senator Pierce Buckman wrapped up the memorial service of the Crossroads State University shootings with an emotional, some might suggest inappropriately political speech," said Lake Northwood in his report from the arena.

"How do we change the frigging channel?" Carl said, his face nearly glowing red as he looked for a remote in the "green room" behind the stage.

On 3N, the senator's emotional 15-minute memorial to the victims was already being replayed in its entirety.

The 3N reporter, Alex Davis, had become an instant celebrity among envious media colleagues by securing the interview with the senator hours after the shooting. It didn't matter that Davis' "good get" interview with the emotional senator who had been the target of the shooting happened only because it was intended to be an expression of the senator's sorrow for the victims.

On the floor of the emptying arena, Davis did a live report minutes following the service.

"The senator, wrestling with his own survivor's guilt of the shooting and his decision to continue his campaign for president as he told us Saturday night in an exclusive interview, paid an emotional tribute to the fallen students and his own friends at a memorial service for those murdered at Crossroads State University just four days ago on this campus moments before a football game."

"The senator, emotional himself at times, is going back into campaign mode again tomorrow, according to campaign spokesman Curt Jaslow. Jaslow reported the senator would be sharing his thoughts about possible gun access ideas very soon with hopes common ground can be found across partisan divides he believes have stalled sensible controls in the past."

Davis' network was running highlights of the senator's memorial service speech every few minutes above a "Breaking News" streamer at the bottom of the screen. In between the memorial services highlights, 3N had political reporters providing analysis.

"He looked presidential today," said one analyst. "He showed he has an emotional side and a spiritual side. He was a voice of compassion when one was needed by these families."

The two black SUVs parked behind the stage backed out of the building and headed to Des Moines to the Iowa hotel headquarters of the senator's campaign. Buckman feared he had been "too political."

"That was just Traditions and Values Network saying that," Carl contended.

There was one more place where the senator's intentions were being questioned. President Rushton's staff had asked Iowa Congressman Montgomery Dumas to represent the president at the memorial service. He wasn't invited to speak, but was prominently seated with families of the victims. The senator had stopped and shaken hands with Dumas. They could be seen in media coverage speaking briefly into each other's ear.

"What did Congressman Dumas say?" Carl asked during the trip back to Des Moines.

"We just talked about the families and how much they lost. It was very quick and cordial. He said he was sorry I was going through this," Buckman said.

CHAPTER 35

A Progressive's View

The first polling following the terrorism and the memorial service was inconclusive. It indicated the senator had not gained any momentum nor lost any.

In the Hawkeye State Poll of respondents who reported they were likely to participate on caucus night, Mike Clarke was at 29 percent, Karla Foster at 27 and Senator Buckman at 24. The rest fell to other candidates or into the undecided category.

"What do the undecided still want to hear?" Carl asked Gerald.

"Maybe nothing. They may just be totally oblivious to the issues, or may not care, so rather than commit, they say they are undecided," Gerald explained. "Undecided is generally for the weak of spirit … I think also the weak of IQ.

"On the day of the caucuses, many of them would still report being undecided. Or … we could be this close to capturing them (holding his thumb and pointer finger slightly apart) and will be engaged by caucus night. That is what we hope will happen in the next six weeks. We're in this. We just have to keep doing what we're doing."

Mike Clarke, who had nearly beaten Rushton once already, was reluctant to debate Foster or Buckman. Neither of the leaders in the polls thought being on the same stage with Buckman was a good idea. Even with progressive ideas putting him widely to the left of themselves, he was known as a fierce debater who could convincingly defend those progressive principles and do so with a sharp wit.

"Ah, they are afraid of the Cue Ball," Kim Wakefield said as they headed to two days of stops in eastern Iowa. "They should be. The little guy can be kind of intimidating."

Some candidates on a debate stage earn points simply by appearance. It's just sociology. Some people believe a taller person is more commanding and powerful. Clarke was 6-foot-3. A woman could influence a debate audience either way. Women could admire her just because she was putting herself out there. If they were less political or less engaged, or less informed, or less educated, they might resent the woman candidate. They might turn against her in jealousy of position and attention.

Clarke and Foster had been able to avoid being on the same stage with Buckman so far. The Iowa Democratic Party was pushing for one January debate in Des Moines. Buckman wanted three debates in three different Iowa cities.

Senator Buckman had a good relationship with Karla Foster. Kassie Foster was due to deliver any day. The senator and Foster talked at least once a week for a few minutes.

"We'll do it without Clarke. How about that?" the senator asked Foster about a debate.

"Well, I think that will at least draw him out," Foster said. "I think they believe they are in a good position and can only hurt their campaign with a debate."

"Do we call him out publicly at campaign events?" Buckman asked.

"It will only take a day of that. Rushton will be jumping on him for not being willing to face the voters. Sure, let's do it," Foster said.

In Marion, Iowa, at a visit to a senior residence center to meet with a 104-year-old veteran of World War II, Senator Buckman challenged Clarke to face off in a debate format. Buckman told the media covering the stop at the care center he should be the one who didn't want to get on a debate stage with Clarke.

"Governor Foster and I will do it alone if he is still reluctant. I'm the one who should be reluctant. Mike Clarke's physical presence will dominate the stage. The guy looks like he could make millions modeling T-shirts. I'm maybe 5-foot-8 on a good day if I'm wearing boots instead of my loafers. I'm pretty much bald ... my wife calls me Cue Ball ... so I shave my head and I'll handicap myself further by wearing my glasses. I'll make the debate production peoples' jobs impossible with my shiny melon. And I promise not to wear makeup.

"But, I will talk about issues. I will talk about sensible immigration policy, equitable taxation so that everyone pays their fair share, a universal living wage and stricter gun laws. I will talk about my vision of a future where everyone has the opportunity to improve their lives and the lives of their children. I will talk about public schools and bringing down barriers standing in the way of success for everyone. I will be happy to talk about how I differ from Mike Clarke and Governor Foster. And, if someone asks if I have ever smoked marijuana, I will answer truthfully ... the answer is 'yes.' And, I will advocate for legalization to decriminalize marijuana to provide funding for thorough medical testing of the possible benefits of cannabis-based products."

"I don't have many secrets. It's all in the book anyway. Available now by the way. Lake Northwood of Traditions and Values, no preview copy for you. You have to buy it to read it."

Looking straight at Northwood, the senator, now on a roll with reporters laughing, said, "No Lake, you are mentioned a few times, we have a book for you, too."

The senator's biography, "A Progressive's Life... Where We Are, Where We Could Be," written by Carl Lyon, was self-published to get it out quickly, but was already selling in the top 200 books on Amazon. There are more than 17 million available so the top 200 was a good start. Carl had agreed to take a quarter of the net from sales after expenses. The senator had vowed to give the rest of the proceeds to progressive causes.

The book was the story of Buckman's life so far. The first several chapters were his account and thoughts about the assassinations of his friends Senator Lansing Landon and Congressman Marion Jackson and the terrorist shooting of the others at Crossroads State. He talked about his serious consideration to withdraw from the race and asking for spiritual guidance. Several more chapters detailed his opinions about thoughtful gun control.

In the middle chapters he talked about his life before politics, his relationship with a gorgeous student who became his wife, and how his world view was cultivated by travels with his parents to foreign lands. He told the stories about being conceived by "The Old Hippies" in the arboretum of Crossroads State University and his favorite story about exploring the Smithsonian in 1976 on the same day the Queen of England visited, wearing strings of pearls and a woman's wide-brimmed sailor hat.

Later in the book he took a deeper dive into policy. He and Carl wrote about policy and what he would do as president. Carl thought the policy chapters had surprising clarity considering how wonky the senator could be when discussing his beliefs.

In the book, the senator added his thoughts about a universal living wage, essentially guaranteed income, which was the most radical of his left leanings.

Mike Clarke committed to the debate the day after Buckman challenged him to come out and play.

Three days before the debate, the senator began debate preparation with his staff on Beatrice in between campaign stops. He was an entertaining professor … at least Kim Wakefield had thought so … and he seemed unshakable in preparation for the debate.

Everyone on Beatrice pressed him on three levels, the basic and hanging curve ball questions, policy, and the "gotcha" moments.

"Cue Ball, did you think your relationship with a student who had previously had a high school fling of about 30 seconds, resulting in a pregnancy and abortion, was appropriate?" Kim asked.

The room went silent. It was another unexpected moment, one of many in their campaign, from the unpredictable candidate and his spirited wife. No one had ever mentioned the senator's wife had undergone an abortion.

"What?" Gerald said. "Wait. Back up to that moment where you mentioned abortion."

"Gerald, he knows," Kim said. "As soon as I found out I was

pregnant and told my parents, they talked with me about options and statistics about being a single mother and college student, which I could have been. They were very understanding. The guy was an ass and was out of my life about as quickly as … well, about as quickly as the act lasted. I made the decision to not have the baby. It was very early in the pregnancy. The guy is still alive and it was bound to come out eventually. My parents were supportive of my decision."

"I know," the senator confirmed. "It was one of the things we talked about in those long conversations when we were still just student and advisor. No reason for the subject to come up and I'm comfortable if it does."

"So now I have a question, which you could likely face before caucus night," O'Malley began. "As a Christian, as you claim to be, do you support abortion rights?"

"You mean a woman's right of choice when it comes to her own life and body? Yes, I believe in a woman's right to choose," the senator said. "Just as simple as that. I know I pray to a heavenly force and it gives me comfort. Kim prays with me and has asked for forgiveness.

"Do you support abortion rights all the way to 25 weeks of pregnancy?" O'Malley continued.

"I support a woman's right to choose, but I will add that the abortion rate in the United States is about the lowest in 50 years, and the teenage pregnancy rate is the lowest since records about teenage pregnancy have been kept. I am sympathetic to anyone who has to consider the difficult choices Kim faced."

"So back to Kim's good question. Should you have allowed yourself to start an intimate relationship with a student who you were advising?" Gerald asked.

"It started as a student-counselor relationship and developed over time into a lifetime relationship. We are still together, have a son we are adore, and we are devoted to each other," the senator said. "Some people probably do have an issue with how our relationship began. I do not. I fell in love and I'm still deeply in love with my wife. I see nothing negative about that."

"In your book you admit that you have smoked marijuana. Given that and the start of your relationship with your wife, should voters question your judgment?" O'Malley asked.

"I question my own …"

"No Senator, you do not question anything about your judgment. Not ever," Gerald interrupted. "I know how honest you are but there comes a time when you need to be slightly less honest. Just tone it down. Relax the honesty a bit. Say you understand that some people may not agree with everything you have done in your life, but it is your life."

CHAPTER 36

Debate

Gerald had hired a veteran producer of Traditions and Values Network to work on the senator's stage presence. Phil Everly had left TVN to start a consulting business.

"Phil Everly? You aren't from Shenandoah, Iowa, originally, are you?" the senator asked, with no hint of a smile.

"Where the hell is Shenandoah, Iowa?" Everly asked.

"If this guy doesn't know who Phil Everly was, we may have an issue with communication and fitting together," the senator said, now with a big smile. "Phil and Don Everly are legendary in Iowa. They were early and great rockers. You keep telling everyone in Iowa your name. It may help us pick up some votes in western Iowa. The real Phil, God rest his soul, died a few years ago."

Gerald didn't know who the Everly Brothers were either. He knew for damn sure he was not about to admit the fact.

Everly urged the senator to reconsider his insistence about wearing his glasses and going on television without makeup.

"The glasses are staying. I will agree to a little touchup," the senator said.

"Cue Ball, you'll need to do something with that head. I'd suggest a stocking cap," said Kim, who was back on the sarcasm trail moments after her campaign-rocking revelation.

Everly also suggested that whenever possible, the senator move out from behind the podium. The podium might make him look even smaller than he was. Everly was not the only one offering an opinion on Senator Buckman's stature.

Rushton, in one of his frequent social media messages from the White House, got in a dig at Senator Buckman days before the debate. He tweeted, "I'm wondering if anyone will see the Senator from Minnesota over the podium?" #tinyguy #professorhemp

Buckman didn't back down when reporters at a campaign event asked him about Rushton's dig.

"At least the president was able to spell everything correctly in this post. Spelling is quite often a challenge for him. This social media thing is complex work for the president," Buckman said. "Unfortunately for the country, what this president lacks in grammar, he also lacks in vision.

"Besides, if people are listening, they won't need to see me. I'll be the one talking about issues, solutions and what I want to do every day for people."

Everly also had more advice.

"Avoid standing next to Clarke except for obligatory pre-debate greetings," Everly added. "Stand next to Governor Foster instead. We'll demand that your podium be next to Governor Foster's with her in the middle."

"Don't go too deeply with policy statements or positions. They may sound more progressive … radical … than they actually are. Tone down the professor and emphasize the pragmatic, progressive senator."

The major news channels – 3N, Traditions and Values and The News Affiliates (TNA) -- planned live coverage with an hour of post-debate analysis.

Ticket access had become a public, pre-debate controversy. Mike Clarke and Governor Foster both had long lists of major donors they wanted seats for up front near the stage. The senator fought for equal distribution of tickets among the three candidates and the top Iowa Democratic officials.

"This is Iowa's major pre-caucus event. The rest of us are outsiders asking for the support of Iowans. I want Iowans to be included in the most prominent seats," Buckman said.

The senator really wanted his supporters near the stage. He had spent nearly 200 days in the state in the past 10 months. He felt it was to his advantage to have a live audience heavy with young, enthusiastic Iowans who wouldn't be sitting on their hands.

Buckman's campaign had invited hundreds of young supporters whom the senator had been courting since the first day Beatrice rolled across the border. The word was out to come to Des Moines, even if you couldn't get into the Heartland Civic Center for the debate. The invitation spread via Buckman's social media platforms and throughout college Young Democrat organizations to blanket Iowa with a door-to-door army of volunteers in the week before the debate. In exchange, they would be invited to a post-debate party at a Des Moines hotel with another party at 100 Iowa Brews and Buns.

Buckman was asked about a brief moment of silence for Senator Lansing Landon and Congressman Marion Jackson and the others lost at Crossroads State before the debate. He asked that the moment of silence take place before the candidates were on the stage. The senator also was concerned about his own emotional reaction to the video tribute to his fallen friends.

"I'd like to at least start the debate before breaking down emotionally," the senator said. "I've seen the video. It's very moving. The video can stand on its own."

On January 20, the day of the debate, the senator started the day on the exercise bike. He went to a breakfast with supporters who arrived from all over Iowa, Minnesota, Illinois and Wisconsin to volunteer to knock on doors.

"No matter what happens tonight and what you read or hear after the debate, I have won," the senator told the crowd he thought was about 300. "We started this endeavor with the goal to shake some stuff up. You all might use a different word than stuff.

"I think we are doing that … shaking stuff up. We are forcing conversations and pressing issues no other candidate, certainly not the president, will talk about. We're talking about improving public schools, not abandoning them. We're talking about universal health care. It's a right of all, not the privilege of the wealthy. We're talking about service in exchange for paid tuition.

"We're talking about taxing the wealthiest Americans

equitably. We're talking about a universal guaranteed income. The wealthiest should not have all the advantages, although Rushton believes they should. We're the ones talking about a three trillion-dollar infrastructure project.

"We're the ones who have spent 200 days in Iowa, meeting Iowans, riding bikes with them, waiting at shift changes to listen to their concerns. And, we have certainly suffered tragedy and dark days along the way.

"Yes, we have already won because of your vision and your faith.

"Tonight, and all the way through caucus night I'm going to ask you to do what you can to make lives better. When you go home, keep making phone calls, keep talking to your friends and if you can, keep knocking on the doors of Iowans. Stick with us all the way through caucus night, when the dorky looking senator from Minnesota with the glasses and his grassroots campaign shocks them all.

"Thank you for your support and your hard work on my behalf. You humble me."

Most of the people in the room couldn't see him. He knew that and made his security scramble again as he waded into the crowd to shake hands, take pictures and personally thank dozens of supporters before the Secret Service detail could convince him to head out the back way from the union hall.

He made 12 more stops to ask for support and listen to Iowans before heading to the Heartland Center.

He added new policy at one of the many stops. He explained the thought that inner city schoolchildren may be deeply impacted by lead-based paint and lead exposure in their homes. He promised a national lead abatement plan as part of his proposal to invest in the infrastructure of the United States.

"Imagine if we could identify children whose learning was impaired by exposure to lead in their homes. Imagine if their development was harmed by that exposure. We can do something about that," he said. "It would be a national solution, not only a quick fix to known problem spots like in Flint, Michigan," he said, referring to the crumbling lead piping polluting that city's water system. "What if we can have a real impact on lead exposure and how it could improve the academic progress of at-risk children in older cities?

"We can do this and much more."

The debate featuring the Democrats still running seriously in Iowa was the first time most Americans, flipping between the Iowa debate, reruns of movies they had seen a dozen times and, home improvement shows, would see the Senator from Minnesota.

Outside the venue, hundreds of college kids from throughout the Midwest waved Buckman signs. Others had caricatures of his shaved, round head and black glasses on another version of Buckman support signs. They had already discovered 100 Iowa Brews and Buns in the afternoon before the rally.

Buckman wanted to go out and meet supporters before the debate. The Secret Service didn't even consider the idea. Security entering the Civic Center was extremely tight. People with tickets were funneled to redundant security checks. No bags or signs were allowed in the seating areas. There were seats available to only a few reporters. Buckman had asked for much better access for the media but lost that fight to the other two candidates. Most of the reporters were in an adjacent media center that the candidates would visit after the debate.

Mike Clarke, as anticipated, looked presidential and tall. Karla Foster was immaculately dressed and composed. By comparison, Senator Pierce Buckman was dressed down. He wore a blue button-down shirt and a navy blazer. He had on loafers. No socks. Everly had expressed concern about the appearance of the senator's ears, which had been damaged by years of wrestling.

"What the hell is wrong with your ears?" Everly had asked during a debate coaching session. "Can we do something with them?"

"Cauliflower ears from damage done over years of wrestling. Very natural for wrestlers to have them. Surgery can help somewhat and the damage may heal somewhat. Or not. Mine aren't that bad. I'm afraid we're stuck with them. Lincoln was a wrestler. Even he may have had cauliflower ears."

"Yeah, well the Lincoln-Douglas debates were not being

watched by a few million people, or whatever the number is," Everly shot back.

"I know I'm better looking than Lincoln," the senator joked. "And Douglas was a lot shorter than Abe."

"Yeah, and how did that go for Douglas?" Everly said.

"He might have won the debates and the election if he'd had the toughness and confidence of a wrestler," the senator said.

The debate seemed predictable at first. All three candidates spent more time targeting President Rushton and his Republican cronies than they did each other.

There were two prime opportunities for Buckman to contrast himself with Foster and Clarke.

Clarke went after him on what he called "the shallowness of the senator's campaign promises."

"College tuition, infrastructure, guaranteed income, public school spending ... these are all massive programs he is proposing. But, the senator has yet to explain how this is possible without raising taxes. He won't tell you tonight he will raise taxes, but it is impossible to do what he is advocating without raising taxes," Clarke challenged. "He will raise taxes as president.

"My observation of the senator is that he started this campaign as the humble professor from Minnesota. He has gotten beyond the humble part. He is now proposing everything for everyone and suggesting he is the one who can provide this pipe dream. And remember, it is a pipe dream."

It was a hard, effective shot.

Buckman moved out toward the center of the stage a couple of feet from behind his podium. He started out quietly.

"I have been talking about these issues with Iowans for months, and I have explained numerous times how to pay for this vision shared by so many people. Public service in exchange for college tuition, schools without barriers that will not only improve the future of the students within them, but their parents, siblings, grandparents and the neighborhoods around them.

"If I am elected president, I will fight every day for the neglected, forgotten and underserved. I will fight to make quality health care a right for every American, not a privilege of the wealthy.

"But, you must believe we can do big things as this country has in the past. If we are handcuffed by politics, as we have seen, little is accomplished. I think Iowans understand what we have been talking about. They want the restrictions of political handcuffs off and tossed away permanently."

For the first time all night, some of the Democrats rose to their feet, applauding.

"I will advocate for a multi-trillion-dollar infrastructure project to rebuild roads, airports, bridges and aging city services. At the same time, we will create jobs for years to come.

"We can do it all. Here is how: As president I would ask for immediate reduction of budgets by 10 percent. If possible, staff reductions will be made through retirements and attrition. I will ask for equitable taxation so the wealthiest Americans are paying their fair share and the burden is lessened on the middle class.

"Yes, I support a progressive vision. That vision will not change for political expediency, to be elected, or to appeal to donors who may not share the same vision. I won't change who I am to win votes. I am what I am … a husband, a father, a son, a U.S. senator, a progressive and an educator. I believe if we have compassion and an inextinguishable will and spirit, we can improve the lives of millions who are being left behind."

The senator's young supporters watching on big screens in the cold winter air outside the civic center celebrated their candidate with chants of "Buckman, Buckman, Buckman" as they waved their signs.

There was one more opportunity for the senator to distance himself from Rushton more than from his Democratic opponents.

Lake Northwood, who had been chosen as one of three media representatives moderating the debate, made his personal case questioning Senator Buckman's judgment, citing his relationship with a student, his Iowa Agricultural Exposition appearance in extreme heat, resulting in deaths, and his "radically progressive" policy statements.

"Senator, the millions of viewers of Traditions and Values are asking if you have the judgment or values to be president or even the nominee of the Democratic Party."

Buckman walked slowly from behind the lectern toward the center of the stage, this time even farther in front. His facial expression was not different than at any other point in the 90 minutes under the lights.

When he spoke, he was precise in his selection of words.

"Our worst day of this campaign was the tragedy at Crossroads State. The second worst day was the day of the fair, which was so torridly hot. People died of heat-related illnesses that day across the country. Many of the same people we've talked about throughout this endeavor in Iowa … the impoverished, the left behind, the uninsured, the forgotten … were among those who died.

"People did die at the Expo that day. It had nothing to do with our campaign event there. Our event was no different than any other candidate's similar event at the Expo over the years. It's a tradition of the Iowa Caucuses. The problem was the heat, not the event itself."

He headed back toward his lectern but wasn't done. Not nearly.

"I would ask 'Whose traditions and whose values are we talking about?' It used to be traditional in his country to practice slavery. It used to be tradition to discriminate against minorities. They couldn't own property or vote. They couldn't control their own destiny. They couldn't advance their careers because of the color of their skin. Displacing American Indians and taking their lands was traditional in this country. Extreme wealth of some, often at the expense of others, still appears to be a value of this country. We devalued women. We didn't allow them to vote. Those were traditions and values of this country. There is a different path … a different vision … and I believe Iowans share different values.

"You and many others have asked about the ethics of a college professor having a relationship with a student. I fell in love with an adult graduate student, who is the love of my life, whom I married, who is totally supportive of my campaign. We have a fantastic baby boy who I believe may be the happiest, smartest child in the world. I may be biased, though. If some believe my personal story should disqualify me as a viable candidate for president, that is not only acceptable to me, I would encourage them to find the candidate right for them. I will not apologize for having a fantastic life."

Senator Buckman's supporters outside the Civic Center cheered wildly. Inside, much of the crowd gave the senator a standing ovation.

Then he returned to the lectern.

Karla Foster continued to hammer Senator Buckman on how he would pay for what he was promising.

"The Senator can continue to be the fantasy candidate, promising an agenda that is impossible to pay for without a massive tax increase. This is not fantasy land. When you make promises, they are very hollow unless you can pay for them," Governor Foster said. "This vision he continues to talk about gets very blurred when you start talking about how to pay for everything."

Post-debate analysts generally agreed Senator Buckman had won because he had the most to gain.

Former Congressman and Gulf War veteran Carlton Cromwell, now a political analyst for 3N (National News Network), seemed to sum up the night by saying "on caucus night in Iowa, candidates must be 'viable' to earn delegates. That essentially means they need enough support to earn delegates. If he wasn't before, and I personally believe he was, Senator Pierce Buckman of Minnesota became viable tonight with his debate performance.

"I think it was an impressive performance. The criticism about how to pay for what he is talking about will continue to be an issue for his campaign. Some of these ideas may be pipe dreams. No question.

"But if you serve up a hanging curve ball to the senator the way Lake Northwood did tonight, he is going to take it deep. He is smart and showed passion and compassion tonight."

Senator Buckman and Kim briefly attended a post-debate rally at 100 Iowa Brews and Buns with hundreds of supporters.

"How do you think we did?" the senator asked, anticipating the raucous response he received. "Yeah, me too.

"But, do you know what was really important tonight? Your enthusiasm and support. You were incredible tonight. Karla Foster and Mike Clarke are probably already on their private jets heading home. What am I doing? I'm staying in Iowa.

"In the remaining weeks before the caucuses, our message will not change. We're going to continue to talk about initiatives and programs to improve the lives of the forgotten, neglected, impoverished and underserved. This is the fairness campaign. We're going to continue to outwork other candidates. We're going to be at as many factory gates as we can schedule, schedule as many college events as we can, call thousands of Iowans who we know will caucus and will support us.

"For the first time in the Iowa caucus process you will be able to participate remotely. From your own home. It might be 20 below, it might be the worst ice storm on record in Iowa, you might have a sick baby, you might need a baby sitter and don't have one. Our supporters will be there at the caucus sites or at their computers wherever they are because they know the importance. We're the campaign that can make the lives of people better.

"I need your help. Volunteer to make the phone calls, knock on doors, come to our events, tell your friends to participate on caucus night. Set up caucus parties on your floors in college or go to your caucus site. Just participate.

"I ask you again to join us… white, black, Hispanic, American Indian, straight, gay, transgender, wealthy progressives, you folks the opposition calls the radical left, old hippies like my parents, whom you will see much more often in the next two weeks, people who go home from work with the grime of their job on their hands and their clothes, and especially people who are tired of a president who builds barriers, a president who sits in the White House with his mobile device, sending out social media posts … sometimes even grammatically correct posts … and appears to do little else. He is the Divider in Chief. His idea of vision is to deport and separate families of people who are productively employed and help drive the economy. He can say a lot, he just can't seem to DO ANYTHING," the senator said, his voice rising.

"I think we can do better. We can do more. Thank you for your support tonight. Now get your butts back out there in morning. I will be out there with the message."

By 6 a.m., after 45 minutes on a stationary bike, the senator was at a factory gate during shift change. Both the candidate and his staffers voiced their opinion there was a different feel this morning. Workers congratulated him on his debate performance. More of them were telling him they would "be there on caucus night."

For the next 14 hours he had four speaking engagements around central Iowa. He also visited two diners to talk with patrons and showed up unannounced at a teachers' union event.

"This president wants to dilute the incredible strength of teachers. You know it, I know it. He wants to give up on public schools. He doesn't believe in your schools in diverse neighborhoods, your students who haven't had the advantages of safe neighborhoods, supportive families, experiences that make them better students. We will break down those barriers. We will build better schools and give you the tools to help students be productive adults who will drive this country and economy for decades to come.

"This president has made it clear: he will short-change you and your students. He is willing to leave them and you behind. We've tried that. It doesn't work. I need your support on caucus night. If you can believe we can do better for your students and your neighborhoods, I ask for your support."

CHAPTER 37

Timmy Caucus

Two weeks remained before the Pierce Buckman campaign would either move forward or be unceremoniously disbanded and forgotten. He had staked his campaign on one often confusing, sometimes contentious, sometimes controversial, grassroots voter event. They would support his vision and push it forward or reject it with a resounding defeat. For Buckman's campaign, there was no middle ground. Without the boost of funds for an Iowa Caucus winner, there wouldn't be money to advance to New Hampshire.

The old hippies, Jane and Robert Buckman, understood the situation as they joined the campaign for the last two weeks before caucus night. The senator looked forward to spending time with them. Kim was eager for them to help take care of Owen, who was also going out on the road for the last two weeks.

"Pierce, how is it *really* going?" Jane asked. "You OK? It looks like Clarke and Foster have the money for the long haul. What's your financial picture?"

"Actually, we've got plenty of money to get through caucus night. We have money for television in Des Moines, Cedar Rapids, Waterloo, the Quad Cities and Council Bluffs. We have a pretty good operation going in The Warehouse. Gerald tells me it's going well.

"And, we seem to have the caucus day organized. We have dozens of caucus parties planned where people will caucus remotely."

Timothy Cashton, a former graduate student in statistics and computer science at Crossroads State, had shown up at the Buckman for President headquarters in the extended stay hotel in West Des Moines. He said he wanted to volunteer. It wasn't that simple anymore. Not for anyone who would have access to the candidate. Not after Crossroads State.

Crossroads State was why Tim Cashton wanted to join the campaign. He was in his dorm room studying ... he had no interest in football nor any real interest in presidential politics at the time ... but he knew one of the young people killed that day. Annie Able was as close to a love interest as anyone ever in his life. They had studied together, gotten coffee together and shared pizza and a movie in her off-campus apartment. They had kissed. The relationship hadn't become intimate, so far, but Tim thought he might be in love.

Cashton was interviewed initially by Gerald O'Malley; whose first question was always "What skills do you have to help the senator become president?" Sometimes, passion and idealism were enough for O'Malley and he would pass the candidate on to the FBI for a background check. O'Malley hated the complexity of the process and how long it could take. When he wanted someone, he wanted them immediately. The tragedy at Crossroads State had complicated his hiring process.

The FBI check on Cashton revealed he was from an average family background in South Dakota. He was an accomplished student with an aptitude for numbers, analysis and computers. His academic record at Crossroads State was exceptional.

O'Malley sensed that with his background and his emotional investment in the campaign growing out of the Crossroads State massacre, Timothy Cashton could help identify Iowans most likely to show up on caucus night. And if they showed up, would they stand up in support for Senator Buckman? O'Malley wanted Cashton close by to go to for analysis and updates.

In a long, rambling interview, O'Malley became lost in Cashton's lingo. O'Malley was way outside his scope of knowledge. He wanted the kid badly for exactly those reasons.

It didn't take long for Cashton to be a spectacular addition to the "Campaign Kids for Buckman," a tight, relatively small group of young people who focused on identifying and stratifying supporters who would show up on caucus night. Stratification of support – unlikely, possible, likely, dead-lock cinches – was as important as having the personal data on Iowans. It went beyond that when Cashton started with the "Campaign Kids." He took all the data, added in voting history and caucus participation of the Iowans who had been identified as possible Buckman supporters and came up with categories of commitment.

He had done it by working 20-hour days. His sleeping quarters and office were the same place -- in a meeting room in the West Des Moines extended stay headquarters. He was sleeping on an inflatable mattress.

Cashton came up with a database of Iowans stratified not only by level of commitment to the senator but by likelihood of showing up. The focus could then be more strategic.

"We should focus on levels C and D, those likely to vote, but with only 'casual' or 'possible' support of the senator. More contacts with these people and less contact with levels A and B, who are already fully engaged with the senator. Think of it as a cone. More contacts at the bottom, fewer at the top," Cashton had suggested in a widely distributed email within the campaign. "Feed the beasts at the bottom with more direct contacts. More phone calls, more direct mail, more invitations to the website and to events in their area. We need to get after these people for the remaining days."

The candidate had seen Cashton's email to staff about a strategy for the two weeks remaining before caucus night.

"I want to meet this kid and thank him. I've seen him around but haven't met him," the senator told Gerald.

"They've started calling him Timmy Caucus and Timmy Money," O'Malley reported. "He is always here. Let's go find him."

Timmy Caucus was where he usually was, in the meeting room standing face-to-face with a bank of computer screens.

"Tim, Pierce Buckman. I understand you are doing some great analytics and coming up with terrific strategies to focus on the right people before caucus night."

"Senator, nice to meet you," Timmy Caucus said.

"I'm guessing we have a lot in common. Umm ... I was always considered kind of a nerdy kid," the senator said.

"Me too, Senator. Now look at us. You are going to be president of the United States and I'll be one of the nerds who helped you get there. It's a nerd's world."

The senator laughed.

"What are you working on now?" Buckman asked.

"A dummy database."

"Explain and let's see if I understand," the senator said.

"Bad people have been trying to hack into databases like these and not only steal the data, but use the data to flood voters with imaginative, crude, racist, effective misinformation to meddle with elections. The gun advocates like the people Jericho Brooks was hanging around with could hack in and send information to your supporters accusing you of all sorts of bad things. They want to influence the results because they fear your candidacy. It may be your own party opponents, opposing campaigns, including Rushton's campaign, or foreign entities. What we're working on are fake databases. The names may be correct, but the addresses and phone numbers, email addresses, social media addresses, will all be fake. Hack in all you want, we don't think you will get data helping you in the slightest."

"There are also several accurate databases available to your staff. Each one is different in some way, but still accurate.

"Not sure you want to know all of this, but you have staff who are not only fighting hacks, but maybe, possibly, are looking at entry into the data of your opponents, including Russian bots who are just messing around with you right now. The Russian bot farms probably don't think you can win yet. They are practicing in case you do win the nomination, which I think you just might.

"You have a cybersecurity team in addition to a social media team. They are spending a lot of time protecting the integrity of your campaign finances, your supporter lists and the integrity and security of your social media platforms. They have definitely bought in to the campaign. They are invested in you fully. They are a ruthless group."

The senator took it all in.

"I understand this is going on and has been. I've been told some of the comments on our social media platforms are coming from fake accounts. They may be foreign, they may be domestic, correct?" Buckman asked.

"Yes, but more importantly, on caucus night, we will get your supporters to participate either at sites or anywhere really and stand for you and we will know who the supporters of Clarke and Foster are, and there are possibly ways to discourage them from showing up. But I didn't suggest that. I know, this isn't the way democracy should work. Even I know that, and until a few weeks ago, I didn't care at all about Rushton or any other candidates. By the way, I now think Rushton is evil because of his stand, or inability to take a stand, on controlling weapons made to kill humans."

"Tim, keep up the great work. Gerald, make sure our nerds are at least getting food and T-shirts. Tim, can we win the Iowa Caucuses?"

"Yes sir. You will win. I guarantee it," Timmy Caucus said. "Our people will turn out if the end of the world is on the horizon."

"Well, let's hope it doesn't come to that," the Senator smiled as he turned and left the room.

O'Malley was shocked by the conversation. He thought Senator Buckman was by far the best Democratic candidate. He believed the senator would make a great president. But he also knew the senator to be incredibly honest, almost to a fault, by political standards. The honesty bar is not that high in politics. The guy was only taking funds from one political action committee, the one set by the Holtons and their wealthy friends when the senator first disclosed he was running. Buckman was trying to do something remarkable, beat big-moneyed candidates and beat them with true grass-roots campaigning. Their campaign was traveling Iowa on a beat-up motorhome that had broken down repeatedly, including that tragic day at Crossroads State, while the other Democratic candidates traveled by private jets and when in Iowa, in luxury motorhomes. Was Buckman looking the other way when told his staff might be bending campaign ethics? O'Malley wasn't about to ask.

O'Malley did ask Timmy Caucus about a recent event on the campaign trail when 150 people showed up for a Mike Clarke event in northwest Iowa and Clarke wasn't even in the state. It was an embarrassment for the Clarke campaign. Even Buckman had suggested publicly they "may not have their stuff together."

"Did our folks do that?" O'Malley asked.

"Maybe," Timmy Caucus conceded. "Pretty easy to get people to turn out when you go on a candidate's social media page and a college's social media sites to promote an event you know won't happen. Ok, guilty. Just did it that once to see if we could. Once was enough. It was successful. We knew we could do it if we needed to respond to dirty tricks. All these people waiting for an event that didn't happen. They scrambled to get a surrogate there. It was classic. The media story of the day was the mix-up. The senator's nerds won the media day.

"We know foreign and domestic troublemakers will try to meddle in our campaign and even in the Iowa Caucuses, especially now when you can participate remotely. Our feeling is that Senator Buckman will be more of a target than other candidates because he is different. That worries people who fear outsiders. They think he might gain momentum by being different. We've done a good job of keeping his opponents at bay with some creative meddling of our own. It was particularly noticeable and ugly after the Crossroads State massacre. We had people expressing regret the senator hadn't been there and had avoided the assassination attempt. One post said the bus would be bombed. We filed a report with Secret Service and FBI but we were able to turn public opinion in the senator's favor. That wasn't difficult. There was, and is, a lot of sympathy out there for him."

O'Malley warned Timmy Caucus to not repeat their conversation.

CHAPTER 38

Bombshell

The Senator Pierce Buckman for President campaign had visited dozens of Iowa towns, had been in 82 of 99 counties. He had been advised to not spend any time in northwest Iowa. He went anyway and talked with hundreds of college students and professors. In that region of the state, he had met workers at the gates of meat packing plants who were natives of African and Caribbean countries, of Mexico and Central America.

He had hosted Biking with Buckman events all over the state, attracting as few as six bikers on a chilly, windy day to more than 700 in a ride from Des Moines.

He had started with little name recognition. Opening Iowa Caucus preference polls showed him at about 3 percentage points, far behind several other candidates and far behind "undecided."

He became a father for the first time.

He had taken media questions on an impromptu basis what campaign staff estimated to be 250 times, knowing his campaign required free media for name recognition. He had agreed to only a few extended interviews with national media, except with his own biographer, Carl Lyon, who wrote his book.

"I'm too busy in Iowa," he claimed when asked to come to Washington, D.C., or New York for extended media interviews.

He nearly ended his campaign in the aftermath of the tragedy at Crossroads State. His odd campaign motorhome, now nearly covered in messages written in permanent markers, had broken down 17 times in Iowa. He may have survived an assassination plot only because the bus broke down that day.

The candidate, an advocate for access to mental health services, struggled with his own moments of depression.

The polls now suggested he was within range of Mike Clarke and Karla Foster, who at one point were expected to get Buckman out of the way before the caucuses even took place.

His biography sales indicated he was gaining attention outside of Iowa. "A Progressive's View ... Where We Are, Where We Could Be" was now a top 50 book nationally.

He had introduced the most progressive policy statements since Franklin D. Roosevelt.

He was himself: the bald, savvy, engaging, liberal professor from northern Minnesota.

The entire campaign had been shadowed by the unexpected. Just before the campaign finale, the reason they had spent all this time in Iowa, there was another defining, unexpected moment.

On the night before the Iowa Caucuses, Traditions and Values chose to broadcast the news the campaign had known might come out at some point. On the screen were the words "Senator Buckman's Wife Had Abortion as a Teen."

3N reported the same news minutes later but said it had been unable to independently confirm the news. Essentially that meant they were monitoring Traditions and Values and had stolen the news from a rival.

It was a last-minute bombshell meant to slow or destroy what appeared to be Buckman momentum. Who knows where it came from? Maybe from Foster, who had been on friendly terms throughout the campaign with Buckman, especially after her daughter started a relationship with the Buckman staffer, Ryan Holton, and now had a granddaughter. Kassie Foster may have inadvertently let the secret out. She knew about Kim Wakefield's previous pregnancy. She had become close to Kim when the senator's wife was pregnant at the same time as Kassie.

Maybe the story came directly from the White House from "opposition research." It was not exactly a secret. Kim Wakefield's family, friends and those who were unfriendly to Kim certainly would know and may have been found by the Rushton campaign. The guy involved in the fling was out there somewhere.

Spokesman Curt Jaslow's phone quickly lit up with media calls. At first, he issued the stock non-answer of "I don't know but I will try to find out for you," although he did know it was true.

Jaslow suggested to O'Malley the senator would have to go on national television. So would Kim.

"Sir, let's handle this as quickly as possible," O'Malley said when he informed the candidate. "There are people out there who believe this will be the stumble that gets you beat tomorrow night. And they know that unless you have a very strong showing, they won't have to worry about you for the rest of the campaign" O'Malley said. "Will Kim appear with you?"

"I think so. You know she hasn't hidden it from anyone inside the campaign. You all know and we'll say that this is not a secret, we just didn't think it was anyone's business," the senator said. "I will ask Kim. Set it up as quickly as possible."

Kim Wakefield took about two seconds to decide. She was angry about the invasion of her privacy.

"Not only yes, but hell, yes, even though this is no one's business and that is one of the things I will say. Sweetheart, you believe in a woman's right to choose, even though I know you are personally opposed to abortion. It's contradictory but you can explain your thoughts," Kim said.

Less than an hour later, Jaslow and O'Malley had returned media calls and said the senator would talk publicly in the room Timmy Caucus was using for his clandestine operation. The computer whiz was nervous about exposure of his operation. He made sure all the screens were off, and the papers strewn across the room were secured out of sight.

"Timmy Caucus would be the better story than something very private that happened what, 15 or 20 years ago but this will be big news for media?" O'Malley said.

O'Malley was right. This was apparently big news. Reporters from all over the country gathering in Des Moines to cover caucus night had broken away from their bar tour of Des Moines for this. O'Malley counted 15 television cameras in the tight meeting room.

O'Malley was on his way to the senator's suite to get him and Kim when Ridge and Brynn Powell and their burly security guard, Lincoln, headed down the hall toward the room guarded by Secret Service.

"The Powells to see the senator and Kim," Lincoln said in a deep, quiet voice.

"Of course. No weapon, right?" one of the field agents, recognizing the Powells, as most people would, asked Lincoln. "We'll still have to wand you. Also, the Powells."

A couple of minutes later after a call into the suite, Brynn was allowed to knock on the door.

"Oh my gosh," Kim said, hugging Brynn first, then Ridge.

The senator kissed Brynn on the cheek and hugged Ridge.

"We have this little thing going on downstairs," the senator said.

"We heard. We're coming. This is ridiculous," Brynn said.

"We weren't asked, Brynn," Ridge said.

"We want you there," Kim said. "We're so glad you are here."

The Powells had made five campaign tours throughout Iowa already with the senator. Each stop had drawn huge crowds appropriate for Hollywood royalty, starting with the appearance at the Expo. They had every intention of going out on caucus day to campaign with the senator.

The group, flanked by two Secret Service agents and Lincoln, walked into the meeting room where the press conference had been set up. There was an audible reaction of reporters to the presence of the Powells. The senator spoke first.

"When Kim was a teen, she became pregnant. After talking with her parents and a school counselor, who has been very influential in her life and continues to be, Kim considered her options. The unambiguous truth is this … teen mothers often face a lifetime of struggle," the senator began. "Kim decided she would terminate the pregnancy very soon after she found out she was pregnant.

"I have to tell you, I hardly think it is coincidence that the night before the caucuses and, in reflection of polling suggesting we are doing well, this suddenly becomes an important story. I do not enjoy Kim having to expose a difficult time of her life because someone wants to play politics. It is cruel. I guess we now have come to expect this type of politics.

"I believe in a woman's right to choose. Let me repeat … I am pro-woman and pro-choice. The rate of teen pregnancy by the way, is at an all-time low. I believe that is positive. Statistically, women are more likely to finish high school, attend college, build a career, if they are not single parents.

"Kim is now a fantastic mother. She was ready to be a mother. She has a master's degree. She was admitted to law schools and still may attend someday. I am very proud of my wife."

Kim spoke on her own behalf.

"I made the most difficult choice of my life quite a few years ago now. I think about my choice often. But it was my choice, which is a fact to remember. I broke no law," Kim said. "Fortunately, teenage girls now have a very low birth rate and have a number of family planning options available to them. At the time, it was the decision that was right for me. In this country, women do have choice, and if Pierce is elected, he will fight for that right, even though I know he personally is opposed to abortion as a form of birth control."

They weren't through. One of the reporters asked Brynn Powell about the issue. She obliged. If the last-minute bombshell news was intended to move support away from Buckman, she was about to move it back.

"The senator was restrained. I don't have to be. I am not running for anything. The future first lady of the United States, Kim Wakefield, is the best mother I know. She made a difficult choice and was able to because women in this country have a right to choose, although if Jack Rushton wins another term, he will do his best to take choice from women. That is why it is so important to support Senator Buckman tomorrow. We need reasonable voices in Washington who support women, respect women and believe women are able to make appropriate decisions about our own bodies."

Brynn Powell flashed a recognizable grin and said, "I wish she would have told you all it was none of your damn business because I believe you all know … it's none of your damn business."

The senator and Ridge Powell, standing next to each other, both applauded the spirited women they knew and loved.

"OK, let's go to Iowa Brews and Buns now," Ridge Powell whispered to the senator as the media left.

"Right behind you," Buckman said.

The Buckmans, the Powells, Buckman's parents, Gerald, Carl and Susan Lyon, Ryan Holton, Kassie Foster and spokesman, Curt Jaslow, plus two Secret Service agents and Lincoln the bodyguard piled into Beatrice the Bus, which was running as well as could be expected. Lincoln insisted on driving.

Buckman for President had recruited hundreds of volunteers to blanket the state at caucus sites. About a third of them appeared to be in Iowa Brews and Buns even before they knew who was about to show up. The bus unloaded. Lincoln checked out the inside quickly and arranged to take everyone in the back door.

"Way too crowded up front. Seems a bit crazy, but they are your people," Lincoln reported.

The place erupted as the group appeared. Young campaign volunteers, most wearing their caucus night T-shirts and eating sandwiches the campaign had paid for, were dumping beer on each other. The place was a mess. The senator's security detail was having trouble controlling the candidate, who wanted to wade into the young volunteers with Ridge Powell. The agents had their arms in front of Buckman shielding him from the wildly responsive kids.

"*Buckman, Buckman, Buckman*," they shouted.

Beer was flying. The senator and Ridge Powell were already soaked when Buckman climbed up on the bar with the cheap megaphone out of the bus. His Secret Service agents, plus Lincoln, were also on the bar.

"Settle down for a second. Settle down. OK, be respectful to the owners here. Don't throw the beer around. It's OK to drink it if you aren't driving," Buckman said. "Thank you all for coming. I know you made this trip with your own money and are probably skipping school to be here.

"I don't know about all of you, but I think something surprising is going to happen in Iowa tomorrow night. All across the state, because of all the work you have done on our behalf, we are going to stun the shit out of people.

"I probably shouldn't have said shit, should I? Is media here? Oh, well, I said it. Nine months ago, no one cared what I said. I could have said it then and no one would have noticed. We got to this point by being different and we'll keep being different.

"If we are successful tomorrow, it will be because you all share the vision of a different country which treats everyone fairly and does everything possible to make their lives better. No one is going to be left out of the progress if I am elected. We will have equitable taxation, we will provide college tuition for public service in this country and globally. We will provide quality, affordable health care for everyone. We will protect Social Security, Medicare and the safety net programs for the poor and forgotten. We will have vision. Thank you for sharing the vision.

"Tomorrow night across Iowa you will be working to share that vision with everyone. I see the T-shirts and I know you've had training about how this odd caucus system works. When you participate tomorrow night, I ask you to be advocates for everyone Jack Rushton wants to leave behind. Advocate for productive natives of other countries who are contributing greatly to our economy. He wants to deport them. Be advocates for people who work hard and still need those safety net programs he wants to cut. Be advocates for those without a voice.

"Be advocates for those who look different and sound different than you do.

"Be advocates for mental health.

"Be…advocates…for…change. It is on the horizon.

"Thank you all, bless you and be safe tonight. Don't drive, walk."

The crowd exploded again with the chanting and more flying beer like it was the winning team's celebration after a huge victory.

The senator and Ridge shook as many hands as they were allowed to shake by their security, which now included four city officers who had been called by the worried management team

315

of Iowa Brews and Buns.

Brynn Powell took charge, as usual. She wrote a check for $5,000 to Brew and Buns to pay for any cleanup and to cover more beer and sandwiches.

Ridge and Brynn stayed to share pitchers of Iowa craft beers with a couple of tables. Lincoln and the four Des Moines police officers stayed close to the Powells.

"Sir, you are leaving, right now," one of the Secret Service agents insisted, making it clear there would be no negotiation this time.

The senator waved and disappeared out the back door by the Secret Service agents and two more Des Moines police officers into a waiting black SUV instead of Beatrice.

"No matter what happens tomorrow, this has been some ride," the senator said to Kim and the Old Hippies. "Those kids humble me with their passion. Jack Rushton just doesn't understand what is outside his life in Washington. It's out here."

"You aren't going to cry again are you, Cue Ball?" Kim chided.

CHAPTER 39

Caucus Day

Ridge and Brynn Powell had helped close down Iowa Brews and Buns, which was still jammed at 2 a.m. Only four hours later they were still recovering when the senator, flanked by his Secret Service detail, climbed on the treadmill. After 45 minutes he went to the sauna.

"How many years have you been following this routine?" one of the Secret Service agents asked the senator.

"Probably since I was a sophomore in high school and I got serious about wrestling," Buckman said. "I just read a story that said saunas are good exercise. They open up your blood vessels, the heat gets your heart pumping and it lowers your blood pressure. We used to come in with heavy plastic suits, jump rope, stationary bikes, to get down to weight. Now we know that wasn't safe, and wrestlers don't do it anymore. At least they don't admit to doing it."

The only companion the senator could usually find for his early morning workouts was his security detail and Carl Lyon, who explained, "I'm old, I wake up early."

Lyon couldn't keep up physically with the senator but was at least willing to make some attempt on most mornings. Carl had discovered the workouts and sauna were great places to interview the senator for their book project. Buckman was wired from the exercise and his brain was sharp following a workout. The senator shared a lot of stories Lyon could use, and others he couldn't, in the sauna, where the senator was so comfortable.

Carl showed up late, 7 a.m., on the morning of the Iowa

Caucuses.

"At least you showed up," the senator said. "What do you think about today, Carl?"

"Campaign all the way to the finish, sir," Carl said. "And it's going to be a hell of a finish. I can feel it. Let's go listen to some people and get them to stand for you tonight."

"Crossroads State," the senator said.

"You know you won't be allowed to do that," Carl said.

"You may not have noticed, but I do what I need to do. I need to go to Crossroads State today," he said.

"Am I the one who is broaching this idea with your security detail?" Carl asked. "They won't go for it."

"I got it," the senator said.

As anticipated by Carl and the senator himself, the Secret Service initially said the trip from their campaign headquarters to Crossroads State was not possible.

"Oh, it is possible. Kim will go with me. Carl will go. I'll drive Beatrice," the senator said, knowing the Secret Service detail was reluctant to have him go anywhere in the distinctive motorhome.

After a couple of calls to Crossroads State security and administration and University City Police, the Secret Service detail was considering the senator's request. The Secret Service said it must be a small group, not a major campaign event. And, no media.

"After last night, I'm tired of them. Kim and I, the Old Hippies and Carl Lyon. That's it," the senator said. "I need to go."

Buckman and the rest of the small group was taken out the back of the extended stay headquarters to a string of three SUVs already running. Media was already hanging out in front but not at this particular exit. They could hardly miss the caravan of government issue SUVs leaving the parking lot.

There had been a lengthy investigation of the site of the Crossroads State assassination and mass killing. Evidence still had to be gathered to be able to prosecute Marin Gabbard, who was now nearly always referred to as Magda by the media, which is the nickname Jericho Brooks had given her. She was in

Polk County Jail awaiting trial for her role and was likely facing prison for the rest of her life.

Waiting for the senator in University City were law enforcement officers from the county and the university. University President Dana Moore was also there.

"Dr. Moore, thanks for allowing us to do this. I needed to be here. You know I haven't been allowed to come here even on the day of the memorial service," the senator said as he shook Dr. Moore's hand. "I have seen media coverage of the memorial site but wanted to visit myself."

The site was now covered by thousands of flowers and hundreds of handmade messages and remembrances.

"We're planning a permanent memorial on the site," Dr. Moore said.

A female student carrying a backpack was immediately spotted by the security detail. The Secret Service agents trotted to the startled student to check out the backpack. Inside were books, a laptop and a wallet. She explained she was headed about a mile away to a basic newswriting course.

The senator walked solemnly around the site. He read some of the messages. He whispered to Kim and held her hand. Carl snapped a few photos on his phone.

After several minutes, the senator asked the young student who was allowed to watch from a distance what the mood of the campus was after the tragedy.

"It took some time to get over the fact that something so terrible could happen here," the student said as she cautiously approached the senator. "Sir, I'm a journalism major. Can I ask you a few questions about that day?"

The senator agreed.

They were questions he had been asked repeatedly except the reporter found out this was the first time he had been to the actual site.

"As you might imagine, it's very emotional for Kim and I to be here. I think about what happened every day and probably will for the rest of my life. I was the target that day and fate intervened. I believe things happen for a reason," the senator said.

"Why do you think you survived?" the young woman asked.

"I struggle with that every day. It's an unanswerable question. To be a father to Owen, a husband to Kim, to do what I can to possibly make the lives of some people better in some small way. Maybe that is it or maybe it will be something that happens much later in my life," he said. "I have survived a heart attack and was not here when this tragedy occurred. I guess I'm supposed to be here right now."

"Will you win tonight?" the young woman asked.

"I believe we've had a message people in Iowa have responded to about helping the disaffected, the needy. We've talked about gun control, college tuition in exchange for public service, universal health care, universal living wage, Schools Without Barriers and equitable opportunities. We believe we've done what we can to be the progressive candidate in Iowa."

The journalism student asked if she could take a photo of the senator and Kim with the memorial in the background on her phone.

The Secret Service looked more closely at the phone before allowing the photos.

The excited student had a story. She knew it was a good one.

Buckman's entourage drove across campus to where he had started his Iowa campaign. At the Crossroads State University arboretum, they got out again.

"Oh dear, I do remember this place," Jane Buckman said. "Robert, remember?"

"Um, kind of unforgettable. Let's go for a walk," Robert said.

"Senator, no way you are going," one of his Secret Service agents said.

"I understand. Thanks for letting us do this today. You want me back in the SUV?"

"That would be good, sir."

The Old Hippies, Jane and Robert Buckman, walked on the groomed path cleared of snow. It was a beautiful setting with the snow on the ground and clinging to evergreen trees. Art students frequented the arboretum. It was quiet. The Old Hippies sat on bench for a few minutes. Kim was with them. They kissed. Kim hugged both of them and tears came to her eyes.

"Pierce, thanks for bringing us here. You know we haven't been back here since we were teaching school here during graduate school," Robert said when he got back in the SUV.

"You know the story is in the book. A few hundred thousand people know the hanky panky that went on here," the Senator kidded his parents.

"Oh, Pierce," his mom said.

There were scheduled events the rest of the day. The media caught up with Senator Buckman as he knocked on doors for an hour in inner city neighborhoods of Des Moines. He spoke at a luncheon, urging the crowd of several hundred to participate in the Iowa Caucuses.

"Regardless of what happens tonight, this journey has been one of the highlights of my life. I love Iowa, I love Iowans, and I will be back here," Buckman told the lunch crowd.

He visited a social services agency with a food pantry, child care, employment center and free lunch for whoever showed up. He read "Pete the Cat" and "Marcus and the Magnificent Margo" to kids in child care with media looking on. The senator did a commendable Marcus voice for the kids, who seemed mesmerized.

"If I am fortunate enough to be elected president of this great country, we will become a nation emphasizing early childhood education," he said to reporters. "Here is why it is important: Parents need dependable, safe care for their children so they can work and support their families. We can also start working early with children who may be considered at-risk because of where they live and how they learn. There is just so much more we could be doing."

"Will you win?" a reporter asked.

"We already have," the senator said. "We have met fantastic people, engaged with bright students, listened to the stories of people who need assistance, spent a lot of time in a beautiful place with wonderful people. We've won already."

The sound bites and the video of the senator reading to the young learners made the newscasts in the final hours before the caucus meetings. Also making the national news was the story and photo of the young reporter from Crossroads State

University who by chance came across the senator's visit to the memorial. The photos taken from the student's cellphone made all of the newscasts, local and national.

One of the photos was taken at an angle showing the solemn faces of the senator and his wife.

CHAPTER 40
Shocker

Without hundreds, maybe thousands, of white-haired senior adults there might not be such a process as the Iowa Caucuses. Few, it seems, really understand the process like the dedicated white hairs who show up on every election day in Iowa to provide a semblance of organization to the chaos.

The Iowa Caucuses had always been neighborhood meetings in schools, meeting halls, churches and sometimes peoples' homes. They would be different this time with participation available online to make the event more accessible and more diverse in nature.

The night starts at 7 p.m., or maybe a bit later if not everyone has been registered yet. The caucuses start with a recitation of rules, a few introductions and announcements.

If there are city or county officials attending, they are introduced. A party activist or two rally the crowd and explain the process. Supporters of the individual candidates then make the case for their candidate. There may be jeers or shouted questions disparaging the candidate from supporters of a rival candidate. This is when the friendly neighborhood caucuses can get nasty and unneighborly. The time is approaching when most everyone takes a stand. There may be hundreds of participants at a single caucus location. They are finally asked to divide in separate locations around the room based on the candidate they support.

There is a count of the various groups. A candidate who does not have at least 15 percent of those attending a caucus site is considered "not viable." Support those supporting a candidate determined to be "not viable" and those who have shown up as undecided become the prey of supporters of other candidates who are viable.

In small groups, supporters of one of the viable candidates try to convince the undecided and those without a viable candidate to move their support to their side. They may be offered a T-shirt or a sugary baked good.

The Iowa Caucuses typically attract a diverse crowd; diverse as Iowa gets, anyway. The Democratic version of the Iowa Caucuses will include the white hairs, single-issue advocates, blacks and Hispanics, young families with babies in strollers or in baby sacks, progressives, "do gooders" tree huggers, community activists and first-time voters.

After a period of time for attracting the non-viable supporters and undecided, there is a new count of supporters of the remaining viable candidates. This time online participants would be counted, too. Those raw numbers of support for a candidate are translated through what can be some confusing mathematics into delegates to the county convention. Each of the 1,681 precincts of Iowa are given a number of delegate spots to fill with supporters of the candidates. Delegates won by each viable candidate are the numbers reported to state party headquarters.

From those number of delegates, percentages of support for each candidate are determined. Finally, there is a winner. Maybe.

Some Iowa Caucuses have clear-cut winners, others do not. Favorite son Tom Harkin pulled 76 percent of the delegates from the 1992 Iowa Caucuses. Barack Obama was a surprise winner in 2008 with 38 percent of the delegates to 30 percent for John Edwards.

In 2016, there was mass confusion about who won between Hillary Clinton and Bernie Sanders. Clinton was deemed the winner with 49.8 percent of the delegates to 49.6 for Sanders.

Two people besides the white hairs who run the show in many Iowa precincts understood and had studied the history of

Iowa Caucuses. Senator Buckman's campaign had them both: Gerald O'Malley, who had helped Mike Clarke start his path to the nomination before losing to Jack Rushton in the general election, and Timothy Cashton, aka Timmy Caucus and Timmy Money.

Using the database built over months in Iowa, the campaign had amassed a large base of volunteers. The tireless Buckman supporters in The Warehouse had lined up at least two supporters to act as surrogates in many of those 1,681 precincts. In larger counties, they had an extra observer to watch over the count from online participants. They would be the lead supporters for the senator and would also be watchful for anything on a list of shenanigans that could be expected, including simple math errors or online malfunctions. With their phone calculators and their pink Buckman for President T-shirts, they were prepared. They had been sent additional T-shirts to hand out to those who came over to the Buckman corner. The Buckman campaign wasn't only attracting young progressives. The campaign had enlisted the help of a diverse group.

Buckman's campaign had been accused of bringing outsiders into Iowa for the final weeks before caucus night. And they had, but all of the caucus site volunteers had been checked out by Timmy Caucus. All of them had Iowa residency, although dozens of them were out-of-state college students, many of them attending school in Minnesota and other Midwest colleges.

Clarke was the primary source of the criticism of Buckman's organization in Iowa. Clarke hadn't said much when O'Malley had gotten him 42 percent with a similar organizational effort four years earlier.

There are various political theories about who turns out in good weather or bad weather. The high temperature on the clear, sunny day was an unseasonably warm 42 degrees. Teddy Thermal, who had showed up the night before the Iowa Caucuses at the Des Moines hotel headquarters, boasted about hitting the high temperature on the number. He spent caucus day doing weather reports.

By 9 p.m. at a Buckman watch party at Kingdom Foods

Events Center, hundreds of people who had been working for the senator in Iowa, some of them as volunteers for months, were drinking beers. There was also a haze of marijuana smoke in scattered corners of the venue. Some supporters waved rainbow and pink flags with Buckman name or face on them.

Early numbers started popping up on the screen. Buckman 30 percent, Foster 23 percent, and Mike Clarke, also at 23 percent. Four other candidates shared 24 percent. There were hundreds of caucus sites still unreported. There were also uncounted online supporters but for a first effort, online participation seemed to be working.

The candidate sat in the suite that had essentially been his home for months with his parents, Kim and their son, Owen, who was playing on the floor with his grandmother. Buckman was calm as his political career hung in the balance. He got down on the floor beside his mother and marveled at the smiling Owen. He was only paying attention to the television in brief spurts. He paced around the room when he was paying attention to the results.

"I want to go for a walk," he said.

"Not possible, sir. We've doubled your security. There are four agents outside your room and Des Moines officers downstairs and outside the building. You will only be able to leave to go to the event," said the female Secret Service agent, Krista Kuhn, who had become his shadow.

O'Malley and Timmy Caucus had moved their caucus night operations back to The Warehouse in the Twin Cities, where 200 volunteers and paid staff, supporters and downtown neighbors gathered around big screens. O'Malley led the discussion and the drinking with booming hoots every few minutes. Timmy kept him updated with reports from their own precinct watchers in Iowa. The reports were good.

"This is going to happen," Timmy whispered to O'Malley. "We're getting good reports from a lot of unreported turnouts, especially online. People are waiting an hour or more to get into some caucus sites. They are our people. He is going to win this freakin' thing."

"What's going on with social media?" O'Malley asked.

"Right up until caucus times, there was a lot of what appeared to be bot traffic on the sites of Mike Clarke and Karla Foster. Hundreds of posts accusing them of trying to keep turnout down, posts giving their supporters in certain areas wrong caucus site addresses and wrong online directions and posts saying they were having an affair. That was a favorite," Timmy reported.

"Our bots?" O'Malley asked.

"Not all of them. Possibly some," Timmy reported. "Oh, and a doctored photo of Mike Clarke shooting an AR-15. We thought that was a nice touch but we don't know who did it. It wasn't us."

"And people believe that shit?" O'Malley asked.

"If they want to believe, they will," Timmy Caucus reported.

"What about on our own sites?" O'Malley asked. "What's going on?"

"Probably the most potentially troublesome is the talk about the senator being clinically depressed following Crossroads State," Timmy said.

"There have been rough periods," O'Malley conceded. "I guess we have all experienced survivor guilt. I've thought about it myself. I wasn't there either."

Surprise guests showed up at the Buckman post-caucus event. The updates and cheering indicated it was time for the guests to be introduced.

Buckman 32 percent, Foster 30 percent, Mike Clarke 28 percent. The number of unreported precincts was rapidly dropping.

Ridge and Brynn Powell walked out from behind the simple staging of a blue curtain with a lectern and a 40-foot-wide, 15-foot-tall Buckman for President banner. There were huge screens scattered throughout the venue to follow the results. The senator was still fighting the flag waving typical of presidential campaigns to make the stage attractive for television. There was one Iowa flag, one United States flag.

Brynn was suddenly the favorite surrogate of Buckman among

supporters after coming to the defense of Kim Wakefield about her teenage abortion. She received an ear-ringing response as she picked up a microphone from the lectern.

"Oh, thank you. You are very sweet. I have one thing to say: Senator Pierce Morrison Buckman is going to win and it's because of all of you," she shouted above the din. "We have a great big surprise for you.

"With more country entertainer of the year awards than all the awards Ridge and I have, here from Beaumont, Texas is the big man ... be still my heart ... country music superstar Beau Cole."

Cole walked out with a guitar and a stool, without his band.

He got as noisy a reception as Brynn Powell, who was now standing next to Ridge, waving to supporters.

"I wouldn't have missed this night. We're here for Senator Buckman and Kim and for you folks who have done so much to support the Iowa campaign of the senator," Cole said. "I used to call myself a Republican but I figured out I am really a Buckman Republican. His ideas about schools and public service are ideas I can relate to and maybe that's the thing, everyone can relate to his ideas."

"We'll sing a couple and see what happens the rest of the night."

Cole sang and played three of his biggest hits for the crowd growing in numbers. The crowd pressed forward as he sang. Reporters were not confined to a certain area. This was a Buckman event. They were roaming around. Several reporters talked to the Powells during Cole's acoustic performance.

The room became increasingly hazy with marijuana smoke despite repeated reminders smoking was not allowed in the building.

Cole finished at 10 p.m.

At the hotel headquarters, the Secret Service was preparing to leave with the senator and his family.

Buckman hugged his parents, kissed Kim, and they all hugged.

The 10 p.m. local news was playing on two televisions. The

senator had 34 percent, Foster 29 percent and Mike Clarke 27 percent. All but one caucus site was reporting.

"First Cue Ball to win the Iowa Caucuses," Kim shouted, tears streaming down. "You did it."

She could tell he was thinking about Crossroads State. At times since the tragedy, especially in the two weeks following, Kim thought the senator was becoming depressed. She had asked several times if he thought he might need counseling. But then he would get through his dark periods, usually when he was around Owen.

"You have people waiting for you. Did you see that crowd? Brynn and Beau have them all wound up," Kim said. "You deserve this moment. Let's go."

Senator Buckman had thought about what he might say to supporters. O'Malley had shown him polling suggesting he would hit 32 percent. He did better.

There were supporters outside the hotel who had waited for him to make the trip to the Kingdom Foods Events Center. Buckman insisted on shaking hands, taking photos and hugging them.

"Thank you very much for coming out. Your support is humbling," the senator said.

"Pierce, we have to go. People are waiting for you," his mom said.

He waved as he climbed into one of the waiting SUVs for the 15-minute trip to the Events Center. They were flanked by police vehicles. Krista Kuhn had urged him once again to wear a light ballistic vest under his blue shirt and black blazer. He refused.

Cole's mini-concert concluded.

Speeches continued but were largely ignored. The crowd was watching the senator leave the hotel headquarters on a local television station that had posted a video crew outside the hotel.

The caravan of SUVs arrived at a secured building attached to the Events Center. They were able to drive directly into the lower level.

Senator Buckman, his parents, Kim, Owen and a large

security contingent walked through the otherwise empty building. He could now hear the full force of the celebration ahead of him. He broke into a big grin. He kissed Kim, who walked out on stage with Owen and the Old Hippies.

Ridge Powell had been asked to introduce the senator. Brynn hugged Kim, the senator's parents and gave the drowsy Owen a kiss. Ridge first went over to hug Kim and the senator's parents.

"Folks, I have been around politicians in my life," Ridge began his introduction. "Most I have been disappointed by. They were full of crap I discovered. None of them were anything like Senator Pierce Buckman. As you probably already know, he is one of a kind. There are none like him. He is a public servant who cares.

"He is going to make a great president."

"It is my great pleasure to introduce the next President of United States ... Senator Pierce Buckman!"

He walked out slowly from behind the curtain, soaking up the celebratory crowd. He stopped at about center stage and waved, looking into the lights and the crowd. He was beaming.

The celebration went on for a couple of minutes before he raised both his arms, making a first attempt to quiet the celebration. Kim and Owen and his parents were at his side. He hugged them all.

"Thank you, Iowans. Thank you...Thank you all very much." He waited more than a minute for the reaction to calm slightly "Thank you ..."

"Thank you for opening your hearts, your imaginations and your homes to us. I have a secret ... I'm in love with Iowa and the people who live here.

"When we began this campaign last March, we started with about as much support as we had funds. We had little of either. Ask my staff how little money we had. They pretty much were paid in pizza and free breakfast buffets.

"What we did have was a message. It was, and still is, a message of inclusion, a message of compassion, a message of promise that no one willing to make some sacrifice, willing to participate, would be left behind."

The senator strolled around the stage as he spoke. It was like watching a play. He walked to various points of the stage to wave or point at supporters he recognized.

"Listen, listen, this is important … I want to take a minute to honor the memory of my friends, Senator Lansing Landon and Congressman Marion Jackson. I miss them deeply and I have to tell you there have been some difficult weeks. As you celebrate tonight, please remember everyone we lost at Crossroads State. We lost leaders, we lost children, grandchildren, we lost the incredible potential of young people that day.

"Those were dark days. As dark as I have experienced in my life. I seriously considered just going home to Minnesota to get a teaching job. Without the resolve and never-ending support of my fantastic wife, Kim, I would have ended my campaign. She kept reminding me that people would continue to be left behind unless someone spoke up for them.

"So, this campaign, you've heard it called 'A Pink Revolution,' continues. We put everything into Iowa and we're moving forward. We're going to New Hampshire and regardless of what you might hear from the news networks, we will not adapt our messages based on where the campaign is next. This is not a one-and-done campaign, which is what was predicted.

"I want to also congratulate Governor Foster and Governor Clarke for a competitive, spirited campaign. We'll do it again in a few days.

"We were told we were gaining momentum because I was close to my home state. We were told we were doing well because Iowa Democrats have always liked a progressive message. We were told we wouldn't even make it to caucus night. Well, here we are and the message will be the same in New Hampshire and all the way to November.

"The president lacks ideas. The president lacks compassion. The president lacks vision. The president lacks the will to do the difficult thing, or the right thing. The president doesn't care about the people in this room tonight. He would call you socialists, radicals, impressionable young people who have somehow been fooled by our campaign promises.

"Let me ask you something, have you been fooled? Have you been the victims of some sort of mind trick from our campaign? I didn't think so.

"You have informed the country with a loud, enthusiastic voice that cannot be ignored that you share a vision of better schools, better health care, better economic opportunity, better immigration policy and an expedited route to citizenship. We are the campaign talking about public service in exchange for college tuition. We are the campaign talking about the environmental stewardship and the protections necessary to protect our land, water and air.

"You may have heard the president's people refer to me as Senator Tulip, Senator Begonia, even Senator Hemp. Not sure what that last one is all about …"

The reference to Senator Hemp was a joke everyone in the room understood. First there was laughing, then hooting and hollering and finally the chant of "*Senator Hemp, Senator Hemp.*"

"I will say that I wish you wouldn't smoke in this room. You all know better.

"Finally, let me say again thank you for your support, thank you to my great staff and campaign director Gerald O'Malley and everyone in The Warehouse in the Twin Cities. Thank you all for sharing a vision of a different, more compassionate, more equitable country where everyone has a chance to succeed and no one faces discrimination holding them back from reaching their full potential. A country where public schools serve entire neighborhoods with services, a country where everyone has a right to high quality, affordable health care and a country where public service is valued and rewarded.

"That is our vision. Come along with us. God bless you. God bless Iowa. Thank you for sharing our vision."

The senator waved his family, the Powells and Beau Cole toward him on the stage. Owen slept in his grandfather's arms. The senator wanted to shake hands with supporters, but the large security force around him prevented him from leaving the stage.

Buckman continued to share the stage with his family and high-profile supporters. After about five more minutes of waving, they all walked backstage and through the empty building to the vehicles already running for the trip back to the Iowa headquarters.

Ridge, a beer in his hand, and Brynn stayed on stage and engaged with the senator's supporters. Lincoln Zion was watching closely.

CHAPTER 41

New Hampshire Next

The senator's routine was virtually uninterruptable. He pulled on workout clothes, a pink Buckman for President t-shirt and shorts, was careful not to wake up Kim or Owen, found his glasses in the darkness and went to the workout room. He rode the bike for 45 minutes with Krista Kuhn on a bike beside him, then got into the pool for more exercise by swimming laps underwater. He then got back on the bike to cool down. He stopped by the breakfast room for a newspaper and a cup of coffee.

He had been following the same routine throughout the months in Iowa.

"Buckman's Stuns Iowa Field," "Buckman Shocker," and "Buckman Wins Out of Nowhere," blared the banner headlines in morning newspapers.

The "Breaking News" television headlines were similar. He stopped for only a few seconds to look at the television. Only his Secret Service shadow, Krista, was with him. He found the coverage surreal.

"You won. Shocked the heck out of them," his Secret Service agent said. "Congratulations, sir."

"Yeah, weird to see it after all this time getting to this day. I feel like I should have a schedule today. I guess I do. We're going back on the road. Kim and Owen and the Old Hippies are headed home for a few days. I'm headed to New Hampshire. You're going, right?"

"Yes sir. For the duration of the campaign. You are not to be trusted out there alone. We know that," the agent said.

"When do you see family? When do you get a break?" the senator asked.

"In the protective detail, your family is the people you work with. It's difficult to have relationships outside of your career," she said. "It's just part of the profession."

Before leaving Iowa, there was a conference call meeting. There were details to consider and plans to make. The superstitious candidate would not participate in New Hampshire planning prior to Iowa Caucus night. His staff, though, had been working on the next stop all along.

"The key question is do we have funds?" the senator asked.

"Senator, we brought in about $2 million in small donations, $100 or less, just in the last couple days when it appeared you would do well," O'Malley explained. "We've got about $6 million total. It gets more complicated now. You are going to need additional paid staff here in the Twin Cities and we've had a team on the ground in New Hampshire for a few weeks. It started to look like you were doing well so we started investing in New Hampshire. We just didn't tell you. You wouldn't have wanted to know.

"We'll do television ads in New Hampshire. The primary comes up quickly."

They discussed logistics and the fact the senator needed to be in New Hampshire as soon as possible.

Ryan Holton asked about the future of Beatrice the Bus.

"Want me to sell Beatrice now or put her in storage for safe keeping? The bus apparently has historical value now. It's worth maybe $10,000 or $15,000 and we have an offer to buy it for $75,000. We could sell it," suggested Holton, a new father himself who was still driving Beatrice most of the time.

The senator had a different plan. He was quietly thinking.

"No, Beatrice is going to New Hampshire. You may not have noticed, but I'm superstitious. I'm driving it to New Hampshire," the senator said, apparently seriously.

"Senator, that isn't happening," Carl Lyon said. "Things changed last night."

"I didn't," the senator said. "Someone better be down here to

335

drive Beatrice or I will. We're headed East."

This was all very new to the senator. He didn't realize how naïve it now sounded to make a three-day drive, and that was if Beatrice cooperated, to start campaigning in New Hampshire.

"Sir, you can't. We have you scheduled for morning shows tomorrow. You are flying to New Hampshire," O'Malley said. "Will you at least agree to first class? You should have a private jet."

"No, in coach. With my people. Yeah, the thought of driving sounded kind of scatterbrained, didn't it?"

Teddy Thermal was predicting the winter storm of the year in the East. He expected hundreds of canceled flights and hundreds more flights delayed.

Beatrice did make it to the border of Illinois. In the middle of Interstate 74, between the Quad Cities and Galesburg, smoke erupted from the old girl's engine and the warning indicators on the console started dinging and pinging. Beatrice the benevolent bus was pulled off to the shoulder 15 miles from any garage capable of fixing her again.

CPSIA information can be obtained
at www.ICGtesting.com
Printed in the USA
FFHW020614201218
49942076-54593FF